P9-CFY-147

Heir Apparent

By the same author

Leading Lady
Pretty Women
Living Color
Perfect Order
Fame and Fortune

KATE COSCARELLI

HEIR APPARENT

St. Martin's Press / New York

Design by *Charles Davey*

Library of Congress Cataloging-in-Publication Data
Coscarelli, Kate.
    Heir apparent / Kate Coscarelli.
        p.   cm.
    ISBN 0-312-09305-5 (hardcover)
    I. Title
PS3553.O737H4   1993
813'.54—dc20   93-3681
                                      CIP

First edition: July 1993

10   9   8   7   6   5   4   3   2   1

To my husband, Don—for all the love and caring through the years.

Acknowledgments

Many thanks to my son, Don, for his expertise and advice on scuba diving and the harbor, and the same to my seafaring friends, Frank Viault and Gayne Rescher.

My heartfelt gratitude to Tom McCormack for seeing the possibilities and helping me realize them, and to Jenny Notz for her hard work and sharp eyes.

Ongoing appreciation to my agent, Joan Stewart, for her abiding encouragement.

Thanks to Mary Rosenberg, R.P.T., for briefing me about lupus.

And to Greta Andersen, the extraordinary channel swimmer, my eternal thanks for teaching me the stroke that's carried me through miles and miles of friendly water.

Heir Apparent

His touch was light and feathery as he caressed her knees, and she felt a small shiver of familiar desire. Silkily his fingers drew tiny circular patterns on her thighs, her hips, and her abdomen, and when he lifted her gown, her body relaxed in helpless surrender to his soft, insinuating touch.

A small gasp escaped from her lips as his hand closed over her breast and his thumb rested on her nipple. Still on the crest of slumber, her body responded with aroused passion, and she turned from her side to her back and let her legs fall open. She felt an urgent longing for his touch to descend downward to the crown of her ardor, but his movements were leisurely. His gentle hands traced a delicate path from the hollow of her throat to her chin, around the outline of her opened lips, and over the curve of her cheek and her closed eyelids.

He continued his slow fingertip tour of the surface of her body, sliding across the fine bones of her shoulders and descending both her arms.

She sprang to a sudden and complete wakefulness, and her eyes opened wide. Gone was the lassitude and the desire in the instant she felt the cord slipped around her wrist.

"No!" she whispered. "Not tonight . . . please, I don't want that!"

L acey hesitated before her reflection in the foyer mirror of the Gallagher mansion and ran quick fingers through curly brown hair frosted with gray. She wished she'd had time for a haircut and manicure, but she was too busy nowadays to worry about her personal appearance.

She squeezed her lips together to even out the hastily applied lipstick, and for a moment her determination wavered. She was anxious to get to the office, because there was a lot to be done, but she hated to leave her father. She was about to change her mind and stay when the reflection of the tall, handsome figure of her younger brother, Scott, appeared in the mirror and grinned at her.

"Go, Lacey, go!" he commanded. "What the hell are you worrying about?"

"Easy for you to say. Suppose he wakes up and wants me? He'll be confused if I'm not—"

"Look, I promised you I'd stay right here in the house. Swear to God I won't play tennis, and if Dad needs me, I'll be there to hold his hand and soothe his fevered brow. Besides I need a day off, and so do you. So go. Do your Gallagher's Best and have fun." With a sardonic grin, he took her by the shoulders, aimed her toward the front doors, and gave her a light shove.

"If he should have a lucid period, tell him it's Saturday, or he'll worry about your not being at work, okay?" Lacey replied as she opened the front door.

"Go already! I can manage things here on the home front. That new nurse from the cancer center has upped his pain medication, and he's resting easily for a change. You're needed more at the office than you are here. I have no idea what the hell I've been signing the last two weeks, and you better check things out and make sure I haven't made any spectacular goofs. Okay?"

"Promise to call me if Dad should take a turn for the worse?"

"Cross my heart, now quit dithering and go! You've been a devoted daughter and a wonderful nurse, but you can't save him, kiddo. The old geezer's gonna die one of these days, probably sooner than later. Get used to the idea."

"Take care of him, Scott. I'll be back by five."

Lacey hurried out the door and ran down the steps.

"Good morning, Salvador," she greeted the chauffeur waiting beside the limousine. "Let's go to the office."

Happy to see Lacey arrive, Brett Marchbanks, vice president in charge of sales, was the first to appear in her office and plop down in the chair in front of what had been her father's desk. A tall, slightly overweight man with thinning hair and a cherubic face, he was a crackerjack employee and was married to Penny, one of Lacey's closest friends.

"What's up, Brett?" Lacey asked, scanning the list of that morning's calls.

"I've tried to get some answers out of that schizy brother of yours, but he spends all his time here ducking around corners and trying to avoid making decisions. Can't you get in here at least once a week?"

"I'm lucky I make it at all. Scott hates the company, Brett. He always has. You know as well as I do that he only came home because I asked him to help out while Dad was ill. If . . . when . . . Dad dies, he'll never come near this place again."

"What's wrong with him? Gallagher's Best is a great place to work."

Lacey laughed. "That's the problem. Scott hates any kind of work." She picked up the agenda sheet and got to her feet.

"They're waiting for you. Let's go," Brett said as he opened the door.

With Lacey busy scrutinizing the backup documents, they walked together in silence to the elevator that would take them to the floor where the boardroom was located. When they entered the large room, she smiled and shook hands with the staff members closest to the door, but she wasted no time starting the meeting.

"Thank you all for coming. Sam, I know it was an imposition bringing you all the way in from Ohio, but we want to help with the problem you've got out there. Let's start with that first."

Sam Jacoby got to his feet and gave the group a quick summary of his difficulties with a member of the Teamsters' union. In finishing, he said, "And that's why we haven't been able to get any Gallagher's Best products on the shelves of Dayton's big supermarkets for almost a week now."

"Are we talking about a kickback?" Lacey asked.

"That's it," Sam replied. "Mick Hayden wants a fee for every carton he transports. It's highway robbery."

"He demanded it outright?" Brett asked.

"Not in so many words, but I got his drift pretty quick."

"Well, it's too expensive to stonewall him, so we either expose him or knuckle under," Lacey stated. "What do you suggest?"

"If I call him in and have the police put a wire on me, we can probably nail him, but I won't feel safe walking the streets of Dayton again. Mick's a mean son of a bitch. If we pay up, word will spread that we're an easy mark, and everybody will want in."

Lacey looked around the room. "Any ideas?"

No one had any suggestions to offer.

"All right then, this is what we'll have to do," Lacey said, making the decision for herself. "Bill, I want you to call up the national president of the union. Tell him we're having trouble with one of his locals, and we need to talk. Ask him if he'd like to come out here for a little vacation. Tell him to bring his family. Put him up in a suite at the Ritz-Carlton in Laguna-Niguel, all expenses paid. Tell him we'll send the plane to pick him up. What do you think?"

Bill Harris, who was the director of labor relations, nodded. "Worth a try. But what about Sam? The guy's going to be pissed when he finds out we went over his head."

"Right," Lacey replied with a nod. "Sam, we've got an opening in Vancouver. It's a lovely city, almost crime free. Want it?"

Sam grinned. "You bet I do. Margo's family is from Seattle, and she'll be thrilled."

"Good. I'll replace you with Arnie Simpson. My father recruited him from the Teamsters ten years ago, and he's still got a lot of friends in the union. Just stay away from that crook until you're out of there," Lacey said. "Now, who else has a problem that needs attention?"

Margaret Ferguson, the director of advertising, got to her feet. "NBC's raising the rates drastically for 'Crime and Punishment' next year."

"It's a good show. Where did Neilsen rank it for the season?" Lacey asked.

"It came in fourth overall, but it hit first place on several Thursday nights and almost always carries its time slot. The demographics are good too."

"Maybe it's worth more, especially since we're going national with two new products next year. Cynthia Slayton is the big attraction on that show. Have they signed her to a new contract yet?" Lacey asked.

"All set. She's even considering doing a couple of commercials for us, if we'll go for her price."

"That's great! How come?"

"She bought a horse farm in Ireland, and refurbishing the hundred-room mansion is costing her a fortune. She needs the money."

top drawer. She rang the office of Carl Robinson, who handled public relations.

"Carl, my father died this afternoon. Will you take care of notifying the press? Send out the statement they prepared with the bio and pictures. I'll be at home if you need me." Just saying the words made Jack Gallagher's death seem all too final.

Lacey apologized to Jean Atwill on her way out.

"I'm sorry I gave you the news so abruptly, but I was upset that it happened while I was away from home."

Jean looked at her with cold eyes. "I wouldn't worry about that if I were you. Jack's son was with him, wasn't he?"

Lacey was puzzled by the eerie smile of triumph on Jean's face. Good Lord, she thought, this woman had been her father's personal secretay for almost forty years. Why was she looking so smug and self-satisfied at a moment like this? The poor man had just died.

"Yes, Scott was . . . at home. I'd appreciate it if you'd see that everyone on the staff is notified. I'll call you as soon as the time of the funeral is arranged."

Lacey's eyes stayed dry until she was alone in the backseat of the limousine, and then the grief she felt for the loss of the most important man in her life overcame her. She cried all the way home.

I t was almost over. Within minutes the casket of John Joseph Gallagher would be carried into the family mausoleum, where it would be sealed up forever. Lacey stood silently beside Scott and watched through eyes swollen by two days of tears.

The six honorary pallbearers, all men in their sixties and seventies, moved away, and the professionals from the funeral home stepped forward. They grasped the handles of the heavy bronze casket and lifted it off the wheeled stand with some difficulty. Struggling under the weight of the heavy load, they inched up the steps and through the narrow doorway. One of the men lost his grip and the load lurched to the right, smashing against the marble doorway and creating a large dent in the side of the gleaming, highly polished coffin. An audible gasp of shock rippled through the mourners present. The men, distressed, glanced at one another and then continued their journey inside.

Managing to suppress a smile, Scott whispered from the corner of his mouth, "If the old codger is watching, he's probably pissed off. Imagine the great one having to spend eternity in a dented box."

Poor Dad, Lacey thought. He would have hated what just happened. Jack Gallagher could tolerate anything except imperfection.

Lacey and Scott returned to their limousine to lead the way back to the Gallagher estate on the Palos Verdes peninsula. As they waited for Erin and JJ, Lacey's children, and Sasha, Scott's wife, to catch up with them, they talked quietly.

"Well, he's gone, but I haven't seen you shed a tear yet," Lacey said.

"I wouldn't put it past that old God-fearing law-abiding crook to make a pact with the devil so he can come back to haunt us for the rest of our lives."

"That's pretty insensitive, even for you, little brother."

"You think so? Well, he's been pulling our strings for so long I'm not sure that either of us can even walk by ourselves, let alone lead independent normal-type lives."

"So what are you going to do with the rest of your life anyway?" she asked.

"You mean after Sasha and I spend a month skiing in Aspen? I'll have to give it some thought."

"The will stipulates that it be read on the day of the funeral, so you should be a rich man tonight and you can do anything you want. As for me, I'll be happy to get back to work. Will you do me a favor?"

"Such as?" he asked, watching the mourners retreat to their cars.

"When people offer their condolences this afternoon, lay off the wisecracks. Try to look a little bereaved, will you?"

"It won't be easy, but for your sake I'll give it a try." He squinted his eyes and turned down the corners of his mouth.

Lacey shook her head in dismay at the grotesque expression on his face. "Are you ever going to grow up?"

"Why would I want to? Santa Claus is coming today and it's only March."

Lacey shook her head in despair. "Sometimes you're as hardhearted as Dad was."

"Forget that," he said with a sigh. "All my life I've been looking in the mirror and praying to God not to let me look like him or talk like him, and especially not think and act like him."

"He was a great man," she began, but he raised his hand to silence her.

"Please, I heard enough eulogies at the funeral. Let's go home and get this show on the road."

★★ 3 ★★

Brett held open the door of his new white Lincoln Town Car and helped Mary Gallagher into the backseat. Without waiting for his assistance, his wife climbed into the front passenger seat and turned to face Mary.

"Did you see the dress on that Ivana Trump clone? My God, it was halfway up her ass!"

Mary laughed at her perky red-haired friend's bitchiness. "That's the style, Penny. Don't criticize. Even *your* knees are showing. And by the way, you look great in that suit. Is it a Chanel?"

"Looks like but isn't. Brett makes a good salary but not that good," Penny said, before her husband got into the car.

When all three were settled and on their way, Mary asked, "Brett, why do you suppose Mr. Brennan wants us at the reading of the will?"

"I suppose we're all mentioned in it, but if I know Jack Gallagher, it's only a mention."

Mary shook her head and looked out the window as she answered, "Well, he's always been generous with me. Thanks to him, I've been able to stay at home and work on my sculpture. That is, when I'm not having a flare-up of the lupus."

"You've been okay lately, haven't you?" Penny asked.

"I've been feeling terrific since I've been able to afford a physical therapist, thanks to Jack and Lacey. He insisted on paying all my medical bills."

"After what his son did to you, it was no more than right," Penny remarked.

"It's in the past, Penny."

"Scott's spoiled. He always has been, always will be," Brett declared. "Thank God I'll be working for Lacey and not for him."

"How have things been the last few months with Scott in the front office?" Mary asked.

"Mary, you're so obvious," Penny said, making a face. "Every time his name comes up, you beam right in on it."

Mary laughed. "Look, it's no secret that I still regard him as my

10

husband, even if he's already on his third wife. After all, I am Catholic and I don't believe in divorce."

"To answer your question, he's not doing too well," Brett interjected.

"Brett's being too nice," Penny declared. "His performance has been dreadful. You know how lazy he is, and he has the attention span of a gnat."

"You think anything Scott does is dreadful, Penny. What about it, Brett, was he as bad as your wife says?"

"He was present in body only. Never got much involved in things. I took a few big buyers into his office and he was cordial, but he didn't have the faintest idea what was going on, and he didn't seem to care much." Brett paused and then added, "About a month ago, however, when it became apparent that Jack wasn't going to survive, Scott started asking questions."

"What kind of questions?" Penny asked.

"Basic things, stuff you'd have thought he already knew about profit margins and foreign sales."

"Probably counting up his inheritance," Penny remarked.

Brett turned onto the road that led into the gate to the Gallagher estate, and they found themselves in a long line of cars slowing to be admitted.

"Seems as if everybody's coming to the house to pay their respects," Mary noted. "There goes the governor's limousine!"

"Politicians never wait their turn. Look at him up there crowding into the front of the line!" Penny exclaimed.

"If I had to go to as many funerals and weddings as they do, I'd push into line too," Brett remarked.

The guards at the gate finally waved them through, but Brett did not follow the crowd to the assigned parking spaces. Instead, he took the first right turn past the tennis court, followed it up to the service area, parked beside the caterers' trucks, and within minutes he was hustling the two women into the house through the kitchen.

"Close friends have privileges like politicians do," he declared.

Lacey and Scott were standing at the door greeting the arriving mourners, and Brett waved to them as they passed through the hallway.

Lacey winked and inclined her head toward the library, where drinks were being served. Brett headed in that direction, but Mary held back.

"I'll catch up with you later. I want to express my condolences."

Penny shrugged. "Lacey knows how we feel, but suit yourself," she said and followed Brett.

Mary moved to the back of the receiving line to wait her turn. She never passed up an opportunity to talk to the man who had once been her husband.

★★ 4 ★★

After most of the callers had taken their leave, Lacey went looking for Scott. She spotted Sasha, the tall blonde Russian who was her brother's third wife, and she moved out to the glass-walled solarium to talk to her.

"Sasha, dear, have you any idea what happened to that husband of yours?"

"I saw him walking toward the tennis court with Tom more than an hour ago, but now there's no sign of either of them anywhere. The fog is rolling in, and it's difficult to see much."

Sasha was the self-described daughter of a Russian diplomat who had been influential enough to keep his daughter with him in London. She said she had attended the best schools there, which accounted for her accent-free English. Although Sasha reluctantly admitted she'd once been a Communist, she had adapted readily to the comforts that great wealth can provide and had a taste for the finer things.

"I have to stop upstairs for a minute, so I'll check your room, in case he decided to take a quick nap," Lacey said. She was so tired her legs felt like lead weights as she climbed one of the twin curved staircases.

She checked the large room where Sasha and Scott had slept for the past half year. Finding no one there, she went through her own smaller room into her white marble bathroom, where she noticed her pantyhose wrinkling around her ankles. She would have to order some in a smaller size now, since she had lost so much weight in the last few months. She ran a brush through her short hair and decided that tomorrow for sure she would have her hairdresser come to the house to touch up the color. She also needed her eyebrows tweezed and her nails manicured. Now that she was head of the company, she would have to pay more attention to her image. "An untidy appearance is the sign of a disorganized mind" was one of her father's frequently repeated homilies.

She was putting on a bit of pink lipstick when there was a knock. At her call of "Come in," Mary Ryan Gallagher's face appeared at the door.

"Mary, come on in. God, it's good to see you."

The two women embraced, and then Mary dropped down into the satin slipper chair beside the vanity.

13

"Are you doing all right, Lacey?" Mary asked.

"I'm feeling a lot better than I look. Do you know of a good plastic surgeon? I think I need a few tucks." Lacey grimaced at herself in the mirror.

"You're exhausted, that's all, and stay away from hospitals and doctors if you can. All you need is a vacation."

"That I can't afford. I've got to get back to the office. There're so many things I've postponed doing these past few months." She sat down on the bed and appraised her friend. "You're certainly looking good. Did you talk to Scott?"

"No, not that I didn't try. Every time I got anywhere near him, he ducked out of the room and went elsewhere. I hope he's not upset that Jack has apparently mentioned me in his will."

"Well, that shouldn't come as any surprise. Dad still considered you his daughter, if not legally at least spiritually. Have your checks been coming regularly?" Lacey asked.

"Like clockwork. One of these days I might even be able to get off the Gallagher dole. You know that commission I did, the one of the little girl? Well, I finished it, and two other women called me and wanted me to do their daughters. Isn't that great?"

"That's not your kind of art, making kiddie portraits. Why are you doing it?"

"I can't go on being dependent on your family, Lacey. I need to support myself," Mary replied.

"Will you stop that? There was a time when all great artists had patrons to support them. They didn't consider it charity, and neither do we. Besides, you're family. Scott divorced you; we didn't."

"I hope he doesn't mind that you and I are still close friends."

"Who cares if he does."

"Poor Scott. He hasn't found himself yet—" Mary began, but Lacey shushed her.

"For goodness' sake, Mary, Scott's almost forty years old. If he doesn't find himself soon, I'm afraid we'll have to report him as permanently missing."

They both laughed.

"Mind if I use your bathroom?" Mary asked.

"Be my guest. I'm going on downstairs."

Lacey arrived at the foot of the stairs and found herself face-to-face with Steve Haines, her ex-husband and the father of her children. What in the world was he doing here?

"Steve! When did you get here?"

"Just now. I'm sorry the plane was late and I missed your dad's funeral. Are you all right?"

"I'm fine, and it was nice of you to come. Erin and JJ will be happy to see you."

The tall, muscular man took both of her hands and held them against his chest while he gazed down at her tenderly. "How about you? Are you happy to see me too?"

Lacey pulled away. She couldn't bear to look into his dark brown eyes. There were too many painful, emotional memories there.

"Of course, I'm always happy to see you, Steve. You should visit the children more often," she said, her manner formal. "They miss you." The butler was walking past them and she spoke to him. "Gordon, will you go find my children and tell them their father is here? They might be in the pool room."

Turning her attention back to Steve, she asked, "How're things at the ranch?"

"Hard times, Lacey, hard times. I keep thinking that tomorrow it'll get better, but it never does. People aren't eating beef like they used to. Hell, I can't blame 'em with all that stuff about saturated fat and cholesterol killing you. I'm even trimming the fat off my own steaks nowadays. Keep that a secret, will you?"

"Well, whatever you're doing, it seems to be agreeing with you. You look remarkably fit."

As they walked toward the library, Steve draped his arm around Lacey's shoulders. Although it was a natural and affectionate gesture, its familiarity made her uncomfortable. They had been divorced for more than four years and separated for six, and she didn't like his behaving as if they were still attached.

"You look thin and all worn out. Are you feeling okay?"

"We've all been through hell," she replied, easing herself away from him. "Dad suffered terribly. He struggled to hang on, and he fought against taking the pain medication because he wanted to stay alert and on top of things."

"Figures. He was the toughest son of a bitch I ever met in my life. He sure wasn't afraid of anything in this world."

"He was afraid of dying. He wouldn't admit it, but he was."

"The tough bastards always are. If they've figured wrong and there really is a heaven and a hell, they know they're in big trouble come reckoning day."

That was apparently enough of that subject for him, because he grasped her hand and said, "I sure as hell could use a drink. How about you?" He led her toward the bar in the solarium where he opened the icemaker, put ice in two glasses, and splashed dark whiskey on top.

"Here, drink this down. It'll get you through what's to come."

Lacey took the glass from his hand and asked, "What do you mean?"

"The reading of the will, what else?"

"How did you know about that?"

"Tom Brennan called me yesterday and said that Jack wanted all beneficiaries present at the first reading, and it seems I'm one of them. Is that a crock or what? The old bastard did everything in his power to break up our marriage and get you back here and then he names me in his will."

If Steve was surprised, Lacey was even more so. Jack had been wary from the moment she had first brought Steve home during her freshman year in college. Her father's dislike for the young man intensified when he caught him at his desk reading Jack's financial statements. Steve offered the lame excuse that he had been looking for the business section of the newspaper.

That incident and her father's response to it distressed Lacey. She had fallen in love and assumed that her father would respond well to Steve's drive and ambition. Instead, Jack called him a money sniffer, which didn't do much for Lacey's self-image.

She married Steve in spite of her father's opposition, and although he tried to find his niche at Gallagher's Best, her new husband found that he couldn't fit in. After a few years of trying to impress his father-in-law, Steve at last concluded that he'd never gain Jack's respect unless he went out on his own and became a success. The young couple borrowed against Lacey's trust fund and bought a ranch in Texas.

It was the worst decision he could have made. Jack was furious that his daughter and grandchildren had been spirited out of his orbit, and he got his opportunity to get even when his wife, Maude, became ill. Lacey came home with the grandchildren to be with her mother through her surgery.

It had been an unhappy time for Jack Gallagher. He'd had a terrible fight with Scott, who had left home in anger and gone to live in New York, swearing never to return. So Jack offered to anoint his daughter as his successor at the helm of Gallagher's Best, the company he alone had built from a small restaurant with a few good recipes into a megacorporation.

Even though Lacey had always been fascinated by the business, she had grown up assuming that it would be Scott, the only son, who would inherit their father's position. When the coveted job was offered to her instead, she accepted eagerly, and to her father's delight and surprise, she made no effort to bring her husband back with her. She never talked about Steve to her parents and eventually filed for divorce from a marriage that had given her two wonderful children and several years of heartache and hardship. With her father's unquestioning support, she was able to retain sole custody of the children.

Now painful memories hovered over them both as they stood sipping their drinks and talking while the late afternoon fog gradually obscured the view of the garden through the tall Palladian windows.

"Was it worth it, Lacey? Was it all you expected? Or was it less?" he asked.

Lacey knew he wanted her to express some regret for having left him for a position that he himself had coveted. There he stood, big and handsome and sexy. Any normal woman would be flattered by his attention, but she could not lie, even to save some tattered shred of his pride and masculinity. The truth would always have its way with her.

"The company? Better than I expected," she murmured.

Steve laughed. "I had to ask, didn't I? You're too much like your dad. I wish you'd been more like Scott."

As his name was spoken, Scott stepped through the door and signaled her to follow him. He and Steve greeted each other warmly and walked down the hallway chatting like old buddies. Most of the seats in Jack's grand library were already filled. Erin, who was now all of sixteen years old, was sitting on the couch beside her thirteen-year-old brother, JJ, and beside them was Silvana, the woman who had overseen the housekeeping for the Gallagher family for more than thirty years. Gordon, the butler, stood behind them. A dozen or more folding chairs had been set in rows in front of the giant mahogany desk, and they were filled with an assortment of relatives, most of whom were fairly advanced in age. Jack had apparently left nothing to the children or grandchildren of any of his cousins.

Lacey was startled to see Brett and Penny Marchbanks sitting beside Mary in the back row. She went over to talk to them.

"Did Tom invite you all here?" Lacey asked.

Brett stood up. "His office called this morning. I got along well with the old man, but I sure never expected to be named in his will."

"It's the least he could do after working you half to death for the past fifteen years." Penny grinned and winked at Lacey, "Think we're gonna be rich now?"

"Who knows? I don't even know if I am. Dad kept the contents of his will a closely guarded secret. But if anybody deserves to be rewarded you three do. Brett, last month's sales were fantastic."

"I love my job, Lacey, and I'm sure looking forward to working for you."

Lacey sat down in a chair between her brother and ex-husband, smiled at her children, and turned her attention to the team of lawyers that had taken their positions behind the desk. Tom Brennan was seated in Jack's big brown leather chair, and, papers in hand, he wasted no time in getting started.

"Please bear with me," he began as soon as the principal heirs were seated. "The document is long, and I'll read it through once and then answer questions any of you might have. Everyone in attendance is named in the will."

As he began to read, his deep voice resounded throughout the room and bounced off booklined shelves shining with a priceless collection of first editions. He raced through the assorted bequests to charities, which were generous, and to the distant relatives, which amounted to a token one thousand dollars each. For Silvana, he had endowed a trust fund ample enough for her to retire and return to her native Sicily as a relatively wealthy woman. The other household servants received sums not large enough to permit them to quit their jobs.

With that out of the way, Tom turned to the important bequests:

"To my beloved son, Scott, who made it possible for me to leave this world in peace by making my most cherished dream come true, I bequeath my home and gardens as well as my controlling stock of Gallagher's Best and its attendant buildings, factories, and holdings, on the condition that he assume the presidency and run the company himself. If, however, he is incapacitated or chooses to decline the responsibility, then his entire inheritance passes on to my daughter, Lacey. As a further inducement to Scott, I hereby stipulate that if he chooses not to abide by my wishes, then the sum total of his inheritance will be limited to one thousand dollars in cash.

"I hereby leave to Stephen R. Haines the sum of ten million dollars. Such money is to be paid only upon the occasion of his remarriage to my daughter, Lacey. It has always been my belief that the family is stronger when the money and control are in the hands of the husband, and with this inheritance, Steve will no longer feel that he is powerless in relation to his wife's family.

"With my son, Scott, firmly entrenched as the president of Gallagher's Best, my daughter's duties there will no longer be needed. A successful company cannot have divided leadership, and so for the good of the business and to reflect the vision of one person, it is better that Lacey have no continuing function in the corporation whatsoever. It is instead my fondest hope that she will resume her life as wife to Steve and mother to my grandchildren. I am deeply grateful to her for all the sacrifices she made on my behalf; however, she knows how important it was for me to be able to turn Gallagher's Best over to my only son. If she chooses not to remarry Steve, then the ten million dollars will be placed in a trust fund for her to be administered by the Ocean Pacific Bank. This trust will provide her with a generous monthly allowance. In either event, she is also to receive title to our ranch in Jackson Hole, Wyoming, as well as the house and land in Maui.

"To each of my beloved grandchildren, I bequeath a trust fund of five million dollars for their health, welfare, and education. The Ocean Pacific Bank will administer the trust without invading the principal except for emergencies until each of the grandchildren reaches the age of thirty-five, at which time they will assume control of the principal.

"To see that the terms of this will are carried out according to my wishes, I am appointing my trusted friend and longtime confidante, Jean Atwill, as executor. For this service, she is to be paid an annual salary of two hundred and fifty thousand dollars, plus expenses as she deems necessary. In the unlikely event that my son refuses or is unable to accept his responsibility and his total share reverts to my daughter, then it is my wish that Lacey also assume the role of sole executor. Jean Atwill will then relinquish that position and will be paid the one-time sum of five million dollars."

Jack's will also bequeathed to both Brett Marchbanks and Mary Ryan Gallagher the sum of five hundred thousand dollars each, and there was a statement of explanation:

"Although money can never be sufficient compensation for lifelong devotion, I am leaving a significant sum to my good friend and loyal employee. Without Brett Marchbank's brilliant endeavors over the past fifteen years, Gallagher's Best would never have become the giant that it is. He deserves more, but I don't want him to become too rich to continue working.

"When Mary Ryan married my son, I was the happiest of fathers. Because I believe in the sanctity and permanence of marriage, I still consider her to be my rightful, blessed daughter-in-law. This small bequest can never right the mortal wrong that was done to her by my son's defection from the church and his marriage, but I want her to know that I still love her.

"Although I have never been one to believe in a hereafter, I now find myself facing eternity with a fervent hope in my heart that someday we will all meet again. Until that time, I bid you farewell. May you enjoy good health and prosper."

The attorney cleared his throat and laid the papers down on the desk. "There is an addendum of procedures to be followed as well as line of succession, but this is of little interest to anyone except the executor."

All eyes in the room focused on Jean Atwill, the petite gray-haired woman who had entered after everyone had been seated. Her eyes were red-rimmed from weeping, but she was perfectly dressed in a black wool Valentino suit and Chanel pumps and handbag. Her only jewelry was a rope of large pearls around her neck and a diamond-studded gold Rolex on her arm. When her name was spoken, she lifted her head and looked straight ahead, her chin at a defiant tilt.

Tom Brennan had a few comments to make. "I know the terms of the will come as a shock to some of you, but I want you to know that it was written only after great thought and discussion and much soul-searching on the part of the deceased. Whether you agree with Jack Gallagher's final decision or not, rest assured that he did only what he thought was best for everyone concerned."

There was a long, heavy silence in the room. Lacey could not bring herself to look at her brother, so filled was she with rage at her father's betrayal and his godlike meddling in their lives. The relatives and servants shuffled to their feet and began to file out of the room.

Scott stood up and looked anxiously at his sister. She avoided his eyes and muttered, "Wills can be broken."

Tom Brennan heard her and retorted, "Not this one. Jack added a codicil stipulating that anyone who contests the will or any part of it is automatically disinherited. Sorry, Lacey. You should know by now that Jack Gallagher was not one to be easily thwarted."

Scott continued to stare at his sister, the one person who had given him nothing but love and support his entire life, but when she raised her eyes to his, he saw only a sickening frustration and disappointment. He knew with dreadful certainty that nothing would ever be the same between them again. In death, Jack Gallagher had managed to drive a deep and mortal wedge between his daughter and son, a feat he could have never accomplished in life.

Scott cast his eyes downward, turned on his heel, and strode from the room. Sasha followed, her stiletto heels clicking along the marble halls and piercing the sullen, pervasive silence that had settled on the house.

Steve reached over and tried to take Lacey's hand, but she recoiled. "Don't touch me!"

Raising his hands in mock surrender, Steve replied, "Hey, don't take it out on me! It was your father that shafted you."

"You must be very happy with him now. He's offered you ten million dollars to marry me again, hasn't he?" she asked, her words glacial.

"Not really! Whether or not I get that money is your decision, not mine. He knew damned well you'd never come back to me, even with that kind of price on my head. Suffering and pain didn't turn that bastard into a saint after all, did it now?"

She stared at him in stony silence.

Steve got to his feet, and the fury that was seething inside him boiled over into his words. "Think it over, Lacey. Maybe it's not such a bad idea after all."

He turned from her and walked to Erin and JJ to give them each a hug. "You can always come stay with me at the ranch if it gets too tough around here, remember that." Then, without a backward glance, he left the room.

Lacey got out of her chair and approached Tom Brennan. "Does this mean that I can't even sit on the board anymore?"

"Not while Scott's alive, I'm afraid. The terms of the will are explicit. Either he runs the company himself or he's disinherited, and you know, nice guy that he is, he has no intention of taking the vows of poverty. Even if he was so inclined, I'm afraid that wife of his wouldn't let him."

"He doesn't know or care about any of it. He'll run Gallagher's Best right into the ground."

"I tried to point that out to your father, but he wouldn't listen to me. He was convinced that his son would rise to the occasion. Jack was a pragmatic man, but he had a blind spot as big as the moon where Scott was concerned. He cut you out because he knew that if you were around, you'd do all the work and let Scott off the hook as usual. Jack didn't want that. He wanted Scott to have to make all the decisions himself."

"My father lied to me, Tom. He promised me when I came back from Texas that I would succeed him as head of Gallagher's Best. Now it seems that it didn't matter that I was smarter or worked harder or cared about him and his damned company," she said. "All that mattered to him was that I had the misfortune not to be a son." She spoke the words as if they were poison in her mouth.

"He did what he thought was best for you."

"I hope there's a hell, Tom, and I hope to God he's there!" she declared and strode out of the room, followed by Mary and Penny. Brett stayed behind to ponder his future at Gallagher's Best. The prospect of working for Scott was not a happy one. Brett decided then and there that it was time to look for a new job. He got out of his chair and stomped out of the room.

Tom watched Lacey and her friends leave and shook his head. "I do believe she inherited her father's steel balls," he murmured to his associate.

"What do you think will happen now?"

"There's nothing she can do. I made sure of that. Jack Gallagher is going to get his way in death, the same as he did in life."

"Personally, I'd put my money on the dame. The son looks like a wimp."

Tom Brennan shook his head. "That would be a serious mistake. They've both got killer genes."

Throughout the discussion, Jean Atwill had stayed in her chair in the back of the room, watching and listening. As soon as Lacey left the room, she stood up and walked toward the desk where Tom was now gathering up his papers.

She and Tom stared at each other for a moment. A glimmer of a smile passed between them.

"I'd appreciate it if you'd send me a copy of the will tomorrow." Her tone was courteous and pleasant.

Tom smiled. "As you wish."

She turned and left the room.

When she was gone, Tom's associate asked, "Is that the broad Gallagher's supposed to have been shacking up with for the past thirty-five years?"

"That's the bitch all right."

"She musta been a great lay."

"Maybe, but she's smart too. She knows where all the bodies are buried."

"How come he didn't leave her anything in the will if they were so close?" the associate asked.

"Two-fifty a year plus expenses is nothing?" Tom asked as he picked up his briefcase and strode from the room.

5

Mary Ryan Gallagher and Penny and Brett Marchbanks stood at the bottom of the staircase, trying to decide what to do. Penny wanted to go up and comfort Lacey, but Brett held her back.

"She's not going to want to talk to anybody for a while. Let her alone."

Penny looked up at her tall husband and noticed the muscles jumping in his cheek. Even though he had said nothing after hearing the will read, it was apparent, to her at least, that he was angry. Trying to lighten the situation, she said, "For a man who just inherited half a million dollars, you don't look very happy."

"Let it rest, Penny. You know exactly how I'm feeling right now."

Mary listened to the frustration evident in both of her friends' voices and asked, "It doesn't make sense, does it, Brett?"

He shook his head in tight little jerks as he responded in a burst of aggravation.

"It doesn't make sense at all! Jack Gallagher must have been nuts at the end to do such a damned stupid thing as to cut Lacey out altogether. God, what was he thinking? To give Gallagher's Best to that good-for-nothing bastard! Scott will destroy everything that Jack worked all his life to build."

The two women watched him fume, and they both thought of Lacey and how betrayed she must be feeling.

"Come on, Mary. Let's go upstairs and see if she wants to talk," Penny insisted, taking the other woman's arm and starting up the stairs. "Brett, do you want to come too?"

"Go ahead if you must, but count me out. I'm having enough trouble dealing with this thing myself. I'm going to walk around the garden for a while and cool off. Take your time. I'll meet you back here in the foyer."

He turned and walked out of the house.

"It's damp and foggy out there," Mary protested, but he was already gone.

"Let him go. He needs to work off some of his anger. I've never seen him in such a state. He looks like he's going to have a stroke."

The two women climbed the stairs, and Penny hesitated for a moment before knocking at the door to Lacey's bedroom.

"Who is it?" Lacey called.

"Mary and Penny. Want some soft shoulders to cry on?" Penny responded.

The door was opened by a tense and drawn Lacey, and Penny moved right in and took her friend in her arms.

"Your poor thing! You must be miserable," she said, and sympathetic words from one of her dearest friends melted the icy anger that had enveloped Lacey. Tears trickled down her cheeks as she choked on a suppressed sob.

Mary, who was standing close by, murmured, "Go ahead and cry, Lacey. It won't change anything but it might make you feel better."

Lacey's crying spell did not last long, and when it was over she went into her bathroom and splashed cold water on her face. Her friends waited on the mauve velvet bench at the foot of the bed. Lacey at last settled herself in the boudoir chair, and there was a long moment of silence, which Lacey herself broke.

"Brett must be feeling almost as bad as I am, isn't he?"

"He's outside stomping around in the fog, trying to cool down," Penny replied, and then added, "what in the world got into your father to do such a dumb-assed thing?"

Lacey shook her head in bewilderment. "I have no idea. He was happy to have Scott back, but I'm not so sure he was as happy as I kept telling him he ought to be. He never had any confidence in him, never. It's unlike him not to have warned me."

"Men!" Penny said disgustedly. "They always band together against the women. It makes me sick."

Mary, who had said little, spoke up. "I'll bet Scott is as upset as you are, Lacey. I think you ought to talk things out with him. You two have always been so close. Don't let the damned will change that. Talk to him. Work things out together."

Penny agreed. "That's a great suggestion. Nothing can be served by you two being enemies."

"It sounds like a good idea, but right now I'm not sure I can talk rationally. I'm too upset and angry."

"But you're not angry with Scott, Lacey," Mary insisted. "Remember, he's been victimized too. He doesn't want to run Gallagher's Best. He hates it there."

"That's true. Maybe we ought to talk."

"And be sure you're alone, Lacey, alone. Keep that bitch wife of his away. All she's interested in is money, and now her hubby's got bundles of it in his own name," Penny warned. "Talk to your brother alone."

The three women chatted for half an hour. When Penny and Mary at last took their leave, Lacey felt better and was considering approaching Scott.

The women had to wait almost fifteen minutes in the foyer before Brett came in from the early evening fog.

"That must've been a long walk," Penny observed, seeing that her husband looked much calmer than he had when he left.

"I feel a lot better now. I was a little panicky there for a few minutes. Come on, let's drive down to Rive Gauche for dinner. A nice meal and a bottle or two of good wine should make us all feel better. How's Lacey doing?"

Mary smiled. "I think she's going to live."

"Well, that's good news."

As they headed toward the French restaurant on the peninsula, Mary offered her own perception of the day's events.

"I know you're both feeling hostile to Jack Gallagher, but I'm grateful for all he's done for me, and leaving me a half million dollars was, well, it was so generous of him. Brett, don't you feel even a little bit thankful and pleased that he left you that money?"

"Yeah, I'm happy to get the money. I guess."

"You were worth a lot more than he paid you," Penny said. "Other men in positions as responsible as yours have a lot of perks that he refused to give you. He wouldn't even let you fly first-class."

"He ran a tight ship, Penny, and he kept operating costs down," Brett responded. "That's why Gallagher's Best is as successful as it is. But I don't want to talk about him anymore. He's dead and gone. Let's let him rot in peace."

6

A

fter Mary and Penny left, Lacey got into the shower to relax
some of the tension and refresh herself. As she stood under the cascade
of warm water, she began to formulate an approach to Scott. Surely the
two of them could come up with a plan that would be mutually bene-
ficial. As selfish as her brother might be, she was sure he was as uneasy
about inheriting everything as she was with being excluded almost entirely. What the devil had happened to her father's mind?

By the time she emerged and was toweling her hair and her body dry,
she had decided that the next morning she would definitely speak to
Scott. She had nothing to lose.

She pulled on a clean pair of sweatpants and a shirt and went down
to the kitchen. Gordon and Silvana were sitting at the table having coffee.
The cook was nowhere to be seen, and there seemed to be no prepa-
rations for dinner.

Both servants jumped to their feet.

"Please sit down and relax," Lacey said, motioning them back into
their chairs. "I thought I might like a cup of tea and a sandwich."

Gordon was flustered. "Miss Lacey, I'm so sorry, but I thought, well,
Mr. Scott said he and his wife were going out to a restaurant to celebrate.
I asked him about you and he assured me that you wouldn't feel like
eating anything tonight. Consequently, I gave the cook the night off. I'm
so sorry. What would you like to have?"

Gordon's words shocked Lacey. How could Scott be so damned cavalier about everything? He could at least have made a gesture of concern for her feelings, but no, he went out to have a good time. Typical.
In that moment an idea that was lurking in the back of her mind came
forward and she grasped it. She would hire herself the finest team of
lawyers in the country and she would break the rotten will. She didn't
give a damn whether or not she lost what her father left her. She'd rather
fight injustice and lose than to give in to a decision that must have been
made when her father's mind was twisted by disease and medication.
If her mother were alive this would never have happened.

"Ma'am, are you all right?" Gordon asked.

Lacey snapped out of her reverie. "Oh, yes. Absolutely, Gordon. I'm fine. Don't be concerned. I am a little hungry, though. If we have any sliced chicken, I'd love a sandwich."

"There's some good chicken salad left over from the reception. You like a sandwich outta that?" Silvana asked.

"That'll be great. And some Darjeeling tea."

The two servants began to scurry around, and Lacey seated herself at the table. "Why don't we have a snack together?" she asked. "Like old times."

For the first time since the will had been read, Lacey felt like a whole person again. Tomorrow morning she would talk to Scott, and if he wasn't cooperative, she'd fight him every step of the way.

Unable to sleep, Lacey was propped up in bed watching an old movie on television when there was a knock at her bedroom door, and she heard Scott's voice calling to her. She got out of bed, saw that it was almost one-thirty, pulled on a robe, and opened the door. A slightly tipsy Scott was standing there grinning at her. He was wearing his monogrammed silk pajamas with no robe and his feet were bare. In each hand he held a bottle of wine from the cellar. He grinned and held up the bottles for her to see the labels.

"Look, '61 Petrus—one for you and one for me."

Lacey shook her head. "You're already tight. You don't need to drink anything else."

"No, I'm not! I only had two, maybe three glasses of Dom Pérignon. Sasha drank most of it. She's already asleep. I wanted to drink the old man's important stuff with you and talk. You're not mad at me, are you?"

Lacey looked at her brother and remembered the thousands of times he had asked her that question. Even as a small boy, he could never stand for her to be angry with him. He would commit the most egregious of sins and then become contrite in the face of her displeasure. She always forgave him.

She smiled and moved through the doorway.

"Okay, but we're going to open only one of those bottles. Come on, let's go down to the study."

The wine was indeed wonderful. Jack Gallagher had been an aggressive collector of rare vintages, and he had one of the finest cellars in the country. Both of his children had been taught the nuances of wine appreciation, and they swirled and sniffed and marveled over the heady bouquet.

"I'll bet the old guy's turning over in his grave right now. We didn't even wait for the sediment to settle, but what the hell, so it's a little chewy," Scott remarked.

They were on their second glass when the subject of inheritance came up, and Scott was appropriately discomfited.

"I'm sorry it turned out this way, Lacey. Honest to God, I am. I never thought he'd do such a terrible thing to you, to both of us actually. You know I don't want that job."

"I know you don't, but it's my life, and I'm going to take it back, Scott. I've decided to break the will."

Her brother was startled. "You're not serious. If you lose, you'll lose everything. That would be insane."

"I've already lost almost everything anyway. The children have their trusts, so I'm not risking their futures." She grinned wickedly, took a sip of the wine and added, "Besides, I'll have a very rich brother who would never throw me out on the street."

Scott grew more agitated. "But you'll get everything all tied up in court if you do that. It could be bad for the business."

"True. It'll probably be devastating and take years. You know how slow the courts are. But what the hell, it'll give me something to do."

"Tom repeatedly told me the will was ironclad. There was no way it could be broken."

"When did you talk to him about it? I thought he left right after the reading."

"I, uh, he called me . . . before we went out."

"I see. Now he's your lawyer I suppose. Tom always goes where the money is. I'll hire my own firm anyway. I think I'll go for Callaghan, Bernstein, and Wickham. They're terrific litigators. If anybody can break that damn thing, they can. It might take some time, but you won't have too much to lose. If I win, the court will probably decide that we should share the estate equally. Then I'll use my cash to buy you out of the company, if the lawyers leave us anything to divide, that is."

"Don't do this to me, Lacey. I hate the thought of having our whole lives dragged through the courtroom."

"I hate it too, but I've been left no alternative, unless . . ."

Scott refilled his glass with what was left of the first bottle. "Uh, sorry, Lacey. Did you want some more? Want me to open the other bottle?"

"Why the hell not? It's your cellar now. Why shouldn't I enjoy the best you have to offer." She got up from the couch. "Here, let me do it. You never get the corkscrew in straight."

As she peeled the lead seal off the top of the bottle, Scott sank down into the chair and asked, "What did you mean by 'unless'?"

"I've been giving it some thought, and I've figured out a way for us both to begin living our lives free and clear of that stupid will."

"How the hell can we manage that?"

"I don't have all the exact figures, but I can make an educated guess," Lacey began, choosing her words carefully. "Dad's stock in the company is worth about eight or nine hundred million, a little more, a little less. At the time he died, Dad had cash and other investments outside the business that added up to at least two or three hundred million, all in his own name. That doesn't count the real estate, the boat, Mom's jewels, or the art collection. Suppose you refuse to accept the job. You'd get one thousand dollars, and I'd get everything else."

"Why would I do that?"

"Because then I would be in control of everything. I took Dad's copy of the will out of the safe this evening, and there's nothing in there that says that I can't dispose of the inheritance anyway I choose, if I become the beneficiary, of course. You could go off skiing, travel, do anything you want, and you could go right away. I would take steps to transfer everything that wasn't part of the company to your name. That would mean between two and three hundred million in your control immediately. I'd then split the company stock that was in Dad's name almost down the middle. Fifty-one percent to me, forty-nine to you, keeping me in control. I'd sign over the titles to all the properties, the house, the boat, but not the plane. The company needs that, but you could still use it. I'd give you the art collection and all of Mom's jewels, except her engagement ring. She wanted me to have that."

"I don't want Mom's jewelry. You can keep all of it." Scott was quite obviously warming to the idea.

"So what do you say, have we got a deal? We can each then draw up a new will. If anything happens to me, you'll be the beneficiary, and you could do the same for me. You know you can trust me. Have I ever once reneged on a promise?"

Scott was excited. His sister was pulling him out of a jam as she always did.

"It's a great idea. Let's put it down on paper right now. We'll sign it and wake Gordon up to be a witness."

"I don't think that would be wise," Lacey said. "The papers should be drawn up by an attorney."

"Not Tom, I don't want Tom. He'll try to stop us."

"Why would he?"

"He'll think we're trying to subvert Dad's wishes. I know he will. He was one of Dad's cronies. He'll fight us every step of the way."

"You're probably right. Tomorrow morning I'll call up Mickey Callahan and we'll go see him together." She raised her glass in triumph. "Here's to the Gallagher heirs. When we stick together, nobody can defeat us."

Scott clinked his glass with hers and added, "Even the old Gallagher himself."

"If he's watching, I hope he's impressed with our creativity," Lacey added with a sigh.

"He's probably pissed out of his mind."

Brother and sister said good night at about three-thirty in the morning. Scott tottered off to bed carrying half a bottle of Petrus. He said he was going to wake Sasha up and tell her that they were still going to be rich but they were also going to be free. His sister promised him that as soon as the papers were signed, he could take the plane to wherever the spring skiing was the best.

Lacey knew it would be pointless to try to go to sleep. She was exhilarated and anxious for the morning to come so she could set her plan in action. It had all been so much easier than she had expected it to be.

She stayed in the study reading the will and going over in her mind all the things that had to be written into the agreement. She made several pages of notes.

When dawn turned the sky from black to gray, she went upstairs to put on her suit and get ready for a nice long swim in the pool. It would be the most relaxing thing she could do. There was no point in getting into bed and staring at the ceiling.

She was surprised to find the door to her bedroom shut. She was almost certain she had left it wide open when Scott had come to get her. She opened the door and snapped on the light, but everything looked as it had when she left. She slipped out of her nightgown and into a tank suit. The morning was chilly but the water would be warm. It took a few minutes to find her goggles, and then she wrapped herself in her terrycloth robe and headed back downstairs.

★★ 7 ★★

Sasha was sound asleep when Scott returned to their bedroom. Taking a swig from the wine bottle, he snapped on the overhead light and sat down on the edge of the bed. He put his lips to his wife's ear.

"Wake up, my little Russian doll. Wake up. Daddy's brought you some good news."

Sasha opened her eyes and squinted in the glare of the light.

"What the hell are you talking about?"

"Look, I brought you some of the old fart's Petrus. Here taste it," he said, shoving the bottle toward her.

She pushed it away irritably. "For God's sake, didn't you have enough to drink at the restaurant? Get in bed."

"Can't. Gotta get my clothes on and go to the lawyer's office with m'sister."

His words brought her to instant wakefulness.

"What are you talking about?"

Scott giggled. He loved to torment his wife, who had little sense of humor.

"Gonna sign away my inheritance. Give it all to Lacey." He hiccupped and laughed again.

"You're drunk. Go to bed."

"Nope. Gonna go down to the fancy lawyer's office today and sign the papers. Promised her I would."

Sasha sat bolt upright in bed. "Have you been talking to Lacey tonight?"

"Yep, all night. Hours and hours and hours. Great gal. Smart's a whip. Gonna set everything straight for both of us. She gets the comp'ny, I get the money and the houses and the boat and the art collection. Is that a good deal or what?"

"What in God's name do you think you're doing? The will gave you everything. You don't need Lacey to straighten things out, understand?" Sasha was furious. She had always resented the hold that Lacey had over her husband, and she had been afraid something like this would happen. Scott was such a damned jellyfish.

She snatched the bottle away from him. "Give me that. You've had enough to drink. Now get out of your pajamas and get in the shower." She sprang out of bed and marched into the bathroom to pour the rest of the wine down the sink, when she was struck by an alternative thought. Why wake him up at all? The best thing that could happen right now was for Scott to go to sleep and give her a chance to get help. If he was out cold, he couldn't do anything stupid.

She opened the medicine chest and took the sleeping pills she'd been given to help her through the last weeks of Jack's illness. With Lacey and the nurses tramping about at all hours of the night, she'd had trouble sleeping. Two usually did it for her, but the longer Scott was out, the better. She popped four pills into her husband's water glass, filled it with wine, and swirled the liquid with the handle of her toothbrush until she was certain the pills had dissolved. She then poured a small amount of wine into her own glass and carried both glasses back into the bedroom.

Scott was still sitting on the edge of the bed, but his chin was on his chest and his eyes were closed.

"Wake up, darling. I'll help you into bed, and then we'll have a little nightcap."

Scott fumbled his way between the sheets, and then she put the glass of doctored wine into his hand.

"Here's to us, darling, and the good times ahead."

"Good times. Here's to m'sister. Tomorrow we're gonna be rich. Get papers signed, 'nd ski on the plane. I mean . . ."

"I know what you mean, darling. Now drink this wonderful Petrus. Chugalug, now."

His heavy eyelids were drooping, and she was afraid the glass would slip out of his hand. She set her own wine down and wrapped her fingers around his.

"Here you go, darling, down the hatch." She lifted the hand that was holding the glass to his mouth, and he opened his lips and drank it all. He grimaced at the taste but swallowed anyway. She then took the empty glass and helped him down to his pillow. She tucked the covers around him. A tidy person, she carried both glasses into the bathroom, washed the wine out with soap, rinsed them, and returned them to their holders. She left the unfinished bottle of wine on the sink and climbed into bed.

She was too worried to go back to sleep. She needed to talk to Tom Brennan. As soon as daylight broke, she'd get ready for her morning job and make her call from the telephone in the Ferrari. That way she'd make sure nobody overheard her. Tom would know what to do. He was more than a match for that bitch Lacey. She had a lot of nerve trying to wheedle an unfair agreement out of Scott. She wasn't going to let her get away with it.

8

The water was a perfect eighty-six degrees, and when she stepped into the pool, it seemed to wrap itself around her body and gather her into its relaxing warmth. Lacey had always loved to swim. Maude had to watch her constantly because even as a toddler, Lacey would jump into the deep end and never feel the least bit threatened. When she was ten, her father had the old kidney-shaped pool dug out of the yard and replaced with a long rectangle. Three lanes wide, it was twenty-five meters in length and always kept at a warm temperature. Maude called it Lacey's playground because she and her friends were always in it.

Submerging herself, Lacey's thoughts turned to memories of her mother. As she adjusted the goggles on her face and stretched her body on the surface of the water to begin her extended, smooth stroke, she remembered her mother sitting in the garden chair, an umbrella protecting her from the sun as she watched her daughter do her daily two thousand meters. Maude was always there, morning, afternoon, or evening, needlepoint in hand, glorying in the athletic ability of her only daughter.

Lacey moved slowly. It had been at least a week since she'd had time to do her laps, and she wanted to prepare herself for a long, easy workout. She was in no hurry. By the time she had finished twenty laps, her muscles felt loose again, and she began to pick up the pace. She wondered how many thousands of miles she had swum in this pool. Stroke, breathe in, pull, exhale, kick, kick, kick. At each end, she did a graceful flip turn and glided back into the rhythm of her stroke. She could tell that her heart rate had elevated, and it felt good to be pushing her body to perform.

She was on her fortieth lap when she picked up the scent of perfume in the air. When she reached the end of the lap, she looked up before she did her turn to see if there was anyone around, but she saw no one. She continued swimming and wondered if Scott had been sober enough to explain to Sasha the agreement they'd made a few hours ago. It didn't matter. Scott didn't want a protracted legal battle, and neither did she. They'd work things out together. That's the way it had always been, and she was sure their relationship would not change now.

Lacey swam for more than an hour, and when she finished, she floated on her back and looked up at the now blue sky. The sun had risen, and it was going to be a beautiful day.

Lacey pulled her body out of the pool, wrapped herself in the terry-cloth robe, and hurried through the chill morning air into the house past the kitchen, and up the back stairs. As soon as she entered her room, she stripped off her suit and stepped into the shower. She shampooed her hair and soaped herself down. Although she was vaguely aware of some noise and commotion, the sound of the water distorted and almost obliterated all other sounds. When at last she turned off the shower, she heard a pounding at her bedroom door.

"Who is it?" she called as she pulled a big towel from the warming rack and wound it around her body.

"It's Gordon, ma'am. Please come out. Something terrible has happened." His normally controlled, modulated voice was hysterical.

Lacey shoved her feet into her mules, grabbed a robe from the chair beside her bed and hurried to the door. What could have happened that would upset him like that?

"Yes?" she said as she swung the door open.

"It's Mr. Scott . . . ," he began.

"Is something wrong? Where is he?" Not waiting for an answer, she pushed past him and strode down the hall toward the large room she had given up to her brother and his wife.

"I'm afraid he's . . . he's dead, ma'am," Gordon called to her back, stopping her.

She whirled around to face him. "Oh my God!" she exclaimed and turned once more toward the room.

"Don't go in there! Please don't! I beg you."

Lacey's knees went weak and she reached for the banister to steady herself. Gordon's words were pounding in her ears but she couldn't bring herself to believe them. It had to be a mistake. She'd go in there, and Scott would apologize for causing such a row. He was always getting himself into scrapes and coming out unscathed but leaving everyone else shattered in little pieces.

She continued toward the closed bedroom door and lifted her hand to knock, then, realizing her error, grabbed the knob and turned it. The large, beautiful room with its antique walnut furniture was in disarray. Sasha's pink silk nightgown and negligee were draped across the brocade chaise longue by the window. The silk coverlet was partially pulled from the figure in the large four-poster bed, and Lacey could see Scott's curly brown hair on the pillow.

In repose, he looked young and angelic, as he always did when he was asleep. Untimely death would surely not leave such a peaceful expression on his handsome face, but there was an unmistakable chill of death in the room. She had to be sure he wasn't merely asleep, and as her slippers carried her across the pale blue carpeting and closer to the bed, her eyes pulled away from his face, down his slender neck, to the hilt of a small knife protruding from the middle of his chest. There was a long, red stain of blood draining from his wound, streaming down his flesh to the sheets. She stopped, transfixed by the sudden and absolute certainty that her brother was gone forever.

She tried to scream, but no sound would come. She attempted to breathe, but her throat was closed tight. Suddenly she felt a strong hand laid on her shoulder and a voice hissed into her ear, "It's all your fault! It's all your fault!"

Lacey whirled around and looked into the face of her sister-in-law. Sasha's eyes were wide and crazed, and she shouted, "You're the cause of it all!"

Lacey wanted to speak, to refute the vicious and untrue words, but she could not utter a word. Her throat was paralyzed, and Sasha's words hung in the air, creating waves of ugly, oppressive sound that coiled around her like a snake, threatening to crush the life out of her. Lacey turned away and forced herself to go to her brother.

The walk to the big bed was eternal, and when she was close enough to touch him, she put her shaking hand on his cool brow, and tears streamed down her face. She wanted to kiss him good-bye. She had to. She leaned down and pressed her lips to his cheek, and then her knees gave way altogether. Silvana came into the room just as Lacey was collapsing, and she rushed forward and grabbed her in her strong arms.

"There, there, cara mia. Silvana is here. Hush, bambina, hush," she murmured as she led her from the room. Out in the hallway, Lacey was still struggling for air. Her throat hurt, and she felt as if she were suffocating. At the head of the twin curving staircases, she found herself unable to walk any farther. Her head whirled with the vision that would haunt her forever, and she lost her equilibrium. Her upper body pitched forward. If Silvana had not been gripping her arm, she would have crashed down the long stairway, head first, but the older woman pulled her back. Gordon leapt forward and helped, and between them, the servants managed to lower the distraught woman to the floor of the upper gallery.

She was lying helpless in her distress, barely able to draw air into her lungs, when the figure of her sister-in-law loomed over her again.

"You bitch! Stop playacting! You're glad he's dead! Now you'll get it all!"

Silvana moved her heavy body with a speed and grace only severe emotion would wring from it. She got to her feet, drew her arm back, and slapped the hysterical young woman across the face.

"Be quiet, *putana!* She loved him more than you ever loved anybody but yourself!"

Her cheek reddening, Sasha stepped back, and her manner switched from hot to cold. "I'm calling the police!"

"It's already been done," Gordon said, squatting on the floor and cradling Lacey's head in his hands.

Sasha stormed back toward her room, but remembering the horror that was there, she whirled about and raced down the stairs instead. The two servants watched with contempt apparent on their faces, and then turned to the task at hand.

"Give us a little help, Miss Lacey," Gordon urged, "and we'll get you back to your bed."

9

Filled with grief, shock, and confusion, Lacey returned to her room, but she refused to return to her bed. Now was the time to find out if she possessed the strength and fortitude she would need. Assisted by the supportive Silvana, she dressed, and when the police arrived, it was she who directed them to the room where her dead brother's body lay. It was not long before the house was swarming with officers in uniforms and plainclothes detectives, as well as several men from the coroner's office. At Lacey's insistence, Cherry Dolan, the detective assigned to the case, put an officer at each entrance to keep the members of the press outside. After a brief look at the corpse and the scene of the crime, Cherry Dolan and her partner, Chuck Bascombe, approached Lacey.

"Miss Gallagher, we'd like to have a few words with everyone who spent the night in the house, but one at a time, please. Is there a place where we could do that in privacy?"

Lacey was numb with grief but she wanted to be cooperative. These people were there to find out who had killed her brother. "Of course. Come, I'll show you to my father's library."

"Your father's funeral was yesterday, wasn't it?" Chuck asked.

Lacey nodded.

As they approached a library door, a policeman came in and announced that there was a Tom Brennan outside who insisted on being admitted to the house.

"Who's he?" Cherry asked.

"My father's attorney."

Eyebrows raised, Chuck looked at Lacey and asked, "You called your lawyer already?"

Lacey shook her head. "No, but I'm sure someone in the house did. He and my father were very close friends."

"Let him in then," Chuck told the officer.

Within moments Tom Brennan was striding toward them, bristling with annoyance.

"Lacey, have you said anything, anything at all to these people?" he asked, putting his arm around her protectively and glaring at the two detectives.

Before Lacey could reply, Cherry responded, "So far, she's merely been asked to direct us to a room where we can conduct an inquiry, so relax, sir. We have no intention of violating anybody's rights."

The testy exchange startled Lacey. Was it possible that one or both of them might seriously think she had anything to do with Scott's death?

"Good," Tom replied, "however, I need a few moments alone with my client first."

"But, Tom, I have nothing to hide . . . ," she began to protest, but the attorney shushed her.

"I know that, my dear, but this gentleman and the pretty little lady don't, so if you'll excuse us," the attorney declared, taking Lacey's arm and leading her away.

A shared look of displeasure passed between the detectives, and Chuck quipped, "Well, 'pretty little lady,' let's go talk to the coroner's men and see what they have for us."

Cherry made a face at him, and they walked away.

Once inside the library Lacey protested, "But I told them they could use this room." Tom slammed the door behind them.

"Let 'em find someplace else to do their job. They're the enemy now, Lacey, remember that."

"Why in the world would you say that? I want to help them find out who killed my brother! I want whoever killed Scott put into the gas chamber or locked away forever. Why are they my enemies?"

Pulling her over to the big leather couch, he sat very close so that he could speak softly.

"Listen, my dear, the police are as much interested in finding someone to accuse as they are in finding the culprit. Believe me, I know how they work, and you, my dear, will be the obvious suspect."

"Me?"

"Yes, you, because you had the most to gain from Scott's death. I knew the terms your stubborn father concocted would cause trouble, but he wouldn't listen to me. Remember, you were in the house not more than a few yards from Scott, and you alone had millions to gain from his murder."

Her situation sharply clear, Lacey protested, "That's crazy! I could never have harmed Scott! I loved him. All of our lives, we've been as close as a brother and sister can be. We told each other things we could never have told anyone else. My life will never be the same without him." Tears streamed freely down her face. Tom put his arm around her, cradled her head on his shoulder, and encouraged her to weep.

When her tears were spent at last, he went to the desk to ring the kitchen. Gordon responded on the intercom.

"Bring some coffee into the library," he began and then turning to Lacey asked, "have you had anything to eat today?" When she shook her head no, he asked Gordon to bring toast too. Returning to the couch with a box of tissues, he commented, "I'd have had him bring something heartier, but you probably wouldn't be able to swallow it. Now tell me everything that happened after you left the library in a huff yesterday. Did you talk to anybody?"

She blew her nose and wiped her eyes and nodded.

"Who?" Tom asked.

"Well, Mary and Penny before they left the house. I had a sandwich in the kitchen with Gordon and Silvana in the evening and last of all Scott. It was after one when he knocked on my door. I was watching television and thinking about trying to break the will when he arrived."

"That would have been a stupid thing to do. So you let him come into your room?"

"No. We came here to the library. He'd gone down to the cellar to get some of Dad's rare wine to drink. He said it all belonged to us now, and we might as well enjoy it. He brought back two bottles of '61 Petrus—two, for God's sake. Dad would have turned in his grave if he'd seen us depleting his precious collection."

There was a soft knock on the door, and Gordon rolled in an antique tea cart on which there was a silver pot of coffee, two Limoges china cups and saucers, a silver rack filled with several kinds of bread toasted to perfection, a basket of rolls, curls of sweet butter, and a small bowl of homemade strawberry conserve. In a house built by food, only the finest was ever served. The butler started to pour the coffee, but Tom waved him out.

"Thanks, Gordon. We'll take care of it ourselves."

Gordon hesitated, his eyes fixed on Lacey. "Are you all right, ma'am?" he asked.

Lacey nodded and looked away. She had never been able to accept sympathy of any kind without tears rising in her eyes, and she did not want to cry anymore, at least not until she was alone.

When Gordon left, Lacey nibbled a piece of toast and sipped the steaming coffee, but it was too hot to drink. She continued her story.

"Scott opened the first bottle and poured us each a glass. We felt as guilty as two kids behind the barn smoking cigarettes. Dad was so possessive about his wine collection, you know. The Petrus was great, and it also helped relieve the pain we were both feeling. We drank one whole bottle while we reminisced, trying to top each other with stories about how Dad had controlled our lives."

She paused to ruminate, and Tom asked, "Did you talk about the mess your father made of things?"

"Of course. Both of us were shocked by the will."

Lacey did not notice the expression of disbelief on the lawyer's face.

"We decided on a plan to circumvent Dad's will."

"How did you manage to do that?"

"It was all so simple, really. Scott didn't want to run Gallagher's Best and I did. If he agreed to give up the company, I promised to share the estate with him." She then sketched out the terms they'd agreed on. She went to the desk and showed him the paper on which she had made notes.

"Everything would go to you," Tom Brennan said as he scanned the paper.

Lacey nodded. "Exactly. I checked out the will and it didn't say anything about what I could do with the money when I inherited it, did it?"

"Well . . . no, not really."

"That's it, you see. Would it have worked?"

Tom thought about it. "Much as I hate to admit it, but yeah, you could have given your brother anything you wanted. Did he really trust you that much?"

"Absolutely. You know how close we were. I would have done anything for Scott, and he would have done anything for me."

"So, when you went to your own room in the early hours of the morning it was all settled between you?"

Tears had started to roll down Lacey's cheeks again.

"We planned to tell everybody this morning. We intended to have new wills drawn up making each other the beneficiary."

"It'll be tough convincing people he was actually going to give up everything when it was already his," Tom conjectured, but Lacey intervened. "No, it won't. Not when I tell them that I had decided to sue to break the terms of the will. Scott knew I could have tied up the estate in the courts for years. I actually gave him an easy way out."

"Did you mention this scheme to anybody?"

"When would I have done that? We both went to bed at about three-thirty this morning. I was too excited to sleep, so at dawn I got out of bed and went down to the pool for a swim. I was in the shower when Gordon came to tell me Scott was dead."

She tried hard to swallow the lump in her throat.

"Dad always told us that if our family stayed together, nothing could ever defeat us. That was why the will came as such a shock. It's still hard for me to believe that he would create something so divisive as that damned will was. The cancer must have spread to his brain."

"Is there anything else I should know?"

As Lacey shook her head, she looked down and saw that she had ripped the lace edging from the handkerchief she was holding.

"All right then, I'll tell the detective that he can question you now. But you are never, never—understand?—never to talk to any policeman or district attorney without my being with you." His words were laden with a sense of doom.

"I'm not going to talk to anyone at all until I've had a chance to tell my children. Silvana's gone over to their wing of the house to make sure they stay in their rooms until I get there. They're going to be devastated. They loved Scott too."

"They've gotta grow up sometime. It's a rough world out there."

"Everybody has a right to be safe in their own homes, Tom," Lacey declared, annoyed that the attorney could be so callous about the loss of a beloved brother and uncle. "I haven't got any more time to talk. My children need me."

As Lacey rushed up one staircase, Sasha sauntered down the other. She saw Tom and hesitated. Then, as soon as Lacey was out of sight, she hurried toward him. She was about to say something when Cherry Dolan came out of the library and beckoned to her.

"Mrs. Gallagher, would you mind stepping in here for a few moments? We'd like to talk to you."

Tom spoke up. "Give me a few minutes to express my condolences, and she'll be right with you."

Cherry nodded and returned to the library, leaving them alone.

10

Lacey was relieved to find neither of the detectives in the hallway. She mounted the stairway leading to the wing where her children's rooms were located and opened Erin's door. Her daughter was sitting in the window seat looking down onto the circular driveway now clogged with vehicles. The slim, fragile young woman with long blonde hair jumped up and ran into her mother's arms.

"Mom, what's going on down there? Silvana came in a few minutes ago and told me not to come out of my room. Where's JJ?"

Lacey gave her daughter a long, reassuring hug and murmured, "It's okay, honey. Come on, put on your robe and we'll go see if JJ's awake."

Without knocking, they walked into the boy's room, which had the distinct odor of old tennis shoes, and picked their way across the clutter of dirty T-shirts, canvas shoes, magazines, and balls of various shapes and sizes. The servants were rarely allowed in JJ's room to clean up, because he enjoyed living in what he called his comfortable mess. He was still asleep, his long gangling legs sprawled across the bed and one foot propped up on the bedpost.

"Oh God, open the window!" Erin whispered. "How can he breathe in here?"

Lacey pulled open the draperies and let the morning sunshine stream into the littered room. The young man growled and pulled the pillow over his head. Lacey sat down on the edge of the mattress and put her hand gently on her son's shoulder, thinking how much he was beginning to look like his father.

"JJ, honey, wake up. I have something to tell you."

At the sound of his mother's voice, JJ responded, removing the pillow and opening his eyes.

"Hi, Mom, what's up?"

"Erin, JJ . . . ," she began, trying in vain to soften the terrible words she had to say to them.

Sensing the intensity of her emotion, JJ scrambled to a sitting position and put his hand on her arm. Erin sat down very close to her mother.

"Tell us, Mom," she whispered.

"Your Uncle Scott is dead," she said, foregoing any attempt to euphemize the dreadful message.

"My God, Mom, how?" Erin exclaimed.

"Did he have a heart attack or something?" JJ asked.

"No, no, nothing like that. It seems . . . he has apparently been . . . murdered." She had said the unsayable, and the terrible words left a wretched taste on her lips.

The impact of her message was as profound as she had expected. Erin started to cry, but JJ wanted more information. "How did it happen, Mom?" he asked, swallowing hard and trying not to be affected by his sister's tears.

Lacey put her face into her hands and pressed her fingertips into her temples. She didn't want to give voice to that awful moment when she saw the knife, but her children had to know, and she had to be the one to tell them.

"Somebody . . . stabbed him during the night."

"Where?" JJ asked.

"In his bed. Please don't ask me any more questions about it, because I don't have any answers to give you." As she said the words, she felt an overwhelming need to know more herself.

"Who would have done such a thing?" Erin wailed. "He was always so nice to everybody."

"I know, I know," Lacey said, and she began to cry. Erin and JJ were not accustomed to seeing their mother in tears and it unnerved them both. Lacey had always been their rock and their support, and it was frightening to see her emotionally vulnerable. Watching their mother's despair, they felt naked and unprotected.

Awkwardly, JJ patted her arm and Erin tucked her head into her mother's shoulder, but even that small surcease of tension was to be denied. Silvana burst into the room, her dark eyes wide with fear.

"Madonna," she gasped, making the sign of the cross. "That *diavola!* She tell them it was you!" The elderly woman's voice was charged with fury.

"What? My God, what are you saying, Silvana?"

"I listen. When I leave the library, I turn on the thing on your father's desk, you know the little box . . . and I listen in the kitchen."

"Grandpa's intercom," JJ explained. "I learned a long time ago that if you put it on monitor, you can go to any station in the house and hear what's being said in there."

"Are you talking about Sasha?" Lacey asked.

"Si, the *bagascia,* the beetch!" Silvana's portly figure was quivering in righteous indignation. She and Sasha had hated each other on sight, and the older woman had suffered great indignities at the hands of the imperious young wife, who treated her not as a beloved retainer but as a lowly servant.

"How could she say such a thing!" Erin cried.

Lacey could sense that the situation was getting out of hand. "She's upset, that's all. She knows I couldn't have killed my brother. What else did she say?"

"The man . . . the policeman ask her where she go this morning."

"She said she went out for her usual run, didn't she?" Lacey asked.

"No, more. She say she run more today. Ate too much food yesterday."

"I see. Then what did she say?"

"She say in very loud voice police should arrest you."

Lacey's mind was racing. It was true that she had stomped out of the room after the will was read, and everyone had seen her disappointment and anger. She supposed she was the logical one to be accused, but it was ridiculous. She would have given her own life to save Scott's, if necessary.

Lacey looked at her children and Silvana, and she knew that the people who really mattered would know the truth.

"JJ, go take a shower and get dressed. You too, Erin. Then I want you both down in the kitchen in half an hour. Silvana, have Cook fix them some breakfast."

"What are you going to do, Mom?" Erin asked.

Lacey took a deep breath and looked at her children. This was no time for anything but honesty.

"I haven't the faintest idea right now. But I'll think of something."

11

Lacey appeared at the top of the stairs unnoticed by the two detectives as they emerged from the library. She found herself eavesdropping on their conversation.

"Wow, how'd you like to have a bitch like that brought into the bosom of your family?" Chuck commented.

"Funny you should use the word *bosom*."

"Yeah, well, she's got quite a pair there. They were a little hard to ignore."

"What do you suppose Lacey Gallagher Haines did to deserve that much vitriol from her sister-in-law?"

Chuck shrugged his shoulders. "Seems fairly obvious. Her meal ticket's dead. Now all the millions go to her sister-in-law. Under the circumstances, you'd probably be pissed off too."

"Are you sure about her getting nothing? The order of death can be a tricky proposition when it comes to inheritance."

"You're right, and if that lady with the bosoms might be the beneficiary, then she's also a prime suspect herself."

Lacey made her presence known and startled the two detectives. "I've read the will, and it's explicit," she stated. "Sasha gets nothing. It might not be fair, but that's how Dad wanted it. My father considered her a temporary member of the family because she was my brother's third wife. Dad was a good if not very pious Catholic, and he considered Mary Gallagher, Scott's first wife, to be his true daughter-in-law."

Lacey descended the stairs, and she was at the bottom when she finished speaking. "Did you want to talk to me now?"

Somewhat taken aback by her directness and candor, the detectives nodded.

"You'll want your lawyer present?" Cherry asked.

"Not necessarily, but he'll probably insist on it. I intend to cooperate with you fully, however, since I have a greater interest in finding my brother's killer than you have." Lacey's voice reflected sincerity, and she looked weary and distressed.

While they waited for Tom to finish a telephone call, the coroner was given permission to remove the body from the house. Lacey's pain upon seeing the gurney wheeled past them and out the front door was palpable. She swayed slightly but managed to keep her balance and emotions in check.

When they were all settled in the library, Lacey related how she first learned of Scott's death. She then went on to tell the detectives the story about her late-night meeting with her brother and their plans to subvert their father's will. When she finished, she went to the desk to show them the paper on which she had scribbled notes about her proposed division of the estate. It was not there. The top sheet of the notepad was blank. Confused, she searched through the drawers, but she could not find it.

She looked at Tom. "It was there just a little while ago. I showed it to you. Did you take it?"

Tom looked bewildered. "No, of course I didn't take it. Perhaps one of the servants threw it away."

There was an awkward silence in the room, and for the first time Lacey had the terrible feeling that nobody believed what she had told them. She rang for Gordon, who appeared almost immediately.

"Gordon, have you or any of the maids been in here to clean up this morning?"

"No, ma'am. Everyone's been pretty upset since Mr. Scott's body was found. I'm afraid not much work's been done, because we've all stayed pretty much together in the kitchen."

"There's a piece of paper missing from the notepad on the desk. You haven't seen it, have you?" Lacey asked.

"No, I haven't."

Gordon left the room. Lacey turned to Tom. "You saw it, Tom. Tell them what I had written on it."

Tom shook his head. "I'm sorry, Lacey. I remember your mentioning something about it, but I honestly can't remember even looking at the paper."

Lacey looked at the detectives, then back at Tom. It was apparent that nobody believed her.

Tom got to his feet. "Detective Bascombe, Dolan, will you excuse us for a few minutes, please? My client and I have to talk something over. She's a bit distracted right now, which is understandable under the circumstances. She'll need some time to get her thoughts together."

"No, I don't need to get my thoughts together. Tom, you must have taken it without realizing what you were doing. Let's check your pockets." She got up from the couch and moved swiftly toward the lawyer. Tom shook his head in disbelief but stood quietly while Lacey rummaged through the pockets of his suit coat. The paper was not found.

Frustrated, Lacey insisted that he empty his pants pockets, but he produced nothing but a wallet and car keys. It was a difficult and awkward moment for everyone.

At last Tom shepherded the detectives from the room, insisting that his client was in no condition for further questioning. He promised he would make her available later. When they were alone, he patted her on the shoulder.

"There, there, my dear. You've had a miserable day and night. Your confusion is natural, but stop worrying about that damned little piece of paper. In a court of law it would be meaningless. It doesn't prove that Scott agreed to anything. So forget about it. If you had it, fine, but apparently you don't, so I suggest we chalk it all up to anxiety and confusion. Now I think we should get Dr. Preston over here to give you a little something to relax you."

"I don't need a doctor, and I haven't finished answering the detectives' questions yet," Lacey protested but with little conviction. She was beginning to have doubts of her own.

"You're in no shape to answer any more questions today. They can come back tomorrow when you're feeling better. You didn't kill Scott, and anybody who knows you knows that."

Tom rang for Gordon who appeared within the minute.

"Gordon, get Silvana in here to take Lacey up to bed. She needs time to pull herself together."

Lacey allowed the motherly housekeeper to take her up to her room, although she had no interest in being put to bed or going to sleep. She wanted to sort things out in her mind.

"Thank you, Silvana, but I feel fine. I'm going to sit here at my desk and look out at the garden and think for a while."

"You sure you no need me here with you?"

"I'll be fine, but keep an eye on JJ and Erin. What are they doing now?"

"They in kitchen. Cook fixing them her special French toast."

When the woman had gone, Lacey opened the curtains wide and let her body fall into the chair at the Victorian writing desk that had once been her mother's. She was gazing out the window to the lush greenery below, when her consciousness detected an inconsistency in her surroundings. Something was wrong. She pulled her eyes back from the garden and focused on her desk. The first thing she noticed was the Steuben Excalibur her father had given her on her twenty-first birthday.

It was an exquisite and costly chunk of perfect glass that usually held a small silver and gold sword. Suddenly, her mind flashed back to the vision of Scott's dead body and the small gold and silver hilt protruding from his chest.

Her heart began to pound and her hands shook. "Oh my God!" she whispered. Scott had been stabbed to death by her own letter opener!

12

Brett and Penny learned of Scott's death from Mary, who heard it on the all-news radio station. Penny immediately dressed and hurried over to be with Lacey. When she arrived at the gate, however, she had to park her car outside and make her way through the jam of reporters and cars trying to gain entrance. She managed to convince a policeman that she really was a friend of the family; he called up to the house and Gordon gave permission for her to enter. She had to walk up the hill. Gordon was waiting at the door.

"There's a terrible mob of reporters down at the gate," she said, gasping for breath.

"They brought in even more officers to patrol the perimeter of the property. Reporters were climbing over the walls and trying to get into the house."

"I'll bet," Penny answered as she hurried toward the staircase.

Out of breath as she was, she took the stairs two at a time. Lacey was sitting at the window in her room, obviously in great distress. Penny put her arms around her friend's shoulders. Neither woman spoke until Lacey took a long shuddering breath and said, "Penny, I'm so glad you're here. I've got to talk to somebody I can trust. Look what I found." She pointed to the Excalibur.

"Looks like somebody took your letter opener."

"Yes, and that's what killed Scott."

"Oh, my God, how horrible! How do you know?"

"I saw it sticking out of his chest, but I didn't recognize it until I sat down at my desk and noticed it was missing. The police don't know yet that it was mine."

Penny's mind was moving fast. "Are you thinking the same thing I am?"

Lacey nodded. "Whoever killed Scott wanted me to be blamed."

"Obviously. A butcher knife would have been a helluva lot more efficient, but the killer wanted to use something of yours. Listen, you ought to be the one to tell the police about it. For God's sake, don't let them find out on their own. I'll go with you. Come on," Penny said, getting to her feet.

"Tom's gone, and he's forbidden me to talk to them without him."

"You didn't kill Scott. You have nothing to hide."

Lacey got to her feet. "That's exactly the way I feel. Come with me, Penny. I'm sure we can find the detectives around here somewhere."

She reached out to grab the piece of glass, but Penny stopped her. "Hey, I've seen enough episodes of 'Columbo' to know that you don't pick up anything in your bare hands. Wrap it in a hanky."

Lacey did as Penny suggested, and they went downstairs. They saw Chuck and Cherry listening to a man who was apparently the coroner. "From the rectal temperature probe, I would guess death occurred between six and seven A.M. Blade of the letter opener was about five-and-a-half inches long. As far as I can tell, the killer shoved it right between two ribs, straight into the heart. Had to have strong hands. The hilt's too little to get a grip on. Almost had to use just a couple of fingers."

Cherry noticed that they were being overheard.

"Mrs. Haines, are you feeling better?" she asked, but the words Lacey overheard had painted a sickening picture in her mind, and she didn't respond. Penny did it for her.

"No, she's not feeling any better, but she found something in her room, and she wanted to show it to you. Here."

Penny took the heavy chunk of crystal and handed it to the detective.

"What's this?" Cherry asked, opening the handkerchief and looking at the object.

"It's a very expensive piece of glass. Jack gave it to Lacey when she was twenty-one. Usually it holds a gold and silver letter opener. It's a replica of the sword in the stone, you know, in the story of King Arthur. A few minutes ago she noticed the letter opener was missing. She wanted to let you know."

"Did you touch it, Mrs. Haines?" Chuck asked.

Lacey shook her head. "Not since yesterday or the day before."

"Have you got any idea how long the opener has been missing?"

"I'm sure I would have missed it if it had been gone very long. I use it all the time."

"We'll have it checked for fingerprints. Thanks for bringing it to us," Cherry said. "Are you up to talking some more?"

"My attorney would be very upset if I talked to you without him being here."

Penny put her arm around Lacey and led her back up the stairs to her room. She insisted that Lacey stretch out on the chaise longue and try to relax.

"Does Mary know yet?" Lacey asked.

"She heard it on the radio this morning and called me," Penny replied.

"Oh God, that's awful. Is she all right?"

"She's fine. Don't ask me to explain it, but she is."

"Really? I thought she was still in love with him."

"She is, and I'm sure she'll have a bad time for a while. Like everyone who loved him will. But she's free now. I know it's not very kind to say that your brother's death might be good for somebody, but it's true."

She paused and then asked, "Lacey, who do you think did it?"

"I hope it wasn't somebody who thought they were doing me a favor."

"That's a strange answer," Penny said, frowning.

"What other reason was there? Scott inherited everything; I was cut off. So whoever killed him probably didn't like the way the will was written. I didn't kill him. I could never have harmed him. Never. He meant more to me than anyone in the world except my children. In a way, Scott was actually like my first child. I've been taking care of him and getting him out of scrapes ever since we were kids."

"Remember the dent in your father's Mercedes convertible?" Penny asked, realizing that Lacey wanted to talk about her brother.

One corner of Lacey's mouth lifted in a rueful grin.

"Oh God, do I ever?" she said, turning her gaze out the window as she recalled the unhappy incident. "I took the blame, because if Dad found out Scott had done it, he would never have let him go scuba diving with his class that weekend at Catalina."

Penny remembered it all, and gently she reminded Lacey. "Yeah, and as a result of that magnanimous gesture, you missed our senior prom. And that was the end of your romance with Pete Cunningham, remember? He was furious with you for being a patsy for Scott."

"I never expected Dad to punish me so harshly."

"But your spoiled brother never came forward and told the truth, did he?"

For years, Penny had watched and fumed at her friend's unwarranted loyalty to her selfish sibling, but she had never dared express her feelings. Lacey loved Scott too much, and Penny was too wise to risk their relationship. Even now, she wasn't sure how Lacey would react to the reminder.

Lacey did not take offense. She knew Scott was pampered. She even accepted some of the blame for it, but she loved her brother in spite of his failings.

"No, he sure didn't. He went to Catalina and had a grand time. Probably didn't give me a second thought. I never wore that pink satin dress, you know that? In fact, I gave it away because I couldn't bear to look at it. It represented too much heartbreak."

"And you never went out with Pete again either, did you?"

"No. He was furious with me, and I was angry with him for being so angry. He accused me of ruining the prom for both of us. I wanted an apology from him and he wanted one from me. We were both so young and stupid. After graduation, I spent the summer in Europe, and he went on to Harvard. By the way, I talked to him the day Dad died. Did I tell you?"

"No, what's he up to nowadays?"

"He's the CEO and chairman of Kettlecup. We need to acquire his company because they're getting all the choice soup shelf space. He doesn't want to sell. I said I'd try to convince him."

"He's probably grown fat and bald. By the way, where are the kids?"

"Cook is treating them to their favorite breakfast."

"Come on, let's join them. You look like you need some nourishment, and I'm starved."

Lacey shook her head. "I tried to eat some toast earlier, and I couldn't swallow. Oh God, Penny, the police and everybody else think I did it."

Penny looked at the sadness on her friend's face, and her heart ached for her. "Well, that's not going to hold up, so you can stop worrying about that right now. Come on. If you can't eat, you can at least watch me. I'm hungry and I'm planning to stay as long as you need me."

13

The police spent most of the day searching and probing about the house, and Lacey retreated to the living room with her children after Penny left. They talked about happier times. At twilight, when the men had all gone, Lacey asked Erin and JJ the question that had been nagging at her all day.

"Would you two prefer to go down to Texas to stay with your father until this mess is cleared up?"

"No way, Mom. We're not leaving you here all by yourself in this big house. No way," JJ stated. The Texas ranch was only a dim memory for him and not a very good one.

"He's right. Besides, I don't want to change schools in the middle of my junior year at St. Martin's," Erin concurred.

"Things might get difficult around here," Lacey warned them.

"You're talkin' about Sasha, the bitch, aren't you?" JJ asked.

"I don't like you calling people names. Even if they deserve them."

"Well, she is a bitch. She married Uncle Scott for his money, and now she's got the nerve to insinuate that you might have killed Uncle Scott. Remember the time she accused me of trying to steal when I was only in her dumb room looking for my own blouse!" Erin chimed in, her words scorched with dislike.

"She is pretty nasty about making unfair accusations. But then people can't always be held accountable for what they say when they're upset. When she calms down she'll realize that I could never have hurt my brother."

"Where'd she go?" JJ asked.

"I'm not sure. After the detectives questioned her, she took off in the Mercedes alone."

"Is she coming back?"

"I would assume so. After all, she's Scott's widow, and this has been her home for the past six months. All her belongings are here."

"When are we going to have the funeral?" Erin asked.

"We'll have to find out when Scott's body will be released for burial, and then I'll have to talk to Sasha."

Lacey hated to discuss the gruesome details with her children, but they seemed to accept the grimness of it all better than she did, and so she went on to explain what she had heard so far, which was very little.

"I think Sasha did it herself and she's trying to put the blame on somebody else," JJ asserted, flinging the tennis ball he had been fiddling with into the fireplace. It caught fire and shriveled into a sticky mess that sent a terrible odor of burnt rubber wafting into the room.

"Now you did it!" his sister complained, getting up from her chair. "I can't stand that smell."

JJ was embarrassed and he apologized.

"JJ, why did you say that about Sasha? She had no reason to kill Scott," Lacey said.

JJ and his sister exchanged guilty glances, and Lacey noticed it. "What's going on that I don't know about?"

"I wasn't supposed to tell you," Erin said with her eyes cast down. "I think Mary and Scott were going to get back together again."

"Where did you get that idea?" Lacey asked.

"About two weeks ago, you know, I spent the night at Mary's so she could help me work on my bas relief for art class. She sort of hinted around about him."

"It's wishful thinking on her part, I'm afraid. Scott hated the fact that she had lupus, and that's not something likely to change. Now give me a hug and go get ready for bed."

"Sleep well, my angels," she whispered to their retreating backs.

When they were gone, Lacey wandered into the library, where she sank down into her father's chair. It had always given her great comfort to curl up in its soft leather cushions and imagine that she could draw her father's strength from it.

The Westminster chimes in the tall grandfather clock in the foyer were tolling the hour of eleven when Lacey finally pulled her tired body out of the chair and headed for the stairs. Approaching the now-sealed door to the room where Scott had been killed—its yellow tape a garish reminder of the crime—she quickened her pace, her heart pounding as she rushed into her own room and slammed the door behind her.

Breathing heavily, she looked around. The room had been cleaned up since this morning. There were fresh linens on the bed and a newly picked Sofia rose in the cut crystal bud vase on the night table. A pale lavender nightgown stretched across the foot of the bed, with her peach satin robe beside it and the matching mules on the floor. Everything was just as it always was, but nothing was the same. A new terror suddenly invaded her life.

What had she been thinking of? She turned, and running as fast as her legs would carry her, she dashed down the hallway. Someone had killed her brother. No matter what anyone said or thought, she was the only one who knew for certain that she was not the one who had done it. There was a murderer somewhere, either here in the house or elsewhere, and because the motive was unknown, there was every chance that she and her children were at risk. Good God, how could she be so stupid? How could she have let her grief blot out the frightful reality of it all?

Her hands trembling, she rushed to her daughter's room and called, "Erin, come out here this minute!"

Then she hurried across the hall and did the same at her son's door. Within moments both children were standing beside her, fearful and shaken by her frantic tone of voice.

"What is it, Mom? What's happened?" they asked.

Struggling to get her voice and herself under control, she tried to speak calmly. "Look, Erin, JJ, you're not children, so I'm going to treat you as adults. The fact is, someone killed our Uncle Scott. Someone unknown. Someone either already in the house or who knew how to get in."

"Mom, you're right! We don't know who did it," JJ, an avid TV watcher and moviegoer, responded.

"You think we might be in danger?" Erin asked, her eyes widening in horror.

"Until we know for certain who killed Scott and why, it would be foolish to think otherwise. Now, we'll all sleep in the same room tonight."

"There's only one bed in my room," JJ said.

"I have two but that's not enough," added Erin, looking around the hallway fearfully.

"And we can't all sleep in the single bed in mine either. Let's go. We'll all sleep in Grandpa's big room," Lacey decided.

"Oh yuck, Grandpa Jack died in there just a few days ago," JJ wailed.

"I know. But all the hospital paraphernalia has been removed, and it's been thoroughly cleaned and aired. It's got a king-size bed as well as a big couch. Erin and I can sleep in the bed and JJ can sleep on the couch. Besides, there's a call button by the bed that rings all over the house. Let's go to the linen closet and get some bedding."

When they had finished making up the beds, Lacey checked all the windows to make sure they were secure. She then went out to the security panel in the hallway and armed the entire system, including the motion detector unit, which had never been used. She returned to the bedroom and locked the door behind her.

Erin, who was just coming out of the huge bathroom asked, "Mom, Grandma and Grandpa never did share the same bedroom, did they?"

"Not that I remember. Why do you ask?"

"Well, there's a tub and a shower, and the beige marble and mirrors are gorgeous, but there's no dressing table. Only a shaving mirror on the wall by the sink."

"As far as I can remember, they always had their own room and bath. The big bedroom across the hall was my mother's. I think that's the way the house was planned when Dad built it. Scott and I were just babies at the time."

"Did they get along all right, Mom?" JJ asked as he snuggled down under the blankets on the couch.

"Neither of them ever talked about their private lives or personal relations. Mom tended to withdraw from the world. She loved to read and listen to classical music. She'd sit in the solarium downstairs every afternoon, playing her records and either reading some new book about mystical things or doing needlepoint."

"I'll say she did a lot of needlepoint," JJ said with a laugh. "The house is filled with it."

"I cherish every piece. She tried to teach me to do it when I was young, but I found it tedious and boring. I'm going to take a hot shower and try to relax before I settle in. Are you two okay?"

"It's just like a slumber party," Erin said with a chuckle as she climbed into bed.

"Give me a break," JJ moaned and pulled the covers over his head.

Lacey kissed both of them good night and turned out the lights. She then went into the bathroom to undress, but even though she had her children close by, she still did not feel safe. There was a murderer somewhere, possibly even inside the house.

Soon after Lacey finally fell into a restless slumber filled with dreams of her brother calling for help, she was awakened by a sudden and frightening noise.

All three of them sat up, startled by the sound.

"What's that?" Erin asked, frightened.

"I think it's the burglar alarm," Lacey replied.

"What do we do now?" JJ asked.

Lacey switched on the light and said, "Nothing, absolutely nothing. Sit tight where you are. The servants have undoubtedly been awakened, and if the alarm isn't switched off in the next sixty seconds, the police will dispatch a car."

"You think somebody tried to break into the house?" JJ asked.

Lacey decided to be honest. "I have no idea."

Within moments, the alarm was turned off and there was silence. Then they heard a scurrying of feet on the stairs and a knock at the bedroom door.

"Miss Lacey, are you awake?" Gordon asked.

Lacey jumped out of bed and rushed to the door. Turning the key in the lock, she opened it.

"What happened, Gordon?"

"It was only Miss Sasha coming in the front door."

"I'm sorry I didn't warn you that I had turned on the alarm," a relieved Lacey said, "and thank you for letting us know. What room did she go to? The police have sealed . . ."

"She's waiting in the library for me to prepare the guest room in the children's wing for her. I'll go do that right now."

"As soon as everybody is settled again, I'd appreciate it if you'd reset the alarm."

When he had gone, Lacey decided to go down and talk to Sasha. She put on her satin robe, ran her fingers through her hair, stepped into her mules, and got ready to face the woman who had suggested she might have murdered her brother. It was not going to be an easy conversation.

"Try to go back to sleep, if you can," she told the children.

"Mom, I'm wide awake. D'ya mind if I turn on the TV for a while?" JJ asked.

"Me too. I need something to take my mind off things. Okay?" Erin asked.

"Of course. I might be gone for a while, but stay in bed. The remote control's in the left bedside drawer."

Lacey stepped into the dimly lit hallway. Walking briskly over to the light panel at the head of the stairs, she flipped all the switches, and the house sprang to life with light. The huge crystal chandelier in the entry hall twinkled festively.

"That's better," she murmured to herself. This, after all, was real life, not some murky horror movie. From now on, they'd damned well keep the lights on all night.

14

Lacey found Sasha curled up on the couch in the library, sipping on a generous pouring of brandy. The woman looked up, and it was apparent that she had done a lot of weeping. Her eyes were red-rimmed and swollen, and even though she had evidently tried to repair her mascara, it had begun to run again.

When Lacey approached her, Sasha turned her head and stared into her sister-in-law's eyes and preempted the conversation with defiance. "We have nothing to say to each other."

Lacey sighed, walked over to the big leather armchair that had once been her father's favorite, and sat down.

"You're wrong, Sasha. You might have said all you wanted to say to the police, but I've got a lot to say to you."

Sasha looked down into her glass sullenly as Lacey continued. "I don't believe for a minute that you think I killed Scott. You, as well as anyone, knew how much I loved him and how much we meant to each other. You're angry because he's dead and you need to blame somebody. I happen to be the easiest target."

"You also had the most to gain by his death, and I know how much Gallagher's Best meant to you. Scott once said you'd sacrifice your first-born to get your hands on it."

"That was a joke, Sasha, and you know it. Scott joked about everything. Nothing was safe from his particular kind of humor."

There was a long silence in the room, but Lacey was encouraged. Maybe she and Scott's widow could find some common ground on which to share their sorrow after all.

"Sasha, I know Scott's death is a great loss for you, and you feel as if you've been cut off and sent adrift. I want you to know that when things are settled, I'll certainly see to it that you're well taken care of. I know Scott would have wanted me to do that."

"What do you mean?"

"You won't have to change your life-style."

"So the rich bitch is now going to try to buy off the poor little beggar of a wife, is that it?" Sasha asked, and when she looked up, Lacey saw a nasty glitter in her eyes.

"Well, that just doesn't cut it," Sasha continued. "Scott inherited the estate, and I'm his widow. I talked to a lawyer tonight, and he feels I've got a very good case to claim everything, especially since I'm not even mentioned in the will. So I've got nothing to lose, now have I?"

Lacey's jaw dropped in surprise. Good Lord, all the woman cared about was the money.

"It's a free country, Sasha. You can do anything you want, and we have nothing more to talk about. I'm going back to bed." Lacey got up and started to walk out of the room.

"You're going to jail if I have anything to say about it!"

Lacey whirled around angrily. "You want me in jail for something you know I didn't do? Is that what you want?"

"You're the one with the reason to kill him," Sasha snapped back.

"Ah, but you're wrong! Why would I want to kill my own brother when he had already agreed to turn over the entire inheritance to me?"

"Nobody in his right mind would believe that!"

"If it were true, however, then you might be the one under suspicion. It could easily be reasoned that you killed him in anger because he insisted on giving everything away." The thought was on her lips before she was fully cognizant of its meaning, and it startled her. Could it be possible? Had Scott gone back to his bedroom, found Sasha awake, and told her about their agreement? Knowing Scott's penchant for teasing, it was highly possible that he might have tormented his wife by telling only half the story and neglecting to mention that he was in reality selling out his inheritance for most of the money and half the stock.

"You'll never get away with putting the blame on me. Never!" Sasha exclaimed.

"Me? I don't intend to put the blame on anyone without knowing for sure, but it does seem a bit odd, doesn't it? Scott was killed in your bed. You're the one who found him. You're every bit as much under suspicion as I am."

"That's ridiculous! I lost everything when Scott died."

"You will have a motive if you succeed in breaking the will and becoming Scott's sole heir—a motive and the opportunity," Lacey replied levelly. "As a matter of fact, I don't think I want you in this house. You might actually be a threat to me and my children. So get the hell out."

"My attorney says this is my house now. It belonged to Scott when he died, and as his widow, I'm entitled—"

"You're entitled to nothing. I take back what I said about taking care of you. The only way you're going to get a cent from this estate is through the courts. So pack your bags, all of them, and—"

"You can't put me out. I won't go!" Sasha said, but she sounded less sure of herself.

"Oh no? Well just watch me. I'll have the servants pack up your things and put them outside the gate. And if you won't leave, I'll have Salvador pick you up bodily and throw you out on your backside beside your luggage."

"They won't do that!"

"Do you think anybody who works here won't be delighted to get rid of you? You've been nothing but a pain in the neck to all of them with your arrogant demands."

"You've forgotten something," Sasha said, modulating her voice.

"What?"

"Scott's funeral."

Lacey, who had been pumped up with anger and indignation, was instantly deflated. Oh God, how could she have forgotten? This was no time for petty squabbles.

"You're right," she murmured, backing off from her anger and her ultimatum. "But we can't talk about it tonight. I'll see you at breakfast in the morning, and we'll make the arrangements then."

"So I can stay?" Sasha asked meekly.

"We'll talk about it tomorrow. Now go to your room and stay there until morning."

"What's the rush?" Sasha asked, her confidence somewhat restored.

"Because Gordon is waiting to rearm the security system, and if you so much as step a foot out into the hallway, it will go off. Take the bottle of brandy if you think you need it."

Knowing better than to tangle with her sister-in-law any further, Sasha slammed the Baccarat brandy glass down on the coffee table and got unsteadily to her feet. She brushed past Lacey on somewhat wobbly legs and headed for the stairs.

Lacey returned to the bedroom to find both JJ and Erin sound asleep with the television still on. She retrieved the remote control from Erin's hand and turned it off. Drawing the covers over both her children, she tucked them in warmly and got into bed herself.

Sleep was a long time away, however. She had a lot to think about, not the least of which was her poor, dead brother, vital and alive yesterday, and now lying on a cold slab in the coroner's office. Life was so tentative. She found herself praying to God to watch over her children. Who would take care of them if the police could not find the real killer and instead pointed the finger of accusation at her?

15

Chuck and Cherry were summoned to the office of Bill Snyder, their immediate superior.

"So what have you got?" he asked.

Cherry looked at her partner and nodded. "You first."

"No sign of forced entry anywhere. Security system in place and operational but not armed. Deceased's wife left him alive and asleep and took her usual morning run. Left the house at approximately 6 A.M. Didn't deviate from the three-mile course measured out on the grounds of the estate, except that she ran it almost twice. Said she needed to work off extra calories. It takes her down to the stables where they used to keep horses but don't anymore, eight times around the track, back around the tennis court and swimming pool, then down to the gatehouse and back. Returned to her room a little over an hour later. Found her husband with his sister's letter opener stuck in his chest. Dead."

Cherry picked up the summation. "They've got a video camera at the gate, but the tape didn't show anything unusual. The gates can be opened by remote control from the kitchen, the library, and also from the master bedroom."

"All the windows and doors were checked and everything was secure, but that doesn't mean much either if there's a murderer or a collaborator in the house. Doors and windows can be unlocked and locked again," Chuck added.

"Did the coroner have any snap judgments to offer?" Snyder asked.

"He suspects the guy might have been drugged. There's no sign of movement . . . no flailing . . . no death spasms," Cherry responded. "And last night on my way home, I stopped at the supermarket. I took the letter opener from my desk, which is not as sharp as the murder weapon. The butcher let me try slipping it between some beef ribs to see how hard it would be. It took a certain amount of force, but I managed to do it without too much strain."

"Good deal," Chuck remarked. "And I checked with Tom Brennan to find out who's next in line for the dough if something happens to Lacey. Her kids are to share the estate equally. If all three of them die and there are no other descendants at the time, the company gets sold off and the proceeds deposited into the Gallagher Family Trust, which doles money out annually to a list of charitable organizations as long as your arm."

"Do you think it's possible the Gallagher son might only be the first victim?" Snyder asked.

Chuck shook his head. "When all the facts are in, I feel sure we're going to conclude that Lacey Gallagher Haines iced her brother. The murder weapon came from her desk and her motive was clear-cut. Cherry doesn't agree with me."

Snyder looked at Cherry. "Why not?"

"I certainly don't have any hard and fast evidence to back up the way I feel. Yes, the woman did have motive and opportunity and a weapon, but I don't think she did it. She's too smart to do such a clumsy job and incriminate herself."

"If you arrest her, can you make it stick?" Snyder asked.

Chuck nodded but Cherry shook her head.

"Well, I'm tellin' you two right here and now that if she did it, I want her nailed. I don't care how much money or influence the broad has, she can't get away with murder. Not on my beat. But you sure as hell better have the goods on her before you make an arrest and get us committed. You hear me?"

His two subordinates nodded.

"Now get out there and build a case against her. Talk to Patrick Williams in the D.A.'s office and lay it all out for him. See what he has to say. When you put the cuffs on her, be damned sure we're gonna get a conviction. I'll authorize overtime. See you in the morning."

For a long time after Chuck went home, Cherry sat alone in her office reading through their notes. She always got nervous when the solution to a case was too patently obvious.

16

The alarm sounded, and Jean Atwill turned it off. Although it was only six-thirty in the morning, she was already awake. For thirty-nine years she had been getting up at this hour every morning, so she would be in the office by eight-fifteen, before Jack Gallagher arrived, always before Jack Gallagher arrived. He had liked his cup of coffee steaming on his desk alongside the daily computer sales charts, the *Wall Street Journal,* and *Barron's.* Not only had he built Gallagher's Best from a small restaurant into a huge, multiproduct foodstuff supplier, frozen, canned, bottled, and boxed, but he had also developed a successful chain of franchise restaurants where consumers could eat the very products that were also available on the shelves of supermarkets all over the world. And Jean Atwill had been there, as his executive secretary and assistant, most of the way.

Now that he was gone, she had no intention of changing her routine in the least. Scott Gallagher would be the new president and chief executive officer of Gallagher's Best, and he would be as dependent on her as his father had been, if not considerably more. The company was her profession, her family, her life, and since she was only fifty-nine years old, she had at least six or more good years in which she could help put young Scott on the right path. Gallagher's Best would continue to grow. At least one of its products would be on every table in every home at every meal in the United States in the years to come. Much as she mourned her employer's death, she was looking forward to the future.

She took a quick shower and put on her makeup. She then decided her navy blue St. John three-piece suit would be a good choice for her first day back in the office, now not just as a secretary but as the executor of the Gallagher estate. She'd had her hair done the day of Jack's funeral, and it was still in good shape. She ran a brush through the thick, wiry, and very short coiffure, which fell into place immediately. It was getting whiter, she knew, but that was all right with her. She'd never resort to that awful black dye that made aging brunettes look like witches.

When she was ready, she walked down the long hallway from her bedroom suite to the modern white-on-white kitchen of her spacious condominium overlooking the harbor and the *Queen Mary* in Long Beach. While she made herself a cup of herbal tea and fixed a small bowl of shredded wheat with nonfat milk, she exulted once more in the view from the wraparound windows through which she often watched the sun set.

She'd hired Holly Withers herself to decorate the roomy condo with contemporary furniture in pale mauves and powder blues. The twin couches in front of the fireplace were done in luxurious down cushions, and the dining room table was shining glass atop a white marble base. The only solid wall in the living room was hung with original lithographs that Jack Gallagher's art dealer had gotten for her: a Picasso, a colorful Chagall, and a surrealistic Dali.

At exactly seven-thirty, she exited the elevator into the lobby and strode through the front doors to find the parking attendant waiting with her car, the motor running.

"Good morning, Fernando. Thanks for having the car serviced yesterday," she said, pressing a ten-dollar bill into his hand and getting behind the wheel.

"They say car was overdue, Mees Atweel," the small dark Latino man warned her.

"Yes, I know it was, and that's one of the reasons I took the day off yesterday. I'm thinking about buying a new car. What kind would you suggest?" Because she had so few friends, Jean tended to be conversational with service people.

"I dunno, Mees. Most people in this building drive Lincolns or Cadillacs or Mercedes. They all very nice. You should have one a' them."

"Good idea." She rolled up the window and drove off into the traffic. After pulling onto the main highway, she turned on the radio to get back in touch with a world she had shut out for more than twenty-four hours. She'd spent much of the previous day reading through the will and making notes of questions to ask Tom Brennan. She was fairly sure she understood her responsibilities as executor, but she was meticulous in her preparation for every task she undertook. She wanted no one asking questions she could not answer properly.

The main offices of Gallagher's Best were located in the South Bay, a region north of the Long Beach and Los Angeles ports. Jack Gallagher had bought the land forty years ago when there was nothing nearby, but Gallagher's Best was now surrounded by industry, commercial developments, and many housing tracts.

The Gallagher family lived on a large estate in Palos Verdes, the upscale residential peninsula twenty-five miles south of Los Angeles, but Jean had chosen to live in Long Beach, where she had been born and raised. It was less than a half-hour's drive to her work.

She was only half listening to the newscast, her mind preoccupied with plans for the coming day, when the sudden impact of Scott Gallagher's name brought all her senses to instant alert. She turned the volume up, but it was too late. Frantically she punched the station buttons, trying to find another program to fill in the missing information, but all she could get was rock music. She made a desperate search of her own mind, trying to will her subconscious to regurgitate the words that her ears had heard but her mind had failed to register. Had she really heard the word *police*? Had something happened to Scott? Fearful thoughts raced around in her mind, overlapping and colliding with one another. She pressed her foot down on the accelerator, now in a hurry to get to the office and find out what the devil was going on.

At exactly eight o'clock, she pulled the car into the reserved space in front of the office building, ran up the six granite steps, and strode through the big glass doors. Without stopping to speak to the receptionist, she hurried into the elevator and punched the sixth-floor button.

Arriving at her floor, she hastened down the corridor to the private entrance to Jack's office, slipped the key into the lock, and entered without having to talk to any of the personnel in the front area. By habit, she first opened the blinds of the big window and then strode through Jack's office to her own, where she sat down to check over the newspapers that had accumulated on her desk for the past three days.

She put on her reading glasses, set aside the old papers, and began to scan the morning's edition. Suddenly, there it was.

HEIR TO GALLAGHER FORTUNE MURDERED

With heart pounding and hands shaking, she read the article. Her eyes were frozen to the page, but the enormity of the crime was too great for her to process the information.

This couldn't be true. Scott was young and strong and beautiful, and God would not let him be destroyed in this sordid fashion. He was born to greatness. He was not destined to be put into a cold grave while still a young man. Not yet. Not now.

She read the account once. She closed her eyes and opened them, but the words on the page had not changed. They were still there, staring back at her, mocking her dreams of the future.

Jean closed her eyes again and prayed, "Please, dear God, don't let this be! Don't let this be!"

There was a knock on the door, softly at first and then more insistently. As in a trance, Jean opened her eyes and reached over to press the button that unlocked the door.

It was Marge Melady, the head of the secretarial pool, a woman who had been with Gallagher's Best for more than twenty-five years.

"Hi, Jean. Isn't it awful? I tried to call you at home as soon as I heard the news yesterday, but there was no answer."

"I had the telephone turned off. It's the first time in my life I've ever done that, but it seemed all right now that Jack was gone and would no longer need me." Her eyes had a strange watery look and her gaze was unfocused.

"You look sick. Are you okay?" Marge asked, approaching the desk.

"Not really. I just read this."

"I was afraid you might not have heard. Isn't it awful? Who do you suppose killed him?"

Jean slowly shook her head. "Who would want to? Everybody loved him," Jean said, numbly gazing toward the window but seeing only the awful picture created by the newspaper article.

"There's a detective outside named Cherry Dolan. She'd like to talk to you. She called here yesterday and left a message that she'd be in first thing this morning. Feel like seeing her?" Marge asked.

Jean Atwill's eyes focused again. She looked up at Marge. "Of course I'll talk to her. In Jack's office. See if she wants coffee."

Seconds later, Cherry Dolan was shown into the sumptuous office paneled in burnished mahogany. Jean walked around the desk to shake the detective's hand.

"I'm so glad you've come, Miss Dolan. I have a lot of questions to ask you."

Cherry followed Jean's lead over to a group of leather chairs arranged around a small table in the bay window overlooking the landscape below. Both women sat down. Marge arrived shortly, bearing a tray with two cups, one coffee, one tea, and an assortment of delicious-looking miniature pastries.

"My, that looks good," Cherry commented, taking the coffee and helping herself to a small cinnamon-raisin roll. "When she asked if I wanted coffee, I didn't expect such a nice treat."

"Gallagher's is a house of food, and we not only sell it, we serve it with almost everything," Jean replied, reaching for her cup of tea. Her hand shook so violently that she had to use both to steady the cup as she lifted it to her lips.

The movement did not go unnoticed. "I suppose you know why I'm here," Cherry asked.

"Yes, of course. It's about the . . . murder." The word stuck in Jean's throat. "I hope you'll excuse my distracted state, but you see, I didn't find out about it until this morning. I was home alone all day yesterday and had both the television and the telephone turned off."

"I'm sorry. Would you rather I came back another time?"

"No, no, I'm perfectly all right," she said, knowing it was a lie but determined to get as much information as possible. "Could you give me a quick rundown on the facts? The newspaper, well, I don't trust news-paper accounts anymore. So often they misrepresented things pertaining to the company that I lost faith in them."

Cherry had learned that if she was open and forthcoming with people they would respond in like measure, so she briefly delineated the status of the case, describing the crime with as few of the grisly details as possible. As she talked, she watched Jean's reactions and tried to take a reading of her responses. The woman was obviously shaken, but she had her emotions under tight control.

When she finished, Jean asked a question that surprised Cherry.

"Do you know if he suffered at all?"

Cherry was reassuring. "We're pretty certain he was unconscious at the time the weapon . . ." She paused. The words were having an extreme effect on Jean Atwill.

"Are you sure you feel like talking right now?" she asked again.

"Yes, yes, please go on. And thank you for all the information. What can I tell you?"

"I understand that you're the executor of the will."

"Was."

"Was? You aren't anymore?"

"No, I was to be the executor only if Scott was the inheritor of the estate. If something happened to him, I was to be replaced by Lacey."

"No kidding?"

"Mr. Gallagher felt that Scott would need all the help he could get, and that was the reason I was made the executor. If anything happened to Scott, as it apparently has, then it was Jack's—Mr. Gallagher's—wish that his daughter take charge of everything."

"He didn't think she'd need your help?"

"No."

"He thought his daughter was more capable than his son? Right?"

"He always underestimated Scott's abilities."

"But he left everything to Scott anyway?"

"It was always his dream that his son would someday take his place at Gallagher's Best."

"I understand you got a big chunk of money for being executor. Will that be taken away from you too?"

"Not entirely. In place of the annual stipend for serving as executor, I was to be retired with a trust fund of five million dollars."

"Whew, some trust fund."

"Mr. Gallagher was very generous to those who were loyal to him."

"How well do you know Lacey Gallagher?" Cherry asked.

"Haines. Her married name is Haines. What do you want to know?"

"What kind of woman is she?"

"That's hard to say. The word *unnatural* comes to mind."

"Unnatural?" Cherry asked, bemused. "In what way?"

"She gave up her home and the man she loved, the father of her children. She gave up everything that a normal woman holds dear for her father and this company."

"I thought her father wanted his son to run the company?"

"He did, but he and Scott had a difference of opinion. It was one of those things that could have been avoided, but there were pressures that caused it to escalate."

"Pressures? What kind of pressures?"

"I really wouldn't want to say."

"Miss Atwill, it is Miss is it not?" Cherry asked.

Jean pursed her lips together and nodded, and Cherry continued.

"We're conducting a murder investigation, and you're not on the witness stand, so it's perfectly all right for you to give me your opinions and impressions of things, understand? Now what kind of pressure are you talking about?"

"I always suspected that Maude, Mr. Gallagher's wife, showed a distinct preference for her daughter. I think she wanted to see Lacey take over the company and run it," Jean declared.

"What gave you that feeling?"

"Oh, little things. I also believe that Maude was instrumental in breaking up Lacey's marriage. She wanted her back here to protect her position in the company."

"She was still alive when Lacey returned home?"

"Very much so. Lacey had been home about three months when she had her fatal stroke."

"I see, so you think that Mrs. Gallagher encouraged the rift between father and son?"

"More or less. I wouldn't want to be quoted on that, however."

Cherry let an awkward silence hang in the air for a few moments. When she began her questions again, she pursued the subject further.

"Which one of the children did you feel was better equipped to be CEO at Gallagher's Best?" she asked and was startled by Jean's ready and quick response.

"Why Scott, of course. He was the son."

Cherry could tell that Jean was about to lose control. Her eyes were filled with tears, and there was a nervous shaking of her shoulders.

"Is there anything else you'd like to tell me that might be helpful?"

Jean shook her head.

"I see. Well, I won't impose upon you any longer. Here's my card. Call me if you think of something." Cherry got to her feet. Jean seemed not to notice. She sat staring stonily ahead.

"Thank you for talking to me," Cherry said and moved toward the door. She was about to leave when Jean spoke.

"You haven't asked me who I think killed him."

Startled, Cherry took a few steps back toward her. "Do you want to tell me?"

"She did it."

"She?"

"His sister."

"Why do you say that?"

"Because of the money—the company and the money."

"Anything else? Has Lacey ever done or said anything to make you believe she might actually commit such a serious crime?"

"She's ruthless. Like her father."

Jean refused to say anything else, and for a long time after the detective had gone, she sat immobile. Then as her tightly held reserve disintegrated, she began to moan and weep.

She attempted to wrest her arm away from him, but it was too late. He already had the silken cord wrapped around her wrist, and with one swift movement he stretched out her arm and tied it to the bed post.

"Turn over!" he commanded in a low and forceful whisper, pulling the cord so taut that the pain in her arm was almost unbearable. She clawed with her free hand in a futile attempt to release herself, but he was too strong for her. He seized her unfettered arm and pulled it until he had forced her to turn over and lie facedown on the bed. Although she struggled, she could not prevent him from tying her other arm to the opposite bed post. Turning her face away from the pillow, she pleaded for him to stop.

"You've made them too tight! My fingers are numb," she begged. "Please loosen them a little." He did not listen to her.

She felt his hand grip her ankle and she realized that he was not going to stop with just binding her arms.

"I don't want to do this!" she protested in vain, kicking at him with her leg. "You mustn't do this to me!"

Within seconds, he had her completely spread-eagled on the bed, each arm and leg securely bound to a bedpost, and she was helpless. There was no way she could free herself. He could do anything he wanted to her now. He could even kill her.

In anger and frustration and fear, she buried her face in the down pillow and became silent, afraid that if she protested too much, he would only be stimulated to more cruelty. There was nothing she could do but submit. She didn't even dare to scream.

17

L acey was about to leave home for the office the next morning when she received a telephone call from her ex-husband.

"Lacey, my God, I just read about Scott in the morning's paper. You must feel awful."

"I'm numb, Steve. This is the worst thing that's ever happened in our family."

"How are the kids taking it?"

"Better than I am. They insisted on attending school today, so I'm going to the office. Sasha drank too much last night, and she's in bed with a migraine. I need to get away for a few hours."

"Look, you shouldn't be alone. I'll drive right back to the airport and hop on the next plane for L.A. I'll be there before you know it."

Lacey tried to protest. "Steve, no, that's not necessary . . ." she began, but he had already hung up the telephone. She sighed and headed for the car.

It felt good to be out of the house, even if she could only stay at the office for a few hours. She intended to call Pete Cunningham and set a time for them to meet. Her financial vice president had advised her to get the merger going because they were in a cash-rich position, so now would be an appropriate time to make an acquisition as big as Kettlecup.

She arrived at the office to learn that Jean Atwill had left immediately after a visit from Cherry Dolan. This suited Lacey, who was far more at ease dealing with Marge Melady. Her call to Pete was put right through.

"Lacey, I'm surprised to hear from you. I read about Scott's death in the paper this morning. I'm really sorry. Is there anything I can do?"

"I know what a busy man you are, Pete, and so I wanted to get a lunch date on your calendar sometime this month. Have you got a free day for me?"

"I'm at your service, Lacey, although I'm not scheduling anything too far in advance. We're opening a new production facility in the Bay area, and I often have to drop everything and fly up there on short notice. I'm free today, however."

"Today?" Lacey responded. With everything she had on her mind, she doubted that she could be effective in presenting her company's case to him.

"I'm sorry; that was insensitive of me to push you into something at a time like this. You name the date, and I'll do my best to be available."

Listening to his voice brought back old memories that had been long forgotten. Pete had always been a kind and considerate person. She felt a sudden desire to see and talk to him.

"I'm afraid I'm not in good enough shape to make a persuasive pitch today, but let's have lunch anyway. I'd love to have an old friend to talk to. Would it be awfully inconvenient for you to come down here? We have a great private dining room which we'll have to ourselves."

"My customers have told me all about that private dining room of yours. What time would you like me there? It'll take me only about forty-five minutes on the freeway. Our main offices are in downtown L.A. now."

"Would one o'clock be convenient? Do you remember where we are?"

"Lacey, my dear, everybody in the food industry knows where Gallagher's Best is. See you at one."

All morning long, the staff members filed into the office one by one to express great sadness about Scott's death. Lacey detected from most, however, a sense of relief and gratitude rather than sorrow.

When she was alone again, she picked up a copy of the morning newspaper and read the front-page account of Scott's murder and the bizarre terms of the will. The reporter went out of his way to indicate that the victim's sister, who was in the house with him that night, was the only one to benefit by his death. Lacey tried not to let the story upset her, but she knew that anyone who read it would assume she was guilty.

She was happy for the diversion when Brett stopped in for a chat. He sat in the chair beside her desk and told her that the best people in the company had confessed to him that they would have quit rather than work for Scott.

"I still don't understand your dad, Lacey. It wasn't like him to be that unrealistic."

"What about you? You wouldn't have quit, would you?" she asked him.

"There's no way I could have worked for your brother. I know it's bad to speak ill of the dead, but he was incompetent."

Pete arrived fifteen minutes early, before Lacey had a chance to comb her hair or check her appearance in the mirror. Since she thought it would be impolite to keep him waiting, she had him sent right in.

As Marge ushered Pete into the office, Lacey noted that he had aged well. A tall man, he was trim and broad-shouldered, and although his hair was graying, it still showed signs of sun bleach. His tan skin had been weathered by the wind and the sun, and the crinkles around his bright blue eyes had deepened.

"Pete, it's so good to see you after all these years," Lacey exclaimed, standing up and smoothing her hair with her hand.

"Good to see you too, Lacey. You haven't changed much."

They shook hands warmly, and he sat down in one of the chairs closest to her desk and segued right into an easy conversation.

"Sorry I'm early, but my driver has a heavy foot. I remember visiting this office with you on many occasions, and I was always impressed with the sense of power your dad exuded. It's not going to be easy for you to fill his shoes."

Lacey nodded. "I thought that inheriting his office and his position in the company would be the greatest thing that ever happened to me. It didn't turn out quite that way."

"The *Times* went into a lot of detail about the will. Where did they get their information?"

"Not from me, I can assure you. We've been fending off reporters ever since the police were called yesterday morning. One of the women in the office said that Scott's murder was discussed by some ghoul on a morning radio talk show. He was actually asking listeners whether they thought Scott's sister had killed him for the money."

"That's disgusting. Let's not talk about it anymore," he said, changing the subject. "What do you say we go back in time and pretend we're in high school again. I'll bet I can remember more names of old friends than you can."

Lacey laughed. "You're on, but I have the advantage you know. You went to the other coast, and I stayed right here."

When they left the office together, Lacey told Marge she could be reached in the small dining room. "Tell them we're on our way up."

They stepped into the polished brass and dark walnut elevator and were whisked to the tenth floor.

"I thought there were only nine floors in this building," Pete said.

"Only one elevator goes to the tenth floor. It's where we entertain our big clients."

The doors opened and they stepped into a small walnut-paneled foyer. An attractive young woman sitting behind a handsome burled-wood reception desk smiled and got to her feet.

"Hello, Pam. We're ready for lunch," Lacey said.

"It's good to have you back, Ms. Gallagher. Although it was short notice, we have a wonderful meal planned for you."

Lacey introduced Pete and then Pam pressed a button that opened one of the huge double doors.

"On this side of the floor are the private dining rooms. We have three of them. One seats twelve, another seats six, but we're dining in the most exclusive one. It seats only two." They walked down the thickly carpeted hallway, and Lacey opened the doors so that Pete could see into each dining room. Both were furnished handsomely with crystal chandeliers, Chinese Chippendale chairs, and magnificently appointed tables set up with silver, china, crystal, and centerpieces of fresh flowers.

"It looks like they're going to be used today," Pete observed.

"They're in constant use. You see, we not only entertain here, but we also allow our clients to use the rooms to show off to their friends and customers."

"Do they pay for it?"

Lacey smiled and replied enigmatically, "One way or another."

At the end of the hallway was a door, and when they stepped through it, Pete inadvertently drew back.

"Good Lord! I thought I was stepping off the end of the world," he exclaimed, looking in wonder at the view surrounding them.

The private dining room was circular and enclosed by floor-to-ceiling panels of mitered glass; it seemed to be perched out beyond the building, looking down over the surrounding lands. It was a clear day, and they enjoyed a spectacular view of the Pacific.

In the center of the room was a small round table set with white damask, red roses in a silver vase, and exquisite china and crystal.

"This is amazing," he commented, holding Lacey's chair for her. "Where does the food come from?"

"It comes through the same door that we came in. This is the farthest room from the kitchen, but that's all right because only two people need to be served. So what do you think of my room?"

"Your room?"

"Yes, absolutely. It was my idea to build it, and Dad went along with it. When it was finished and was such a hit, he claimed it as his, of course, but then that's always the president's prerogative, right?"

"If you say so, prez," Pete said. "And I love it. Can I make a reservation for tomorrow too?"

Lacey shook her head and smiled. " 'Fraid not. Brett Marchbanks has first claim. He was going to use it today, but I pulled rank."

Almost as if on cue, a waiter appeared, poured water in their glasses, and asked if they would like some wine.

Pete shook his head. "No, thanks, I never drink at lunch."

"We don't have to drink it, but it's fun to do a little tasting. We always try something new and interesting up here. Join me. Is the new bottling of Chalone Chardonnay in yet, Walter?"

"Yes, ma'am. Mr. Middleton sent one up to be chilled for you."

"Fine, and I'll also have some iced tea. How about you, Pete? Would you rather have mineral water or . . ."

"I'm a fiend for iced tea."

"Good. We blend and package some of the finest Darjeeling tea you'll ever taste."

Within seconds, a wine steward appeared and poured a very small amount of the Chardonnay into each glass. Lacey picked up hers, covered it with the top of her hand, and swirled the liquid for a few moments. She then quickly brought the glass to her nose and sniffed.

"Hmmm, lovely fragrance," she commented. She took a sip, let it rest on her tongue for a moment, and before swallowing, she inhaled through her nose. "That is a really good one, don't you think, Pete?"

Pete tasted the wine with an amused expression on his face, swallowed, tasted again, and agreed.

"It's good. It's extremely full-bodied and complex. Obviously it's had a second malolactic fermentation."

Lacey laughed out loud. "Great. You speak the language of wine."

"I do, but being a bit of a snob, I prefer reds, especially Burgundy, the wine of kings."

"My father has an exceptional cellar. He's been collecting for years. He was a real miser about it too. The night after his funeral my brother and I opened two bottles of his precious Petrus, '61 no less." Lacey's face clouded as she remembered her last conversation with Scott.

Pete sensed her change in mood and he tried to make light of the situation. "People don't actually drink Petrus, do they? I thought they just invested in it."

"Only on very special occasions. Did you know that we've acquired about thirty acres of land adjacent to our property here?"

"Brett mentioned something about a restaurant and wine shop."

"Yes, we're going to build a beautiful garden restaurant, glassed in and heated so that it can be open all year-round."

"Except when it rains," Pete said, and Lacey laughed.

"Even when it rains, because we'll have an indoor facility also. We've been acquiring wines for five years now. We'll have a list that will rival anyone's, and a shop where you can go in and buy a red that's really ready to drink."

As they talked, waiters arrived and served them lunch. They started with a delicate pasta, little round raviolis stuffed with mushrooms, in a delectable sauce. This was soon followed by baked Chilean sea bass, topped with mashed potatoes flavored with a hint of fresh horseradish and sitting in a coulis of red pepper with pearls of zucchini and carrots. The third course was a salad of baby lettuces dressed in a light vinaigrette.

Lacey found herself enjoying the conversation immensely. They talked about food and the products made by his company, and she was amazed at his intimate knowledge of ingredients and processes. He in turn asked which of the items they were eating were actually Gallagher's Best products, and she explained that the pasta sauce was reconstituted from a dry mix, and the vinaigrette dressing was bottled under their name.

"It's great to work with a product you can actually use and enjoy yourself," he commented.

"Do you eat your own soup?"

Pete grinned, and she noticed that his smile lighted up his face. "Every night. Well, almost every night. Especially when I've had a sumptuous lunch like this. And you know what I have with it?"

"Crackers?"

"Nothing so mundane as crackers. I have Gallagher's Best Hard Sourdough Pretzels."

"Pretzels go with beer, not soup," Lacey said, making a face.

"You must come over to my place some evening. There's nothing better than Kettlecup garden vegetable soup with pretzels and a glass of Gewürztraminer."

"Where are you living now?"

"My parents' house came back on the market two years ago, and I bought it. Cost me almost twice what they sold it for. I've been renovating it since escrow closed, and I don't think it's ever going to be finished."

"Can you believe it? We're both back in our old homesteads and neighbors once more. How do you like living behind the Rolling Hills's gates again, and how come you haven't called me?"

"It's been a long time, Lacey. And we didn't part on exactly friendly terms, if you'll remember."

There was a long, awkward silence, and then Lacey asked, "Is that why you've refused to accept our offers to buy your company? We've been extremely generous."

Pete shook his head and laughed. "If you're suggesting I'm still angry about the senior prom, I'm not. No, that's not the reason. I don't want to give up the company. Things have gone exceptionally well since I've been running it, and I'm having a great time. I can't give it up to sit around on my duff and count up the money I made on the stock. Kettlecup still has a long way to go."

"If we owned it, I'd give you a free hand in running the company."

"But then I'd be working for you, and I'm already virtually my own boss. Because of the escalation of the stock value, my board of directors treats me as if I'm Jesus Christ."

"And you don't even have a beard," she said with a wry smile.

"Ah, but I do preach a lot." He looked at his watch. "Good Lord, I've got to get on the road. Can we continue this conversation another time? Some evening for dinner perhaps?"

Lacey shook her head. "I don't think I'll have any free evenings for a while. Things are grim at our house. Because of my brother's murder, I keep a close watch on the children. I've even got them sleeping in the same room with me."

"Why don't you move somewhere else until they catch the bastard who did it?"

"The police have searched the house from top to bottom and found nothing. And it's our home."

"Well, I'm not far away." He reached into his pocket, took out a business card, and wrote on it. "Here, keep this with you. It's my private number at home. I'm no more than fifteen minutes from you, and I know the way."

When Lacey took the card, he grasped her hand and held it.

"Let's be friends again, Lacey."

Tears filled Lacey's eyes as she looked into his. She had almost forgotten what a nice, decent human being Pete was.

"I'd like that."

"And don't give up on the merger. I enjoy being courted."

They both laughed and got up from the table. Lacey went down the elevator with him and walked him to the entrance where his limousine and chauffeur were waiting.

"I had a wonderful time. Thanks for calling," he said.

"Old friends, like vintage wines . . . ," she began, and he finished it for her, "improve with age."

Lacey stayed at the door until his car had pulled away, and then she hurried back upstairs to her office. As she rushed past Marge's desk, her secretary said, "Homer's pacing in your office."

"How long has he been there?" Lacey asked, not stopping.

"Fifteen minutes. He's been out here twice demanding that I page you . . . but I didn't."

"Thanks, Marge. I owe you one," she replied and disappeared into her office to confront the vice president and comptroller of the company.

When she was gone, Marge let out a low whistle and said to herself, "We oughta package whatever it was she had for lunch."

18

At the Los Angeles airport later that day, Steve rented a car and made the thirty-mile drive to the Palos Verdes peninsula, where the Gallagher estate dominated the rolling hills that rose up from the sea.

"Mr. Haines, how good of you to come," Gordon greeted him with a smile. "I'm sure Miss Lacey will be happy to see you. This is a very difficult time for her."

"Does she have company?" he asked, inclining his head toward the cars parked in the circular driveway.

"Not really, sir. She just arrived home from the office, and the detectives have some people here again."

"Are the children at home?" Steve asked.

"We had a rather restless night, but they insisted on going to school. Why don't you wait in the library, and I'll go up and tell her you're here?"

"That'll be fine," Steve said, but it rankled him to have to wait to be announced to the woman with whom he had once been so intimate.

He did not have to wait long. In less than five minutes, Lacey appeared at the door.

"Steve, it was nice of you to turn right around and come back." Her eyes were rimmed with red and it looked as if she had been crying.

"Are you all right, honey?" he asked, taking her hands and holding them against his chest.

"In the daylight, I feel like I can handle things, but now that it's getting dark again, I start worrying."

"About what?"

"Oh, God, everything. I know some people believe that I'm the one who killed Scott, but I know that I didn't. So who killed him and why? And are the children and I in danger too?"

Steve gave a long low whistle. "Whew, that's right. Baby, I know for sure you could never have hurt your brother, and I'll tell 'em so." He led her to the couch where they sat down together, and he continued to keep his arm around her.

"Tell me everything that's happened," he said, and Lacey described the past two days. She told him about her meeting with Scott and their agreement, about her reaction to seeing his dead body, and Sasha's accusation. Then she told him about her fears.

"Last night it suddenly occurred to me that I might be next—and then the children. There might be some maniac trying to wipe out the entire family."

"I'd like to comfort you and tell you that you've got nothing to worry about, but the fact is, you do. If the reason for Scott's murder isn't to benefit you, then you probably should be frightened."

"I know. That's why I've got the children sleeping with me in Dad's old room. And I worry about them going off to school, but I'm not really comfortable having them here in this house unless they're in the same room with me."

"I'm not so sure it was a good idea to send them to school today," Steve said. "Maybe I better drive over and pick them up. Come along with me."

"Salvador's already there. I instructed him to stay parked outside the school all day and wait for them, and then I called the principal and told her I wanted them watched closely. It's a private school and not very big. They'd be home by now but there was some kind of special activity after classes today."

"How did the police treat you when you were questioned? You were questioned, weren't you?" he asked.

"Yes, and Tom Brennan was there beside me every minute to make sure that my rights were not violated in any way."

"Good for him."

Lacey sat up straight. "Oh God, in the excitement of seeing you again, I almost forgot what I was on my way to do."

"What's that?"

"Detective Bascombe told me when he came in this afternoon that Scott's body would be released for burial tomorrow, and we've done nothing about the funeral. I have to talk to Sasha about it."

"She's still here?"

"She came in late last night and said she wasn't leaving. She's got an attorney who says that as Scott's widow she's entitled to everything that Scott inherited."

"Ballsy bitch!"

"I thought it over last night, and I don't much blame her. I know exactly how it feels to be completely left out," Lacey said, getting to her feet. "However, she's a real tiger. Want to go with me into her den?"

"Why not?"

The two went upstairs and found Sasha standing in front of her old bedroom and arguing with Detective Bascombe, who was apparently being patient but firm.

"I'm really sorry, Mrs. Gallagher, but I'm not yet ready to have anything removed from that room," he said. "I know this represents a hardship for you, since all your clothes and cosmetics are in there, but I'd like for you to bear with me for another day or two."

"Detective Dolan brought out a few things for me yesterday. I don't see why you can't do the same now. I can't very well wear the same clothes every day, can I?"

Chuck Bascombe was relieved to have the conversation interrupted, and he looked up as Steve and Lacey approached.

"Detective Bascombe, this is my hus—My ex-husband, Steve Haines. He just flew in from Texas this afternoon."

"How do you do, Mr. Haines," the detective said as the two men shook hands. "I'm sure Mrs. Haines is happy to have you here."

"Hello, Steve," Sasha said, her voice cold. "Here to make up with your wife now that she's got all that money in her name? Well, you're wasting your time. She's going to court one way or the other. Either the police will get her for murder or I'll manage to break that damned will and turn her out onto the street where she belongs."

Steve smiled through clenched teeth. "Good to see you too, Sasha."

A twitch of a smile passed across Chuck Bascombe's mouth.

"Sasha, we've got to plan Scott's funeral," Lacey said, trying to keep the animosity out of her voice. "But first, I think we should declare some kind of a truce until it's over. Now, how about it? I won't call you a money-grubbing bitch and you don't call me a murderer, okay?"

Everyone's jaw dropped at Lacey's unusually coarse language.

"How dare you call me a—" Sasha protested, but Lacey cut her off.

"And how dare you accuse me of murdering my own brother? Now, stop it. We have things to do. I'm planning to call Morningside Mortuary, if it's all right with you. They can pick up the body and prepare it for burial. Although Scott hasn't seen the inside of a Catholic church for years, I'm sure that Father O'Brien at Our Lady of the Sea will—"

"No! Scott always told me he wanted his body cremated and the ashes scattered at sea," Sasha protested.

The remark took Lacey completely by surprise. "But Scott was raised a Catholic, and—"

"Scott no longer considered himself a Catholic, and you know that as well as I do. What's all this religious business anyway? You rarely go to Mass, and neither did your father until he got sick."

"That might be true, but my father was grateful to have Father O'Brien visit during his illness, and he received the last rites before he died."

"He always hedged his bets, didn't he?"

The two men listened with fascination as the women went at each other.

Lacey shook her head in dismay. "All right, Sasha. Tell me what you want. You are, after all, his widow."

"I'm glad you're coming to your senses. After the service, I would like for the family to take the *Santa Maria* out to sea. When we get well out into the Catalina channel, I want to scatter his ashes on the water. That's what he'd have wanted. Then we'll have several airplanes fly overhead and drop flowers over the spot where Scott is laid to rest."

"Sasha, please, think about what you're saying. My father built that large mausoleum out at Morningside so that we could all be there to-gether...," Lacey began, but Sasha would not be persuaded.

"Scott hated being hemmed in by the family, and you know it as well as I do. He loved the *Santa Maria,* and he loved the sea." For the first time since Scott's death, Sasha sounded like a caring human being, and Lacey found herself responding. She was right. Scott had always been a free spirit. He had never marched in step with his father.

"Maybe you're right," Lacey conceded. "Dad would have had a fit, but then he doesn't have anything to say about it now, does he? I'll call Billy down at the marina and have him get the boat ready. Is it all right with you if we have a memorial service here in the garden before we take him out to sea?"

Sasha's eyes suddenly filled with tears and her brittle demeanor melted. "That would be perfect." She looked up into Lacey's eyes and added, "Thank you."

"Would it be all right if we let some of our friends follow us in their boats?"

Sasha nodded. "Scott always liked being surrounded by people." Her emotions got the better of her, and she turned and ran down the hallway to the bedroom where she was now sleeping.

Steve put his arm around Lacey, and they walked down the stairs as Chuck Bascombe watched with great interest.

"It's hard to believe it, honey, but I think you've finally broken free," Steve said.

"What do you mean?"

"For the first time in your life, you made a decision that would def-initely not have met with your dad's approval. Keep it up. You're your own woman now."

"I did it for Scott, Steve."

19

Dad, it's so good to see you!" Erin said, rushing into Steve's arms, and even the more circumspect JJ had trouble restraining himself.

"Glad to see you, Dad," he said awkwardly.

Without a second's hesitation, Steve shot out his long arm and grabbed his son into a three-way hug with Erin.

"Real men might not kiss each other, son, but they sure as hell hug, and don't you forget it."

"You gonna stay, Dad?" JJ asked hopefully.

"I'm gonna stay right here in this house as long as you and your mom need me."

Erin snuggled into his arms. "That's wonderful," she exclaimed.

"Isn't it awful about Uncle Scott?" JJ asked.

"I'd like to get my hands on his killer. I'd make him sorry, you can bet your sweet a . . . life on that."

"Where's Mom?" Erin asked.

"She and Sasha are on the telephone arranging a memorial service here in the garden tomorrow. Your uncle's being cremated tonight, and we'll scatter his ashes at sea."

Erin looked shocked. "Mom wouldn't do that!"

"Why not, honey?"

"Our family's Catholic. We don't believe in cremation. We're taught that it's a sin."

"You'll have to talk to your mom about that."

Erin went to find her mother.

"I know, darling, but other people believe differently," Lacey replied when she heard Erin's objections. "Your Uncle Scott rejected the Catholic faith years ago, and Sasha wants it this way. I've accepted her decision."

"But, Mom, what will my teachers at school think?"

"It's none of their business, Erin. The matter is closed," Lacey said softly but very firmly, and Erin knew that further argument would be futile.

"Can't we at least have a Mass said for him?" JJ offered by way of appeasement.

Lacey sighed. "It's fine with me, but I suggest you don't mention it within hearing distance of Sasha. She's so antireligious that the only person she would approve to lead the memorial service is Chief Justice Nicholas."

"Have you asked him yet?" Steve inquired with raised eyebrows.

"I called him an hour ago."

"And the chief justice of the supreme court of California is coming down from San Francisco?" Steve asked.

Lacey found his tone irritating.

"Of course he's coming. He was a good friend of my father's, and Dad was a big donor to the governor who appointed Nick to the bench."

"Well, does His Honor know anything about Scott? Did he, in fact, ever even meet him?" Steve asked, sarcasm dripping from his words.

"I hate it when you use that tone of voice, Steve," Lacey said in annoyance. "No, he never met Scott but I've briefed him thoroughly. I would have preferred Tom Brennan or you to do it, but Sasha insisted on somebody with more prestige. So we compromised."

"I think the Gallaghers have met their match in this Sasha. What's the compromise?"

"All of us are going to get up and say something about Scott after Nick finishes. I want this memorial service to be personal, and I want each of us to express what Scott meant to us." She looked over to her children and said, "Erin, JJ, wouldn't you like to say something about your Uncle Scott?"

JJ looked stricken. "Get up in front of all those people and talk? You mean it?"

"I think it's a great idea, Mom," Erin announced. "I'm going upstairs right now and type up some ideas."

"Oh right!" JJ howled. "Miss Captain of the Speech Team gets off on that stuff. Mom, you're not gonna force me to make a fool of myself, are you?"

"Nobody's going to force you, JJ, but I would like you to think about it. Promise?" Lacey asked.

JJ nodded and began to shuffle toward the door. "Okay, Mom. I'll try, but can I just read it? I don't have to memorize it too, do I?"

"Of course not, darling. Let me know if you need some help."

When they were alone together, Steve sat down beside Lacey and asked, "You don't really want me to say anything, do you?"

"Scott liked you a lot, and he was very upset when I divorced you."

"He certainly never said anything like that to me. Oh, he was jolly enough when we saw each other, but our conversations were always superficial. To me he was nothing but a spoiled, rotten kid who threw away every opportunity to make something of his life."

"If that's the way you feel, forget it," Lacey replied, her words edged in frost.

"How can you be so blind to Scott's faults? All he ever did was goof up. He was never the dashing hero you made him out to be."

Lacey bit her lip and remained silent.

"It's the truth," Steve insisted, "but I didn't dislike him. He had the funniest damned sense of humor of anybody I ever met, but your dad's money ruined him. And I worry a lot about the same thing happening to JJ."

"Only JJ, not Erin?" she asked.

"Nah, she's a girl and she's just like you."

"And what does that mean?"

"She's got to prove she's every bit as good as JJ, in spite of the fact that she was born with different sexual equipment. Like you've been struggling all your life to prove to Daddy that you had more balls than Scott did. Scott didn't have to prove anything." As he spoke, he got up from the couch and walked over to the bar and mixed himself a Scotch and soda.

Lacey resisted the urge to talk back, and Steve continued to goad her. "Case in point: You were the loving, unselfish daughter, and your father humiliated you in his will. Good Old Dad cut you almost completely out, didn't he? And he did it in spite of the fact that you loved his damned company and were a lot smarter and more capable than Scott ever was. But Scott was the son, sweet, ineffective, and totally incompetent, but the son nevertheless. Everything was his for the taking."

"JJ and Erin have different personalities. Just as Scott and I had."

"Right. Look at her, president of the junior class, captain of the speech team, straight-A student. JJ's grades are above average, but all he wants to do is throw a ball around. He's like Scott. He's got nothing to fight for. It's all waiting there for him on a silver tray."

Lacey thought about what he had said. After a few minutes of silence, she responded. "I don't want to push either of my children into any kind of mold. I do agree that Erin's more motivated than JJ, but boys mature later than girls do."

"Maybe, but it'd be good for both of them to get out of this pampered life-style for a while. Let 'em see how real people live."

"How should I go about that?"

"Let me take the kids back to Texas to live on the ranch. At least, let me take JJ. He needs his father."

"I couldn't bear the thought of living without my children, Steve. I just couldn't."

"But you've got everything else you ever wanted now, Lacey. The company, the money, the control. Let me have Erin and JJ. I'll give 'em the time and attention they need."

"Don't ask me to do that, Steve. I can't."

"You might have no choice. Unless the police find out who really killed Scott, you'll be the one they'll come after. You'll have no time to be a mother. After all, I'm their father, and if something should happen to you, I'm the one who'll be responsible for their welfare."

"Oh God, Steve, you don't really think that anyone could seriously believe I killed Scott!"

The expression on Steve's face became extremely somber. "I know it's a terrible subject to bring up, but the fact is, you're the only suspect they have right now. If I didn't know you at all, I'd certainly believe you did it. Do you really want our kids present when you're arrested for murder?"

His words had a devastating emotional effect on Lacey. "Don't do this to me, Steve. Not now. The children need me—and I need them."

"I only want you to face facts. There's no point in kidding yourself that everything's going to be hunky-dory. You've got to look out for yourself, and now it's my job to take care of the kids."

Lacey looked at him for a long, long moment, and she realized that as hurtful as his words were, they were uncomfortably close to the truth.

20

W̲hen the receptionist called Jean Atwill and told her that Lacey was on the telephone, Jean's eyes clouded over with loathing. Slowly, very slowly, she turned away from the computer. She got up from the desk, walked around it for a few moments as she tried to rein in her emotions, and then she sat down and picked up the telephone. She punched the button for line three and said, "Hello, Lacey."

Lacey seemed not to notice her icy tone. "Jean, we've decided to have a memorial service for Scott here in the garden tomorrow afternoon at three. There'll be a very small reception afterward, and then on the following morning at ten, the family is going to gather at the *Santa Maria*. We'll head out to sea to scatter the ashes. We'd be happy to have you join us."

Jean was shocked. "You're not having a funeral Mass at the cathedral?"

"No, Sasha insists that Scott be cremated."

"He's not going to be placed in the family tomb with his father?" she asked.

"I'm afraid not. Sasha feels very strongly that this is what Scott would have wanted. Will you join us?"

"I . . . I . . . think that's appalling!" Jean managed to exclaim, her throat constricted with barely suppressed anger.

"I beg your pardon?" Lacey asked, not sure she had heard correctly.

"I said that I think what you are doing is appalling. What right do you have to keep Scott out of the family tomb? Are you saving that honor for yourself alone?" The hatred Jean felt for the woman on the other end of the line was almost uncontainable.

Thinking that Jean was perhaps not quite understanding the situation, Lacey tried to explain it again.

"Look, this isn't my preference. If it were up to me, we'd have a funeral Mass at Our Lady of the Sea and burial alongside Dad, but Sasha is adamant, and I can't fault her reasoning. After all, she is his widow, and we—"

"Since when has anyone outside the immediate family ever had any influence on any of the Gallaghers' decisions or desires? You all do just what you want to do and the rest of the world be damned."

88

Lacey was stunned by the words Jean Atwill was spitting at her through the telephone.

"Jean, we're all just trying to do what's best. I can assure you that nobody has any ulterior motives. Is it the idea of cremation that bothers you?"

"You're what's bothering me, Mrs. Haines. If all your decisions are as wrong-headed as this one, then Gallagher's Best will soon be Gallagher's Worst."

"I think it's very unfair for you to attack me like this," Lacey replied, suppressing her anger.

"I know what you did. You killed your brother because you wanted everything he had! But you won't get away with it. Not if I have anything to say about it!"

It was Lacey's turn to be aghast. Jean Atwill was openly accusing her of Scott's death. But why?

"That's a terrible thing to say to me! Anybody who knows our family as well as you do should certainly know how much I loved him. I would have given my life for Scott," Lacey said, wounded by Jean's ugly words.

Caution told Jean to retreat, to restrain herself; although she was almost out of control, years of practice at keeping her feelings in check helped her to overcome her fury. Biting her lip, Jean gripped a pencil and snapped it in two, and then she said words that tasted like poison on her tongue.

"I'm sorry, Lacey. I shouldn't have said what I did. I don't know what came over me. I'm so distressed over everything. First losing your father and then to have Scott killed like that. I needed to lash out at somebody. I wanted somebody to blame."

The turnabout was so sudden and unexpected that Lacey hardly knew how to react.

"We're all very upset, Jean," she said, her voice barely above a whisper, but she was not yet prepared to forgive the dreadful accusation.

"Of course I'll be there tomorrow. Thank you for including me," Jean added, trying to gentle her tone of voice.

"I also need to know if you'll be on the *Santa Maria*. Space is limited and—" Lacey began, but Jean interrupted.

"I'll be there. I've known Scott ever since he was a baby."

"Fine. We'll see you tomorrow."

"And Lacey, I'll have my desk cleaned out by the end of the week. Would you like for me to find someone to work for you when I leave?"

"Since you feel the way you do, I agree it would be best for you to leave. Marge Melady will work out fine as my secretary. See you to-morrow," she said, concluding the conversation and hanging up.

Jean set down the receiver and put her face in her hands. Her life was over now. Whatever chance she had of staying on at Gallagher's Best had been shattered by her own intemperate words. How could she have been so stupid? Now she had nothing left. Nothing at all.

When Marge Melady's knock was not answered, she opened the office door and went in.

"Jean, are you all right?" she asked as she approached the desk. When there was no response from the woman whose head was resting on her arms, she went closer. "Jean? Are you sick?"

"Go away," came a muffled voice from the depths of despair.

"Jean, you're taking this too hard. Come on now. Get yourself to-gether. I'll pour us some coffee, and we can talk. Come on now, get moving," she said, going over to the coffee pot, which was always full and ready to be poured.

"Good grief, it's empty. How much of this stuff have you drunk today?"

Slowly, Jean lifted her head and pulled a tissue from the box on her desk. Using a mirror, she wiped the smudged mascara from her eyes and blew her nose.

"Too much, I guess."

"Let's go for an early lunch, what do you say? Come on, it'll be my treat. We'll go to Madeo's."

Jean shook her head. "No, uh, I think I'd rather eat in the company restaurant since it looks like this will be my last full day here."

"What? Are you kidding me?"

"It seems I just got my marching orders from her majesty."

"After all these years, after all you've done for the Gallagher family, you're out of a job? Why we haven't even had a chance to give you a retirement party yet—or even get you a going-away present!"

"Well, that's the way it is with the Gallaghers. Once they feel you're of no use, out you go."

"That's the meanest thing I've ever heard. She simply called and told you to go. That's it?"

"That's it. Of course she also invited me to the private memorial service at the house tomorrow. They're having Scott cremated and scat-tering his ashes at sea. She's not even going to let him have a place in the family mausoleum."

"Maybe she's following his wishes," Marge said pragmatically.

Jean's voice got nastier. "Oh, of course she says it's all the wife's idea, but I know better. That high and mighty bitch always wanted her father to herself."

Marge was put off by the characterization of Lacey Gallagher as a bitch, and she said so.

"Look, Jean, I know you always favored the son, but Lacey was the brains in the family, and I kind of like her."

"Well, you better like her. It seems you've been anointed to take my place. I hope she treats you better than she treated me."

Jean's words changed everything for Marge.

"Me? Are you joking? She actually said that?" she asked, her eyes glistening with pleasure.

Jean realized she might have missed an opportunity and took immediate steps to rectify it.

"Well, it was my suggestion, actually. She had planned on bringing in a stranger, but I told her she couldn't find anybody better than you."

"And she agreed?" Marge said, trying to keep her eyes from wandering around the luxurious office that would soon be hers.

"It wasn't easy, but I convinced her. Come on, let's have lunch. I'll meet you outside after I freshen up."

Resentfully, she watched Marge take one more proprietary look around the office and then leave, and Jean closed the door firmly behind her.

"It's not yours yet, bitch," Jean whispered as she headed toward her private powder room to repair the havoc of her emotional storm.

21

Brett, are you all right?" Penny asked when her husband arrived late to the breakfast table.

"I overslept."

"I've never known you to oversleep."

"Get off my back, hon, please. I want to eat my breakfast and read my newspaper in peace."

"I talked to Lacey last night after you went to sleep. Steve's back."

"Well, she's a rich woman in her own right now. He won't have to put up with Jack Gallagher anymore," Brett said with some rancor. "I always suspected he was after her money."

"When's the funeral?"

Penny outlined the schedule, and added, "Lacey's invited us to be aboard the *Santa Maria* when they scatter the ashes."

Brett let out a long audible sigh but said nothing.

The telephone rang, and Penny hurried to pick it up. It was Mary.

"Hi, Penny. Am I interrupting breakfast? You can call me back."

"Not necessary. I haven't got anybody else here to talk to," she complained, pointedly looking at her husband. "How are you feeling?"

"Not great. I hope to God I'm not on the verge of another flare."

"You probably went out in the sun without a hat or sunscreen yesterday, right? Mary, you know with that condition of yours you can't take the sun!"

"I only went for a walk."

"Are you taking your medicine?" Penny asked. She had been a close friend of Mary's since she was first diagnosed with lupus, and she tended to monitor her friend's health.

"Lay off, Dr. Marchbanks," Mary said with a short laugh. "I should never have let you read the material from that medical journal the doctor gave me. Now you're an expert on the disease. Give it a rest."

"God, what would the people around me do if I didn't take care of you all?"

Penny was a woman with a strong maternal instinct but no children. When, after many years of trying, she finally learned that she could not conceive, she and Brett had tried to adopt with no success. He adjusted to the disappointment by pursuing his career with a vengeance, and Penny had thrown her energies into volunteer work and her friends.

"Well, I, for one, wouldn't do very well at all if you weren't around to nag me. So, will you and Brett take me with you to Scott's memorial service?" Mary asked. "I don't want to go by myself."

"Silly question. Of course we'll take you."

"Did Lacey tell you that the family members are going to get up and say how they felt about Scott?"

Penny sensed Mary had something on her mind.

"Yes, she did. She even asked me if Brett wanted to say something, but we talked it over and decided against it. I know Brett sort of represents the company, but Scott was never part of Gallagher's Best, not really."

"I want to say something about Scott at the service. Do you think Lacey will mind?"

"Mary, don't be an ass. You've got no business intruding on that family's privacy. If Lacey wanted you to say something, she'd ask you."

"I feel as if he were still my husband, and I need to mourn too, you know," Mary argued.

"Scott was not your husband when he died. He was Sasha's. Please don't do something that would upset or embarrass Scott's family—or yourself."

Mary was not easily persuaded. She continued to press the matter.

"If you were a Roman Catholic, Penny, you might see my point of view. Morally, that so-called marriage of his to that Russian had no validity whatsoever."

Penny groaned inwardly and wished for words that would knock some sense into Mary's metaphysical head.

"Look, Mother Teresa, I know how much you loved Scott; I know all about your feelings about still being married to him. God knows I've heard it often enough. But right now, I want your promise to be a good little mourner and stay seated during the service, or so help me, I'm going to call Lacey and tell her to uninvite you."

"That's very disloyal of you. What kind of friend—"

"A good friend, honey, a good friend, because I'm trying to keep you from making a laughingstock of yourself. Go to church, by all means. Get down on your knees and pray, but for God's sake, don't get up at the memorial service and make like you're the bereaved wife."

"I'll do what I have to do," Mary said stubbornly. "Are you still going to give me a ride, or do I have to drive myself?"

Penny sighed in exasperation. "God, you're a tough cookie, Mary. You know that?"

"I've had to be tough to make it with the hand I was dealt."

There was a long silence while the import of her words sank in, and at last Penny conceded defeat.

"Thank God, it's not my funeral. Sure, we'll pick you up."

Penny put down the telephone and turned to her husband to tell him about her exasperating conversation, but he had gone. Although he had drunk all his coffee, his cereal and toast were untouched. Curious, Penny went up to the master bathroom and was relieved to find that he was in the shower.

"Brett, is something wrong?" she asked when he stepped out to dry himself.

"Yeah, I wished somebody dead—and he is."

★★ 22 ★★

After dinner, Steve made a suggestion. "Look, there's no reason for you three to be cooped up in one room. Suppose JJ and I bunk together?"

"That's a great idea," JJ responded enthusiastically. "We can sleep in my room."

Steve frowned. "Afraid not, son. That place is messier than any bunkhouse I've ever seen. I'd rather bed down in the garage than sleep in that clutter."

Erin chimed in. "God knows what creepy, crawly things might be hiding under his bed. The maids go in there to change the sheets once a week and scrub his bathroom, but he won't let them pick up or vacuum, not that they really want to."

"I can't ever find anything if I let them straighten up," JJ protested.

"JJ's room is too far away. I'd feel a lot more comfortable if the two of you would sleep in Mom's room, across the hall from me," Lacey said, realizing that the decision had been taken out of her hands. "We can move the extra twin from one of the guest rooms in there."

"By the way, where is the czarina? Didn't she want to have dinner with us peasants?" Steve asked with a grin.

"She's having dinner in Beverly Hills with her attorney," Erin replied.

"She's serious about breaking the will, eh?" Steve asked, savoring the last few drops of Chambertin in his glass.

Lacey dismissed it with a slight wave of her hand. "Well, she is now, but I'm not letting that happen. She's entitled to a portion of the estate, and I intend to see that she gets it. She's Scott's widow, and she shouldn't be left with nothing."

"How much are you going to give her?" he asked.

"Whatever she asks for, within reason, of course."

Steve fingered his empty Baccarat wineglass and then reached for the bottle of wine sitting beside him on a cork-lined silver coaster. He lifted it up to the light and saw that it was empty.

"Mind if we open another one of these?"

"Of course not," Lacey replied and pressed the foot button to call Gordon, who responded immediately.

"Can I get you something, Miss Lacey?"

"Would you mind going down to the cellar and bringing up a second bottle? Steve would like another glass."

Gordon looked pained. "But ma'am, the wine won't have time to breathe if I pour it immediately."

Steve and Lacey looked at each other and resisted the urge to laugh.

"Don't you worry, Gordon," Steve replied, his eyes twinkling. "As soon as you pour it, I'll give it mouth-to-mouth resuscitation."

Even Gordon could not help but laugh at the joke.

"I'll bring it right away, Mr. Haines."

After the children excused themselves to go do their homework, Steve remarked, "We've got great kids, Lacey. I wish we'd had more."

"Sometimes even two seems a lot to be responsible for," Lacey replied.

Gordon appeared with the wine, which he had decanted, and poured a glass for each of them. When he was gone, Steve returned to the subject of Sasha.

"I don't think you ought to offer Sasha any money voluntarily."

"Why?"

"She's already accused you of killing Scott, and moreover she probably believes you might have done it," he said, his tone serious.

"You're wrong," Lacey replied flatly. "Do you think for one minute that she'd have come back here to stay in this house with me if she thought that I was capable of murder?"

"That's an interesting idea. So if she's not afraid of you, and you're not afraid of her, then neither of you thinks the other is guilty."

Lacey nodded.

"Why don't you think she did it?" he asked.

"She had too much to lose."

"But you had everything to gain. Do you suppose she knows something we don't?"

"Interesting question. Maybe I'll ask her the next time I see her. And I fully intend to give her a share of the money. However, she'll have to forego any plans for a lawsuit. I don't need that hanging over my head along with everything else."

"If it were my call, I'd let her bust her butt in court trying to break that damned will, which she'll never manage to do in a million years. But do what you have to do. It's your decision."

"What makes you think she can't break the will?"

"Because I know your hardass father. He wasn't the kind to leave loopholes. Remember what a tough time he gave me at the time of our divorce? I still can't believe I won a point off him."

"What point did you win?"

"That if anything happened to you, I'd become the kids' guardian."

Lacey shook her head. "I was the one who insisted on that. Much as I loved my dad, I wouldn't give him precedence over the children's own father."

Lacey sipped on her wine thoughtfully and then added, "I thought I understood him so well. He was hard and he was tough, but I never knew him to break a promise. I never knew him to go back on his word before."

She looked down but Steve could see that her eyes were filled with tears as she continued to talk.

"Oh God, Steve, I loved them both so much—and now they're gone forever."

Steve drew his chair alongside hers. Taking her hand, he murmured words of comfort, but she didn't hear them because she continued pouring out her own grief.

"Dad promised me everything, Steve, everything. He said he had come to the conclusion that I was the only one he'd trust to run the company. He apologized to me for thinking that it should be Scott. Oh God, he said all the things that I had wanted so much to hear all of my life. And I believed him because he was a man of his word."

Steve listened solemnly. Jack Gallagher had always been a thorn in his side, and he was gratified to hear Lacey describe her father in less than adoring terms. Perhaps he had been too aware of his own shortcomings in comparison to the powerful, self-made multimillionaire, but he never doubted that throughout their entire marriage, he had played second fiddle to a man twice his age and half his size. Not that Steve didn't have a good opinion of himself. He was a big man physically, tall and well muscled, and always attractive to women. Lacey was the only woman he'd ever met who hadn't swooned over him. From the time they had first dated, he was the one who'd had to do all the pursuing.

As he sipped the rare and expensive wine, like Scott taking perverse pleasure in depleting Jack Gallagher's prize collection, he thought back to all the years of frustration that Lacey Gallagher had brought him. Now both of his rivals for her affection were gone. Would she turn to him, or would she find everything she needed in the damned company and in their children?

Gordon came in to announce that the bedroom was ready.

"You'll be more comfortable in Mom's room than Dad's, Steve," Lacey said getting to her feet.

"Your mother wasn't particularly fond of me either, if you'll recall."

"We must warn JJ not to marry a woman who's too much Daddy's girl," Lacey said wryly.

As they walked out of the dining room together, Steve again draped his arms across her shoulders, but this time, it didn't bother her.

23

Three days after the killing of Scott Gallagher, Cherry Dolan was almost convinced that Lacey was going to have to be charged with her brother's murder. The coroner's report had confirmed their suspicion that the victim had ingested a considerable amount of sedative, buta-barbital sodium, approximately two hours before his death, which was about the same time he had been drinking with his sister. The murder weapon had one partial fingerprint on the hilt, too smudged to be identified. A search of the house turned up an unmarked bottle of pills in the medicine chest in Scott's bathroom. Unfortunately, the wineglasses Lacey and her brother had used had been picked up by the maid early in the morning and washed before the body was found.

Cherry, however, was not happy with the case as it now stood. Everyone she questioned—the gardeners, the housekeeper, the maids, the cook—had all described Lacey as a saint who loved her brother too much for her own good. Only Sasha and Jean Atwill had bad-mouthed her. Cherry understood Sasha's feelings, but Jean was something else. The detective decided to go back to the offices of Gallagher's Best and question some of the people who worked there.

Marge Melady was more than willing to talk about her employer.

"What kind of a boss was Jack Gallagher?" Cherry asked her when they were alone in Jean's office.

"It's hard to say. Most of us didn't have much contact with him. Everything went through Jean. She got really mad at anybody who approached Mr. Gallagher directly."

"Did he pay well?"

"Yeah, I guess so, but Lacey was the one who got all of us in the secretarial pool a raise last year. Jean advised against it. She always said stenos were easily replaced, but Lacey went to her dad. Gosh, was Jean furious."

"So you really like Lacey?"

"I think she's great. I feel honored that she picked me to be her executive secretary."

"Did Jean have any other reason not to like her?"

"Hard to say. They had such different styles. Lacey was, well, accessible would be the word. You could tell her anything. Jean was tough, and sometimes she could get real mean if you crossed her. She and Lacey clashed every now and then.''

"Anything else?''

Marge looked down at her hands and thought. "She gave Jean her marching papers yesterday. Jean was real upset.''

"Jean wanted to stay?''

"Yeah, I think so. But Lacey apparently didn't want her to.''

Cherry spent the next couple of hours talking to people at the company, but the response was invariably the same: Lacey was a saint; Jean was a pain in the ass.

Cherry decided to go back to the Gallagher estate and ask around some more. If she really stuck that letter opener into her brother's heart, Lacey couldn't be as good as everyone said she was. It was noon when Cherry arrived and announced herself to the intercom at the gate.

Cherry was admitted, and she drove up the long and winding driveway to find caterers' trucks parked in the service area as well as two big trucks from Abbey Rents.

Chuck was waiting for her at the circular drive.

"What's going on?'' she asked.

"They're having the memorial service here today. I got here two minutes ago. Come on, let's walk around and see what's going on.''

"This place is like a piece of heaven. Look, is that a great view of the sea or what?'' Cherry commented, and the two stopped for a few moments to indulge themselves in the beauty that stretched before them.

The magnificent Tudor-style home behind them had been built on the crest of a gently rolling hill, and although there were trees aplenty, they had been planted to frame the view of the sea rather than obstruct it. The grounds of the Gallagher house sloped gradually down to the rocky shore below, and white caps could be seen as the waves rolled in. Although fog was a frequent visitor to the Palos Verdes peninsula, this was one of those days when the sky was perfectly clear and blue, and the sun shone warm and bright, making colors intense and shimmering.

"If I didn't know about the tragedy inside, I'd be tempted to envy, wouldn't you, Chuck?'' she asked.

"I don't have a spread like this,'' he said, shaking his head, "but from the bedroom window of my little house, I can see that same sea. Even the Gallaghers don't have an exclusive on that,'' he replied.

"There's the butler. Let's go talk to him.''

Gordon was talking to the man unloading folding chairs from a truck.

"How many people are you expecting today?" Chuck asked as they approached.

"About a hundred."

"Would it be all right if we hung around for the service?" Cherry asked.

"That's up to Miss Lacey. I'll ask her when I have time." The butler turned back to his conversation with the delivery men.

"Rows of twelve, please. About a hundred and fifty chairs will be more than sufficient. Six on one side and six on the other and an aisle down the middle." Then turning to Cherry, he said, "I'll be back shortly."

"Do you get the feeling that he'd throw us out if he could?" Chuck asked. Cherry nodded.

Gordon returned within a couple of minutes.

"Miss Lacey said it would be all right if you stayed. However, she asked that you blend in with the crowd and not tell anyone who you are or why you're here."

"No problem. What time is it scheduled to start?" Cherry asked.

"At two o'clock," Gordon replied and then raced off to oversee the unloading of a caterer's truck.

"You'll have to stay by yourself, Cherry. I've got a two-thirty appointment with Patrick Williams in the D.A.'s office. He's getting anxious to go after somebody. Think we've got enough to go with it?"

"I'm not convinced Lacey's guilty, but nothing else makes sense. She had motive, opportunity, and the weapon, but I wish we'd at least have gotten a fingerprint."

"I'll lay it all out and let him decide."

"Fine. I sure as hell don't want to do it," she said.

"It'll be interesting for you to have a look at the family and their friends all in one spot," Chuck said.

"Do you suppose that guest house over there is open?" Cherry asked, picking up her pace. "I want to look inside."

The front door was locked, as was the door off the patio area of the guest cottage.

Cherry jiggled the knob, which was pulled out of her grasp as the door opened abruptly.

"You knocked?" Lacey asked, her expression slightly amused.

"Uh, no, not really. I had no idea anyone was inside," Cherry said.

"Come in, by all means. I was sitting here by the window watching those people turn my serene garden into a beehive of activity."

She opened the door wide, and the two detectives followed her into the sitting room.

"My goodness, this is beautiful," Cherry murmured, her eyes quickly circling the room and taking in the richness of its antique furnishings.

"Exquisite, isn't it?" Lacey agreed. "It had started to look a little seedy when I came home from Texas, so I had it spruced up."

Cherry found herself asking about the decoration of the house. Experienced as she was, she felt uncomfortable acting friendly toward a woman she was probably going to arrest for murder without being convinced of her guilt.

"I love the color of the walls," Cherry said, somewhat lamely.

"We scraped off the old wallpapers and washed them with that light apricot color. We replaced the heavy draperies with modern blinds and sanded and bleached the hardwood floors. Look over there in the bedroom and you'll see what bringing in a little light can do for a room. That beautiful window over there used to be a wall with a mirror. What could anyone see in a mirror that could possibly equal that?"

The visitors both nodded in agreement. A large hemispherical window had been cut into the wall and the magnificent view of the ocean was now literally at the foot of the twin beds.

"It's quite a view, Mrs. Haines," Chuck agreed, also feeling awkward.

"Don't call me Mrs. Haines," Lacey said. "Ever since I came home from Texas, I've been called by my first name or Ms. Gallagher."

"You don't use your married name?" Cherry asked.

"Not much. At the children's school, of course, and in signing legal documents, but that's about all. My father wanted me to take back my maiden name legally after the divorce, but I didn't feel it was fair to the children."

"This is used as a guest house, isn't it?" Cherry asked.

"Now it is, but Dad originally built the cottage to be a playhouse for Scott and me. Both rooms were always cluttered with toys. Steve and I lived here for a while after we got married. When Erin was born, we had to move back into the big house because there wasn't room for a baby and a nanny here."

"And you still like to come here to get away from things?" Cherry asked.

"Not really. I came down this morning to think about Scott and all the happy days we had playing in here." She looked up and her eyes were filled with tears. "It's so hard for me to say good-bye to him."

"I'm sorry we intruded on you, Miss, er, Gallagher. We'll leave now," Chuck said and started to move toward the door.

"Don't go. I was leaving anyway. Make yourself comfortable. I have to get back and make sure the children are dressing properly. JJ'll have on tennis shoes and jeans if I don't watch him. I've told Gordon to give you access to anything you want to look over."

With those words, Lacey seemed to disappear into thin air, so swiftly and silently did she move out the door.

"Jesus," Chuck said, exhaling the word. "She's truly a great manipulator. She's almost got me convinced she wants to help us find the criminal who killed her brother."

"Yep. I know exactly what you mean."

A few minutes after Lacey had left them, a knock on the door interrupted their conversation. It was a maid bearing a silver tray.

"Miss Lacey thought you might enjoy a glass of lemonade and some cookies," she said handing the tray inside the door to Chuck and turning to rush back toward the main house.

"Well, well, a bit of Gallagher's Best to refresh us," Chuck commented.

"I just can't see that woman murdering anybody," Cherry said, picking up the cut-glass pitcher and pouring the icy pale yellow liquid into two tall crystal glasses.

"She's trying to seduce us, partner," Chuck said as he bit into one of the thick, chewy oatmeal cookies.

"More power to her. God, I love cookies with raisins in 'em."

24

The chief justice's eulogy was literate, appropriate, tasteful, and intelligent, but it was also dry, humorless, and distant, and no more captured the spirit of Scott Gallagher than an obituary notice in the newspaper. As the emotionless words drifted out over the audience, it seemed to Lacey that they floated over the heads of the mourners and out to sea, touching no hearts as they passed. She looked over at the proud gray-haired Father O'Brien and, remembering his thrilling and dramatic tribute to her father, felt that she had failed her brother. Surely he deserved a few tears of farewell. Jack Gallagher had lived a full and long life before he died, but Scott had been deprived of his best years.

As the chief justice gathered up his notes and prepared to abandon the lectern, Lacey reached over the children and squeezed Steve's arm. He was the first family member to speak. Steve covered her hand warmly and got up to say his farewell.

Watching his tall figure, so rarely dressed in a dark suit, white shirt, and necktie, Lacey felt a lump begin to swell in her throat. For the past few days, Steve had returned to being the man she had married, not the man she had divorced, and she was grateful for the support he'd given her and the children.

Steve cleared his throat and took a couple of three-by-five cards from his inside jacket pocket. He started to read:

"Scott Gallagher was my brother-in-law, but he was also my friend. He could make me laugh when there was nothing to laugh about. No matter how serious the situation, Scott could always find some humor in it. He could make me laugh when I needed cheering up, and he could also make me giggle when it was inappropriate to do so, and he always found my embarrassment amusing."

He looked up from his notes and began to speak extemporaneously: "I wanted to get up here today and tell you a story, a funny one. Something that would make you laugh, and in your laughter you would remember Scott at his best, his most humorous best. But I couldn't think of anything that would be as witty or as humorous as Scott was, and I didn't want to dishonor him with a lame or an unfunny joke. When

Scott died, a lot of laughter went out of the world, not only for me but for everyone who knew him."

Lacey was surprised by the simple elegance of his words, and she was moved by the understanding of her brother that they conveyed.

JJ went next because he had begged not to have to follow his sister, whose prowess on the school's speech team was legendary. Lacey patted his arm and whispered, "Just read what you've written, honey. You'll do fine."

Shaking noticeably, JJ made his way to the microphone, and he looked very young and vulnerable in his tweed jacket and dark blue trousers. His hair was combed neatly, but his tie was slightly askew.

Holding the crumpled paper on which he had scribbled the message, which no one had helped him write, he hesitated. Then looking up at the audience, he offered a simple explanation of what he was about to read.

"Mom told me to write down the things I would always remember best about Uncle Scott, and that's what I did." Then looking back at the paper he began to read:

"Uncle Scott played tennis with me, he took me skiing, and he tried to teach me to play golf, but I didn't like it much. What I'll remember most are the days we went sailing together. A couple of months ago we were out on the boat and I asked him how come he didn't have any kids of his own, and he said that he didn't need to have kids because me and my sister were so great and he loved us so much that it wouldn't be fair to have children of his own who would feel they had to compete with us. I knew it wasn't true, but it made me feel good to have him say it. Uncle Scott always said things that made me feel good. It's hard for me to believe that he's not going to be around when I grow up."

There were tears in JJ's eyes when he returned to his seat, where Steve put his arm around him, gave him a reassuring hug, and whispered, "That was fine, JJ. Just fine." Lacey took his hand and squeezed it, but she was fighting off her tears and couldn't say anything.

Erin rose from her chair and walked majestically to the lectern. An accomplished speaker, she had memorized everything she intended to say. She looked at the rows of mourners, made eye contact with several, and began to speak with great assurance and her head held high.

"Scott Gallagher was my uncle, my only uncle, and I treasured him. No matter what the dispute was between my mother and myself, Scott always took my side. Always. More than any other adult I've ever known, he remembered exactly what it was like to be young, and he was so sympathetic. I could talk to him about things I could never discuss with my mother or my father or my grandfather, and he would take the time to listen, but more importantly, he would understand. I know in my heart there's a heaven somewhere and that Uncle Scott is there, and if it's possible, he's watching over me right now, cheering me on, telling me to go for it, that life is for the taking and the enjoying. I loved him with all my heart. I will always remember him. I hope that he can still remember me."

Now it was Lacey's turn, but she was so emotionally unsettled by the strong feelings her children and her husband had expressed that she hesitated to get up from her seat when Erin sat down.

"That was great, darling," she said and wiped her eyes.

"You okay?" Steve whispered to her. "You don't have to say anything if you don't want to, babe."

"But I do. I do," she whispered, more to herself than to anyone else, and she gathered her own emotions inside her and stood up. Slowly but deliberately she walked to the microphone, and like her daughter, she carried no notes. She intended to speak from the heart.

She rested her forearms on the podium to steady herself, and she looked out over the group waiting to hear her. Jean Atwill sat in the rear with her lips pursed tightly together, hatred glittering from her tear-stained eyes. Next to her, Chuck Bascombe and Cherry Dolan were also waiting to pass judgment on her performance. After a long pause, Lacey found her voice, thready and weak at first, but gathering strength and purpose as she proceeded.

"Scott Joseph Gallagher was more than a brother to me. Much, much more. He was my closest friend. My confidant. My strength. We were born less than a year apart into a family of extraordinary people, and we were expected to measure up to them in whatever we did. It was a burden that weighed heavily on us both because so much was expected all the time. My mother counted on me to do everything better and sooner than anyone else. I had to be the very best for her. Our father expected as much, if not more, from his son. I struggled to fulfill their expectations, but Scott rebelled. He found life too much fun to be taken all that seriously, and he never toed the line for anybody, particularly not for Dad. I don't know how either one of us would have survived the pressure if we hadn't had each other. I did my best to cover for Scott and help him avoid the retribution that his transgressions invariably invoked. And Scott helped me to keep life in perspective. He said I didn't know how to play, and I said he didn't know how to work. We were like two halves of a whole person. When he died, I felt that the better half of me died too. I will never see a rainbow or a bright sunny sky or a fancy, expensive car or drink a rare bottle of wine, or hear laughter without thinking of Scott. He has always been there when I needed him. I hope he left some part of his joyful spirit inside me. And I pray to God that he doesn't find heaven too boring."

By the time Lacey finished speaking, tears were running freely down her cheeks, and Steve jumped up to walk her back to her seat. She had barely sat down when Sasha hurried to the lectern with an unseemly urgency. It appeared that she was afraid she might be denied her opportunity to speak.

"Scott Gallagher was my husband," she began as she unfolded the piece of paper on which her notes were written. "Although I didn't have a lifetime of experience with him, as the others have had, my love for him was as deep as anyone's. And unlike the others, I have lost everything." She paused to let that remark sink in. "Tomorrow morning when we embark on his beloved *Santa Maria* to scatter his ashes on the sea, I will be saying good-bye to the only man I have ever loved. No one can take his place. Sleep well, my darling," she said, and her eyes shimmered with tears and amusement as she looked up at the sky. "I'll wake you up when I come home, as you always did me."

She smiled gently and left the lectern, and there was a long moment of silence before people began to stand up. Steve leaned over and whispered to Lacey, "Now I know why he married her. She's got as bawdy a sense of humor as he had."

"Scott would have loved it," Lacey said. "I'm glad she said what she did. The rest of us were so damned gloomy."

Sitting in the back row Brett and Penny had positioned themselves on either side of Mary; they had managed to restrain her from getting to her feet after Lacey had spoken, but they had prepared themselves for a real battle after Sasha's talk. It didn't happen. Something that Scott's widow said stopped Mary cold. Even when all the people began getting to their feet to gather around the family and convey their condolences, Mary continued to sit, staring ahead in pensive silence.

"You all right, old girl?" Penny asked in a whisper.

Mary nodded her head and then abruptly shook it.

Brett and Penny exchanged concerned glances.

"Tell me about it, honey," Penny said sotto voce, but Mary got to her feet without saying a word. Big tears of sorrow filled her eyes as she walked with her friends toward the gates.

"Mary, come on. We have to go see Lacey. What will she think if we leave without talking to her?" Penny asked.

Mary did not stop her exodus, but she finally said a few words. "Thanks for being my friend. Tell Lacey I couldn't talk. Take your time. I'll wait in the car."

She pressed a piece of paper in Penny's hand and then hurried away from them.

Perplexed, Penny opened the paper, and Brett read it over her shoulder:

"Everyone thinks that Scott and I were divorced, but I knew that in the sight of God in His Heaven, we were still married. Not only were we married in His Holy Church, but we continued to know each other physically in spite of his subsequent pseudo-marriages. He told me he continued to love me. I believed him then. I believe him still. I also believe we will be reunited, and spend eternity together. I look forward to that day."

"My God, she was actually going to read this!" Brett exclaimed.

Penny looked up at her husband and asked, "Do you suppose it was true? Do you really think Scott continued to sleep with her?"

"Why would that surprise you? The guy was an alley cat. You're not going to show that thing to Lacey, are you?"

Penny shook her head, crumpled the paper, and stuffed it into her handbag. "Good grief, no. That's all Lacey needs to hear. What a rotten thing to do. No wonder she clung to the hope that one day he'd come back. Poor baby."

"Like father, like son."

"What's that supposed to mean?"

"Everybody knows that his father had a babe or two on the side," Brett snapped. "Don't act so innocent. You know the Gallaghers as well as I do."

Penny raised her eyebrows and muttered, "Apparently I don't know them as well as I thought I did. Come on. Let's squeeze in the line and say a fast few words of condolence. I don't want to keep Mary waiting in the car too long."

The waiters appeared with glasses of champagne, and the quiet air of solemnity that had settled on the crowd during the service evaporated as people began to talk to one another.

The detectives too got to their feet to move to a better vantage point when Jean Atwill pushed past them in an aggressive manner.

"Whoa . . . where's she going in such a rush?" Chuck asked almost loudly enough for Jean to hear.

"That woman's got something on her mind. She's the old man's secretary," Cherry whispered so as not to be overheard by anyone in the crowd milling about them.

"Did you notice her throughout the service?" Chuck asked. "She couldn't take her eyes off Lacey, and if looks could kill, the coroner would be carting the poor woman off right now."

"She really believes Lacey killed Scott. What did you think of the service?" Cherry asked as they walked toward the gate, separating themselves from the visitors, who were clustering around the family members, and moving toward the refreshment tables set up near the gazebo.

"It was nice. Look, I hate to leave," Chuck said, looking at his wristwatch, "but I've really gotta get going. I'm late now. Stay and look things over. I'll see you later."

After Chuck left, Cherry took a glass of Perrier from a waiter and moved closer to the crowd near Lacey. She wanted to see how she handled herself with other people. She seemed too good to be true. The little talk she'd given had been damned near perfect, and even Cherry had found herself near tears.

Suddenly, Jean Atwill's face appeared at Lacey's shoulder, and Cherry reflexively began to move toward them, anticipating some kind of action. The woman looked desperate.

Without even thinking, Cherry put her hand inside her jacket and flipped open the snap holding her gun in its holster. In case she needed to pull it out quickly, she wrapped her fingers around the butt. At the same time, she tried to shove her way toward Lacey, who was busy talking to someone and not at all aware that Jean was behind her. Unfortunately, Cherry was unable to get the well-wishers to move fast enough, and so she used her voice.

"Lacey!" she called loudly, startling those around her and calling attention to herself. "Lacey! Could you come over here, please. Right away!"

To her satisfaction, not only did she get Lacey's attention but Cherry also succeeded in getting Jean Atwill's. The older woman looked up in surprise as she recognized the detective pushing rapidly through the crowd toward her.

"Yes?" Lacey replied, startled by the detective's sudden demand.

"I need to speak to you right now. Please, come with me."

"Why, of course," Lacey replied, smiling apologetically at the people to whom she had been talking.

As soon as the two women were close enough to talk, Cherry took Lacey's arm and steered her away from the crowd. Speaking in an undertone, Cherry said, "I'm sorry I had to interrupt you that way, but Jean Atwill moved up behind you and I had a terrible feeling she was about to do something rash."

"Jean Atwill . . . what do you mean?"

"Can we go inside where we can talk in private?" Cherry asked, looking over her shoulder and noting that Jean was standing there and staring at them with her hand in the purse hanging from her shoulder.

"Look, I'm going back to speak to her. Stay away from her until we can talk, all right?" Cherry requested and walked quickly back where the woman in question stood.

When Jean Atwill realized that Cherry was headed her way, her hand came out of her purse and in it was an embroidered handkerchief that she used to dab at her eyes. She then quickly zipped the handbag shut, turned, and headed toward the entrance to the yard. Cherry closed the distance between them, however, and reached the woman before she could leave.

"Miss Atwill, may I have a word with you?"

"I'm in a hurry," Jean replied, but she stopped and turned to face the detective. "I thought you were so anxious to speak to Lacey," she added with sarcasm.

"No, actually, I was asked to call her to the telephone. Miss Atwill, what are you carrying in your purse?" she asked, noticing how tightly Jean was holding on to the handbag.

"It's none of your business," the woman snapped back at her.

"I think it is. May I see what's inside, please?"

"I know my rights. I've done nothing to give you any reason to suspect me of any wrongdoing."

Cherry knew the woman was right. All she had to go on was her own instinct about the woman's behavior. Jean had actually done nothing.

"Miss Atwill, why are you so angry with Lacey Gallagher?" she asked, changing the subject.

"She killed Scott. Isn't that reason enough?"

"Do you have any information that could help us prove that?" Cherry asked. "If you do, then I'd really appreciate it if you'd tell me about it."

Jean Atwill's eyes flashed with anger.

"If I had any proof, she'd be rotting in jail right now instead of standing there looking bereaved and shedding crocodile tears. She's not sorry Scott's dead. Now she gets everything, and he gets burned into a pile of ashes that she'll throw out to sea tomorrow."

As she spoke, her anger seemed to convert into sorrow, and the glint of hatred in her eyes dissolved in tears. Cherry watched the transformation in astonishment, and the antipathy she felt toward the woman dissipated. Jean Atwill was more than merely a hateful woman. She was desperately grief-stricken, but why? Why did she love Scott and despise his sister?

Gently, Cherry led Jean to the guest house. "Come now," she murmured. "There's a bathroom in here and you can pull yourself together. Here's my card. Call me at anytime, and they'll reach me. I'll be happy to hear anything you have to say, understand?"

Jean nodded and went into the small cottage. Cherry took a deep breath and started to walk away. She was no more than ten feet from the house when she heard her name called.

"Detective Dolan," Jean Atwill called to her from the steps of the cottage.

Cherry turned around. "Yes?"

"Did you really think I intended to harm Lacey?"

Cherry thought for a minute, and then she replied, "I don't know. Did you?"

Jean smiled cynically, said nothing, turned away, took two steps toward the gate and stopped. Slowly turning back to face the detective, she said, "I won't have to take the law into my own hands, Ms. Dolan, because you and your partner are going to see that the guilty person is punished. Aren't you?"

"We're going to try."

There was a strong sense of threat in Jean's response. "You have to do better than that."

25

L acey waited only a couple of minutes, and when Cherry Dolan did not immediately return, she decided to go back to the garden gate to talk with her departing guests. She stepped out the front door and found herself face-to-face with Pete Cunningham.

"Pete!" she exclaimed. "I didn't know you were here."

"I hope I'm not imposing. I called over to your office this morning, and your secretary told me about the memorial service. I felt like I had to come and pay my respects. I wanted Scott to know I wasn't still holding a grudge."

"What a kind thing to say."

"I hope when I go, there'll be as many nice words spoken about me. If Scott's listening, he's probably impressed."

Lacey looked up at him with tears in her eyes. To her surprise, the years she and Pete had been separated seemed to telescope into nothingness. She felt as at ease with him in that moment as she had when they were teenagers. She took his arm and they walked down the garden path toward the gate.

"I'm afraid the sun is gone for good," Lacey commented, gesturing out toward the sea where a bank of fog was rolling in.

"Want my jacket?" Pete asked, but Lacey shook her head.

"No, thank you. I'm fine. I'm as accustomed to this kind of weather as you are."

Pete stayed at her side until the last guest was gone, and then he took his leave.

"Thanks for coming, Pete. We're going to scatter Scott's ashes at sea tomorrow. If you're free, I'd love to have you join us."

"From the *Santa Maria*?" he asked.

Lacey nodded.

"If you want me to be there, I will. What time and where will she be docked?"

Lacey gave him the information, and he left.

Cherry Dolan was waiting for her at the house.

"Ms. Gallagher, you and Jean Atwill don't like each other much, do you?"

Lacey shook her head. "She's never liked me, and I don't know why."

"Can you think of any reason she might want to do you harm?"

"No, I can't, why?"

"I had a feeling she was going to attack you this afternoon. That's why I called out to you as I did. I must have been mistaken. Thanks for letting me stay."

Cherry made a quick exit, and as Lacey turned to go into the house, she saw Steve watching her, a sour expression on his face.

"Who was that tall guy you were talking to?" he asked.

"An old friend."

"Of yours or Scott's?"

"Mine. He's now CEO of a company we're trying to acquire."

Steve seemed relieved. "Oh, it's only business."

She nodded, and they went inside together.

26

Six Years Ago

Startled, Lacey looked up from the pile of bills on the kitchen table as another bolt of lightning crashed through the Texas night sky, and she automatically began counting. She had barely gotten to three when thunder boomed across the landscape, sending a shudder through the timber of the creaky old ranch house. Within seconds the rain began, and it was not tiny, poetic drops pitter-pattering on the roof, but a deluge of water that assaulted the shingles over her head and threatened to dislodge them.

She rushed to the service porch to gather up an armload of buckets and plastic wastebaskets, which she deposited in all the usual places. The roof of the house was in terrible shape and with each new rainstorm, it seemed another hole opened up to let water pour into the house.

Within seconds, the kerplunking sound of raindrops leaking through the roof and falling into the receptacles, drop by drop, began what she called her "rainy night symphony." The water falling into the plastic created a low-toned bass sound that harmonized nicely with the high-toned plink of the drops falling into the galvanized metal buckets.

She then tiptoed into the children's bedroom and draped two plastic dropcloths over each of their blankets. Although she and Steve had positioned the children's beds away from the leaks, she could not be sure that the rain wouldn't find an alternate way to intrude and soak their blankets. If there had been another, drier room in which the children could have been moved, they would have done so, but there was no place in the old ranch house where the roof was secure. They had done little to modernize the decrepit building, which was on the property when they bought it, because they had planned to build a new house as soon as possible. Almost two years had passed, however, and they didn't even have enough money to fix up the roof. They barely had enough to buy food.

She leaned down over JJ's bed, gently put her hand on her seven-year-old son's forehead and breathed a sigh of relief. The fever was gone, thank God. Then she walked softly over to tuck Erin's leg back under the blanket, but as soon as she touched her, her ten-year-old daughter's eyes flew open.

"Mommy!" she whispered. "Is that you?"

"Sh-h-h, go to sleep, honey," Lacey answered, leaning down close to her daughter's face.

"The thunder woke me up," she replied, and then she began to cry. "I hate these storms, Mommy. I want to go home."

"Honey, please be quiet," Lacey whispered, sitting down on the side of her daughter's bed and putting her arms around her unhappy child. "JJ's fever has finally broken, and he needs his sleep."

"I can't help it, Mommy. I want to go home to Grandma and Grandpa's house so bad. I want to sleep in my own room again. I hate it here. Please, please can't we go back?"

Lacey tried to comfort her daughter, but she knew it was futile. How could she lie to her children and tell them it was better to live down here on a ranch in a house that was small and barren, with a roof that gave them no protection from the elements, rather than live in the comfort and security of her father's mansion? Whenever she tried, which was often, her words had a hollow ring, probably because she understood too well her children's feelings. So she soothed her little girl by holding her close and crooning softly until the child was sound enough asleep to tuck her back in bed.

Back at the kitchen table again, Lacey once more tackled the stack of bills. It took every cent they had to feed and care for the livestock and maintain the equipment on the ranch, not to mention the string of unfortunate breakdowns that had consumed all of their capital. The collapse of the dam their first winter had been a calamity, but it was only the first of a series of misfortunes. Now there was no money whatsoever for the things they needed to make life a little more comfortable for themselves. Ever since they had left California to move here, she and Steve had worked night and day, and they weren't making any headway at all. For each step forward, they went two or three steps back. Each month she found it necessary to go back to her father for financial help, and the amounts of money they needed from him were escalating.

It was almost midnight when she finished writing the checks and completing the day's ledger entries; she was exhausted and depressed. Tomorrow she would have to call her mother and ask her to intercede with her father. Last month, after she told him that she wasn't bringing the children home this summer for a visit because Steve said it was too hard on them to adjust to ranch life when they returned, her angry father had declared that he was not going to subsidize their folly anymore. The adventure had failed, and it was time to cut their losses and sell, he said. Steve refused to go back unless her father agreed to give him a vice presidency of the company, and Jack Gallagher declined to be coerced. Her only hope now was that her mother could change her father's mind, because she knew that Steve would never give in.

To make matters worse, little JJ had been sick almost constantly since they had come to Texas, and their medical bills had been enormous. Her son had developed severe allergies, which had triggered asthma attacks, and the once robust child was now delicate and sickly.

Although she knew she should get some sleep, she hated the thought of going to bed. Steve might still be awake, and she was too tired for sex. She put the kettle on the stove to make herself a cup of chamomile tea, and as she sipped the warm, sweetish liquid, she was filled with despair. Nothing was as she had planned or wished it to be, because she had fallen in love with a man whose approach to life was so different from hers. Now she was living it his way and doing a perfectly miserable job of it. The ranch, which was mortgaged to the rafters, was eating them both alive, bleeding them of all their energy and resources, and depriving their children of the comforts that they themselves had enjoyed as youngsters.

The next morning, after Steve had left for town to pick up some supplies, Erin had been put on the school bus, and JJ had been settled down in front of the television set with a box of crayons and some coloring books, Lacey telephoned her mother.

Maude Gallagher was delighted to accept the collect call.

"Mom, how are you?" Lacey asked.

"As well as can be expected, under the circumstances, darling," Maude Lacey Gallagher replied.

"What's wrong, Mom?" She and her mother were extremely close, and it worried her whenever her mother complained because Maude was usually cheerful and upbeat.

"Oh, your father made me go see that cardiovascular specialist yesterday, because I was having those dizzy spells again, and he says that I've got clogged arteries."

"What are they going to do for you?"

"They're putting me into the hospital next week. He says I have to be very quiet and take life easy until then. It seems I'm at great risk of having a stroke. They're going to ream out the affected arteries so the blood can flow more freely."

"Is there anything I can do?"

"Actually, there is, darling. I want to see you and the children before the surgery. I know Steve feels that it's hard on Erin and JJ to return home again after a visit here, but I hope you can prevail on him to let you come."

Lacey hesitated, and then for the first time in a long, long time, she made a decision on her own. After all, the woman asking for a favor was her mother.

"Of course we'll come home, Mom. When do you want us?"

"As soon as possible, darling. Maybe if you tell Steve I'm sick, he won't object."

Maude's words made Lacey's stomach turn. Ever since her marriage, she had found herself in a tug-of-war between the man she married and the family she adored, and she was the rope each side was pulling.

"I'll pack our things and take the first plane I can get out of Austin, Mom. We'll be there before you know it."

"Steve won't come, will he?" Maude asked.

Lacey's response was terse. "He has things to do here."

"Your father will send the plane for you then. It'll be too much of a hassle for you otherwise. What's the closest airport to the ranch, darling?"

The thought of driving the short distance to Bellewether and stepping into her father's luxurious Jetstar was too tempting to resist.

"Mom, that would be wonderful. Tell Dad there's a private airstrip about twenty miles from here that's big enough for Dad's jet. A cattleman built it for his 727, but I understand he's very generous about letting neighbors use it. Want me to call him and ask?"

"You do that, honey. Call your father as soon as you can and give him the information. He said the plane could be ready to go whenever you are."

"We'll be there just as soon as we can. Just last night Erin was talking about her old bedroom, and JJ's been sick again."

"Oh dear, I'm so sorry. Tell my sweet little granddaughter that her room is exactly as it was when she left. Well, you better get started, honey. I can hardly wait to see you all."

To Lacey's chagrin, Steve returned home earlier than expected, and it was obvious that he was annoyed.

"That damn truck blew another tire, and I had to leave it up at the gate. I didn't have a jack with me." He looked at his wife and children all dressed up, with their suitcases packed and ready to leave, and asked, "What the hell's going on here?"

Cursing herself for not getting out faster, Lacey hastened to explain that her mother was about to undergo surgery, but as with every situation that involved his in-laws, he listened with skepticism.

"How long do you intend to stay?"

"I really don't know. Just until Mom's well again."

Her husband rubbed his two-day growth of beard on his handsome face, and a slight sneer passed slowly across his mouth.

"That could be years from now and you know it. You're leaving me, aren't you?"

Lacey didn't want to talk in front of the children, but she had no choice.

"For a while anyway. I need time to think."

Reason departed whenever the subject of Lacey's parents was under discussion. Steve and Jack Gallagher had detested each other from the beginning, and the years of their marriage had not improved the relationship. Steve had taken a bold gamble in removing Lacey and the grandchildren from the grandparents' sphere of influence, and it had not paid off.

"Bullshit! I know how your family operates. They'll figure out some way to keep their darling daughter under their thumbs."

"Don't blame them, Steve. We're the ones with the problems."

"You want a divorce?"

Lacey looked down. For a long time she had been thinking about going home, but she hadn't yet contemplated a step as permanent as divorce. Not until that moment when he suggested it.

"This is not the time for—"

"You're a piece of work, you know that?" he interrupted. "Your shitty father's got a big plane that jets him all over the world, but he's never once come here to see you. Is that how much he loves his daughter and his grandchildren?"

"My parents have never been invited. I didn't want them to see how really squalid this place is." She had spoken the truth, but she regretted the spiteful tone of her voice. "Steve, Mom and Dad have been extremely helpful and generous to us from the very beginning," she continued, trying to be more conciliatory. "I looked over the accounts last night, and they've lent us almost half a million dollars, and we need more. Maybe if I go back now, I can talk Dad into helping you out."

"Help, my ass. They dole out little checks but only when you beg for it, and they've never given us enough money to really get this ranch started so we could make a go of it. They want me to fail, damn it. They've always wanted it."

Lacey looked at her husband and quelled the urge to remind him that he couldn't have it both ways. He couldn't hate and despise her parents and still expect them to give him everything he wanted, but it was risky to escalate the argument. Her father's plane would be landing within the hour, and she wanted to be there when it arrived.

"I have to get going, Steve."

"Your place is here with me. You're my wife. You married me for better or worse, for richer or poorer."

"Please try to understand my position, Steve. My father would never forgive me if something happened to Mom and I wasn't there. And we need his help desperately. We're in serious financial trouble."

"Then leave the kids with me. That way I'll know you won't stay long."

"You don't have time to take care of them and cook and clean and work the ranch too." She was trying to be reasonable.

"I'd take time," he insisted. "They're my kids too, you know."

Panic started to rise in Lacey's throat. She had to stop him from taking a hard, unreasonable position.

"JJ's sick again, Steve. One of the reasons I agreed to go today was so that I could take him to see an asthma specialist while I was in Los Angeles."

"You baby him too much. You're turning him into an invalid."

Lacey looked at her children and saw that they were frightened. Whenever she was tempted to fight back against Steve, fear of upsetting JJ and Erin always caused her to take the path of amelioration. She never wanted them to witness a brawl, and she did not trust her husband to hold his temper in check. She was not about to be bullied, however. Not this time.

"We're going, Steve. Will you drive us over to Bellewether?"

Steve looked at the determined expression on his wife's face, and his irritation mounted. "No! If you're going to leave me, you can damned well walk."

He turned his attention to his children. "You know if you leave with your mother, you'll never come back. Is that what you want?"

"Don't do it, Steve!" she warned. "They're too young to make that kind of decision."

Ignoring her, he persisted, fixing his angry attention on the children. "So, what do you say? You want to leave your father for good so you can live in grampaw's big fancy house?"

Erin started to cry and JJ looked down and began to struggle for breath.

"You son of a bitch! How can you be so cruel to your own children?" She picked JJ up in her arms. "Erin, get the inhaler out of my handbag. Hurry."

The little girl rushed across the room, grateful for a break in the intensity of the dispute.

Steve looked at his family with contempt.

"Damn you all!" he exclaimed and stormed out the front door.

Lacey was too busy to watch what he was doing outside. Although she didn't see him take off in the station wagon in a flurry of dust, she heard, and her determination to leave forever was hardened in that moment. Without looking out the window, she knew that he had left them only the truck with the flat tire, and it was parked half a mile away.

27

T he shining silver jet with its golden brown stripes and the initials "GB" emblazoned on its tail was waiting for them when Lacey and her children drove up to the airstrip in the dusty old truck. The pilot and copilot were standing by the steps.

"We were worried about you. Dave went over to the ranch house and telephoned your place but the line was out of order."

"It's a long story, George. Let's go," Lacey said as she handed over their meager luggage. She looked exhausted. Her clothes were dirty and her shoes scuffed. Her hair had been blown by the wind, and her hands were filthy from changing the tire. The jack had given way while she was pulling off the wheel, and the truck's fender had gashed her arm, but she was pleased with herself. She had done it in spite of everything. Steve had taken their only vehicle and had yanked out the telephone line as he left so she couldn't summon help, but he hadn't stopped her. For the first time since JJ was born, she felt she had accomplished something.

"Yes, ma'am. Let's go," the pilot replied.

The children wasted no time hopping out of the car and racing toward the steps. JJ's eyes were shining as he asked, "Can I look in the cockpit?"

"Son, once we get in the air, George will let you sit in his seat and drive, okay?" the pilot replied.

"Neato!" JJ cried and raced up the steps, closely followed by his equally enthusiastic but a bit more restrained older sister. By the time Lacey joined them in the cabin, both children were already buckled into the plush sand-colored seats, each at a window. Lacey settled herself beside her son, and within minutes, the steps were hauled up into the plane, and the engines were started.

As they taxied to the end of the runway in preparation for takeoff, Erin said, "Mom, this is so exciting! I can't believe we're actually on our way home at last."

Lacey closed her eyes and tried to blot out the ugly scene she'd had with her husband. She could no longer avoid the truth about their marriage. In that moment when she had finally found the physical and moral courage to defy him, she knew with certainty that she was burning the bridge of her marriage behind her and would have to go home and admit to her father that he had been right about Steve's reasons for marrying her. She had wanted to prove him wrong, she had wanted desperately for her marriage to succeed, because Steve had convinced her that he loved her for herself. But she had been wrong. He wanted her only for her father's money.

The plane lifted gracefully off the runway into the blue, cloudless Texas sky, and the children were awed and silent as they watched the ground fall away and become miniaturized by their climb into the sky.

"Mom, look down there! Isn't that our ranch?" Erin asked.

Lacey leaned over to look out the window, but the plane was climbing too fast for her to differentiate between one ranch and another.

"It might be, honey, but I'm not sure," Lacey replied, trying not to see the place they had just left.

The seat belt sign flicked off, and Lacey went into the lavatory to wash up and dress her wound again. She'd have to see a doctor. She might need stitches.

She then checked the galley for refreshments, followed by both children intent on exploring every inch of the beautiful cabin. Expensive beige fabric covered the walls, and there was a thick Berber carpet underfoot. The small galley was done in stainless steel and highly polished white birch, and there was a microwave oven and refrigerator.

Waiting on the counter for them was a platter of fresh fruit on a bed of ice: strawberries, melon, pineapple, guava, and grapes. There was also a tray of sandwiches, a bowl of big fresh prawns with cocktail sauce, and the refrigerator was filled with cans of soda, cartons of lemonade, and chocolate milk. She set them all out on the long side table in front of a banquette that could accommodate more passengers, and they all waded into the delectables. When they were satiated, George took them forward and gave each child a few minutes in the copilot's chair.

It was a pleasant flight, and far too short for JJ and Erin. As they buckled up for the landing at the Long Beach Airport, JJ asked, "Do you think Grandpa might let us take another ride on the plane sometime, Mom?"

"You'll have to ask him yourself, darling," Lacey said, knowing that nothing would please Jack Gallagher more than showing off his elaborate toys to his grandchildren.

After they landed, her father's dependable chauffeur, Salvador, was waiting beside the silver Lincoln limousine just a few feet from where the plane came to a stop, and he hurried forward to greet them.

"Welcome home, Miss Lacey."

"Thank you, Salvador. It's good to be here. Where's my father?" she asked, disappointed that Jack hadn't come to meet her.

"Your mother wouldn't let him come without her, and he was afraid she'd get too excited. They're both waiting at the house, very anxious to see you," Salvador assured her. He was Jack Gallagher's driver and keeper of his cars, and he knew his employer extremely well.

"Is my mother all right, Salvador?" Lacey asked.

"She's . . . well, she's a bit weak, Miss Lacey. She's not the strong lady she used to be."

Lacey got into the limo with Erin, allowed JJ to sit up front beside Salvador, and within minutes after landing, they were on their way home.

Because of traffic, the drive was slow, and the sun had sunk below the horizon when they arrived at the gates to the sprawling Gallagher estate.

Salvador pressed the radio transmitter that opened the heavy iron gates, and a bank of floodlights suddenly illuminated the driveway.

"Those lights are new, aren't they, Salvador?" Lacey asked through the intercom.

"Yes, ma'am. We had some prowlers a while back, and Mr. Gallagher had the entire security system revamped. You can't be too careful nowadays."

As the lights of the house where she had lived for most of her life came into view, tears filled Lacey's eyes. She tried not to let herself be too ecstatically happy about coming home, but it was almost impossible to suppress the surge of sheer joy that welled up inside her.

"Mom, I'd forgotten how big it is," Erin whispered.

"A very big man lives there, darling."

Both her mother and father were waiting with arms outstretched when the limousine arrived. Lacey hugged her handsome father first, noting that he was still strong and vital, and his white hair was bright and full as ever. Then she turned to her mother. Maude Gallagher had aged considerably, Lacey noted with a pang of guilt. Had her departure from home done this to the beautiful and gentle lady who had been her dearest friend all her life?

"Oh, Mom," Lacey whispered taking her fragile mother into her arms. "It's good to see you again."

Maude was so emotionally charged that she was unable to speak, and she clung to her daughter until she recovered her poise. Then she stepped gracefully from her favorite child's arms and leaned down to kiss Erin's upturned and tearful face.

"Erin, my child, why you've grown into a beautiful young lady. Look at her, Jack."

Jack had already gathered his grandson into his arms and was holding him aloft.

"We've gotta put some meat on this kid," he declared, but his face beamed with joy.

Lacey laughed. Now she knew she was really back home, because Jack Gallagher was already mapping out their lives for them.

28

Father O'Brien was the last guest to board the *Santa Maria* before the gangway was pulled and the 122-foot sailing yacht pulled away from the dock in the Long Beach Marina. The black-hulled boat, moving slowly under power, glided majestically past the other large yachts as it made its way toward the channel that would take it out past the breakwater into the open sea. The fog that shrouded the area had lifted slightly, and there was hope that eventually the sun would break through the thick cloud cover and alleviate some of the gloom aboard the vessel.

Scott Gallagher's ashes had been brought aboard by Gordon, who carried the silver urn with the proper reverence and respect. The only other member of the household staff who had been invited aboard for the ceremony was the housekeeper, Silvana, and she busied herself keeping an eye on the two young men from the catering company who served coffee, mimosas, and Ramos gin fizzes and passed trays of miniature breakfast pastries.

In addition to the immediate family and the priest, a number of old friends had been included, as well as Brett and Penny, Jean Atwill, Tom Brennan, and Pete Cunningham. Cherry Dolan had called early that morning and asked to be included, but she was told by the skipper that there wasn't room. She decided to go to the dock anyway and talk her way aboard. She was successful. When Tom Brennan saw her, he was furious.

Taking Lacey aside, he demanded that she eject Cherry before departure.

"Listen, my dear, she is the enemy, understand? Don't let her prowl around in your life."

"Tom, stop treating me like some kind of suspect. I could never have hurt Scott, and the police have to know that. Besides I rather like Miss Dolan, and I want to help her find the person who really murdered my brother." As far as Lacey was concerned, the subject was closed.

As the boat approached the end of the channel, the water got choppy, and a group of less hardy sailors retreated to the main salon.

Soon all the chairs in the light and bright bird's-eye maple cabin were filled.

Lacey, Steve, and the children stayed topside, as did Jean and Sasha. They were soon joined by Pete, who had been on the bridge for castoff. Lacey introduced her old friend to everyone. Although Pete was genuinely friendly, Steve was not particularly cordial. Neither was Jean, although Sasha seemed intrigued. She'd considered Scott to be an extremely handsome man, but this newcomer was even more so. She batted her eyelashes and engaged him in conversation. Jean watched her in silent disapproval. Cherry stayed at a discreet distance, but kept her eyes on them all.

One by one a fleet of private boats joined them on their journey out to the open sea. The Gallaghers were a family of sailors, and they had a lot of friends from the yachting community who wanted to be with them when Scott was consigned to his final resting place.

A breeze came up, and the young man employed as skipper of the *Santa Maria* came forward to talk to Lacey.

"It looks as if we might soon be seeing the sun, Miss Lacey, and the wind is blowing nice and steady from the northwest. Would you like me to raise the mainsail?" he asked, nodding his head toward the tall 140-foot mast that towered above them.

Lacey shook her head. "I don't think so, Billy. The *Santa Maria* cruises too fast for some of the smaller boats to keep up with us, and I'd like to keep everybody together. Steady as she goes for about half an hour."

"As you say, Miss Lacey. It sure is a sad journey. Mr. Scott was a great guy. Me n' the crew are goin' to miss 'im."

"Billy, I told Mal Jacobs to rendezvous with us at about ten-thirty. When you see his plane, head into a circle wide enough to accommodate all the boats," Lacey explained, "and just keep circling until I give you the signal to break it."

"He's Mr. Scott's friend with the Cessna, right, ma'am?"

"Yes, I hope he uses some restraint today. He's a reckless flyer, and I don't want him to frighten anyone. And Billy, I want you to give him lots of room, so make the circle of boats as big as possible."

"Have you taken a count?" Steve asked.

"Yes, sir," Billy replied. "There's twenty-one, not counting the *Santa Maria*." The young man with the curly, sun-bleached hair and ruddy face smiled and returned to his post.

There was not much conversation anywhere on the yacht. People either sat quietly in the salon, sipping their drinks, or stood on deck and watched the land slip from view. When they approached their rendezvous point, Sasha took the silver urn from Gordon's hands and cradled it in her arms. Penny and Brett came topside to watch, as did most of the guests. Conversation subsided. The only sound was the hull of the boat hitting the waves and the hum of the engine. It was a cool, damp Friday, and there were few pleasure boats about other than those in the processional.

Suddenly, another sound was heard, and all looked up to see a small plane approaching.

"That must be Mal," Lacey said, and as she spoke, the *Santa Maria* heaved to port and began the circling maneuver. The other boats followed, and in a few minutes all were rotating in a wide circle. Mal flew across very low and dipped one wing in salute. Everyone below deck came topside to watch the ceremony.

Lacey and Steve joined Sasha and Father O'Brien on the foreward deck. Sasha held the urn, Lacey removed the stopper, and then both Father O'Brien and Steve steadied Sasha as she leaned far out to the leeward side and sprinkled Scott's ashes into the sea. As she was doing this, the plane swooped low and dropped a dozen large wreaths of flowers in the center of the circle. The caterers then passed out long-stemmed red roses so that each of the guests aboard the boat could toss a flower on the water in memory of Scott. Much as he abhorred the cremation, Father O'Brien nevertheless sprinkled holy water and said a blessing. Passengers on the other boats also tossed wreaths and flowers into the sea. As if on cue, the sun emerged from the cloud bank, and the sea sparkled with light. Mal made one last pass over the circle of boats and then headed back toward the Long Beach airport where his trip had begun. The ceremony was at an end.

Lacey raised her hand and signaled to Billy to head back home, and the boats broke rank, each skipper setting his own course back to land.

Now that it was over, the passengers seemed relieved, and the level of chatter escalated. People were now ready to socialize. It had been a beautiful and fitting tribute to a young man whose life had been brutally terminated, but it was time to go on.

Even Lacey, as sad as she was, felt the need to turn her attention to the problems of living. Scott was gone forever. There was nothing more she could do, except of course, find out who killed him. And that, she vowed, would take precedence over everything. Including Gallagher's Best. She headed aft to talk to Cherry Dolan, but was stopped by Tom Brennan.

"It was a nice send-off for your brother, Lacey. He would have liked it," he said, holding her arm so she could not get away from him. "But where the hell do you think you're going?"

"To talk to Cherry Dolan," she replied, trying to pull out of his grasp.

"What do you want to do that for?" he asked, tightening his grip.

"Because I want to help her in any way I can," she declared, still struggling to get free.

"Listen, my lady, you'll stay away from her, do you hear me?"

"I think you're the one who's not hearing," Pete said, wrapping his long fingers around Tom's arm. "Let her go!" he commanded. Surprised Tom looked up at the tall man.

"Who the hell do you think you're talking to?" Tom asked. "I'm her attorney in case you don't know."

"Then abide by your client's wishes and let her the hell go. Do you hear me?"

Pete's voice was louder now, and it drew the attention of everyone nearby, particularly Steve, who moved toward them. Tom found himself surrounded by two very big and strong adversaries. He let go of Lacey's arm.

"If you won't take my advice, then I suggest you get yourself another attorney," Tom said.

"Let's get this settled right now, Tom. Come with me," Lacey ordered and moved rapidly aft where Cherry was standing. Tom followed.

"You don't seriously consider me a suspect in the murder of my brother, do you? I need to know, because my attorney is having fits about my talking to you."

"Well," Cherry replied, somewhat taken aback, "everybody who had access to the deceased is under a certain amount of suspicion."

"Give me a straight answer," Lacey insisted.

Cherry did not like being backed into a corner, and it went against her training to reveal anything to suspects. She knew it would be unfair, however, to lie about something with such serious consequences.

"I'm afraid so."

In spite of everything that Tom said and all the strange things that had happened to incriminate her, Lacey was stunned by the detective's admission. No longer could she deny the appalling possibility that she might be accused, arrested, and tried for the murder of a brother whom she had loved selflessly.

"I'm sorry, but that's the way it is," Cherry added, moved by the stricken look on Lacey's face.

"Now, will you listen to me?" Tom asked with insufferable smugness.

"You're making a terrible mistake," Lacey said to Cherry, ignoring the attorney's question. "By concentrating on me, you might very well make it possible for the real killer to escape."

Having declared her true concern, she turned away, gathered her children to her, and made the rest of the trip in solitary silence, with both Steve and Pete watching over her from a respectful distance.

29

A late lunch was served at the house when the family returned from their trip on he *Santa Maria*, and afterward Sasha went to her room to lie down. She'd had little to say and looked tired.

"I'm gonna do the same," Steve said, standing up and stretching. "I didn't sleep well last night." He'd been unusually quiet and introspective ever since Cherry Dolan had admitted that Lacey was the prime suspect.

Erin and JJ went to their rooms to do homework, and Lacey found herself sitting in the morning room all alone, finishing her tea and trying not to think of the implications of Cherry Dolan's declaration.

She looked out the large window toward the Victorian greenhouse, which her father had given her mother as an anniversary gift more than twenty years ago. She'd been so busy the past few months that there hadn't been a spare moment to browse through it and see how her mother's orchid plants were doing. Pouring herself a second cup of tea, Lacey carried it with her as she walked across the wide expanse of lawn to visit the handsome glass structure.

The greenhouse was a large and imposing building. Its glass walls rose more than twelve feet high, and the peaked roof added another six. Gracefully designed, all the elements curved smoothly together. Constructed of slender ribbons of steel and thick panes of plate glass, it was lined with shelves filled with pots of all sizes. Maude Gallagher had raised some of the finest and most exotic specimen orchids in the world, and the gardener had obviously given them tender care and attention in the years after her death, for there were blooms everywhere. Giant cattleyas—with their deep purple velvet throats and lips with matching lavender petals and sepals—flourished in abundance. There was also a spectacular Green Lady, as well as Pink Champions, with champagne-colored cymbidiums.

Lacey walked slowly through the greenhouse, taking in the beauty and stopping to admire the golden cascade of dendrobium and the junglelike Panhandle. As she drank in the exquisite beauty of each, she thought of her mother.

Maude Gallagher, nee Lacey, was as extraordinary in her own way as Jack Gallagher had been in his. A woman of gentle prettiness, she had been a loving and patient wife, but she had never clung to her husband. Because he was obsessed with his business, she found other things to occupy her time. Unlike contemporary women, she turned her attention to genteel pastimes, most of which could be done at home. Her orchids were her first love, and when she asked Jack to build her a greenhouse, he had given her the biggest and the best.

She also loved to read, and the many novels and first editions that filled the shelves in the massive library were books that she not only had purchased but also had read. Jack had little time for recreational reading.

Then there was Maude's needlepoint. To her it was more art than hobby, for she painted pictures with yarn. She drew all of her own designs, transferred them to the canvas, and then brought them to life with the colors of her wool. She did pictures of the sea, of boats, of gardens, but above all, she did pictures of her orchids. When finished, they became pillows or wall hangings, and there was not a room in the house that did not contain some of her artwork.

Maude was a good sailor, and she loved the sea and the *Santa Maria*. Often when her children were young and Jack was too busy, she would take them on weekends to Catalina. Although they always had a professional crew, Maude occasionally loved to take the helm herself, and she made sure that both Scott and Lacey became knowledgeable sailors with a healthy respect for the might of the sea and the wind.

Lacey sat down on the iron bench, closed her eyes, and inhaled the moist smell of damp earth and plants, and her mother seemed very close. If Maude Gallagher had been alive, her father would never, ever have changed his will and effectively disinherited her, because Lacey had been her mother's favored child. It was a truth Lacey had gradually come to realize as the years had passed.

Maude always encouraged her only daughter to study, to pursue a career, to have an identity of her own. Unlike most women her age, Maude had not scoffed at the women's movement and made no secret of her agreement with much they professed. Lacey remembered her often declaring that she had been born forty years too soon.

Maude and Jack were a handsome couple when they married. Although not tall, he was well-built, with wavy brown hair and broad shoulders. Of medium height and delicate build, Maude had fair skin, large blue eyes, and thick black hair that fell in waves about her face. Her parents called her *mavourneen,* Irish for my darling.

As Lacey grew older, however, she came to realize that her mother's life was a lonely one. Although Jack Gallagher seemed to cherish Maude, his attention was usually elsewhere. She was never heard to complain, however, and she made a happy home for her family.

"Oh, Mom," Lacey whispered. "I hope you're happy now that Scott's with you. Take care of each other."

Tears still in her eyes, Lacey returned to the house and was met by Gordon.

"Miss Lacey, I've been looking all over for you. Mr. Brennan is on the telephone."

"I've been out in the greenhouse. The orchids look wonderful."

"Simon spends a lot of time with them."

She closed the door behind her and strode to the desk. There were two lights on, so somebody must be on another line. Hesitating, she punched line one and started to say hello when she heard a woman's voice talking.

"But, sweetie, you said you'd only be gone a couple of days, and I'm getting tired of sleeping in this house all by myself. You know how I hate to be out here all alone."

Lacey found herself listening in fascination. Who was this woman talking to? And then she heard Steve's voice.

"Hello, hello, is someone there?" he asked.

The woman replied, "Steve, honey, who are you talkin' to?"

"It sounded like somebody picked up the phone."

"I didn't hear anything. So when are you coming home? I miss that big, warm body of yours in bed with me . . ."

Lacey depressed the button on the telephone gently and hung up. Postponing her reaction, she viciously punched the other line.

"Hello, Tom."

"You okay, Lacey? You sound kind of funny."

"I'm fine. What did you want?"

"I don't want you to go worrying yourself about what that detective said. Not that you shouldn't take her seriously. It's best to know what you're up against."

"You've made your point, Tom."

"There's something else. I talked to a friend in the D.A.'s office and got him to promise to give us plenty of warning when they decide to arrest you."

"Terrific," she snapped. "Have you got any other little bits of comfort for me, Tom?"

"Life isn't a fairy tale, Lacey, even if you have been brought up to be a princess."

"Thanks, Tom. You've made my day."

She slammed down the telephone and headed up the stairs. If Tom was right and she was accused, she was damn well going to hire another attorney to defend her. Her father might have liked him, but she didn't.

She was on the landing before she began to wonder why Steve had concealed the fact that he was living with another woman.

30

Feeling restless and irritable, Lacey headed to her bathroom for a shower and a shampoo. The sea air always made her hair feel sticky. She was almost at the door when she heard her name called.

"Lacey, can we talk for a minute?"

She turned around and saw Sasha coming up the stairway.

"I'm not much in the mood right now. Can it wait until dinner?" Lacey asked.

"This is important."

"What do you want to talk about?"

"Not here. In private. Come on over to my room where we won't have to worry about anyone interrupting or overhearing." Sasha headed across the galleria to the children's wing, where she had moved most of her things.

Curious, Lacey followed her.

Sasha opened the door to her room, and they went in. It was one of the smaller bedrooms. Sasha motioned for Lacey to sit down in the antique wicker chair, the only one in the room, and she climbed up onto the tall four-poster bed and sat crosslegged in the middle of it. Lacey noticed the smudges of mascara under her eyes and decided she had probably been crying.

"It was a nice funeral, Lacey. Thanks for doing it the way Scott would have wanted. He didn't believe in much of anything that was Catholic anymore, you know," she said, brushing her long blonde hair out of her eyes.

"That was obvious by the casual way he married and disposed of his first two wives," Lacey commented.

"You were angry with him for divorcing Mary, weren't you?"

"Angry's not the word. Disappointed, definitely. Disapproving too. Mary was very much in love with Scott. I stopped being quite so right-eous about it after I got my own divorce, however."

"Thanks for not inviting Mary to come aboard the *Santa Maria* today."

"I did invite her, just as I said I would, but she wasn't feeling well enough to come. I hope this whole mess isn't going to throw her out of remission. Scott left her, you know, not because he wasn't still in love with her but because of the disease she had. It wasn't one of his finer moments."

"What about his second wife, Bess? How come you didn't invite her too and make it a real party?" There was an acrid edge of sarcasm in her voice.

"That divorce was nasty. Bess didn't go away quietly as Mary did. She actually put a detective on Scott's trail. God, the rotten little things that man turned up. Dad wound up having to buy her off with a lot of money."

"Scott called her a highway bandit."

Lacey shook her head in dismay and looked out the window before responding. She hated to speak ill of her brother, but he had never been a saint.

"That was most unfair of Scott. Bess is a lovely lady, and she resented Scott's cavalier approach to his marriage vows. She went after him, true, but it wasn't only for the money. She felt he deserved to be punished."

"Having his father pay up doesn't seem like much in the way of punishment," Sasha observed with a wry smile.

"She originally wanted Scott to earn the money and pay it himself, but in the end, she settled. I think she got fed up with all of us and decided to get on with her life."

"You liked both of his previous wives, but you don't much like me, do you?" Sasha asked.

"I don't dislike you, Sasha."

"But you don't like me. You never did."

"You haven't been very nice either to me or to my children. There's no way I could be friends with someone who was cruel to JJ or Erin."

"But I found Erin snooping around in my closet."

"She was in your room looking for a blouse she thought the maid might have hung there by mistake, and you refused to listen to her explanation," Lacey reminded her.

"I'm sorry about making that accusation."

"What did you want to talk to me about?" Lacey changed the subject; she was getting bored.

"I heard that conversation between you and Cherry Dolan on the boat today. They're going to arrest you for Scott's murder."

Lacey started to get out of her chair. "Well, if you got me in here to gloat over that, you'll have to excuse—"

"Sit down! I've got something very important to sell you," Sasha said, a smile lurking at the corner of her mouth.

Lacey was startled. "Sell me?" she asked, sitting back down and wondering if she had misheard.

"That's what I said."

"What could you possibly have that I'd want to buy?"

"An alibi, proof positive that you were not the one who killed Scott."

"I didn't kill Scott, and I don't need—"

"Oh yes, you do. You need a damned good alibi. One that's true and not fabricated."

The word *true* caught Lacey's attention, and she was now interested. "Tell me more."

"Suppose I told the police that I saw you swimming in the pool when I left the house the morning Scott was killed, and you were still there when I went back into the house and found his body?"

Lacey's heart began racing as she remembered catching the scent of Sasha's perfume, and she knew for a certainty that her sister-in-law spoke the truth. She actually had seen her swimming.

"You knew all the time I couldn't have done it! Why in God's name did you tell the police I did?"

Sasha's eyes narrowed. "There's no point in giving away something I can sell, now is there?"

Lacey was stunned by the woman's guile. There was nothing she wouldn't do for money.

"But you've accused me of killing Scott. What makes you think the police will believe you now when you say I'm innocent?"

"I was careful never to say you killed him. I simply suggested that everything was your fault."

"It's a fine point the police may not understand. How much do you want?"

"Twenty-five million, deposited in an account in Switzerland."

"The estate may be tied up until the police investigation is over, and it may take a while for me to get that much in cash. I could perhaps borrow ten million."

"I don't intend to bargain. And I'll wait for the full amount. Do we have an agreement?" Sasha asked, and Lacey was fascinated by the glitter of avarice in her eyes.

Hesitating momentarily so as not to seem too eager, Lacey asked, "Do I have any choice?"

Sasha smiled and shook her head.

"Agreed then, but you must call Cherry Dolan first thing in the morning and tell her."

"Of course I will, but the details of our financial arrangement have to be only between us. Nobody will believe a word I say if they find out you're paying me."

Lacey's mind worked fast. "I'm not paying you to say anything, although I do expect you to tell the police the truth. I'm giving you the money to sign a waiver relinquishing all claims to the Gallagher estate. Do we understand each other?"

Sasha looked at her sister-in-law with grudging respect. "You drive a hard bargain, Lacey, but I'm no patsy. It'll cost you five million more to get me to sign that paper. And one more thing. I intend to stay here in this house until the account is squared away and all the money is deposited, understand? I want to continue using my charge accounts, the Mercedes, and the limousine. Deal?"

Lacey knew she had no choice. "Deal. You'll be my honored guest, Sasha. See you at dinner." Lacey got out of the chair and headed for the door.

"Don't worry about anything now," Sasha assured her. "First thing in the morning, I'll have Salvador drive me to the police and I'll sing my pretty little song for them. Don't you have a word of thanks for me, sister dear? I'm the one who's saving your ass."

"And I'm the one who's going to make you a rich woman," Lacey responded.

"Your brother was wrong, you know," Sasha remarked as Lacey was about to leave.

"About what?"

"He said you were the world's best negotiator, but you're not half as good as I am."

A slight sardonic smile hovered at the corner of Lacey's mouth as she left the room. Outside the door, she stopped and took a deep breath. For the first time since Scott was killed, the nagging terror that she might be accused of his murder was gone.

As she walked down the hallway, she contemplated the strangeness of life. Who would have ever thought that Sasha would turn out to be her savior.

31

Lacey felt she had made the best bargain of her life. With a wave of her hand, Sasha, of all people, had banished the frightful specter that had been haunting her since Scott's death. As wildly improbable as it now seemed, she had actually been afraid that the police might accuse her of his murder. Not because she was guilty, but because they might turn to her to conclude an investigation that failed to ferret out the real killer. She shivered, said a small prayer of thanks, and ran down the stairs to tell the children.

Erin was in the library working on a term paper, and JJ was sitting in front of the small television set with his earphones on so as not to disturb his sister.

Lacey pulled the earphones off JJ's head.

"You must have finished all your homework," she commented with a grin.

"I haven't got any."

Erin snickered and Lacey laughed.

"We'll discuss it later. I have some wonderful news to report. I talked to Sasha, and she confessed to me that she saw me swimming in the pool at the time Scott was killed."

"But she accused you of murder! Why would she tell such an awful lie?" Erin asked.

"Let's say she's finally come to her senses. She's going to tell Cherry Dolan first thing tomorrow."

"Who's going to tell Cherry Dolan what?" Steve asked, walking into the library in the middle of the conversation.

JJ told Steve about Sasha's seeing his mother in the swimming pool.

"I hope they'll believe the bitch," Steve commented. Then seeing the crestfallen look on JJ's face, he smiled and added, "Well, it's about time we had some good news around here for a change. This calls for a celebration."

Steve's appearance served to remind Lacey of the telephone call she had overheard, and her euphoria was slightly diminished. What was he up to now?

"I don't feel that today is exactly a day for celebrating anything, Steve."

Steve knew right away what was bothering her, because he had heard a third person on the line. "Lacey, I wanted to talk to you, but I couldn't find you anywhere."

"I was in Sasha's room."

"Can we talk now?" he asked.

"Not now. It's time for dinner. Come on, Erin, JJ, let's go upstairs and freshen up. Steve, would you mind telling Gordon to serve dinner in half an hour? I'll tell Sasha. And I want everyone to be nice to her from now on, understand? All of you?" She looked pointedly at JJ and Erin.

"Sasha left," Steve said. "I saw her go out the door just before I came in here. She told Gordon she'd be back by midnight."

"Fine. See you at dinner," she muttered, not even bothering to look back at him.

As she washed her face, Lacey tried to examine her own feelings about Steve. She wished he had been honest and forthcoming about the woman on the telephone, but he had a right to his own life. After all, she had been the one who left the marriage. She had no reason to be angry with him.

She looked more closely at her reflection and despaired of what she saw. She used to be pretty, with an outdoorsy, natural look. She'd never needed to rely on makeup to be attractive. Her lashes and brows were thick and dark, and because of her love of the outdoors and the sea, she'd always had a tan. She'd spent the past year indoors, however, running the office and caring for her sick father, and she was now not just pale but downright sallow. She'd also lost a lot of weight, and her clothes were too big.

Erin came into the bathroom and found her mother staring at herself in the mirror.

"Whatcha lookin' at, Mom?" she asked.

"Me. I look terrible."

"Mom, you're over thirty-five. Face it, you need a little help. Everybody does," Erin said with a grin. "Want some of my blush? It'll put a glow on your face."

"I need something," Lacey said with a grimace.

JJ and Steve were waiting in the dining room when the women of the family arrived, and JJ was the first to comment on his mother's appearance. "Wow, Mom, you look great!"

Erin smirked with satisfaction. "Thanks to me and my magic make-up kit."

Lacey felt self-conscious. "It was Erin's idea. I feel like a painted doll. I've never had this much stuff on my face before."

"Mom promised to take me into Beverly Hills tomorrow to do some shopping. JJ, you can't come," Erin announced, taking her seat at the table.

"Why not? They've got these great stores with all kinds of good junk in them. Hammacher-something, and The Sharper Image, and there's another one. I can't think of the name but I know where it's at. Come on, it's Saturday, let me go with you. I'll stay out of your way."

"No. Mom and I are going to buy some new clothes, and we're going to have lunch at Neiman's—"

Steve interrupted. "Why don't we all go? You can drop JJ and me off, and he can take me around to the places he wants to go. We'll find someplace to have a hamburger, and then we'll meet you two around four or five for the trip back home."

"That's a great idea, Dad. Boy, wait'll you see some of the stuff . . . ," JJ enthused.

"I had intended to go into the office, but since it'll be a Saturday," Lacey said, "I won't. We'd better take the limo and Salvador, if you don't mind. He can trail us from store to store, and we'll have somewhere to dump the packages. Something tells me this is going to be an expensive day."

"I hope so," Erin said with a grin. She lifted her glass of ice water in a toast.

"Yeah, me too," echoed JJ.

Dinner was the most pleasant meal they'd had for a long time, and when it was over, Erin and JJ went into the media room to watch television on the big set, and Lacey and Steve retired to the library, carrying their wineglasses.

Gordon had made a fire in the fireplace, and they sank down on the big, cushy leather couch.

"You wanted to talk to me about something?" Lacey asked.

"I do. That was you listening on the telephone today, wasn't it?"

"How did you know?"

"Anybody else in the house would have answered when I asked who had picked up, but I figured you would be too surprised and hurt to say anything. How long did you listen?"

"A second or two. I got the idea right away. It seems there's somebody in Texas who's sleeping alone nowadays. You know you're free to go back to her anytime you want," she said, hoping she had not sounded petulant.

"Oh shit," Steve muttered and put his glass down on the heavy wooden end table. "I know you're not going to believe me, but I intended to tell you about Betty Lou."

"Steve, you don't have to tell me anything you don't want to tell me. What you've done with your life is none of my business. Let's talk about something else."

Steve laughed out loud. "Goddammit, you're jealous."

"If it bolsters your masculine ego to believe that, then there's nothing I can do to persuade you otherwise. But you're wrong."

Steve slid his arm across the back of the couch and laid his hand on her shoulder. "I know what you're thinking. I always do. You think Betty Lou is some dumb, young nympho with big knockers who works as a waitress at Monty's. Well, before that image gets too fixed in that big brain of yours, let me tell you the truth. Betty Lou Dunsmoor is over thirty. Her husband, who was an air force pilot, was killed in a plane crash, and she was left in Texas with a widow's pension and two little kids. She's a nice lady, and she likes me a lot. And I like her too."

The conversation made Lacey uncomfortable. He was putting her in an awkward position. When she left Steve, she left everything they shared except the children back in Texas. Hearing about his personal life only served to take her back to a place and time she wanted to forget.

"Please, you don't have to explain your life to me," Lacey insisted. "And I'll certainly understand if you want to go back home."

"I'm not going home while you and JJ and Erin need me here. And I'm not going anywhere until this mess is straightened out and we find out who killed Scott."

He moved a little closer to Lacey as he continued, "As for my situation with Betty Lou, I have to admit that I'd have been happy to have her and her kids move into the ranch with me. I asked her to the first night we slept together because we were real compatible, and it gets awfully lonely. But she refused."

Lacey was curious. "Really?"

"I said right up front that I wouldn't marry her, and she didn't want to put her children into a situation that wasn't permanent. She's afraid they'll get hurt if I get tired of having her around." He picked up his glass and finished his wine.

"Why wouldn't you marry her, Steve?"

"Because I still feel married to you. I've never been able to accept the fact you weren't going to be part of my future."

His words astonished her. She was prepared for anything but a declaration of devotion.

"Oh Steve, I'm sorry."

"It's not your fault, Lacey. I've always felt your father was to blame for the failure of our marriage."

"You're touching a vulnerable spot, Steve. I'm feeling very hostile to him at the moment. It seems I was nothing but a pawn and he was the chess master."

Steve tightened his grip on her shoulder and pulled her close to him. With his lips close to hers, he whispered, "Kiss me, Lacey. For old time's sake, one kiss . . ."

Before she could resist or consent, she found his lips covering hers, and the sensation was both exotic and familiar at the same time. He had the most sensual lips, she thought, kissing him back. Feeling the old stirrings deep down inside her as her body responded to his of its own will, she was afraid she might be swept into Steve's magnetic orbit of sexuality once more. She tried to pull away, but he would not let her go.

The kiss lasted for a long, long time, and when he finally released her, he asked, "You haven't slept with anyone else, have you?"

Lacey looked away. "That's none of your business, Steve."

"You haven't. I know you haven't, and I'm glad," he whispered and kissed her again, and she was grateful that the children were nearby to protect her from submitting to a dangerous urge. When Erin and JJ came in at last to say good night, they found their mother and father merely sitting on the couch and talking, and then they all went upstairs together, Erin and Lacey to their room, JJ and Steve to theirs.

When the lights were out, Lacey vowed not to allow herself to get into another compromising position with her ex-husband. Her life was complicated enough without adding Steve Haines to it again.

32

While Lacey and her family were having dinner together and preparing for their day of shopping, Penny took food over to Mary's.

When the door opened, Penny was relieved to see that her friend was pale but not bent over and hobbling. She had been close to Mary through many of the flares and remissions of the disease, and she was well aware of the symptoms.

"How are you feeling?" Penny asked as she followed her to the bedroom where Mary climbed back into bed.

"Nauseated."

"You think maybe you've got the flu?"

Mary shook her head and closed her eyes.

"It's a good thing you didn't go on the *Santa Maria* today. It was a little choppy and there were a few green faces around but nobody tossed their cookies."

"Don't say that! I've spent half the day with my head in the toilet," Mary said, snatching the damp washcloth from the table beside her bed and putting it over her eyes.

"You really are sick. Maybe I ought to call Dr. Rosenberg," Penny suggested.

"I don't need a doctor for what's wrong with me."

"I guess you don't want any of the food I brought."

Mary wiped her face with the cloth and sat up. "Sure I do. At least I'll have something to throw up next time."

Penny peered at her friend closely as she straightened the sheets and propped her up on pillows. Mary was acting very odd.

After dishing out the food she brought, Penny described the ceremony aboard the boat and gave Mary a rundown of the guests aboard. She set a bowl of homemade vegetable soup on the bed tray along with slices of cheese toast and a serving of fresh fruit salad.

"Think your tummy can handle that?" she asked.

Mary picked up the spoon and began eating the soup.

"No," she replied, "but I'm going to eat it anyway. I'm starved."

Penny went into the kitchen to brew a pot of tea for them both. When she returned, she was surprised to see that the soup was almost all gone, as was the toast, and half of the fruit salad. When they had finished their tea, Penny suggested that Mary take a shower while she was there. Feeling better, Mary agreed, and while she was showering, Penny changed the sheets and threw them into the washer. When at last Mary was back in the freshly made bed, she said, "Thanks, Penny. You're a real friend. I don't know how I would have made it without you."

"I'll tell Lacey you're under the weather, and she'll be here too."

"Did you tell her about me and Scott?"

Penny shook her head. "No way, honey. Lacey's got her hands full with her own problems right now."

Again the thought passed through Penny's head that perhaps it wasn't true that her friend had had a recent affair with Lacey's brother, but then Mary said something that banished that idea altogether.

"She's going to know eventually, I'm afraid. You see, I'm pregnant."

Penny's jaw dropped, and she sank into the bedroom chair, exclaiming, "Oh my God, that's terrible."

"It's not terrible. I planned this, and it's wonderful."

"But what about the lupus?"

"My doctor said that a lot of women like me have normal pregnancies. She'll simply have to monitor me closely, and there's a greater chance of miscarriage. That's why I stayed in bed today and didn't even try to go."

Penny was still aghast. "But what about the baby? I mean, will it be all right?"

"There's a possibility that the baby might have symptoms of a mild case of lupus at birth, like a rash or a low blood count, or maybe a slightly enlarged liver, but these things usually disappear by the time the baby is six months old."

"That's all?"

"Of course there are risks, but then there's always a risk that a child might not be perfect when you bring it into the world."

"You planned this, huh? It wasn't an accident?"

Mary smiled. "Yes, I planned it. You don't suppose I went into this affair with Scott merely to be his afternoon floozy, do you?"

"You seduced him, him the great seducer himself! Oh, God, that's rich. Tell me about it. Every single little detail. Don't leave out a thing."

"If you really want to know. . . .

"I devised the plan the day Lacey told me that Scott and his wife were coming home to live while her father was ill. The good Lord helped me. I'd been in remission for a long time, and I looked great. I was exercising regularly and seeing the physical therapist three times a week. I felt ready for anything, especially a little fooling around.

"I stopped over at the house frequently to see Jack, which made things convenient. I always checked with Silvana to make sure Scott was at home. He went to the office in the mornings, but he was usually back by two or three.

"One afternoon I put on my new bikini and went down to the pool for a swim with Lacey. Scott was on the tennis court, working out with the ball machine, and I made sure he saw us. After Lacey went back to the house to tend to her father, I stretched out on the chaise, under an umbrella, of course, and pretended to sleep. I looked very seductive. The top part of my suit had slipped down on one side, exposing my breast. They've always been my greatest asset, you know. Then I got lucky. Scott came down alone for a swim. I pretended not to hear him splashing about in the pool. Finally, he pulled another chaise right alongside me and lay down on it.

" 'Mind if I join you under the umbrella? I don't have any sunscreen on,' he said.

" 'Be my guest,' I replied.

" 'You look great, Mary,' he said, and I could see that his eyes were glued to my breast. God, it was erotic. When push came to shove I knew I wouldn't have to fake it.

" 'How are you feeling nowadays?' he asked.

" 'Like a new woman,' I told him. 'I went to this great doctor last year, and she put me on an experimental drug. For a while it made me pretty sick, but I stuck to it, and three months ago, I was pronounced cured.'

"I knew he was squeamish about disease and illness, so I decided to sweep that obstacle under the rug right away. It wasn't true, but it worked for him.

" 'That's great,' he said, and he seemed genuinely happy for me. 'How come Lacey didn't tell me about it?'

" 'Lacey never talks about me, or your second wife, for that matter. Haven't you noticed?' I replied, but I was guessing.

" 'Yeah, you're right about that. What do you say I get us something cold to drink. What would you like?'

" 'Iced tea?' I answered coyly but I knew he had something stronger in mind.

" 'That's all? You wouldn't be interested in sharing a cold bottle of bubbly?' he asked, and he sounded flirty as all hell. I almost laughed in his face. Does anybody nowadays still call champagne 'bubbly?'

" 'Well, now that you mentioned it, that would be terrific,' I replied and smiled so the dimple in my cheek would show.

"He was back with a chilled bottle of Taittinger's and two glasses within five minutes. He was a grape ready to be picked, I can tell you.

"We talked about old times and laughed a lot. He drank most of the bottle and didn't notice that I was barely sipping any, especially since I started giggling and acting tipsy. I kept covering up my breast, but the darned thing just kept slipping out. Especially when I lifted my arm over my head, which I did frequently.

"It had been a warm, sunshiny day, but it was winter, and the sun set early. I shivered and suggested we go into the pool house to finish the bottle. He thought it was a great idea, and I heard him click the lock once we were inside. Two minds with the same thought.

"I was still cold, but instead of getting into my clothes, I said I was going to take a quick shower and warm up. I knew as soon as I took off my suit and stepped into that shower stall, I was going to have company. It's so easy to tell if you're making headway with a man. All you have to do is look at his crotch. Poor guys can't hide a thing.

"Sure enough, there he was, ready to go. He stood naked outside the shower stall and watched me for a while. I thought he was never going to come in, but when he did, he came all the way in.

" 'Oh baby,' he whispered in my ear, 'have I missed you.' I spread my legs wide and enjoyed it while it lasted, which wasn't more than a few seconds. I wasn't upset though. I was kind of flattered, actually, because I had excited him a whole lot.

"We got out of the shower and dried each other off. I knew from experience if I waited a little while, he'd be ready to go again soon. And he was. It was more comfortable the second time. We took the cushions off the chairs and made ourselves a nice bed on the floor. We took things real slow, and it was heaven, I can tell you. I knew from the way I felt that the good Lord was blessing that union. Nothing sinful could have felt as good as that did.

"When we were both exhausted, I stayed lying on those pillows for a long, long time. I wanted to make sure those little sperm didn't have to swim uphill.

"I went back again the next day, but it was cold and rainy, so we didn't even make a pretense of swimming. He was in the pool house waiting for me with another cold bottle and a hot fire in the fireplace. We were both having fun.

"When it was warm, we swam or played tennis first, because we were too tired to do anything much afterward. We gave those cushions in the pool house a real workout, I can tell you. It's hard to believe he'd have anything left for Sasha.

"Funny, in a place like that with people and servants coming and going, you would have thought somebody, sometime, would have caught us or gotten suspicious, but it never happened, not that either of us cared.

"When we were making love, I forgot about how much I resented Scott for leaving me and damning me to a life without children or a family. It felt so good and so right to have his arms around me again.

"I found out I was pregnant the day before Jack's death. I was at the pool with Scott, telling him about the baby at the very moment that Jack died. Life's funny, isn't it? He offered to divorce Sasha and marry me again, but I told him I didn't think it was a good idea. He couldn't understand why I was turning him down. I didn't have the courage, you see, to tell him I'd deceived him about being cured of lupus. A few days after that, he was gone. I don't know what I'd do if I didn't believe that having this baby was all part of God's plan. Scott's going to have a son or a daughter now, and I'm going to be the one to have it. Not Sasha. That's why I didn't get up and read that thing at the memorial service. I suddenly felt sorry for her."

When the story ended, Penny was dumbfounded, and for the first time in her life she was at a complete loss for words.

"Say something, Penny. Don't sit there with your mouth open," Mary said, but Penny just shook her head.

33

Sasha dug into her taupe lizard Judith Leiber handbag, one of a dozen of the expensive little purses she had bought since marrying Scott, and fumbled around for a minute or more before finally coming up with a ticket to hand the parking attendant.

"What kind of car, ma'am?" he asked, because there were a lot of cars parked there that Friday evening.

She hesitated. Which car had she driven here tonight? Had she brought the Testarossa or the Mercedes? Her mind had gone foggy. She put her fingers to her forehead and rubbed briskly on the spot between her eyes.

"Uh . . . Mercedes . . . a silver Mercedes SL," she guessed, although she really wasn't at all sure. What was wrong with her? She'd only had two drinks, and for her that was nothing. She was probably worn out from all the misery and tension she'd been through during the past few days.

The attendant brought the car, and she handed him what she thought was a five-dollar bill.

The young man looked at the fifty in his hand and gulped. The most anybody had ever given him was a twenty, and he had been warned by his boss not to take advantage of guests who'd had too much to drink.

"Gee, thanks, ma'am. Are you feeling all right?"

"I think so. Are my headlights on?"

His heart sank. The woman was obviously swacked. Tomorrow she'd wake up and complain because fifty dollars was missing from her purse.

"Look, ma'am. Did you mean to give me this?" he asked.

"What?"

He held out the money, but Sasha gave it only a cursory glance and saw a number five on the bill.

"Sure, which way to the highway?"

Satisfied that he had done all he could, the attendant pocketed the bill and replied, "As soon as you leave the lot, take a right, go to the stoplight. Take another right and you'll be headed west, or turn left if you want to go east."

Sasha nodded, put the gearshift into drive, and accelerated so heavily that the car leaped out of the parking lot and almost collided with the oncoming traffic. Fortunately, the other drivers had their cars in control and were able to avoid a collision. Followed by the angry honking of horns, the Mercedes moved rapidly away. Sasha was getting sleepy, and she was anxious to get home and into bed. She couldn't remember ever being so tired. Her arms and legs felt as if they had been weighted with lead, and she had to focus hard to stay in the right-hand lane.

She rolled down the windows and let the cold night air blow into the car to keep herself awake. Nothing like a blast of the damp, chilled air of the peninsula to get the old eyelids wide open. When she turned off the highway onto the road that led through the hills, she knew she had to be especially alert. It was a winding dark road, and it could be treacherous at night, but she had driven it many times and was familiar with its twists and turns. She was prudent enough to slow down, however, and drive cautiously because she was most definitely under the influence of alcohol, although she was at a loss to explain why she felt as groggy as she did.

She was about halfway up the road when the car behind her began to move up close to her fender. She looked into the rearview mirror and noticed that the driver was getting impatient. She went a little faster, because it was an unsafe area for passing. She glanced into the mirror again and saw that the car was moving closer.

"Get off my tail, you bastard!" she yelled out the window, but the car kept getting closer and closer. What the hell was he trying to do?

She accelerated. She wanted to put some distance between herself and the car behind, but no matter how fast she went, the headlights stayed right on top of her rear bumper.

"You son of a bitch!" she screamed into the night air, but she was not thinking straight. Instead of slowing down and concentrating on her driving, she allowed herself to be goaded. The night was dark, she was on the outer edge of the road, and just beyond the shoulder, the land fell away sharply.

She was driving at better than seventy miles per hour when suddenly the car pulled out and began to pass.

"You crazy asshole!" she screamed, but now she was more afraid than angry. If another car came down the hill, they would all be killed.

The car had pulled up beside her now. She wanted to look at it to see what kind of idiot was driving, but she was afraid to take her eyes off the road. To make it easier for it to pass, she eased up on the accelerator, but the car stayed alongside, and she could see with her peripheral vision that it was getting closer.

Her heart began to race, and her fogged brain was put on the alert by a massive surge of adrenaline as she realized that the driver was trying to run her off the road! Marshaling all her strength, she gripped the steering wheel and tried to remain on course, but the other car had the advantage. Sasha was terrified. For the first time in her adventurous life, she was faced with the certainty of her own violent death.

At that instant, there was a horrible screech of metal meeting metal, and a shock wave passed through Sasha and the car. Good God, someone was actually trying to push her car off the road into the dark abyss!

She gripped the steering wheel tighter and wished to God that she had fastened her seat belt before leaving the restaurant. Whoever was driving that car was risking his own life to take hers.

The car slammed into her again, and she screamed in terror and panic. And then, just as Sasha was approaching a sharp curve, there was another thunderous jolt. The Mercedes's wheels left the road, and Sasha was flying through space.

34

Lacey heard herself screaming, "Don't go away, Scott, don't go away!" Then she found herself sitting up in bed with Erin holding her.

"Oh God, I was having a terrible dream," she whispered, shaking with cold and anxiety.

"It's okay, Mom. You're awake now, and it's all over," her daughter soothed her.

"Was I screaming?" she asked, pulling the covers up.

"Not really. You were thrashing around the mumbling something. Do you want me to get Dad?"

"No, don't wake him up. I'll be okay."

"You were dreaming about Uncle Scott, weren't you?" Erin asked as she too snuggled under the fluffy down duvet.

"It was as if he was still here somewhere, trying to talk to me, to tell me something," Lacey murmured, and hot, wet tears began to trickle down her icy cheeks. She shivered and pulled the duvet tighter around her shoulders. She and her brother had been close throughout their entire lives, she thought, and it was only natural that she would be emotionally upset by his murder.

Lacey had trouble getting back to sleep. So did Erin, who encouraged her mother to tell stories about Scott as a little boy until they both drifted off again.

Everyone was dressed and ready for breakfast before Steve came to wake Lacey up. He sat on the edge of the bed, leaned down, and kissed her softly on the lips.

"Sleepyhead, are you going to stay in bed all day?"

Normally a light sleeper, Lacey came to immediate wakefulness. "Oh . . . what time is it?" she asked.

"It's after ten, and the troops are getting restless downstairs. Are we still on for the big trip to the Land of Material Things?"

"Of course. I promised," she said, sitting up. "I'll take a quick shower and be ready in a jiffy. Have you had breakfast yet?"

"No, but JJ and Erin have already started."

"You join them. I'll be down in a few minutes."

Steve grinned. "Well, I'd rather join you, but since I've had my shower, I better go have breakfast. Don't rush, we've got all day."

True to her word, Lacey was downstairs within twenty minutes. Since her hair was short and naturally curly, she never wore a shower cap, and it took just five minutes to fluff it up with a dryer. Erin had pointedly left her blush and mascara on the dressing table, and Lacey used them. The makeup did make a difference, and certainly made her feel more confident.

When she arrived in the dining room, JJ led a round of applause. "Hear, hear, for Mom, the fastest dresser in the West! Yay."

She smiled self-consciously. "I hope my skirt doesn't fall down around my ankles and embarrass us all to death. I must have lost ten pounds."

"It looks great, Mom. Don't gain it back," Erin assured. "But you need to buy some smaller clothes."

"What do you think of this new jam?" Lacey asked as she spread some on a freshly baked brioche. "We bought a tiny company in France to get the recipe."

"It tastes like ordinary jam to me," Steve replied. "What's so special about it?"

"It's made without sugar. It's simply pure fruit and concentrated fruit juice. I love it."

"Yuppie food," JJ remarked.

Steve laughed. "JJ, every day you sound more and more like me."

"Nothin' wrong with that," JJ responded.

"Has Sasha been down for breakfast yet?"

"I don't believe she came home last night," Gordon remarked. "I set the security system at about midnight, and she wasn't in then."

"Would you find out, please?" Lacey asked.

Gordon left the dining room to go upstairs while Lacey finished her breakfast. She was about to drink her café au lait when Gordon returned.

"I knocked and knocked, and when there was no answer, I used the master key and unlocked her door."

"She locks her door?" Steve asked in surprise.

Lacey nodded, and Gordon continued.

"Her bed has apparently not been slept in."

Steve grinned and winked at Lacey. "I have a feeling that the widow is out of mourning already."

"Let's go," Lacey said, getting out of her chair. "Is Salvador ready?"

"He's been waiting for half an hour," Steve replied. "Come on."

They headed out the front door, and JJ ran down the granite steps yelling, "Shotgun!" Without waiting for Salvador, he pulled open the right-hand front door of the long, silver limousine and plopped down on the seat next to the chauffeur.

"Good Lord," Steve said, "do you suppose we'll ever civilize him?"

"I doubt it," Lacey replied. "Nobody ever succeeded in thoroughly civilizing his father."

"Touché," Steve muttered, climbing in and sitting beside Lacey.

"He really is a barbarian, Mom. He makes such a big deal of commandeering the front seat even when I'm driving and have friends in the car," Erin complained.

It was a clear, sunny spring day, and Salvador manuevered the big car skillfully through the traffic. It took close to an hour to arrive at the famous Rodeo Drive in Beverly Hills. It was almost noon, and the street was filled with shoppers and tourists.

"Stop the car here, Salvador. Dad, that Hammacher place is just down the street."

Steve got out of the car. "Well, have a good time, ladies. Don't buy out the town."

"Wait, Steve," Lacey said, digging into her purse. "Take this credit card and use your own judgment about what JJ buys, okay?"

Steve refused to take the card. "Come on, I can buy my kid a trinket or two."

"Not in this town, you can't, Steve. One of these stores he wants to visit sells Ferraris and private planes."

"You're kidding?"

"No, she's not, Dad," Erin said.

"Okay, give me the card, and I'll buy no fast cars or planes for the kid," Steve promised with a grin. "Where'll we meet you?"

"Mom, why don't we have tea at the Regent?" Erin suggested.

"I know where that is," Steve interjected. "In the lobby, about five?"

"See you then," Lacey said. "Have fun."

It was the first day of shopping that Lacey had ever truly enjoyed, because she took enormous delight in the way her daughter guided her from place to place and picked out clothes for her. It was a total reversal of roles for them, and Lacey realized how grown-up her daughter had become.

They spent a fortune. Lacey bought several Armani suits at Neiman's for herself, and Erin found a pair of jeans she liked and a handsome black and silver belt by Barry Kieselstein-Cord that cost more than a month's rent on a nice apartment. At the Chanel boutique, Erin insisted that Lacey order a remarkable black evening suit that had a price tag of five figures. The shoes and handbag set her back almost half again as much.

They had a quick salad at Neiman's, with one of their enormous popovers and iced tea, and then they headed to Rodeo Drive, where they walked the new complex of stores known as Rodeo II. At Fred Hayman's Lacey found a cocktail dress in deep blue that was stunning, and Erin bought a short black leather skirt with an art deco-styled cashmere sweater. At Giorgio's, they both bought hand-painted sun visors for tennis.

The trunk of the car was full of packages by the time they finished, and they fell into the backseat giggling. It had been an expensive but fun day.

"It's been terrific, darling," Lacey said, but she cautioned, "I can't do this kind of thing very often."

"I know, Mom, but that makes it special. You're a great shopper."

"Only with an expert like you, my dear. What do you think your dad'll say about that cashmere sweater we bought for him?" Lacey asked.

"He'll love it. After all, it's plain old conservative heather gray, and it'll be nice and warm for those Texas winters. You think he'll be upset if he finds out it cost more than nine hundred dollars?"

A slight smirk crossed Lacey's face. "I doubt it. He's always liked expensive things."

Steve and JJ were waiting in the hotel lobby, but they were carrying only one, relatively small package.

"Okay, what did you buy?" Erin asked her brother.

"Something I'd like to have but can't afford," Steve replied, "but I figured, why not?"

"I got my own fax machine," JJ boasted. "And you can't use it!" he added pointing his finger at his sister.

"What a dumb thing to buy! Who are you going to send faxes to?" Erin challenged.

"Buddy Murphy got one for Christmas. Now we can send messages to each other."

"Well, you better learn how to write legibly first," Erin said witheringly.

Deciding that it was a little late for tea, they got into the limousine for the long ride home. They had a lot to talk about, and the refrigerated bar was stocked with soft drinks and champagne. It was almost seven o'clock by the time they drove through the gates. Gordon was waiting at the front door.

"Miss Lacey," he said very solemnly. "There's a policeman here to see you. Something dreadful has happened."

"Gordon, what are you talking about?" Lacey asked, dismayed by his words and manner.

"It's Mr. Scott's wife, Miss Sasha. She was killed last night!"

35

L ate that evening, the family was gathered together in the media room, watching the newscasts, trying to glean some information about Sasha's death. Lacey was in despair. Not only was she mourning the sudden demise of her sister-in-law, but she was thoroughly depressed by the realization that her best hope of being proven innocent had died with Sasha. Gordon came in to tell them that Cherry Dolan had finally arrived.

"It's about time," Steve muttered.

"I left several calls for you," Lacey said the moment the detective made her appearance. "The officer who came here to tell us about Sasha's death didn't know anything."

"I'm sorry I couldn't get here sooner."

"Exactly what happened?" Lacey asked.

"A kid hiking in the hills on the peninsula this afternoon found a Mercedes crashed into a stand of trees at the bottom of a hill off Crest Highway. Sasha Gallagher's body was in it. She must have driven off the side of the road last night."

"Was she drunk?" Steve asked.

"We don't know yet, but I've been told there was a strong odor of alcohol on the body. The car was a wreck. It seems to have smashed into every tree on the way down, but luckily it didn't catch fire. She wasn't wearing a seat belt."

In spite of the fact that Sasha had been unpopular in the family, the details of her death affected them all.

"We've run her fingerprints through the FBI and come up with a blank. Does anyone have any idea who she really is?" Cherry asked.

"We were told she was from Russia," Lacey answered.

"She's not. Did she ever talk about her background, or where she had lived?"

Everyone shook their heads, and Erin said, "She never talked to anybody, not really. She spent most of the days out shopping and in the evenings, she and Uncle Scott were always dressing up and going someplace. I never had a real conversation with her, not that I wanted to."

"Was it an accident?" Steve asked.

156

"We can't say for sure yet. My partner will be here in a few minutes with a court order granting us permission to search through her belongings."

"What are you looking for? Her room was thoroughly searched after my brother's death."

"That was then. This is now. We may be looking for other things," Cherry replied.

"Well, you don't need a court order. Come on, I'll take you up to her room," Lacey said and got up from her chair.

As the two women walked up the stairs, Lacey wondered whether or not she should tell the detective about her talk with Sasha on Friday. Tom would probably object, but then he seemed to object to everything.

She opened the door to the bedroom and flipped on the light.

"I think you should know something," Lacey began.

"Do you mind if I take notes?" Cherry asked. Lacey shook her head and told the entire story of her conversation with Sasha, including the sum they had agreed on. There seemed no point in concealing anything now.

When she finished, Cherry asked, "And where were you about one this morning?"

"Was that the time of the accident?"

Cherry nodded. "Approximate. We'll pinpoint it more accurately in the autopsy."

"I was in bed, but I wasn't sleeping. I had a nightmare and woke up screaming about that time. I couldn't get back to sleep."

"Was anyone with you?" Cherry asked.

"My daughter. She and I talked for most of the night."

"Did Sasha tell you where she was going or whom she was going to meet?"

"I didn't even know she was going out until after she left. The last thing she said to me was that she'd go down to your office this morning and tell you where I was when Scott was killed."

Lacey left Cherry in Sasha's room and went back down to her family. She decided not to tell them what she had revealed to Cherry.

Chuck arrived ten minutes later and was sent to join Cherry in her search. They spent more than two hours in the bedroom. It was past midnight when they came downstairs.

"Any luck?" Steve asked.

"We found her passport taped inside one of her boots," Chuck replied. "Any idea why she went to so much trouble to hide it?"

Lacey shook her head.

"It shows her to be a citizen of the U.S. Well, at least now we can track down her family. We're also taking her date book. We'll check out all the places noted in it to see if maybe she was at one of 'em last night. Did she ever take any medication of any kind?" Chuck asked.

Lacey shook her head. "Not that I know of. Why?"

"Well, it seemed strange there was nothing at all in her medicine cabinet. Most people at least have some aspirin."

JJ, who liked mysteries, spoke up. "Did you find anything when you searched her room after my uncle was killed?"

"Yes, we did, son. We found a bottle of pills."

"What were they?" Lacey asked.

"Butabarbital sodium. The same medication that we found in your brother's body."

"Do you by any chance have a picture of your sister-in-law?" Cherry asked, changing the subject.

"I have some snapshots Scott sent me. Before he married her, he wanted me to see how beautiful she was."

Lacey took an envelope from the desk drawer and handed it to Cherry. In it was a small stack of pictures that were taken on the ski slopes, and Sasha was wearing goggles and a hat.

"Do you have anything better than this?" Chuck asked.

"Only their wedding picture. It's hanging in the bedroom they shared. I'll send Gordon—"

"Don't bother. I'll run up and get it myself," Chuck said and headed for the stairs.

He returned with the framed picture in hand and gave it to Cherry who remarked, "This is an excellent likeness of her. She was quite photogenic."

"Strange, isn't it? Most beautiful women love to have their pictures taken, but Sasha was an exception. I bought a video camera for JJ, sort of as a family diversion while Dad was ill, and my son started shooting everything in sight. Sasha got very annoyed with him. We had one terrible scene. She threw such a temper tantrum that Scott actually had to ask JJ to give him the tape so it could be destroyed."

Eyes narrowing as he listened, Chuck asked, "Did she ever give any reason why she didn't like to have her picture taken?"

Lacey shook her head. "Not really. At least she never gave a good reason. She always looked bandbox perfect, even after her morning run, but she'd complain that she needed lipstick or her hair was messed up."

"Where did your brother meet his wife?" Chuck asked.

"Aspen. They got on a lift together, had a whirlwind romance, and were married three weeks later," Lacey replied.

"Did your brother ever meet any of her family?" Cherry asked. "We need to contact them."

Lacey shook her head. "He wanted to, but she said she didn't want her father to know she was married. I have no idea why she felt that way, and if Scott knew, he never said anything."

"We may have more questions later. Thanks for being so cooperative," Cherry said, and the detectives left the house.

Fearful that someone else in her family might be harmed, Lacey vowed that her first order of business the next day would be to get extra security in the house.

In the Darkness of the Night

She was lying there tied hand and foot to the bedposts, frightened and helpless, when he turned out the light in the bathroom. Now they were in total darkness and she could see nothing. She could hear him moving around somewhere at the foot of the bed. What was he doing, she wondered frantically, and when she heard his shoe drop she knew he was getting undressed.

"Please let me go. The cord is hurting my wrists, and my legs are going numb," she begged.

"We can't have that," he whispered. "I don't want you to be numb anywhere. I want you sensitive to every touch."

She could feel him loosening the cords around her ankles, and although she tried to kick her legs, she was still bound too securely to wrench herself free.

She felt his fingers caressing her legs, moving upward, drawing insinuating circles around the crest of her buttocks and up her spine, but she was not aroused by his delicate touch. She was too frightened and apprehensive. He was going to hurt her, of that she was certain.

When his fingers reached her shoulders, he stretched his body on top of hers and let his hands move out and caress her arms. His weight pressed her deeper into the mattress and caused her arms to be stretched tighter, and the pull was painful.

"You're hurting me," she gasped.

"It's a good hurt, though, isn't it, cunt?" he whispered, and his fingers were on her buttocks again, spreading them apart.

"Please don't do that to me," she pleaded softly, tightening her muscles to keep him out.

"Let go, cunt! It'll only hurt worse if you fight me," he warned her, and so she tried to relax and let him have his way. He forced himself roughly into her, and she felt the hot, searing pain, which grew more intense when he moved, slowly at first and then more rapidly as his passion mounted. He reached around and gripped her breasts tightly in his hands and whispered in her ear, "I know you like this. No matter what you women say, you like it hard and rough."

She could feel the stinging of the tears behind her eyelids as she began to cry. She wanted to scream out in anger and pain that no woman could enjoy being hurt this way, but she didn't dare draw attention to herself and to what was going on there in that bed in the darkness of the night.

160

36

W hen Mass was over, Lacey and her family walked to the car where Salvador was waiting. Although he too had been in the church, he sat in the back pew so that he could slip out first and have the car waiting.

"Let's drive over to the marina and have lunch on the boat," JJ suggested, but Erin protested that she had homework to do.

Steve and Lacey looked at each other, and Steve commented, "Like father like son."

And Lacey retorted, "Like mother, like daughter," and everybody laughed, and she added, "I'm sorry, JJ, but your sister is right."

"Okay, okay, but after I finish studying, let's play some tennis, Dad."

Steve sighed. "Well, okay, JJ, but I haven't been on a court for years. I won't give you much of a game."

JJ grinned. "Great. I love to win."

The first thing Lacey did when they got home was call Tom Brennan, but his wife, Mamie, told her that he had gone to Washington, D.C.

"He didn't tell me he was leaving town," Lacey said indignantly.

"It came up unexpectedly."

"Where's he staying? I need to talk to him today."

Mamie Brennan hesitated. She hated making decisions, but she was afraid to offend Lacey.

"Well, if it's really important . . . ," she said.

"It's very important, Mamie," Lacey insisted with annoyance.

"Oh my, well, he's at the Carlton," she replied, reassured by Lacey's urgency.

"Thank you, Mamie. When did he leave L.A.?"

"Early Saturday morning. He didn't have much sleep. He was at the office working until late the night before," she said, chattering effusively, trying to make up for her previous reticence. "What did you want with him?"

"I need to talk to him about hiring a good security service."

"I wouldn't know anything about that," Mamie said with a small giggle. "I'm afraid I couldn't help you at all."

"You've been a big help already. Thanks, Mamie," Lacey replied and hung up quickly. God, she hated to talk to Tom's wife. She was always pleasant, but she had raised helplessness to a fine art, and Tom seemed to like her that way. He called her his "sweet, little darlin'," whereas Jack Gallagher had usually referred to her as "Vera Vague."

It was after three o'clock when she finally got Tom on the telephone.

"Tom, I hate to bother you, but we need to talk. I thought you'd call me when you heard about Sasha being killed."

"Sasha was killed? My God, when did that happen?"

"Didn't you know? It was in all the papers and the newscasts," Lacey replied.

"No, something came up, and I've been distracted."

"Her car went over an embankment late on Friday night. They didn't find her until yesterday afternoon."

"Was she drunk?" he asked.

"They're not sure it was an accident."

"No kidding? God, I'm sorry I can't be there with you. I'll call my associate, Blake Hart, and have him come right over. I don't want you talking to any of those detectives unless he's with you, understand?"

"Relax, Tom. I'm not a suspect this time," Lacey said with a degree of irritation.

"You can't be sure of that. I wouldn't trust any of those people from homicide. They're tricky as hell."

"Tom, listen to me! At the time Sasha was killed, I was awake and talking to my daughter. Okay?"

"Well, that's good. But still they might claim you hired some-body to—"

"Listen, Tom, shortly before she died, Sasha told me she'd seen me swimming laps the morning Scott was killed. She promised to go to the police and tell them I couldn't have done it. Unfortunately, she didn't live long enough to do that."

"I hope you weren't stupid enough to tell anybody that story," he said.

"I told Cherry Dolan."

"Oh God, didn't I tell you not to talk—"

Lacey interrupted him. She did not feel like being lectured again. "Look, what I called to ask you is this: I want the name of a good security company. Do you know of any?"

"Why?"

"Why? Tom, for God's sake, my brother's been murdered and now his wife's died in a crash that may not be accidental. I want protection, not just for myself but for my family. Bodyguards, skilled ones. Understand?"

If he hadn't been such a close friend of her father's, she wouldn't deal with Tom at all, Lacey thought with annoyance.

"Good idea. Call Tim Coffey at, eh, let's see what's the name of his company. It's a fancy name, oh yeah, P. Itech. That's it. His office is in Hawthorne. He's a good man."

"Can his firm supply enough manpower for me?" Lacey asked. "I want skilled and armed drivers to take the children to and from school. Whoever's done this might resort to kidnapping."

"Of course, but I don't think you have anything to worry about."

"Well I don't agree with you. Scott's murderer infiltrated our house undetected, and he might do it again."

"Call Tim. He's an ex-Secret Service man, used to guard the president. Tell him it's an emergency."

"Will do. Thanks, Tom," Lacey replied, disconnected the call, and dialed information. She got the number of the agency, but when she called, she got only an answering machine. She left her number, said she'd been referred by Tom Brennan, and that it was an emergency.

Five minutes after the call had been placed, Tim Coffey called her back. Lacey sketched out the situation for him, and he assured her that he could provide all the protection she needed.

"Why don't I drive out there this evening and bring a contract for you to sign," he suggested.

"We can deal with the contract anytime you wish. If you want an advance retainer, I'll be happy to accommodate you, but I'd like some men on duty out here before nightfall, understand?"

"Let's start with two for the night shift. I'll be one of them. Then I can go over the house and suggest any changes that might need to be made."

"Come as soon as possible," Lacey said and gave him her address.

"I suggest that you and your family stay inside the house until we've gone over the grounds thoroughly, okay?"

"Fine," Lacey agreed and went to find Steve and JJ to tell them that the tennis game was off.

She was sitting in the library reading the Sunday newspaper's account of Sasha's death when the telephone rang. It was Cherry Dolan.

"Anything new?" Lacey asked.

"I promised I'd call when we got the coroner's report. They found both alcohol and butabarbital sodium in her body."

"Then, it was an accident, after all," Lacey replied with relief.

"No. The left side of her car was damaged and there's several streaks of black paint. It looks like she might have been forced off the road. Does anybody connected to you or the family drive a large black car?"

"None of our cars are black, not even the limousine. Dad hated black cars, said they reminded him of funerals."

"If you come up with anything, give me a call, will you?"

"Of course. Cherry, you're not still thinking that I—"

"I'm not at liberty to say anything at this point. I'm sorry."

"Thanks anyway for calling me about Sasha."

Lacey put down the telephone and noticed that her hands were shaking again. Sasha and Scott had both been murdered by an unknown assailant. But why? And who would be next?

37

J ean Atwill stared at the account of Sasha's death in the newspaper and her thinking took off in a wildly new direction. Sasha's death might be only an unhappy coincidence, but she had to be sure. She picked up the telephone and dialed it. For the second time that morning, Mamie Brennan found herself besieged by a distraught woman demanding to know where Tom could be found. This time, however, Mamie refused to be cooperative. Jean Atwill was nobody important. She certainly wasn't Lacey Gallagher.

"I'm sorry, but my husband's very busy in Washington, D.C. You'll have to call his office tomorrow and leave a number where he can reach you. This is Sunday, you know."

Jean tried to persuade her that it was an emergency, but Mamie had made up her mind. Jean slammed down the telephone in annoyance. Determined to talk to Tom, she began to check the big hotels in the nation's capital. She found him on the fourth try.

"What the hell is going on?" Jean asked him.

"I don't know, but we can thank our lucky stars that bitch is dead," he replied. "I talked to Lacey today, and it seems our little Russian friend made a deal with her."

"What kind of deal?"

"She saw Lacey swimming the morning Scott was killed. She promised to tell the police that Lacey couldn't have done it."

"Was that true?" Jean asked in shock. Old prejudices die hard, and it was difficult for her to let go of her fixation that Lacey had killed Scott.

"I doubt it. Lacey probably bought her off, but Sasha's dead now and won't cause us any trouble. Somebody did us a favor."

"What kind of trouble could she have caused us?" Jean asked.

"Get with it, Jean. The less people alive that know, the better."

"I don't understand," she persisted. "Why is it better for us that Sasha's dead?"

"Because we want Lacey arrested and convicted of her brother's murder; then I'll be in charge and we can move right ahead according to plan."

"I didn't get in this mess to make you rich and powerful. I did it for Scott."

"I know that, and Lacey killed him. Who else would have done it? You don't want her to get away with it, do you?"

"No," Jean replied.

"Good. Then just sit tight there in your apartment. Don't see anybody and don't talk to anybody without checking with me first."

Jean sat at her desk for a long time, reading the article about Sasha's death, and then reading it again, and yet again. The more she concentrated on the story, the more convoluted her thinking became. In her mind, Lacey was the villain, the source of all the trouble. She had killed her brother and then she had conspired to buy off his wife and get herself an alibi. Lacey was evil.

The notion haunted her. The more she deliberated the more certain she became that the object of her hatred would never be brought to justice. Lacey had enormous riches that would buy her way out of everything. Somebody had to stop her. Somebody had to make her pay the penalty for Scott's death.

For the rest of that day and for most of the night, Jean sat in her easy chair, staring out the window and fondling the small handgun she had carried in her purse to Scott's memorial service.

38

Although she felt better about going to sleep knowing that Tim Coffey and his assistant were standing guard, Lacey still did not have an untroubled night. Erin too was uneasy. Usually a quiet and sound sleeper, the young woman now moved restlessly, groaning and muttering and grinding her teeth. Steve mentioned that JJ was thrashing about a lot too.

Lacey sighed and sat up in bed, and in the stillness of the night she heard a small sound in the hall outside her door. Her heart began to beat faster, and she could feel the hair at the back of her neck rise. She looked at the clock. It was almost three in the morning.

Not one to hide under the blankets, Lacey slid out of bed, stepped into her soft slippers, and pulled on her robe. If there was some villain creeping about in her house, she would damn well find out who it was. Grabbing the large, heavy flashlight she kept beside her bed, she moved toward the door and turned the handle.

As soon as she felt the lock release, she swung the door open. The hallway was dark. Someone had turned off the main chandelier they'd been keeping lit all night. She switched on the flashlight and swept the bright beam toward the stairs, and suddenly the figure of a man was spotlighted.

Startled, he asked, "Ms. Gallagher, are you all right?"

Lacey's heart began to slow its racing. "Good Lord, Tim, is that you?"

"I was making rounds. Checking to see if everything is all right. I'm sorry I bumped into that credenza and made a noise."

"No problem. I was awake anyway."

"Don't worry about a thing. Nobody's going to get into this house tonight. You've got an excellent security system, and it's working fine. We checked out the grounds, and everything's quiet."

"I didn't hear the dogs bark."

"We made friends with them first thing. Pets aren't the best protection, I'm afraid."

Lacey smiled. "They're getting old too."

"The next shift will be here at eight," he replied and disappeared down the stairway.

Steve's door opened, and he peered out.

"I thought I heard some conversation out here in the hallway. What's the matter, can't you sleep either?" he asked.

"Not really."

"I'm sorry you're having such a rough time."

"When to God is this nightmare ever going to end, Steve?"

"It may already be over and you don't know it. I've got a strong suspicion that Scott got himself into some kind of a mess and Sasha was part of it."

Lacey shivered. "I wish I knew what the hell was going on."

Steve walked across the hall and put his arms around her. "Stop worrying now. I'm going to stay right here and help you watch over the kids. Nothing more's going to happen."

"Suppose they arrest me for Scott's murder, Steve? What will that do to Erin and JJ?"

"They haven't got enough evidence to convict you. Quit thinking about that. Remember I'll be here and I'll always take good care of our children. I've let you down on other things, Lacey, but I promise you I won't let you down on that."

He held her close and gently kissed the top of her head and said, "Now you go back to bed and get some rest."

Lacey went back into her room feeling that she ought to be comforted, but she wasn't. As the sun started to rise, dispelling the demons of the night, she fell asleep at last.

39

Monday morning, Jean arose from her bed. She tried to follow her usual breakfast routine, but the shredded wheat stuck in her throat and made her gag. She threw it down the garbage disposal. She showered, and after toweling herself dry, she smoothed lotion all over her body. She gave a lot of thought to her appearance that day. Her pictures would be taken for newspapers and magazines, and she wanted to be dressed well. She remembered how dramatic Jackie Kennedy had looked in her pink suit with the blood splattered all over the skirt.

She checked her hair and decided it needed a little freshening. She plugged in the hot rollers and then brushed and flossed her teeth.

Jean took a long time with her makeup. She didn't want to look sallow and drawn in the photographs. She dabbed a little concealer under her eyes to hide the circles created by the last few sleepless nights. When she finished her face, she rolled up her hair.

Her closet contained numerous designer suits. She passed over the chic little red David Hayes, the brown Anne Klein, and the white Chanel. She wanted to make a statement. The peach Armani jacket with the cocoa gabardine skirt and matching chiffon blouse. That was it. Stylish but conservative and elegant. It would photograph well.

She pulled on her Donna Karan pantyhose and plain pumps in beige calf. When she got the purse that matched the shoes, she hesitated. It wasn't big enough, and for a moment she was perplexed. She'd have to choose something else to wear, something that had a matching handbag sufficiently large. She returned to the closet, but nothing pleased her as much as the Armani.

She got the handgun from her bedside table and tried it. It fit snugly into the purse, but there was room for nothing else. What do do?

Inspiration struck. She retrieved her briefcase from the living room closet and emptied it of all the papers she'd been carrying. She threw them in the wastebasket. It was junk that would mean nothing to her from this day forward. Then she packed the case like an overnight bag. Clean underwear, an extra pair of pantyhose, two handkerchiefs, a toothbrush, her medications, makeup and a hairbrush, her wallet, and car keys. Jean opened the wall safe in her bedroom closet and took out a document, which she placed on top of everything else. She was pleased with herself for remembering it.

She finished combing her hair and put on her clothes. For a moment she hesitated about wearing the gold and diamond Rolex watch that Jack had given her on her fiftieth birthday. Somebody would probably steal it, but what difference did that make? She had no one to leave it to anyway. She put it on.

When she was ready, she made one last survey of herself in the full-length mirror of her bedroom and was satisfied. She picked up the briefcase and her purse and opened the door to the hallway. She looked back inside and her eyes swept over her beloved apartment.

"Good-bye," she whispered. "I'll miss you."

40

Lacey was late getting to the office on Monday morning. Although she now had trained and armed drivers to take her children to school, she insisted on going along with them. Upon arrival, Erin and JJ went to their classrooms and Lacey went to the principal's office to request that the staff be especially vigilant.

"Here are the names and pictures of the two drivers in addition to Salvador who will be bringing them to school and taking them home," she said, presenting the identifications.

The nun promised her that they would be careful, and Lacey left the school feeling more secure.

Marge greeted her when she came in.

"Pete Cunningham left a message for you. He said he wanted to be invited here to lunch again. He says he's got a proposition for you."

"Really? Maybe he's given this merger thing some serious thought. Get him on the line for me and tell Raoul I'll need the private dining room today."

Marge came to Lacey's office a few minutes later to report. "I talked to Mr. Cunningham's secretary. He had to go to a meeting, but she arranged the time for him. He'll be here at twelve-thirty sharp."

"Fine. Is the dining room free?"

"It is now."

"Who put this report on my desk about Mrs. Gallagher's grocery stores?"

"Sam Davenport. He told me the stores are doing great. He's got six more locations tied down and ready to go when you are."

"Whew, six, all at once? I want to talk to him."

As soon as he was on the line, Lacey said, "Good Lord, Sam, that'll be twenty-two stores in the last two quarters. Aren't you moving a little fast?"

"Believe me, Lacey, these stores are gold mines."

"Wouldn't it be less risky to franchise them?"

"Less risk, less profit, to quote your father."

"Have you located your produce sources to supply all these stores?

You know if we can't get enough good organically grown produce, it's only another supermarket."

"I've got agricultural teams all over the place, and these stores are great outlets for our Natural n' Good products."

"Okay, do it, but don't get yourself too far out on a limb in case we have to do some tree trimming."

For the rest of the morning, Lacey immersed herself in work and relished every moment of it. She almost forgot the troubles she had at home as time raced by.

It was a few minutes before twelve-thirty when Marge called to say, "Jean Atwill's here, and she wants to talk to you for a minute."

Lacey looked at the clock. Pete would be arriving any time, and she didn't want to keep him waiting. It was important to her to bring about the proposed merger, and she certainly didn't want to be bothered with Jean Atwill. Not now.

"Tell her I've got an important appointment. See if she can come back this afternoon when I'll have more time."

Lacey waited while Marge talked to Jean. "She insists it'll only take a minute," was the message her secretary brought back.

Lacey sighed. "All right, send her in, but if she isn't gone by the time Pete arrives, you come in and get her out of here."

"Will do," Marge responded.

Jean came through the door, and Lacey noted how nice she looked. She was always perfectly groomed, but she looked younger and more stylish today. Her face seemed to glow and her eyes sparkled.

"Come in and sit down, Jean," Lacey said, not getting out of her chair. "You look lovely today. Those colors become you."

"I wish I could say the same for you. You look tired. Aren't you sleeping well?"

"No, I'm not, as a matter of fact. I suppose you read about Sasha's accident?"

"Good riddance, I say."

"What?" Lacey was incredulous.

"She was trash. I don't know why Scott ever married her in the first place. You know she wasn't really the daughter of a Russian diplomat."

"How do you know that?"

"Scott told me. It was only a story he made up to impress Jack. Her father was a poor Russian immigrant who worked in a factory in Chicago. She was nothing but a hustler looking for a rich husband when she latched onto Scott."

"I don't have much time, Jean. What can I do for you?" Lacey was anxious to get the conversation over and done with. Gossip was not on her agenda, and besides, the woman irritated her.

Jean smiled a strange and eerie smile. "You can pay for the life you took." She then reached into her handbag, pulled out the gun, and pointed it at Lacey.

"Oh my God, what do you think you're doing?"

"I'm going to do this at close range, if you don't mind," Jean said, approaching her desk. "I'm not a very good shot and I don't want to miss."

Lacey stared at the barrel of the gun coming closer to her, and she was frantic. Somewhere on the floor under her father's desk was a panic button, but she had to move her foot carefully or Jean would remember it was there and figure out what she was trying to do.

"Wait, Jean, wait! Let's talk about this. Why do you want to kill me?"

"I'm going to punish you because the law won't. You killed Scott, and your money will save you. I know that you successfully bought an alibi from that Russian bitch, and now that she's dead, you'll find somebody else to corrupt with your millions."

"Jean, I swear on the lives of my children that I didn't kill Scott. I loved him, you know that."

"But you loved the money more, and he was in your way. That's why I'm going to punish you. Because I'm guilty too, you see. I gave him the money that caused his death. By shooting you myself we'll both pay for our sins. I'll go to jail or to the gas chamber, and you'll go to your grave."

"What are you talking about? Why was Scott so important to you? You hardly knew him!" Lacey was truly panic-stricken now. The woman was crazy.

Outraged, Jean snapped, "I most certainly did know him, you bitch, you see I—"

At that moment, Marge opened the door, but she could only see Jean's back. "Lacey, Mr. Cun—"

Startled, Jean whirled around, and in that instant, Marge and Pete, who was behind her, saw the gun. Marge screamed and Lacey tried to duck under her desk, but Jean turned back too quickly and squeezed the trigger. The bullet skimmed across the top of Lacey's shoulder. Before Jean could get another shot off, Pete shoved Marge out of the way, threw himself at Jean, and grabbed her. He was so much bigger and stronger that she was no match for him. He succeeded in wresting the gun away from her, and in the scuffle, she lost her balance and fell to the floor.

"Are you all right?" he asked, rushing to Lacey, who was getting to her feet.

"I think so. The bullet went through the fabric of my jacket. Oh God! Marge, get security in here and then call the police!"

Lacey went to where Jean was lying on the floor, glaring at her.

"Why in God's name did you do this?"

"Somebody had to avenge Scott's death," Jean declared with no remorse. The expression on her face was cold and filled with hatred.

"Why you of all people? You hardly knew my brother."

"I knew him better than anyone. He was my son."

41

J
ean concentrated on typing the letter from her dictation notes, but
she was so nervous that her fingers kept hitting the wrong keys. Each
mistake made it necessary for her to rip the piece of stationery out of
the typewriter and start over, because Jack Gallagher would not sign
his name to a letter that had mistakes or erasures on it.

Forty Years Ago

She had finally gotten as far as Very Truly Yours, when she began to
slow her speed. She was almost there, just a few strokes more and the
letter would be finished. By the time she typed her initials at the bottom,
she was pecking at the keys, one at a time.

She finished, carefully rolled the letter out of the typewriter, and
inserted an envelope. At last she was ready to carry it into her employer's
office for his signature, but it was not the only message she had for him
that day.

She knocked discreetly at the door before going in. Jack Gallagher
was on the telephone, but he signaled to her to come in and sit down
in the chair in front of his desk, which she quietly did and waited until
he was finished talking. At last he ended his telephone conversation.

"Here, let me read that. I might want to make a few changes," he
said, holding out his hand.

Jean passed the letter to him, mentally crossing her fingers that it
would meet with his approval. Her heart sank when he picked up his
ballpoint pen and began scratching through some of the sentences and
writing in the margins.

"There, that's better. No sense in tipping our hand too early. When
you're negotiating it's always best not to say more than absolutely necessary. I'll be leaving early today, so be sure it's ready for me to sign
before I go. And send it by messenger. I want it on his desk as soon as
possible."

Jean took the letter and read through the changes he'd made to be
sure she understood them. When she was finished, she raised her eyes
and stared at the man sitting before her. He was the handsomest man
she'd ever seen. A silver streak shot through the front of his thick unruly
dark hair, and there were little crinkles at the corners of his bright blue
eyes. His shoulders were broad and his waistline trim. His hands were

large and square and powerful, and he was self-confident to the point of arrogance, unless he chose to be otherwise. And at those rare times, he could be self-effacing, humorous, and gentle.

Because his secretary did not jump up to do his bidding, Jack knew she had something on her mind.

"What's up?" he asked. When he was in his office, Jack Gallagher was always abrupt and businesslike. There were not enough hours in the day for him to complete everything on his schedule.

Jean looked down and said, "Something awful's happened, Jack."

Her response put Jack on instant alert. It was unlike Jean to intrude on the affairs of Gallagher's Best with problems of her own. Even though she was very young, she was the best, most efficient employee he had ever had, and since the day she had come to work for him more than a year before, his office had run like clockwork.

His voice reflected his concern. "Is there anything I can do?"

Jean looked up, and there were tears in her eyes.

"Jack, I'm pregnant." Like her employer, she was a direct and forthcoming person.

"Good God!" Jack exclaimed. "How could that be? We always took precautions," he said, his voice dropping almost to a whisper.

"I know, I know . . . it must have happened that time a few weeks ago when the . . . the . . . rubber slipped off . . . remember?"

"Jesus, Mary, and Joseph! One little time! Are you absolutely sure?"

Jean nodded. "I'm so sorry, Jack," she replied, and there was true regret in her voice. As much as she loved Jack Gallagher, she had never expected anything from the relationship except a little love and affection, and a very secure position at Gallagher's Best. Now she feared she would be banished forever—sent off with a hefty check and an admonition never to return.

Jack got to his feet and walked to the door. Was he going to open it and order her out of his sight forever?

Instead, he turned the key in the lock and came back to her. Taking her hands in his, he pulled her to her feet and took her in his arms. Holding her close, he patted her on the back and murmured words that comforted and reassured her.

"There, there, now don't you worry about a thing. We're going to see this through together."

Jean began to cry. "Oh God, Jack, what am I going to do?"

"Well, you'll have the baby, and it will be ours. We'll find a nice private place for you to go, someplace where they'll take good care of you . . ."

"Jack, I can't have this baby! I don't want to have a baby. I want to stay on here and work with you. I couldn't stand it if you sent me away."

"I hope you're not meaning that you might do something to murder a child of mine. You're not, are you?"

"Oh, Jack, I'm so miserable I don't know what I mean. I feel like God is punishing me for doing what I did."

"Children are not God's punishment, Jean. I will love this child and take care of it the same as the child that Maude is carrying."

"Oh God, suppose your wife found out about it?"

"We must see that she never does. She would never forgive me."

But Maude Gallagher did find out, and on the very same day that Jean gave birth to a son. A young novice at St. Anne's Maternity Home was directed to call Jack Gallagher and tell him. Eager to convey the exciting news, the novice did not leave word at his office to call her when he came in, but instead she innocently tried to contact him at home.

Maude Gallagher was nursing her seven-month-old daughter when the call came. And when Jack arrived home that night, he was greeted not with a smile and an affectionate kiss as usual. Rather he was met by a cold and furious woman who was now a stranger to him, and it was from her grim lips that he learned that he had a son.

For days after, Maude locked herself away from the world and had words for no one except her beloved baby daughter. When she finally was ready to talk to someone, she summoned a priest. Each afternoon, the devoted man of God would come to the house, and he helped her find a way, not only to exact retribution but also to save the appearance of a marriage.

When she was emotionally ready, she appeared one night in the dining room of the great house that Jack had built for her. They ate in silence, and after coffee was served, Maude addressed her husband with exaggerated politeness.

"Jack, it's time we settled this matter once and for all. In the library, please."

Jack moved to take her into his arms, thinking that perhaps enough time had passed to soften the shock of his infidelity, but his original prophesy proved to be correct. His wife would never forgive him.

When they were seated, Maude asked, "Do you want a divorce so that you can marry that woman?"

Jack was shocked. "Of course not! I'm still a Catholic, Maude, even if I have failed to keep all my marriage vows."

"I see. And how is your son? Is he a beautiful baby?" she asked, and there was a gleam in her eye.

Shamed but nevertheless proud of the fruit his passion had borne, he replied, "Not as beautiful as our lovely littly Lacey, but big and healthy and strong, as a boy should be."

Maude composed her next utterance carefully. "Then I will not deny you your son. He is the only one you will ever have."

"What do you mean, sweetheart? You're still young. We'll have many—"

"We will have no more children together, Jack, because we will never share the same bed again." Her voice was low but it reflected her deadly intent.

"You're not serious," he replied, his eyes angry and his voice cold.

"As God is my witness."

"I will not live in a loveless marriage!"

"Then you will have no marriage at all. I'll divorce you, and I'll take half of everything you own. Gallagher's Best will no longer be all yours. And if my attorney is sharp enough—and I guarantee you that he will be the best that money can buy—I might even be able to take more than half. I can, after all, prove that it was my father's investment in your little enterprise that got you started on the road to the big time. At the very least, I could force you to sell Gallagher's Best and divide the proceeds."

"You wouldn't do that, Maude. Gallagher's Best is mine, and you know it. I took that little restaurant of my grandfather's and turned its recipes and its food into a giant corporation. I did it. Nobody else."

"If you feel so certain of your position, then by all means take your chances in a court of law. However, there's another way we can settle this matter so that you can have your son, your daughter, your company, and what will appear to the world as a happy marriage."

"How?" Jack asked suspiciously. He had always known that his wife was a headstrong and determined Irish woman, and he had admired her for it, but now he was afraid of the glitter in her eyes and the cruel smile that played at the corner of her lips.

"Tell your secretary-mistress to give the child to me. I will raise him as my own son."

"You're talking nonsense. Jean will never give up her baby."

"Tell her what I said. Her son will be raised as an heir to the Gallagher fortune. He will have everything. He will in effect become the *legitimate* son of a wealthy and powerful man rather than the bastard he is now."

"And what about Jean?"

"I don't give a damn about her. I want the boy."

"She'll never do it. She loves her child, she loves her work, and she loves me. She'll never give up everything she holds dear and steal away into the night with a little silver in her purse."

"Whether she goes or stays is of no importance whatsoever to me. Let her give up the child, and she can keep her job, for all I care. She can even be your mistress, if you want her. God knows you'll need someone to provide you with an outlet for passion, because I certainly won't."

"You're mad!"

"Tell her what I said, and then you'll see whether I'm mad or not!" she declared as she swept out of the room, leaving her final words hanging in the air.

Furious and confused, Jack stormed out of the house and jumped into his car. After driving about for an angry hour, he headed for Jean Atwill's apartment. She was the one person in his life to whom he could turn for an answer to his problem.

42

Jean was finished telling her story when the police arrived. Pete turned the gun over to them and explained what had happened.

"If it's all right, I'd like to say a few words to this woman before you take her away," Lacey said. The young uniformed officer said he thought it would be all right and then he belatedly read Jean her rights.

"Jean, you're living in a fantasy world," Lacey began. "I know you were in love with my father; everybody knew it. But nobody in their right mind would believe that ridiculous story you just told. I sure as hell don't."

Jean glared back at Lacey. "Every word I said is true, and I don't give a damn whether or not you believe it, because my son believed me."

"You're lying! Scott loved our mother. He would never have dishonored her memory by believing she had taken him away from you out of spite. My mother was the dearest, sweetest, kindest—"

"Bitch! That's what she was. A mean, conniving shrew who stole my son and then locked her husband out of her bed forever." Jean's eyes bulged with anger and hatred as she spit out the words. "And Scott believed I was his mother when he died."

Lacey stared in revulsion at the crazed woman before her, and suddenly everything came together. Her eyes widened in surprise as she gasped, "Oh, my God, you did it, didn't you? You're the one who killed my brother. He wouldn't buy into your wild story and so you killed him!"

Jean reacted instantly to Lacey's accusation. "No!" she screamed. "I would never have done anything to hurt Scott, never! He was my own flesh and blood. I gave him away because I loved him and wanted him to have everything. And it was because I wanted everything for him that he died. Can't you see that?" In desperation she looked around the room, seeking some kind of support, but all she saw was disbelief and loathing.

Jean's tone changed. She realized it was absolutely essential for her to convince those present of the veracity of her claim, or her son's murderer would go free and she would be accused of the vicious crime. She looked at Lacey again, and their eyes locked in mutual dislike.

"Your father was a liar and a cheat, Lacey Haines. He disinherited my son after promising me he would always be equal to you."

Lacey started to feel some compassion for the woman. She was quite obviously demented. "No, he didn't. My father left everything to Scott, remember? It was I who was disinherited."

A sardonic smile tilted one corner of Jean's mouth.

"Ah, but you weren't. You were always Jack's favorite, and I can prove it. There's an envelope in the briefcase on the backseat of my car." Jean was calmer now. She had proof of her story to present.

The policeman in charge dispatched an officer to bring it in. A few minutes later, Jean handed the document to Lacey, and Cherry Dolan, who had heard the call on her radio, arrived on the scene.

"What have I missed?" she asked.

Pete Cunningham briefed her while Lacey opened the envelope and looked over its contents.

"What is the document, Ms. Atwill?" Cherry asked.

"Jack Gallagher's will."

"I already have a copy," Lacey said.

"Not like this, you don't," Jean declared. "The document you have in your hand is Jack's real will. It leaves everything to you: the company, the homes, the art work, everything."

Lacey was bewildered. "I don't understand."

"The will that Tom Brennan read was a fake. Your father's will was written shortly after you divorced Steve, and only the figures were updated three months ago."

"But what about Scott?" Lacey asked.

"Jack left him only his gold Rolex watch, his diamond signet ring, and the house in Aspen. That's all. Scott was his son, and he left him virtually nothing but a recommendation to you that you pay your brother a handsome salary, but only if he returned to Gallagher's Best and made an honest effort to be a productive employee."

"I find that very hard to believe," Lacey said shaking her head.

"Who cares what you think; it's true nevertheless. When Jack got sick and Scott came back to work, I begged your father to change the will and make it more equitable, but he refused. He said he'd worked for his money, and Scott would damned well have to do the same." The tone of Jean's voice reflected the monumental anger that had long festered inside her.

"But the will? Who changed it?" Lacey asked.

"Tom Brennan and I."

"Good Lord!" Lacey exclaimed. "Did Scott know about this?"

"I told him everything right after Tom proposed changing the will. He was shocked, as you are. At first he didn't believe me either, but I showed him a copy of his true birth certificate."

"You have a birth certificate?" Lacey asked, numbed by this new turn of events.

"Yes, and Scott eventually came to realize that I was his real birth mother. His only regret was that I couldn't also tell him he had a different father. He never liked Jack, you know. He thought it would be funny if I had cuckholded him."

Appalled as she was, Lacey began to experience a glimmer of belief. "But he wasn't in on the conspiracy to cut me out of the will, was he?" Dear God, she prayed, don't let Scott be a villain too!

"At first he wanted no part of it, but when I showed him Jack's actual will cutting him off with practically nothing, he changed his mind."

"Why did Tom want the will changed?" Lacey asked.

Jean sighed and looked away. This was a tale she had never expected to tell. "Oh, he had found a buyer for the company. At least, that's what he said. Some foreign conglomerate. If the deal had been consummated, Tom would have made millions. He has a lot of stock, and he'd also have received a percentage of the deal as a finder's fee."

"And is that why the bogus will cut me out of the company entirely? Because Tom knew I would never sell, and Scott would be more than eager?" Lacey asked, realizing that Jean's version made better sense than the will that had been read on the day of her father's funeral. "But why was my brother killed then?"

"You should know. You did it." Jean's words were bitter.

"No, I didn't do it! Can't you get it through your head that I loved Scott as much as you did? And there was no need for me to kill anybody, because the night before he died, my brother and I had come to a workable agreement. We always managed to solve any problems between us, because we truly cared about each other."

Lacey stared at Jean and tried to quell the urge to shake the woman until she accepted the truth.

Cherry interrupted. "If your story is accurate, then what part did Sasha play?"

Jean's head jerked around, and she stared at the detective for a few moments before answering. She was calmer now.

"Very little. She was too busy shopping, but she did manage to find out the combination to the safe, God knows how. She was the one who took Jack's copy of the original out of the safe in his study and replaced it with the forgery. She also carried documents back and forth on a couple of occasions between Tom and me because I didn't want to be seen alone with him, nor did I wish to have too many meetings for fear someone would get suspicious."

"Whose idea was it to put all that weird business in the will about me marrying Steve again?" Lacey asked.

Jean seemed to relish answering that question. "It was Scott's idea. He said it was eccentric enough to sound believable and would get you away from the company so you couldn't interfere with the sale." Her lips twitched with disdain. "I had a terrible time trying to talk him out of his ridiculous notion to split the money with you after the company was sold."

The information was as hurtful to Lacey as Jean had hoped it would be.

Lacey looked at Cherry Dolan and said, "With Scott dead, none of this makes any sense at all."

"It would if the police did their job and arrested you for murder!" Jean declared.

Without saying a word, Cherry inclined her head toward Jean, and the uniformed officer led her away, with Cherry following close behind.

When everyone had gone, Pete stayed with Lacey in her office.

"I owe you my life, Pete," she said, sinking down into her chair and looking out the window. "I would have been on my way to the morgue if you hadn't saved me."

"It was certainly a revelation for me," he remarked, shaking his head in wonder.

"A revelation? How so?"

"It's not important," he replied, shrugging his shoulders. "Just a little mysticism."

"Tell me. I need a bit of mystical revelation at this moment," she insisted.

"Okay, well, at that single moment in time, I realized that maybe I wasn't meant to die in the air crash with my wife. Maybe I was supposed to be here in this office, today, to keep you from being killed."

Tears filled Lacey's eyes. "Thank God you were or my poor children would be without a mother. I can never repay you for what you did."

Pete shook his head. "You don't owe me anything. I owe you, as a matter of fact. Maybe now I can stop feeling guilty about being alive and get on with my life."

They looked at each other and smiled.

"You still feel like having lunch?" she asked.

"I do if you do."

"Let's go."

Pete kept a steadying hand on her arm as they walked toward the elevators. "Do you think Jean's telling the truth?" Lacey asked.

"Her story's wild enough to be true, I guess. Had you ever suspected anything before?"

"Sort of. I remember my mother pushing me to succeed, and she never did that with Scott, never. She always let him do whatever he felt like doing. When Dad would get angry with him for not finishing something, Mom would laugh it off."

"We're always tougher on those we love."

"I suppose," she remarked as they stepped into the elevator and headed upward.

Lacey continued ruminating aloud. "Mom always held me to a much higher standard than she did Scott, and there were times when I resented it, especially when I was little. I grew up thinking that Scott was her favorite because she indulged him so much, but now if what Jean says is true . . ."

"Don't jump to conclusions too fast. That sort of thing happens in a lot of families. There's a kind of boys-will-be-boys attitude, whereas girls are expected to behave perfectly."

They were seated in the private dining room before Lacey continued the discussion. "Looking back on it, I'd have to conclude that Mom didn't seem to care much what Scott did. It was my father who'd get furious when my brother messed up. It was always Dad who came down on him with both feet. Never my mother. I can't ever remember a time that she got involved in Scott's problems."

"Well, she certainly did with yours. Remember the time she gave me hell for stopping by the house when you were supposed to be writing your valedictory speech?"

"And when I was in college, she got this awful pained expression on her face if I came home with something other than an A. Which I did occasionally."

"I find that hard to believe."

They were silent while the waiter poured them each a glass of Chardonnay.

"I think I'm going to have more than a taste of this today," Pete remarked as he picked up his glass.

"Me too. Let's finish the bottle."

They sipped the wine in thoughtful silence, which Lacey finally broke.

"Funny, but now I want to accept Jean's story because it's important for me to know that Dad kept his word to me."

"Don't forget the woman's unbalanced. She came here determined to murder you."

"But there's that will. I glanced over it before the police took it away, and it looks every bit as authentic as the other one. How will we ever know which one is real?"

"It's a moot question. Your brother's dead, and you're the heir under any circumstance."

They discussed the situation at length, and dessert was being served before Lacey remembered to ask what kind of proposition Pete had wanted to discuss.

"Do you really want to talk business?" he asked.

"My father taught me that in this life you always take care of business first."

"Well, if you insist. My sources tell me that someone is acquiring an inordinate amount of Kettlecup stock. Are you positioning yourself for a hostile takeover of my company?"

Lacey looked away. "God, I hate answering this question, especially now after what you did for me today."

"So it's true? You couldn't even wait a few weeks while I assessed your offer?"

Lacey had the grace to look ashamed. "It was only a feint, Pete. I wanted to apply pressure. I'm sorry if it caused you any trouble."

There was a long silence, and Lacey spoke again. "I'm going to do something now that would not have met with my father's approval."

"What's that?"

"I'm going to give you my solemn promise that if all our negotiations break down, I will not attempt a takeover of Kettlecup. It's the least I can do."

Pete shook his head. "Shame on you. Never show your hand before all the bets are in."

Lacey toyed with her glass. "Perhaps a man wouldn't let a little notion like gratitude affect his business judgment, but I'm not a man . . ."

"Glad to hear that."

"And I have no intention of acting like one. I'll succeed at Gallagher's Best doing things my way, or I'll crash, I guess."

Pete smiled. "I have a feeling you'll make it your way. You're a special woman, Lacey."

"And a live one, thanks to you."

Pete winked at her. "I'll use that as leverage in the negotiations."

Lacey was startled. "You're actually going to consider selling?"

Pete nodded. "That's what I came to talk about today. Your maneuver worked, but the price has to be right, so prepare for a lot of hard bargaining. I intend to make our stockholders very rich. Now, I've got to be on my way. It's after four o'clock."

"I'm sorry. I shouldn't have kept you so long. You're too good a listener."

"I enjoyed every word, every bite, and every sip. We drank that whole bottle of Far Niente, you know. Thank God I've got my driver with me. I've still got to go back to the office and get some work done. I'll give you a call at home tonight in case you feel like talking some more."

Lacey shook her head. "No, not tonight. My ex-husband is still there."

Pete looked surprised. "I had no idea he was staying with you."

Lacey was quick to explain. "He's sleeping in the same room with my son, JJ. He's been nice enough to watch over us until things settle down once more. But the marriage is finished, Pete. It has been for a long time. Call me in the morning at the office and we'll set up a preliminary meeting between your people and ours."

"Good deal. Thanks for a terrific lunch."

"Thanks for my life, Pete."

43

Are you sure you want to go back to that office after what happened there yesterday?" Steve asked Lacey at breakfast the next morning.

"Why shouldn't I? Jean is in police custody undergoing psychiatric evaluation. I can't spend the rest of my life locked up and afraid."

"Well, I have a couple of errands I have to do. Okay if I use one of the cars?"

Lacey's attitude softened. Steve was staying with them out of the goodness of his heart, in spite of the severe financial problems he had back in Texas.

"Of course you can. How're you fixed for cash?"

"I'm not sure I could afford to buy gas if the car needed it."

Lacey opened her purse and pulled out her checkbook. She wrote a check for a thousand dollars and handed it to him.

"Take this to the nearest Wells Fargo bank anytime after about eleven. Marge will approve it when they call for verification."

"Thanks. I know you won't miss it, but it'll help me a lot. I need some shirts and another jacket. I came here so fast, I didn't bring much with me."

"You need clothes? Well that's not enough then. Here's my MasterCard for you to use. Keep the cash for incidentals. Save all the receipts so I can give them to Marge. Okay?"

"You shouldn't be buying me clothes," he protested, but his words lacked conviction.

"Nonsense. See you at dinner tonight."

When he was certain she had gone, Steve hurried to the telephone and placed a call to Tom Brennan's office. He asked for an appointment sometime that day, and after consulting with her employer, Tom's secretary told him to come in at two.

Wearing new jeans, shirt, and leather jacket, Steve arrived on schedule and was immediately ushered into Tom's office.

"What can I do for you, Steve?" Tom asked warily. His old friend Jack Gallagher had detested his son-in-law, and Tom suspected he'd had good reason.

Steve dropped into the chair nearest Tom's desk and said, "Have you talked to the police yet?"

"About what?"

"Forging the will. It's true, isn't it?"

"Yes, I've talked to the police, and no, it's not true. The will I read was the real one. I don't know where the hell Jean ever cooked up that other document. She's a dangerous psychopath."

Steve chuckled. "That's your story and I guess you're stuck with it."

"What the hell do you want anyway?" Tom didn't like the man's smartass attitude.

"I need a little information, and if I have to pay for your time to get it, okay by me."

"Make it fast. I'm not taking you on as a client, because you can't afford me. You're nothing but a piss-poor rancher."

Steve glared at him. "Okay, here it is. If something happens to Lacey, like if she should be arrested and convicted of Scott's murder, what kind of legal action do I need to take?"

"What the hell are you talking about?"

"Custody of the kids. Under the terms of our divorce, it's up to me to raise them. I just need to know what to do. Will the money and stuff be in their names or in mine until they get old enough to handle things themselves?"

Jack leaned across the desk, and there was a strange smile on his face as he replied, "Look, cowboy, it's your kids who're going to inherit the whole ball of wax, not you."

"I know that, asshole. But I get control of them *and* their inheritance until they're of age. That's the way the divorce is written."

Tom laughed out loud. "You're as venal as Jack said you were. Yes, it's quite true that you will become the children's physical guardian in the event that something happens to their mother, which, as things look right now, is a definite possibility. But no, you don't get control of the money, or the company, or the stock."

"Who says?"

"Look, I engineered that whole divorce. I did it exactly as Jack wanted it, and there's no way in hell he'd have given you anything. Lacy insisted on your rights as their father, but that's all you get. Oh, of course you'll be allowed to live at the mansion with your kids, and you can decide where they'll go to school, how late they can stay up, and that kind of stuff, but that's it, buddy. There's not even a provision for you to have an allowance."

Steve was not convinced. "If I'm not going to take care of their inheritance, then who the hell is?"

"The man Jack designated, with Lacey's approval."

"Who the hell's that? You?"

Tom pressed his fingertips together and smiled. "My relationship with Jack Gallagher went back a long, long way, Steve. We were good friends."

Steve got to his feet, placed both hands on Tom's desk, and leaned forward until he was nose to nose with the older man. "You shit! You've been pretending to watch out for Lacey's best interests, and you've been out to nail her every step of the way, haven't you?"

"I've only done what Jack Gallagher wanted me to do," Tom said and rang for his secretary, who responded almost instantly.

"You called, Mr. Brennan?" she asked as she opened the door.

"Show this guy out, and if he doesn't leave immediately, call the police."

Steven straightened up and snickered. "Scared you there, didn't I, asshole? Well, don't feel too sure of yourself. If Lacey goes to jail, I'll damned sure hire another firm to challenge you, got it? And for starters, my wife's hiring another lawyer to defend her."

"She's not your wife anymore, and I could care less, and you know why? Because I think she's guilty. She's going to need the best criminal attorney that money can buy to get her off. And no matter what happens to her, you can forget about getting your sticky fingers on the Gallagher money. You'll be lucky to get enough money to keep you in clean underwear."

Steve was tempted to punch the old man in the nose, but thought better of it.

"This dispute isn't over yet, Brennan," Steve declared as he strode out of the office.

44

Lacey scanned the morning report Marge had waiting for her, but none of the figures in the columns had any meaning. Her mind was too filled with the unsettling revelations of the past day to concentrate on units shipped and orders pending.

All night she had lain awake trying to fit the pieces of the puzzle together. Her brother was murdered, her father was an adulterer, her mother a vindictive child stealer. Sasha was dead, and Jean Atwill had very nearly succeeded in killing her. Who and what was behind all this?

She called Marge into her office. Maybe she could remember if anything strange had happened here while she was tending her ill father.

Marge came in and Lacey motioned her to a chair.

"Marge, you've read the account in the morning's newspaper, and you know what's going on around here. Now, I need you to search your memory. Can you remember anything, anything at all that happened here while both Dad and I weren't around?"

Marge shook her head. "I don't know exactly what you mean."

"Did Jean see somebody or bring somebody in, or did my brother?"

Marge nodded. "Yeah, I do remember something. Tom Brennan brought a group of Japanese businessmen to visit the plant one day about three months ago."

"We've had a lot of Japanese visit. Everyone who's in manufacturing, particularly of foodstuffs, wants to see how we do it."

"True, but this group was different."

"How so?" Lacey asked, her curiosity piqued.

"They stayed for two days. They not only looked at the facilities, but Tom also took them to the accounting department."

"What for?"

"I don't know."

"Did someone authorize them to look at the books?"

"The office buzz said your brother did. People get nervous about a takeover or a merger that might cost us our jobs."

"So you remember what company they were from?"

"No, but if we look through Scott's calendar, maybe we can track it down," Marge replied.

"Good idea. If we find something, it might reinforce Jean's story. About what month was this visit?" Lacey asked as she pulled open the large black leather datebook.

"Look through February."

Lacey began skimming through the pages while Marge looked over her shoulder.

"Thank goodness Jean logged every meeting and telephone call."

"She was a real stickler for detail," Marge observed.

"That's how Dad wanted her to be."

"Oh look, there, Tokoro, could that be it?" Marge asked.

Lacey shook her head. "No, the Tokoro Company furnishes us with the seaweed used to season our shrimp boil."

"Right. I forgot."

They were halfway through February when Marge thrust out her hand and put a finger on the seventeenth.

"That's it! J. Watanabe of the Mashima Company. He was head of the delegation. He spoke stilted English and had an interpreter to make sure he understood everything that was said."

"Look, he's also listed at eleven o'clock on the eighteenth, and from the appearance of the schedule he must have stayed in Scott's office for about an hour."

"He did. See, there's an asterisk beside his name. That meant that Jean held all calls while they were meeting," Marge replied and returned to her chair. "That was her system. I usually sat in for her when she was on vacation."

"According to Jean's notations here, Tom met with Scott and these men on both days. Well, that certainly reinforces Jean's story. Scott and Tom were probably setting up a buyer for the company. Mashima has the capability. Marge, call Cherry Dolan and ask her if she can arrange for me to talk to Jean this afternoon."

"Why would you want to do that?"

"She can answer a lot of questions that nobody else can. Call her."

An hour later, Marge returned to say that the arrangements were all set. "Detective Dolan had only one condition. She has to sit in on the meeting."

"Fine with me. Tell her I'll be there promptly at two."

Jean was brought into a small interrogation room, and they were joined by a young woman from the public defender's office. Jean had refused to call an attorney and so the court provided her with one. Bail had not yet been set.

She did not look like the same person Lacey had known. Her hair was combed back straight, she wore no makeup, and she was in a gray, cotton uniform. Her hands were shackled.

Before she arrived, the young attorney explained that Jean was being held in the infirmary on the advice of the court-appointed psychiatrist, who also recommended vigilance because she might be suicidal.

As Jean was being settled in a chair on the other side of a table, she glared at Lacey. "What's she doing here?"she asked the detectuve.

"She has some questions to ask you, and I figured it might be helpful to all of us if you answered them," Cherry replied.

"Jean, I'm beginning to believe there might be some truth in what you told us, but I need to know more," Lacey pleaded gently.

"Why should I do anything for you?"

"Because it might provide some extenuating circumstances when you go to trial for attempted murder," Cherry interjected.

Jean looked at the detective and said nothing, but after a short interval, she nodded.

"If it's true what you said about Scott's birth, who arranged his adoption?" Lacey asked.

Jean looked down at the table and there was silence. Finally she spoke. "Tom Brennan, and he did a slick job of it. The name of the mother on the birth certificate was Maude Lacey Gallagher."

"How did he manage that?"

"I was admitted into a small, private clinic under that name."

"What was the actual date Scott was born?"

"November 17, 1953. He was a beautiful baby."

"Was that date registered on his birth certificate?" Lacey asked, her eyes bright with interest.

"Yes."

"You mentioned you had a copy of it. Where is it?"

Jean looked over at her attorney, who nodded to her.

"There's a lockbox in the safe in Jack's office. It has my name on it. All my personal papers are in there, including my own will, leaving what little I own to Scott."

Lacey let out a long breath of air. "If it's there and it's genuine, it could prove that he wasn't Maude's child, because I was born on April 16, 1953, just seven months earlier! It's unlikely that a woman could give birth to two full-term babies that closely together. We were always told Scott's birthday was February 17, 1954."

Jean smiled, but her eyes were dead as she said in a monotone. "The clinic closed the year after Scott was born, because the doctor who owned it unexpectedly inherited a lot of money, bought a sailboat, and set out to fulfill his life's ambition to sail to Tahiti."

"My dad bought him out?"

Jean nodded. "When Scott went to apply for his first passport, it seems the clinic had conveniently failed to register his birth, and so the State Department accepted his baptism certificate, which had the February date on it."

"My Lord, my family made the church part of the conspiracy?" Lacey asked.

"Your parents didn't have Scott baptized until he was three years old, and by then a difference in a few months of age wouldn't be noticeable. Your mother and father lied to the priest. They made a big donation at the same time, which discouraged any questions."

"It's really hard to believe that my devout Catholic parents let that poor little boy live for three years without the sacrament of baptism."

"Your parents weren't saints. Scott's soul in particular wasn't very important to Maude, and Jack . . . well, the teachings of the church were subject to his interpretation."

"How many copies were there of the will?" Lacey asked.

"Jack signed three. One was kept in the safe in the office, one at home, the other in Tom's office." She laughed in scorn. "You know the more wills an attorney has in his probate file, the more secure his future."

"How did Tom manage the switch?" Lacey asked.

"It was simple. He figured out some small technicality and convinced Jack that he needed to revise the will slightly. Jack signed three copies, but of course, he only signed the last page of each one. Tom then substituted the phony pages at the front of the will and gave me one copy to put in the office safe. I didn't destroy the original will, however, as I told Tom I had.'

"Why not?" Cherry asked.

Jean shot her a withering look. "Insurance. When you're a woman all alone in the world you tend to hang on to things you might need sometime in the future. That's why I kept the original will and why I also kept Scott's birth certificate. Once the adoption was done, Jack could have fired me, you know, and I'd have been out on my ass without some corroboration."

There was a long silence, and then Jean added, speaking to Lacey, "Because you were named executor on the last page, we had to come up with something. We couldn't very well have you be executor of a will that virtually cut you off. So Tom came up with the idea of naming you executor only if for some reason Scott didn't accept the terms and become the beneficiary or if he died. Tom wanted Jack's actual signature on the document. He knew a fake with those weird terms would never hold up if you contested it, which we assumed you would."

"We? You mean Tom and you and Sasha?"

"No. I mean Tom and Scott and me. Sasha had no input whatsoever."

"Have you any idea how much Tom stood to gain by the sale of Gallagher's Best?" Cherry asked.

"I don't know how much they offered him, but he owns a lot of shares. From the beginning, he took all his fees in stock options. Jack was flattered, and so he was extremely generous. Roughly, I would guess maybe twenty million to as high as thirty or forty."

"What about you? Did you own stock in Gallagher's Best too?" Lacey asked.

"I had to take my salary in cash. It was all the income I had."

"And so you participated in this scheme solely for Scott's benefit?"

Jean nodded.

"Was Mashima the company that was going to buy Gallagher's Best?" Lacey asked.

"That was Tom's territory, not mine. All I cared about was that my son got what was due him as the Gallagher heir." She pursed her lips and refused to answer any more questions.

"Thanks for seeing me, Jean," Lacey said, getting to her feet. "You might believe that I killed Scott, but I didn't. It's as important to me as it is to you to find out who the murderer really is."

Their eyes met, and the gleam of hatred shone through Jean's once more.

"Screw you, bitch!" Jean muttered as she was led away.

45

C herry Dolan and Chuck Bascombe followed Lacey back to the office, where the safe was opened and Jean's lockbox retrieved. Lacey watched in fascination as the detectives opened it and sifted through the papers: insurance policies, the deed to her condominium, the pink slip to her car, her passport, and finally the birth certificate. After looking it over carefully, they allowed Lacey to see it. Everything was as Jean said it would be.

"Do you think it's authentic?" Lacey asked.

"Looks real, but we'll check it out as best we can," Chuck said. "Thanks for the help."

After they had gone, Lacey sat down at her desk to organize her thoughts and put the few known facts into her computer. Tom Brennan's name kept coming up again and again.

She looked at the clock. It was almost six-thirty. She had better call home and tell them not to wait dinner on her. Erin and JJ had to study.

Steve answered the telephone. He sounded agitated.

"What's wrong, Steve?" she asked.

"Are you aware that if anything happens to you, all the kids' money goes into Tom Brennan's control?" he burst out in anger.

"Yes, that's the way Dad wanted it."

"How could you let him do that? The guy's a shyster."

"I didn't have any control over it. You know my father. Who were you talking to?"

"Tom, who else?"

"When did you see him?"

"I, uh, ran into him in town this afternoon."

"Look, we'll talk this over tonight. I'll be leaving here in a few minutes."

Lacey hung up the telephone and looked at her notes again, but it didn't make sense for Tom to kill Scott, who was the linchpin in Tom's scheme. The only person now dead that it made sense for him to kill was Sasha, because Sasha was going to provide Lacey with an alibi. That was it! Cherry had asked her if she knew anyone who owned a big, black car, and Tom had bought Mamie a big, black Mercedes sedan for her sixtieth birthday. Lacey picked up the telephone to call Cherry Dolan.

The other line rang, and she took it. It was Tom Brennan.

"Listen, Lacey, I got another call from those detectives in the homocide division, and they're beginning to annoy me. I'm a busy man, and I don't have time for all these fairy tales this crackpot Jean Atwill is telling."

"You're talking about Dad's will?"

"What else? That kook's filling your head with garbage. Maude Gallagher had two children, you and Scott, and don't you believe for a minute that she didn't. You'd be dishonoring your sainted mother if you did. She was a great lady, and it's nothing but bullshit."

"She produced the original will, Tom, and she also has Scott's original birth certificate, showing him to be only seven months younger than I am."

"They're the real forgeries, damn it. God, I wish to hell your father was here so he could defend himself against this lunatic."

"How much stock do you own in Gallagher's Best?" Lacey said, changing the subject.

"God, I don't know. I don't usually pay much attention to that kind of thing. Why?"

"You don't have to tell me exactly. Give me a ballpark figure," Lacey insisted.

"Two, three hundred thousand shares, more or less. You father was generous when the company first started, and I've been accumulating more through the years, and there've been two splits. I held on, because with Jack Gallagher at the helm, I knew it was a safe bet."

While he talked, Lacey shuffled through the papers Marge had put on her desk to check the most recent quotations on the New York Stock Exchange. GBC closed at 79⅞. She multiplied eighty times 300,000. Good grief, Tom held stock worth twenty-four million dollars. He was a wealthy man. Why would he want more than that?

"Do you still feel that your investment will be safe with me running the company?" she asked.

"That's a stupid question, Lacey," Tom hedged.

"Answer me, Tom. My father never tolerated pussyfooting and neither will I."

"You're your father's daughter, Lacey. Why wouldn't I have faith in you?"

Lacey changed her tactic.

"Tom, if I should decide to sell Gallagher's Best, what kind of a price do you think it would command?"

There was a long pause on the telephone, and then Tom asked, "Seriously?"

"Absolutely. Scott's death has changed my attitude about a lot of things."

"If you didn't wait too long, I would guess you could lock the price in at ninety-two, maybe more. But you'd have to find a big enough buyer, and that could be a problem."

"Got any ideas about who might be interested in it?" she asked.

There was a brief silence on the other end of the line, and then Tom replied, "Offhand no, but I could look around."

"Give it some thought. By the way, how is that suit going on that limited partnership you were involved in. Settled it yet?" she asked.

"That casino thing? Nothin' to it. Those guys haven't got a leg to stand on. They knew what they were getting into. Look, I've got another call coming in. When can we get together so I can lay all the documents out for you to prove that Atwill woman is nothing but a sicko broad?"

"Call Marge tomorrow," Lacey snapped, and punched the telephone key, cutting him off.

She dialed Cherry's number again and the detective answered on the first ring. "What can I do for you?"

"You questioned Tom Brennan yesterday. Did he tell you anything interesting?"

"I'm not really at liberty to talk about that, Lacey. I'm sorry."

Lacey hesitated for a moment, and then she said, "Do you have any way of proving which will is the original?"

"They're checking the signatures, but if Jean's telling the truth, they're both real. It's going to be a tough call."

"By the way, I remembered something today. Tom Brennan bought his wife a Mercedes 560 SL for her sixtieth birthday."

"Is it black?" Cherry asked.

"Yes, and Tom had a good reason to kill Sasha. She knew I couldn't have killed Scott and she was ready to swear to it."

"Why wouldn't Tom want you exonerated as a suspect?"

"Because if I should die, or go to jail, he becomes the children's financial guardian. He'd control everything. And the sale of Gallagher's Best would enrich him to the tune of more than twenty-four million dollars."

"That's important information, Lacey."

"One other matter you ought to look into. Tom Brennan got involved in a heavy-duty fund-raising partnership a few years back. He convinced a few entertainment people to invest a lot of money in a casino that never got built. They lost everything, and then the IRS disallowed the investment as a tax loss. There was a big story in the newspapers about it last year, then nothing. I would guess that Tom's settling things by promising to pay them back."

"With the money he'd realize off the sale of his stock in Gallagher's Best?"

"Exactly."

"How do you know this?"

"I'm guessing. I remember my father mentioning that Tom could be disbarred if all the facts were known."

"How come you didn't tell us about this sooner?"

"My mind was on other things. Call the SEC. I'm sure they've got a file on it. Good night." Lacey put down the telephone and shut off her computer. It was time to go home.

46

L acey was at her desk the next morning when Marge announced that Cherry Dolan was on the telephone.

"Did you check out Tom's car?" Lacey asked.

"It seems that he parked it at the airport early on Saturday morning. When he returned from Washington, D.C., it was gone. Stolen."

"Well, that was certainly inconvenient."

"For us but not for him. It's probably already been dismantled at one of the bandit chop shops and the parts are being sold off as we speak."

"Now what are you going to do?"

"We've circumscribed a broad area that we're checking on a place-by-place basis. We've reproduced pictures of Sasha and Brennan, and if he did have a meeting with her on the night she was killed, maybe somebody will remember seeing them together. She was good-looking enough to draw attention. We're also checking the various places she frequented, according to the date book we found in her room."

"That sounds like a big job. There are hundreds of restaurants or hotels where they might have met," Lacey observed.

"Not as many as you might think. Not all restaurants stay open past midnight. We might not have put such an extensive effort into it if the car hadn't conveniently disappeared and if Jean Atwill hadn't implicated Brennan as a conspirator."

"Have you considered the possibility that Scott went back to his bedroom, told Sasha that he and I had come to an agreement about the money, and she called Tom and told him, either in the middle of the night or early the next morning?" Lacey asked.

"Then Sasha let Tom in and went out on her run?" Cherry asked.

Lacey said yes, but Cherry disagreed.

"We checked all the outgoing calls from the telephones in the house. There weren't any, and Sasha wouldn't have had time to go outside the grounds and call. Besides the camera at the gate did not register her leaving. And one other thing pretty well exonerates Brennan of Scott's murder."

"What's that?"

"He offered the information that he received a speeding ticket that morning. I checked it out. Even talked to the CHP officer involved. He was still wrangling with Tom at the time Scott's body was discovered."

"Well, that settles that, doesn't it?" Lacey said. "Thanks for the information, but I'm more confused now than ever."

As Lacey put down the telephone, Marge rang to tell her Pete Cunningham was calling.

"Pete, I'd hoped you'd call me yesterday."

"Sorry, we had an emergency here at our main plant. One of the gas pipes burst and caused an explosion. Thank God nobody was hurt seriously, but we've had to shut down for a couple of days to make repairs."

"Is there anything I can do to help?"

"Talk to me for a few minutes and let me be comforted by the sound of your voice."

They chatted for ten minutes or so, and in spite of the stress she was under, Lacey could feel herself smiling and enjoying it thoroughly. Pete Cunningham had walked out of her life twenty years ago, and then he had walked back in, and it seemed as if the intervening time had never happened. They were still good friends.

He was called away suddenly, and they had to end their little talk, but for a long time after she had hung up, she sat at her desk smiling. Marge found her thus.

"You looked pleased, Lacey. Want to share the good news?"

Snapping out of her reverie, Lacey became businesslike again. "No, Marge. This stupid grin on my face is strictly personal."

"Mr. Cunningham is a terrific-looking guy. Have you known him long?"

Lacey nodded. "He was my boyfriend in high school. Then we went our separate ways. Call my car for me, will you? I'm going home early today. You can go too."

Lacey was anxious to get home and be with her children. It was already getting dark outside, and even though they were being closely watched, she was uncomfortable when they were out of her sight. She looked with regret at the stack of papers she needed to read, thought momentarily of taking them with her but resisted the impulse. No, she was Lacey, not Jack. She had a life other than Gallagher's Best. She picked up her handbag and left the office. Tomorrow was another day.

She was in the limousine when the sudden ringing of the car telephone startled her. She reached over and picked it up, but before she could answer a sudden inspiration sent her thoughts reeling. That was it! That was the missing information!

"Hello, hello . . ." She heard a voice calling her to attention.

"Hello, Steve," she answered, recognizing her former husband's voice.

"Are you okay?" he asked. "I called the office and Marge told me you had left early."

"Yes. Are the children home yet?"

"We're not at home. We're at the Javalane's bowling alley. Halfway through our first game. Want to join us?"

"No, this is a school night, and they should be doing their homework," she said, with a trace of annoyance in her voice.

"Take it easy, will you, honey? Don't lay your compulsions on your kids. Now, come on over and bowl a game with us."

Lacey looked down at the short tight skirt she was wearing and realized there was no possibility of her doing anything of the kind.

"I can't. Look, bowl only one game and then come home. I want them to have an early dinner tonight."

"You got it, baby. We'll hustle."

Before he could hang up, Lacey had another worrisome thought. "Steve, did you have one of the armed drivers take you there?"

"Of course not. I can take care of my own kids. Relax, will you?" he replied and hung up on her.

Lacey sat looking at the telephone for a moment of uninterrupted irritation. The she pulled her small telephone book out of her briefcase and dialed Cherry Dolan's number. Chuck took the call.

"This is Lacey Gallagher. I wanted to remind Cherry to check the records of our car phones. They're on a separate line."

"Good thinking. How many do you have?"

"There's one in the limo, the Lincoln, the Ferrari, the station wagon, and the Mercedes that Sasha's body was found in."

"And they were all in your garage the night of your brother's death?"

"Yes, they were." Then reading from her directory, she gave him the telephone numbers of each car.

"I think they're all on the same cellular service, and please let me know what you've found out."

"Will do."

Lacey put down the telephone and thought again of Tom Brennan. He might not be Scott's murderer, but he sure as hell had tried to stab her in the back.

47

Gordon met Lacey at the door when she arrived home.

"Miss Mary is on the telephone, ma'am."

"Thanks, Gordon. I'll take the call in the library," Lacey replied, striding across the marble-floored entryway.

"Hi, Mary, how are things going? Are you feeling better?" Lacey asked when she picked up the phone.

"Yes, I am," Mary replied. "Are you busy this evening? I really need to talk to you."

"I always have time for you. Is it something we can discuss on the telephone?" she asked, hoping the answer would be in the affirmative.

"No, no, it really isn't, but if you're busy, it certainly can wait."

"Why don't you come over for dinner tomorrow evening? The children would love to see you, and I know that Steve would too."

Mary agreed that would be fine, and Lacey said she'd send Salvador to pick her up at seven.

"Lacey, will there be time for us to talk alone tomorrow night?"

"Of course, dear. After dinner, I'll send everyone to bed, and we'll have a nice little chat all by ourselves. See you then."

After hanging up, Lacey took one cursory glance at the mail on the hall table and decided it could wait. She hastened upstairs, eager to get out of her pantyhose and high-heeled shoes and into a pair of comfortable slacks and loafers. Now that she was the head of this household, there would be no getting all gussied up for dinner as her mother and father had done.

Clad only in her bra and lace bikini underpants, she was standing in her large walk-in closet when she had the feeling that someone was watching her. She whirled around and saw Steve looking at her. She grabbed a robe off the hanger and held it in front of herself.

He laughed. "Is there something there I haven't seen before?"

"Don't ever walk in on me like that again! We're not married anymore."

"It's the last decade of the twentieth century, Lacey. Get with it. People don't think like you do anymore. Besides, I want to talk to you about something."

202

"It will have to wait until I'm dressed." She would have walked away, but he was blocking the doorway and she didn't want to try to push past him. There was an expression on his face that reminded her of too many other times in their marriage.

Steve was not fazed by her annoyance, and he moved his body so as to block the doorway completely. It was a gesture intended to indimidate her but she would not allow it. Not anymore.

"Get out of my closet, Steve. Now!"

Steve stood there for a moment, and then apparently decided not to pursue the subject. He turned around and walked away. "See you downstairs," he called over his shoulder.

Later at the dinner table, Steve and JJ dominated the conversation talking about their bowling excursion. Lacey noted that Erin seemed unusually subdued.

"You don't look too happy, honey," Lacey said.

"She's pissed because Dad wouldn't let her go to Marcia Winfield's house after school," JJ declared.

"Don't use that kind of language, JJ," Lacey admonished her son. "You had plans to go to Marcia's today?" she asked her daughter.

Erin nodded. "We were going to work on our model city for social sciences. Marcia's dad's an architect, and he brought all kinds of stuff home for us to use, little boxes and trees and things."

"Why didn't you let her go?" Lacey asked, turning to Steve.

"I wanted her to go bowling with JJ and me. I haven't had much of a chance to do things with my kids lately."

"Can you work on your city tomorrow, Erin?" Lacey asked.

Her daughter shook her head. "Marcia's going skiing with her family at Aspen for a week, and we have to be finished by a week from Monday."

"Well, I'll call Marcia's mother and see what I can work out," she said, getting up from the table.

"That'd be great, Mom. Marcia's going to stay up all night to finish it if she has to."

Within a few minutes, she was back.

"Get your things together, Erin. Ruth invited you to spend the night. She said that as long as Marcia was working, you might as well be too. I'll have Salvador drive you."

Erin jumped up from the table and was about to dash out when Steve objected. "Now wait a minute!" he said. Then turning to Lacey, "You're not actually going to let her sleep in somebody else's house tonight without security guards around? Are you crazy? There've been two murders in this family!"

Erin looked anxiously at her mother, her eyes pleading with her, and Lacey understood how she felt.

"Go on upstairs and get ready, Erin."

The young girl flew out the dining room doorway and up the stairs, and Steve was livid.

"Thanks a lot, Lacey. You've always been an expert at making me look like a wimp in front of the kids."

Lacey ignored him and pressed the button on the floor under her chair. Gordon appeared immediately.

"Gordon, ask Salvador to get out the limo and take Erin to the Winfield house over on Lariat. Tell him to see her to the door and make sure she's inside before he leaves."

Lacey picked up her spoon and began to eat her coupe of fresh fruit. She turned her gaze to her son and asked, "Do you have any homework tonight, JJ?"

"I have to finish reading a book, that's all."

"Then as soon as you finish your dessert, get on it," she said in a tone that her son knew he'd better obey.

When JJ was gone and they were alone, Lacey went on the offense.

"I've been raising these children for a long time with no help from you. You can't come in here and change things around to suit yourself."

"They need a little fun in their lives." Steve retorted.

"The kind of fun they have should be their choice, not yours. Erin doesn't even like to bowl."

Steve threw his napkin down on the table in disgust and pushed his chair back.

"Yeah, yeah, I know. It's a blue-collar sport. You want her to ride or play golf or tennis, that's your idea of fun, isn't it?"

Lacey got up from the table.

"Good night, Steve. I have work to do."

"Since Erin's going away, you'll be sleeping alone tonight," he remarked, lowering his voice to an insinuating whisper and running his fingertips lightly up her arm.

She pulled away from him.

"You have to stay with JJ, Steve. Good night."

48

Lacey slept restlessly that night. Not only was she worried about Erin's being away from home, but she was also besieged by what she called her "demons in the night," the daytime worries that assumed larger and more threatening proportions after the lights were turned out.

When the first sliver of dawn cracked the horizon, she got out of bed, pulled on a sweatsuit, a heavy pair of athletic socks, and her old running shoes. She tied a band around her forehead, punched the code numbers in the security system, and hurried down the stairs. Before going out the front door, however, she armed the system again. As she took off down the flagstone driveway, she noted cynically that she had managed to elude the so-called security guards to whom she was paying an enormous amount of money to keep watch on the house.

Although a small voice inside her head told her she was taking a risk being out alone in these early hours of dawn, she dismissed it. If she had an enemy out there, she'd almost welcome an appearance from him or her or them so that at least she would know who it was.

Lacey was walking faster now. By the time she reached the road that curved down toward the gate she should be warmed up enough to break into a slow jog, although she was already feeling her heart rate escalate. She had been in decent shape during the months she cared for her father, because jogging and swimming had been the only respite she allowed herself. She picked up the pace, the soles of her shoes hitting the pavement harder.

She ran and she ran, and as she fought the fatigue and the breathlessness, the effort emasculated her demons, and she felt better. She cut from the paved road to the wide grassy area that ran parallel to the sea. Normally, she would have gone through the gate and followed the path down to the seawall, but she did not want to push her body too hard. She had to reserve some of her energy to deal with the problems of the day, and there would probably be plenty of those.

She was passing the tennis court, which had been sunken to protect it from the prevailing ocean breeze, when she was startled by a figure walking toward her. She could see immediately that the man had a gun in his hand, and she called out to him.

"It's me, Lacey!"

The man waited for her to get near enough so that he could identify her.

"How did you get out here without me knowing about it?" the security guard asked in annoyance.

Lacey did not slow her pace as she called out in passing, "I just walked out the door, Arnold. Where in the hell were you?"

She was long past him when he answered, "I was out here checking the grounds to make sure everything was secure. Christ, I could have shot you! Where was Henry?"

"Find the hell out!" she called back.

It was only during her final approach to the house, after Lacey had slowed her pace, that she allowed herself to remember the encounter with Steve the night before. It had reminded her of a lot of things about their relationship that had faded from her memory.

Henry, the other nighttime security guard, was standing at the front door waiting for her.

"How did you get out of the house, Miss Gallagher?"

"I disarmed the security system from my bedroom, walked down the front stairs, and rearmed the perimeter on my way out. Where were you?" she asked, breathing hard.

"I was in the kitchen fixing a pot of coffee for Arnold and me. Sorry, ma'am."

"No harm done, none intended," she snapped and headed up the stairs.

By the time she had showered and dressed, it was after seven. She left her room, and she could hear Steve and JJ talking in their bedroom. She knocked on their door.

"Get going, JJ. I'll drop you off at school on my way to the office."

The door opened, and Steve appeared fully dressed in a new suit and tie.

"Where are you going?" she asked.

"Thought I'd go to the office with you this morning for a while. Okay?" he asked, giving her a light kiss on the cheek.

"I'm going to be awfully busy today, Steve," she hedged, wondering what he had in mind.

"That's okay. I'll meander around for a while and look the place over, then I'll take off. I thought I might drive by myself. Which car should I take?"

"Take the Testarossa and you can drop me off at school," JJ said, appearing behind him.

"No way!" Lacey snapped. "That car is going back to the dealer. Your Uncle Scott leased it temporarily to try it out, and now that he's gone, we are not going to keep that thing. You can take the Rolls or the Lincoln, Steve, but you, young man, are going in the limo with me. That's the rule."

JJ knew better than to try to argue with his mother, but he did grumble under his breath, "Sure, sure, Erin goes to spend the night with a friend, but I can't even have one last ride in the neatest car in town."

Lacey heard every word and was reminded of her vows to keep life normal, and so she relented.

"All right, you can take him to school in the Testarossa, Steve, but be careful, okay? Come on, let's have breakfast together."

Lacey arrived at the office at eight-thirty, and the place was humming with activity. Before she could settle down to work, she checked to make sure the children had arrived at school safely.

Five minutes later, Marge called on the intercom.

"Your ex-husband's here. Should I send him in?"

"Tell him to look around for a while and come back in half an hour. Show him where the new test kitchen is."

Lacey felt a little guilty about her reluctance to have him at Gallagher's Best. Was it possible she was making him feel as unwelcome as her father had done all those years ago? He had left everything to be here for her and the children, and she was treating him like some kind of interloper. She pressed down the intercom button.

"Send Steve in now. I want to talk to him."

Within moments, Steve was inside the door.

"Hey, I'm sorry, babe. I don't want to mess up your schedule."

"No problem, Steve. Let me show you on the map where I think you should go. A lot of exciting things have happened since you quit working here. You always said we could improve on our technology, and we have. Look, start here . . ."

For fifteen minutes, she explained the changes, and when she finished talking, Steve shook his head.

"Gosh, this could take all day and I've got a few things I need to do in Los Angeles. I've made an appointment to see a guy at First Consolidated Bank about renewing the loan on the ranch."

"That's not going to be easy. Would you like for me to cosign a loan, Steve?" she asked in a burst of generosity tinged with guilt.

"I really don't want . . . ," he began, but she could see his eyes light with pleasure.

"It's no problem. Really. Take out whatever kind of a loan you need to keep things going."

Steve sat down on the edge of her desk and grinned.

"You know, sometimes I think you're just like your dad, and then you turn around and do something warm and generous like this, and you're Lacey again, the beautiful, smart, and affectionate woman I fell in love with."

Lacey realized in that moment that she now had the means at her disposal to solve the problem of Steve. She didn't have to take him back into her life to make him happy. She could simply give him the money he needed to make his dreams come true. But not too fast, the genes that came from Jack Gallagher warned her. A little at a time. No one was ever grateful for gifts that came too easily.

"That's sweet of you to say that, Steve. Now, the light on my intercom has been lit for some time. My first appointment is waiting. Have your banker call me."

"Any restrictions on the amount?" Steve asked.

"Within reason," Lacey replied.

"What's that?"

"Use your own good judgment, Steve. You know what you need to keep the ranch on an even keel."

"You've got a deal."

"So, are you going to take the tour first?" Lacey asked.

"I don't think so. I better sharpen my pencil and figure out some things."

"Another time, then. See you at dinner. Mary's going to join us this evening."

"I'll be there. And thanks for the vote of confidence, babe."

As he walked out the door, Lacey muttered to herself, "Don't call me 'babe.' "

★★ 49 ★★

It was well past four in the afternoon when Lacey received a call from Steve.

"Hi, how did everything go?" she asked, more as an opening to the conversation than out of any real curiosity. Years ago she had shut the ranch out of her mind, and she still had little or no interest in it. The time she had spent there was now only a dim, disagreeable memory.

"Great. Nothing like having the Gallagher name to open doors. I had bankers chasing me trying to hand me money. The papers will be all drawn up and ready for our signatures by day after tomorrow," he replied.

"Terrific. How much are you borrowing?"

"Seventeen million. I hope that's not too much. You said you'd go along with whatever I wanted to do," Steve replied, his tone defensive.

"Seventeen million! I had no idea you wanted that kind of money."

"What are you getting so excited about? It's only a loan. I fully intend to pay it back when the ranch starts producing the way it should."

"That ranch isn't worth that kind of investment." Lacey's voice was cold.

"You sound like your father," Steve said, controlling his anger. "That ranch has a lot of potential. If your father had given us the kind of backing that we needed when we first started it, I wouldn't have to crawl on my knees for help from anybody now. The land alone is worth double the price I paid."

Lacey was still not convinced. "But seventeen million! What will you do with all that money?"

"I've got a lot of debt to pay back; then there's the back taxes. I need to wipe out the mortages, build a decent house and bunkhouses for the hands, payroll for ten to fifteen new employees, stock, feed, a new tractor, a new truck—the old one is a piece of junk—"

Lacey interrupted. "How much debt have you got?"

"In round numbers, maybe two hundred and sixty-three thousand, plus the mortgage and the second."

Lacey had been jotting down figures. She had lived on the ranch and kept the books, so she could estimate what the costs would be for the things he needed. She began punching numbers into her calculator.

"So what do you think?" Steve prodded her.

"How much of a second did you take out?"

"Three hundred and seventy-five thousand," he replied, "but I did that four years ago, and the lump payment is due in six months. I'm also in arrears on the interest."

Lacey let out a sigh and shook her head. Steve had always been so damned cavalier about paying bills on time. She hit the total and pulled the paper out of the calculator. After studying it for a few minutes, she said, "Steve, you can get by with two and a half million, but I'll cosign for five. That's it."

"Oh, so now you want to negotiate the amount of help you're willing to give me," he said sarcastically. "Your tune sure has changed since this morning. You could at least be generous enough to guarantee ten, since you were so eager and willing to hand over thirty million to that bitch your brother married. After all, I'm the father of your children. Even if we are divorced, we're still part of the same family. You mean a lot to me. I wouldn't be here if I didn't care about you and Erin and JJ."

Lacey felt uncomfortable. Steve was trying to make her feel guilty for having money when he had nothing. It had worked for him before, and apparently it was going to work for him again.

"Steve, the telephone is no way for us to discuss this matter. After dinner, we'll talk—"

"Your old buddy Mary's coming tonight. Had you forgotten?"

"No, I haven't, but she won't stay late."

"Well, I'm not going to be there. George Swope invited me to dinner at the Jonathan Club."

"How do you know George Swope?" Lacey asked in surprise.

"The loan officer took me into the president's office to meet him. He's a nice guy. He was raised on a ranch and we got along great. So I may be late tonight."

"Then we'll discuss this when you get home."

"So your answer is no? You're going to make me look very foolish having to go back and tell them that my wife won't guarantee me all the money I need. Think about it overnight, will you? And give me a chance to show you all the figures on paper."

"We'll talk about it tomorrow," Lacey said, not committing herself to anything. "Are JJ and Erin home from school yet?"

"They're here. We're all going for a swim together now. I'm leaving at six-thirty. Will you be home by then?"

"Probably. 'Bye."

Lacey tried to concentrate on the reports on her desk, but she could not, because she was still angry. Steve's attitude should not have come as a surprise to her. He had always expected a great deal from her family, and now she wondered if moving to the ranch hadn't been as much her fault as it was his. When they were married, she had hated the fact that he seemed always to be looking for some kind of handout, and she wanted him to step out and do something on his own. Deep down, she wanted her husband to be independent of her father, and she had detested it when Steve bad-mouthed Jack for not giving him everything he asked for. Now, here she was being put in the awkward position of denying Steve money he wanted, just as her father had been.

She slammed the papers down on her desk and pushed her chair back. She pressed the intercom button and told Marge to go home. It was time to quit for the day.

Before Marge left the office, she stuck her head in to say good night.

"Anything you need?" her secretary asked.

"No. Have you figured out Jean's filing system yet?"

"Not completely. It's unique, that's for sure."

"Keep at it, and pretty soon you'll find out where all the treasure is buried. See you in the morning."

"Salvador's on his way to pick you up, but he's stuck in traffic. He said he should be here by five. G'night now."

When she was alone again, Lacey went into her bathroom to freshen up. She heard a voice calling her name, and she opened the door to see who it was.

"Hi. I had to attend a meeting in Long Beach this afternoon, and I thought I'd buzz over here and see if you were still around," Pete Cunningham greeted her.

"Pete! What a nice surprise," Lacey exclaimed, crossing the room to greet him. "It's a good thing my driver got stuck in traffic or I'd have been gone."

Pete took her hands in his and leaned down to give her a kiss on the cheek. It took her by surprise but she was pleased.

"Any chance you could get away and have dinner with me tonight?" he asked. "We've got a lot to talk about."

"I'd love to, but Scott's first wife is coming to my house. She called yesterday and said she needed to talk."

"I should have known you'd be busy. By the way, how many ex-wives did Scott accumulate?"

Lacey laughed. "He was married three times."

"Only three? From the way he carried on in high school, I expected him to match Bluebeard's record or not get married at all. As I recall he never went steady with less than five girls at once."

"Can I fix you a drink?" she asked.

"A Coke would be great. I've got to drive home, and I need something to keep me awake. I haven't slept much since the explosion."

"When will you be on line again?" Lacey asked, filling two glasses with ice and opening a can of soda.

"Six o'clock tomorrow morning, if everything goes right, which it never does."

Lacey handed him his glass and sat down on the couch beside him.

"Well, good luck and cheers," she said, clinking her glass against his.

They looked at each other for a moment, and Lacey found herself unable to hold her gaze into his. She looked down, and there was a long silence.

"Do you sometimes have the feeling that the last twenty years didn't happen, and we're back in high school?" Pete asked.

Lacey nodded. "Funny you should say that, because I've had the same feelings. I thought if we ever met again, we'd be strangers, but we're not. Next to my family, you were the best friend I ever had, Pete. I thought we'd always be together. Why weren't we?"

Pete shook his head. "I planned to graduate from Harvard and come back to California and sweep you off your feet. I was devastated when my mother wrote that she'd been invited to your wedding. It never once occurred to me that you'd get married before you finished college. You were so ambitious."

"You went away and never once wrote or called me."

"I was angry with you. And maybe a little jealous," he remarked with a sigh.

"Jealous?"

"Yep, jealous. I hated the relationship you had with Scott. You were always looking out for him, putting his needs and concerns way above your own and certainly above mine. I figured you owed me an apology for ruining the senior prom. I still do."

Lacey smiled and reached over and touched his hand.

"I'm sorry, Pete. It was stupid of me, and I apologize. I hurt you, and I hurt myself, and I also hurt my brother. I thought I was being a good sister. I was wrong on all counts. Will you forgive me—finally?"

Pete grinned. "Apology accepted, and I forgave you years ago. I was too full of pride to tell you, and then suddenly you were gone."

"When did you get married, Pete? And who was she?"

"I didn't get married until ten years ago. Melanie was a terrific lady who was an associate professor of English literature at Harvard. I stayed there, you know. Got my Ph.D. in industrial management and taught. When Melanie died in a plane crash, I decided to leave the academic life and see if I could cut it in the world I was teaching kids to conquer. I was lucky enough to land at Kettlecup, and I loved it. I started at the top and stayed there. I tried out all the theories I'd taught, and they worked. In three years we went from a sixty-million-dollar-a-year company to three hundred million. Didn't you read about me in *Fortune* magazine two months ago?"

Lacey listened to his story and was thrilled by it. She had always considered Pete to be one of the brightest people she'd ever known. "No, I didn't, but I promise to get a copy of the edition and memorize it. No wonder you don't want to be swallowed up by Gallagher's."

"My board of directors thinks I'm the second coming, and so when I nixed the offer, they supported me. They're really happy, however, that I'm changing my mind."

Lacey ran her finger around the edge of the glass while she thought about her answer.

"So am I."

"It's going to put me out of a job. You know that don't you?"

"You most certainly will not be out of a job! You'll have as much freedom and control over Kettlecup as you have now, except you'll have a different board of directors to answer to."

"But I'll be one of your employees. You'll be the boss. I don't think I can live with that arrangement."

When she didn't answer, Pete continued. "Let's table the discussion for now, okay?"

Lacey was relieved, and she had the grace to admit it.

"That's fine with me. If everything goes as planned, I should have my ex-husband on his way back to Texas in a day or two. I'll invite you over for dinner then. I'd like you to get to know Erin and JJ."

"I'll be available. How about riding home with me? I'm going your way."

"That would be great. I'll call Salvador and tell him to turn around and go home without me."

50

I t was the most relaxed, enjoyable dinner Lacey had had since the day her father fell into his final decline. Mary arrived looking beautiful and radiantly happy. The cook had prepared a simple dinner of broiled salmon with fresh carrots and baked potatoes, a lightly dressed green salad, and for dessert they had *fraises des bois,* tiny sweet wild strawberries imported from France, with whipped cream. When Mary passed on cappuccino and asked for herbal tea instead, Lacey expressed her surprise.

"Mary, how come? You were the one who talked me into having that espresso machine installed in the kitchen."

"I'm off it for a while. I can't have any caffeine, and nowadays, coffee gives me heartburn."

"Are you feeling all right, Aunt Mary?" Erin asked.

"Right now I feel perfectly marvelous," Mary replied, and the glow on her face put everyone's fears to rest.

When dinner was over, Lacey took Mary into the library so they could talk privately.

"Where's Steve tonight?" Mary asked when they were settled on the sofa in front of the fire.

"He's having dinner with a president of a bank that's agreed to loan him seventeen million dollars." Lacey had always found it easy to confide in Mary.

"Who in their right mind would lend Steve Haines that much money?"

"Anybody, I suppose. As long as I cosign the note," Lacey replied sardonically.

Mary was appalled. "You're not going to do it?"

"Not for that much. I agreed to five, but now he's angling for ten."

"You don't owe that man a cent, Lacey."

"You never liked Steve, did you?"

"He's all right, I suppose. He's certainly handsome enough," Mary remarked, reluctant to respond to the question.

"He's been quite nice since Scott's death. It's been comforting having him here, although I'm about ready for him to go back to Texas."

"It's pretty intimidating to think that somebody sneaked into

214

house and killed a big, strong man like Scott without anybody hearing a thing," Mary declared. "Are you all right now?"

"Not really all right, but better," Lacey responded. "Life can never be good again until we know for certain who killed my brother. So, let's talk about you. What's new and exciting in your life? Any new commissions?"

Mary smiled. "There is something very exciting in my life, Lacey. Penny knows about it, and although I intended to wait until your life was a little less complicated, she insisted that I tell you now."

"Good news has been in short supply around here," Lacey replied. "So tell me."

"Well, I'm pregnant. The baby is due in about six months."

Lacey was astounded. To her knowledge, Mary had not had even a single date since her divorce from Scott.

"Why . . . that's wonderful . . . it's amazing . . . who's the father . . . or is that too personal . . ."

"It's not too personal—Lacey there's not a question that's too personal for you to ask—and it's Scott. You're going to be an aunt."

"Scott!?" Lacey squealed in astonishment. "You were seeing Scott, and I didn't know?"

Mary nodded happily, and Lacey demanded she tell her everything. Mary told the story, exactly as she had told it to Penny. Lacey listened, transfixed and awed by her quiet little Catholic friend's audacity.

"And this is what you wanted from my brother—a baby?" Lacey asked when she had finished.

"I figured he owed me that. It might have been a sin to lie to him about my illness, but in the eyes of the church, it was no sin for me to have sex with him. I still considered him to be my husband," Mary declared defensively.

Lacey reached across and covered her friend's hand with her own.

"Mary, I can't tell you how happy I am that you'll be giving us all Scott's child. Have you any idea how much that means to me to know that something of him will have survived? It's just the greatest gift to me, to Erin and JJ—and even to Jean Atwill. Do you realize she's going to be a grandmother?"

"I know. Penny and I talked that over. I don't want her ever to know."

"Are you sure? She's had so little in her life to make her happy."

"She gave away her child, and she tried to kill you. How can I feel kindly toward her?"

"Scott knew about her. She told him."

"Was he upset about it?" Mary asked.

"If you can believe what Jean says, he accepted it, but he must have been devastated when she told him. I know I would have been, but Scott was, well, you know, he was different."

Mary looked down at her hands thoughtfully and said, "He was very different from you, Lacey. I told him about the baby the night before he was killed. He offered to divorce Sasha and marry me again, but I knew he didn't really mean it. He had such a short attention span."

"Maybe having a baby of his own might have changed him, Mary. Scott would have been a loving father."

The two friends talked until late in the evening. And when it was time for Mary to go home, they embraced each other warmly.

"Mary, I was so happy when Scott married you. You became part of our family and you always will be."

"I was worried you might want proof that it was Scott's baby."

Lacey shushed her. "Don't even say it. Your word is enough for me. And the baby is a Gallagher. Now, what would you say about coming here to live? We have lots of room and a full staff to take care of you."

Mary shook her head. "Thank you, Lacey, but that won't be necessary. I can take care of myself."

"Then I insist on sending you a full-time housekeeper and cook. I'll have Gordon hire someone right away."

Mary tried to protest, but Lacey would not be dissuaded. "You need someone. I know you've told me that having lupus won't interfere with your pregnancy, but it's only reasonable that you have help."

"Penny's been great. She might feel that she's being replaced."

"She'll have to cope with it."

"One thing I didn't mention, Lacey. If anything happens to me, I want Penny to have the baby. I hope that's all right with you."

Lacey hugged her. "Nothing's going to happen to you, my friend. I won't let it." The tone of her voice was so assured and determined that even Mary believed her.

Later, as Lacey was getting ready for bed, she actually caught herself humming. Life had been such a bitch lately that it felt wonderful to have something to be happy about.

Erin, who was already in bed but not yet asleep, heard her mother and called out, "What are you singing about, Mom?"

Lacey appeared at the door to her bathroom wearing her blue silk nightgown and peignoir.

"Mary had some great news, honey. She's pregnant with Scott's child. Can you believe it?"

Erin smirked, "Yeah, I believe it all right. I saw them going into the pool house together a couple of times."

Lacey was startled by her daughter's worldliness.

"You did? How come you never told me?"

Erin laughed. "I didn't think it was any of my business . . . or yours."

"Well, thanks a lot. Has there been anything else going on around this house that you know and I don't?"

Instead of laughing off the question, however, Erin's manner turned quite serious.

"Funny you should ask, Mom. Are you aware that Dad talks long-distance to a woman in Texas every single night?"

"How do you know that?"

"JJ told me. He pretends to go to sleep and then he listens."

"JJ shouldn't spy on his father," Lacey said flatly, but she was curious.

"I know, and he wouldn't if Dad weren't so secretive."

"Look, your father and I are divorced, he has every right . . . ," Lacey protested.

"When he thinks JJ's asleep," Erin forged ahead with determination, "he dials a long-distance number. JJ can tell by the number of buttons he pushes. He lets it ring once and hangs up. A minute later, line three, you know the call-out line that nobody calls in on, well it rings, but he picks it up before anybody can hear it. He talks to her for half an hour or more. JJ and I figured he did it so the calls wouldn't show up on your bill."

"How do you know it's a her?"

"JJ's sure it is, because he says that sometimes they talk about sex."

"Oh my God!" Lacey exclaimed, shocked that JJ's father would be so careless.

"Don't get yourself in a dither, Mom, JJ knows all about the birds and the bees. Besides, he thinks Dad's married to the woman."

"What!?" Lacey exclaimed. "What makes him think that?"

"He says he just sort of put two and two together. JJ's kind of upset about it. He thinks that if Dad really does have a wife, it's mean not to tell us about it."

Lacey was now sitting on the bed listening to her daughter with fascination.

"JJ wouldn't make this up," Lacey observed.

"Of course not. You know JJ," Erin replied, "I was surprised when he told me he was spying on Dad. You know how crazy he's always been about him."

The thought that JJ was suspicious of his own father sickened Lacey, and she felt she needed to initiate some damage control.

"Erin, I want you to talk to JJ and tell him to stop eavesdropping on his father. I can't tell him without violating your confidence."

She was interrupted by Erin, who said, "Forget that, Mom. JJ told me to tell you. He wants you to know what's going on. He loves Dad, but he's afraid he might hurt your feelings. Go talk to him before Dad gets home,"Erin urged.

Lacey got to her feet. She had been acting as both mother and father to her children for so long that she was not at all reluctant to talk frankly with either of them.

JJ was lying in his bed reading with a book propped up on his stomach. He looked up and grinned when she opened the door.

"Hi, Mom. Come on in. When I heard the knob turning I thought it was Dad coming home."

Lacey moved into the room and sat down on the bed.

"What are you reading?" she asked.

"*The Turn of the Screw* by Henry James. I thought I'd be bored but it's kind of neat."

"It's scarey, don't you think?" Lacey asked, smiling at her son. JJ was the kindest, most candid person she had ever known. She hoped the recent tragedies would not change him.

"Not really," he replied. "Not for somebody who's seen as many horror movies as I have."

"Mary gave me some news tonight that I wanted to share with you. It's not to be broadcast, understand? It's strictly a family matter," Lacey began.

"What's up?"

"Mary's pregnant with Scott's child."

JJ grinned and said, "Oh ho, so that's what they were doing in the pool house!"

"Yes, I suppose so," Lacey said with a sigh, and then she plunged into her other mission. "And what's this I hear about your listening in on your father's telephone calls late at night?"

JJ looked down at his book. "I didn't mean to, Mom. The first time it was an accident, but I heard things that made me want to listen more."

"You're invading his privacy, JJ," she began, but her son was swift to defend himself.

"He makes me want to puke! He's lying to us all. He's married, and he keeps telling his . . . wife"—JJ spit out the word as if it were an obscenity—"that as soon as he gets the money, he'll be coming home. He has no intention of staying with us!"

Lacey reached over and stroked her son's cheek.

"He never said he would, sweetie. Your father has a life of his own in Texas. He's only staying because he feels that we need him. It would have been extremely frightening for us if we'd been alone."

"He's not doing it for us, he's doing it for himself!" JJ snapped. "He's only staying so he can get a lot of money out of you. That's why he's here!"

Lacey heard the pain in her son's voice, and she was dismayed. It was a moment of truth that all children of wealth must eventually face when they first realize they are loved not for themselves but for their money. It was loathsome, Lacey thought, that JJ's first betrayal would be by his own father.

"You've only heard one side of the conversation, JJ. Don't judge your father by a half truth," she warned, and then the door was opened and Steve walked into the room.

"Well, well, what's going on here?" he asked jovially. It was apparent from the way he moved and talked that he'd had plenty to drink.

"We were having a little talk about Henry James and *The Turn of the Screw*," Lacey said, getting up and moving to the door.

"Sounds dirty to me," Steve remarked, trying to be funny and failing miserably.

"I presume your dinner with George Swope went well?" Lacey asked but with little interest.

"Swell guy. We're going to play golf Thursday at L.A. Country Club. He invited you to meet us there for dinner. His wife'll be there. I said you'd love to come." As he talked, he was unbuttoning his shirt and getting ready for bed.

Lacey's voice was flat as she refused. "Please don't make any dates for me, Steve. I don't intend to be away from home in the evenings until my brother's murderer has been locked up. Now, good night." She leaned down and kissed JJ on the forehead, and said, "Now, I want you to go right to sleep tonight, JJ. You need your rest."

Her son knew what she meant.

When she returned to her own room, Erin was still awake, but Lacey didn't want to talk anymore.

51

A s soon as her daughter fell asleep, Lacey disarmed the security system and tiptoed down the stairs. She then locked herself in her father's study. Just as Erin had described, the light on one of the outgoing phone lines lit up for a few seconds. It went out, and less than a minute later, a call came in. Lacey carefully lifted the receiver at the same time that Steve did upstairs. With her hand across the mouthpiece, she listened.

"Hi, babe, miss me?"

"I'm gettin' mighty tired of all this shit, Steve. I didn't get married to sleep alone while my husband goes back to livin' with his ex-wife. I'm not gonna stand for it much longer, you hear?" The woman's voice was petulant and cross.

"Hold on now, babycakes. I told you I was sleeping in the room with my son. Lacey's got some weird notion that the killer might come back—"

The woman interrupted, "I thought you said Lacey was the one who did the killin'. Why'd she be worried if she was the guilty one?"

"Shh, now let's not go talking about that anymore. It's all an act, and I've got to go along with it."

"Don't she know you suspect her?"

"I've got that workin' for me, honey child. Once I get her John Hancock on the paper, I'll be on the first plane outta here, and boy are you and me gonna do some travelin'!"

Lacey noted that Steve had lapsed into a heavy Texas drawl.

"First off, we're gonna take a trip, you hear?" Steve continued, his voice so low that Lacey had difficulty understanding what he was saying. "And we're gonna do some fancy fuckin' in all the great hotels in the world. Whatya think about that? Tell me how you miss me, go on. It's been a long dry spell up here."

Listening to the rest of the conversation was almost unbearable for Lacey because Steve and the woman began an explicit and pornographic conversation. It became readily apparent that her ex-husband had at last found a sexual partner who suited him. When the call ended, Lacey held on to the line until she was sure that Steve had hung up, and then she did too. She tiptoed back up the stairs and went to the sink and washed her hands. It seemed the appropriate thing to do. She felt dirtied by her own evesdropping, and she was furious that her son had been exposed to his father's duplicity as well as his salacious conversation.

She sat down in her bathroom and stared at her reflection in the mirror. What was she to do now? Should she give him the money and get rid of him? Or would he spend it and come back for more? And what about her children? The moment Steve took off, they would know for certain that their father cared little or nothing about them or their safety. He was only here for the money. With all that baloney about being independent, he had in reality married her for her family's wealth. But hadn't she always known that? Wasn't that the real reason she had left him? Hadn't she been sickened by the violence of his sexual appetite? And hadn't she always detected a certain level of punishing behavior whenever he made love to her?

Love, what a joke it all was, and how stupid she had been. He had made her feel like such a weak-kneed prude because she was an unadventurous lover, but now she understood why. He got satisfaction from hurting her because he hated her for having so much when he had so little. Damn! And she was the one who had felt guilty for not being as beautiful as Steve was handsome, for not being as sexy as his desires demanded, for not being the woman he really wanted.

A sudden stinging thought occurred to her. Her father had always known! That's why he disliked Steve and refused to let him become a significant part of Gallagher's Best. Her parents had lured her home because they wanted the marriage to fail, not because of them and their selfishness, but because of him. They knew she had made a bad deal. They had known all along.

Lacey became aware of the woman looking back at her—nice-looking, slim. But not really beautiful and not sexy-looking. Merely pleasant. No big breasts, no alluring curves, no big melting eyes or pouty lips. Just Lacey.

She thought about Steve and how proud she had been walking down the aisle to meet him on their wedding day. When he had emerged from the vestibule to wait for her at the altar, Penny had later reported that there was a distinct murmur of appreciation in the crowd. Tall, muscular, handsome, with deep dimples and curly brown hair, he had looked sensational in his morning coat. Her friends had told her there was not a woman present who had not envied the bride. She remembered that he had smiled and taken her hand and squeezed it, his amazing profile posed just right for the photographer to capture it perfectly. Prince Charming had married the wealthy brown mouse. And even though he might have believed she was really Scott's murderer, he was still willing to risk being here with her to get his hands on some money.

She switched out the light and went to bed. It would be another long night.

The next morning she decided to forego her exercise and leave the house before breakfast. She was not ready to face Steve yet. She hadn't decided what she was going to do, but it was a relief to sit down at her desk and confront business problems that had nothing to do with her household. When the first call of the day came, however, she was drawn back.

"Who is it, Marge?"

"It's Steve. He says it's urgent."

"I'll take it," she said and reluctantly picked up the phone.

"Hi, Steve," she answered.

"Listen, babe, I wanted to talk to you at breakfast this morning. What was the idea of rushing out of here before anybody got up?"

"I had an early meeting at the office," she lied.

"Well, look, we've gotta get this loan thing settled. Now I need to know where I stand, damn it. You're making me look like a fool. I've given my word to George Swope and all the people at the bank that you'll cosign for seventeen million and . . ."

Lacey's anger began to build. He was bullying her again, the way he had when they were married.

"I told you yesterday that I would not go for that amount. You'll never pay it back, Steve. You have no intention of ever paying it back."

"I most certainly do!"

"Why don't you come right out and ask me to give you the cash? Why go to all the trouble of taking out a loan, which you'll wind up defaulting."

"Look, I don't want to talk about this on the telephone. I'll tell the bank that you can't get in until tomorrow to sign the papers, and we'll discuss this tonight, after dinner."

"Why don't you stop wasting their time? Call them and say I've changed my mind. I've got to go, Steve. I've got another call waiting." She slammed down the receiver. She then called Tim Coffey.

"Tim, when you have the children picked up at school, bring them here to my office instead of taking them home, all right?"

"Whatever you say, Ms. Gallagher."

"And I'd like an extra security guard in the house tonight—and keep it that way until I tell you differently."

"You got it."

Lacey was relieved. It was time to send Steve Haines back to Texas. The children were better off without him. Whatever the cost, it would be worth it. How was she ever going to teach JJ and Erin that they had value in and of themselves if even their father wanted to exploit them to get at their money? Being rich was terrific, but it had some significant drawbacks.

52

When Lacey arrived home that evening, she was alone. Both Erin and JJ had been sent with the extra security guard to Mary's house to spend the night. It was time to have it out with Steve about the money and his telephone conversations. She wanted to speak freely, without having the children nearby listening. Gordon informed her that Steve had left about an hour before in the Testarossa without telling anyone where he was going or when he would be back.

She went up to her room to change into a pair of slacks. She had come to the conclusion that it was time for Steve to go back to Texas. He might have served some purpose being there in the immediate aftermath of Scott's death, but there was no need for him to stay now. She'd give him some money and send him away. He was not a particularly good influence on the children, and she also wanted to avoid another recurrence of the encounter in her closet.

She hoped there wouldn't be a scene when she told him that she'd decided to pay off his debts and put him on an annual stipend instead of the huge windfall of cash he was expecting.

Lacey was standing in her closet stepping out of her skirt when suddenly she felt herself grabbed from behind. Before she could cry out, a hand closed over her mouth. Her heart began to race and she tried to pull away, but there was a strong arm around her waist holding her and she could feel herself being drawn tightly against a body much larger than hers. She began to struggle and pull at the hand that was shutting off her breath, when the hold went slack. She whirled around and found herself in Steve's arms.

"Sh-h-h-h-h. baby, sh-h-h-h," he whispered, his mouth touching hers. "I know what you want. That's why you sent the kids away tonight, didn't you?" Then before she could protest, his lips closed over hers and his arms tightened around her.

For a long time he kissed her, and when he at last allowed her to pull her face away from his, she exploded with anger.

"Don't you ever sneak up on me like that again! You scared me half to death." She put her hands against his chest and tried to push him away.

"Good. Fear gets the adrenaline going, makes it more exciting. The harder the fight, the sweeter the surrender," he whispered in her ear and then kissed her forcefully again.

His fingers began to glide sensuously down her back and when he had her buttocks cupped in his hands, he pressed her body even closer to his. She could feel that he was eager and ready, but she was not. For years she had suppressed every hint of carnal longing, and she was never going to allow herself to be pulled back into his sexual fantasies again.

She struggled to get free, but Steve was too big and too strong for her. She felt his hand strip off her lace panties, and within seconds, he had forced her to the floor and spread her legs apart. Without once taking his mouth from hers, he penetrated her roughly, and she knew it was too late to fight him off. Her resistance would only make him enjoy the act more. She knew from past experience that nothing stimulated Steve more than the thrill of inflicting pain.

She forced her body to relax. If he was going to have sex with her, he'd have to do it all by himself.

Steve felt her body go limp as he moved inside her, and he was frustrated by her compliance. He snaked his hand up into her hair, wrapped it around his fingers, and pulled it hard. Lacey's head snapped back. She reacted to the pain by arching her back and gasping, and Steve climaxed.

Only a few moments had passed since he first embraced her, but it seemed an eternity for Lacey. Steve stayed on top and inside her, kissing her eyelids and her forehead. He had always been gentle and loving when the sex was finished.

"You still cry when you make love, you know that?" he whispered.

Lacey could feel the tears run down her temples and into her hair, and she turned her face away from his. She should have known this would happen if Steve stayed here long enough, and she hated herself for failing to avoid it. Had she learned nothing in the years they were married?

"We're great together, Lacey. We always were."

She was in no position to argue.

"Let me up, Steve. I have to take a shower. The Marchbanks will be here soon," she lied. "I invited them for dinner." She didn't dare tell him she'd been foolish enough to plan an evening alone, or this coupling would be nothing more than a preamble. She could call the security men and have him thrown out, but she had kept the secrets of their marriage too many years to share them with a stranger now.

"We'll sleep in the same bed tonight, baby. It'll be great. You'll see."

She got up from the floor and went into her bathroom and locked the door before he could follow her in. She turned on the shower quickly and pretended she could not hear him knocking. Dear God, let him leave me in peace, she prayed as she got into the hot water and tried to cleanse herself.

Half an hour later, she ventured out of the bathroom and was relieved to see that he had gone. She ducked into her large closet and locked the door behind her while she pulled on clean underwear, pantyhose, a turtleneck silk blouse, slacks, and a sweater. She felt as if she were donning a suit of armor for protection.

Lacey emerged to hear knocking at the bedroom door.

"Who is it?" she asked nervously.

She was relieved when she heard Gordon's voice.

"It's JJ on line one, ma'am. He's called twice, but you were in the shower and couldn't hear me. He says it's important that he talk to you right away."

"Thanks, Gordon. Where's Steve?"

"He's down in the library watching the evening news. I opened a bottle of Chambertin for him."

"Thanks, Gordon. I'll take the call. Give Steve anything he wants, and tell him I'll be down soon. And Gordon, call Tim and tell him to stay inside the house where I can reach him if I want to, but don't let anybody hear you talking to him, understand?"

She picked up the phone.

"Mom, I need a big favor," JJ said when she answered.

"What can I do for you, sweetheart?"

"There's a list of questions in my room that I've got to answer tonight, and I forgot to bring 'em with me. We're having an exam in history tomorrow, and all the questions will be from that list. Could you find 'em and call me back and read 'em to me?"

"Sure. Where are they?"

"I dunno exactly, Mom. Someplace in my room."

Lacey laughed. "Oh good Lord, now that is a favor. Okay, I'll go in there and dig through—"

"No, no, Mom, not in *my* room. In the room where I've been sleeping with Dad."

"Ah well, that's an easy one. I'll go find it and call you right back, honey."

Lacey went across the hallway to the bedroom that had once been her mother's. It was spacious and comfortable, and in spite of the fact that Maude had been gone for years, Lacey nevertheless sensed her presence there. Maude had been such a strong influence on her life that Lacey always had the feeling she was still nearby. To make sure she would be alone, she again locked the door behind her.

It took her a few minutes to find the paper, and then she went to the telephone on her mother's vanity table and called her son.

"JJ, have you got your pencil ready? I found them."

"Read slow, Mom. I have to copy them down."

Lacey began to read. It was a leisurely process, and as she waited for JJ to write the words, she found herself fiddling with the things on her mother's dresser. The handsome embossed leather jewelry box was still there, although it was now empty. Gently, she lifted the lid and her finger slid easily across the lush velvet interior. It seemed like only yesterday that it had been filled with her mother's finest jewels, which Maude refused to keep in the safe. She could hear her mother's voice responding sharply to Jack's admonition to be more careful with the valuable collection of gems.

"If I have to trot down to the safe in the library every time I want to wear a ring or a necklace, I'll never wear any of it, Jack. I don't want to be a slave to my jewelry. I want to enjoy it."

Idly, Lacey slipped her fingernail under the false bottom of the box and lifted it. That was where Maude had kept the twenty-carat emerald-cut diamond ring when it wasn't on her finger. Continuing to read aloud, Lacey noted with surprise that there was an envelope of some kind under the false bottom. She lifted it out curiously. It was a Delta Air Lines ticket envelope.

Wondering who had left it there, she noted that it had been used. The date and the seat number were marked on the front: the day of her father's funeral. She opened the envelope and read the name, Steve Haines, and then read the information that had been filled out on the ticket. He had traveled coach, and bought a round-trip ticket to Los Angeles, but he had left the return date open, and he had not used the return ticket. It was still intact.

She read the final question to JJ, said good night, and slipped the ticket envelope under her sweater. She returned the false bottom to the jewel case, closed it, and got out of the room as fast as she could. She sprinted across the hallway to her own room, closed the door behind her, and locked it. Then she pulled the envelope from under her sweater and looked at it again to make sure she had read the date correctly. Steve had lied! He said he'd flown to Texas and had come back to be with her as soon as he read about Scott's death. Not true. He must have still been here when her brother was killed. She tried to quell the thought and its dark meaning. It couldn't possibly be true. She didn't want it to be true, because the idea that her children might have a killer for a father was too horrible to consider.

There was a soft knock on her door, and she heard Steve's voice.

"Lacey, when are you coming downstairs?"

Lacey retreated to the bathroom and flushed the toilet before she called, "I can't right now. I'm not feeling very well. Go on down to the library. When I'm finished I'll be there."

Lacey tiptoed to the door and listened for the sound of his retreating footsteps and was relieved to hear him leaving. She had to have time to think.

After staring at the ticket for a few minutes, she realized she had to get the information to the police right away. Now that she thought about it, it was odd that no one had doubted for a moment that Steve had stalked out of the house and gone back to his ranch, and so neither she nor anyone else had considered looking into his whereabouts at the time of the murder. The whole investigation had been focused on the people in the house, and it was reasonably possible that Steve might have remained somewhere on the huge estate.

Maybe he was innocent. Then again, maybe he was not. After all, he had nothing to gain if Scott had been the sole inheritor of the estate. He couldn't even have collected the ten million for remarrying Lacey as stipulated in the bogus will because he was already married to somebody else. So what would he have to gain by Lacey's becoming rich? A lot. He was a master at manipulating her. Now that it was in her power to give almost any amount, he was after millions.

Lacey picked up the telephone and dialed Cherry Dolan's telephone number, but she was not in the office. She asked that Cherry be contacted immediately and told it was urgent she return the call right away. Before Lacey went downstairs, she was careful to hide the telltale ticket by sliding it between the mattress and boxspring.

Steve was waiting in the library, a glass of wine in his hand. A glance at the bottle told her that a good deal of the Chambertin was already gone.

"Hi," he said, flashing her a welcoming smile and getting up off the couch to greet her with a kiss.

Her teeth clenched, Lacey turned her cheek and walked over to the bar cart to pour herself a glass of the expensive wine. She needed something to calm her nerves.

"I see you've been in Dad's cellar again," she said, trying to keep the hostility out of her voice.

"It's not Dad's cellar anymore, darling. It's yours, remember? And we have something to celebrate, don't we? Come on, let's enjoy it," he replied, sitting back down on the couch. "What time will the Marchbanks be here?"

"I'm not sure whether they're coming or not," Lacey lied. "Penny's not feeling well, but she's going to try to make it." Lacey wished it were true. She was not simply dealing with a conniving, manipulative ex-husband with a penchant for rape, she was now dealing with a man possibly desperate enough to have committed murder.

With a slight leer, Steve patted the couch pillow beside him and said, "Then why don't you come sit over here?"

Lacey saw that Tim was hovering outside the door, and she was emboldened. "I don't think so, Steve. In fact I think that after dinner is over tonight, you should pack your things and go to a hotel. Your visit with us is over. I don't want you here anymore. What happened upstairs was unforgivable."

"What are you talking about?"

"You know exactly what I mean."

Steve laughed and took a swallow of his wine. "Now let's not go getting all coy on me, Lacey. You planned that. You know you did. Why else would you have sent the kids to Mary's for the night if you hadn't wanted us to get together again?"

Lacey cursed her own stupidity. She should have realized she might be sending him the wrong signal.

"Look, I know you're married, Steve. I listened to your telephone conversation last night with Betty Lou. I sent the children to Mary's because I didn't want Erin and JJ here when I gave their father his marching orders, understand?"

"You've never worried before about humiliating me in front of them."

"God, your arrogance never ceases to astound me. Did you really think you could have those lewd telephone conversations in the same room with JJ and he wouldn't tell me?"

"You're jealous, aren't you?" he said with a grin.

At that moment Gordon came back into the room carrying a tray of canapés. Lacey was happy to see him. She was stalling for time, hoping that Cherry would get the message and hurry here.

She took a canapé and asked Gordon to open a bottle of champagne for her. "Do you have a bottle chilled?" she asked.

"I believe there's one in the kitchen, ma'am."

She didn't want him to leave the room. "On second thought, why don't you mix me one of those terrific martinis Dad liked so much. I haven't had one of those in years."

Gordon went to the bar cart to do as she asked, and Lacey went over to watch him. The silence in the room was charged with tension. The drink was in her hand much sooner than she had wished, and then Gordon was gone. Steve spoke the moment they were alone again, this time with less hubris.

"I'm sorry, Lacey, really I am. I'd have been a lot more careful if I'd had any idea the kid was spying on me. Well, you've finally got what you wanted. My son probably hates me."

Although she didn't want to escalate the argument, she could not resist an appropriate response.

"Not true, Steve, not true at all. JJ has always adored you, but the only times you've ever bothered with either of them was when you wanted to extract more money from me. As soon as you got it, it was so long and good-bye to JJ and Erin."

"I guess you're not going to cosign the note for me now."

She wanted to tell the truth, but caution prevailed. She didn't want to deal with a man who had nothing to lose.

"I'm still considering it, Steve. I'm not comfortable with the idea of my children's father being penniless and in debt. Bring all the papers to my office tomorrow, and we'll go over them with one of my accountants. Rather than go through the bank, maybe I can lend you the money directly. That way, there'll be no third-party involvement. If you default, you'll only have to answer to me."

"How much are you going to cut me back?"

"Not as much as you might think" she lied. "I'll have to see what amount my accountant says I can comfortably release right now."

The telephone rang, and she rushed to answer it before Gordon did. She did not want him to come into the room and announce that the detective was returning her call. And she especially wanted to find some way to keep Steve from going to his room and discovering that the ticket was missing from the jewel box.

"I'll get it," she said. "JJ's having a test tomorrow, and I've been helping him on the phone."

It was Cherry Dolan.

"Well, hello. How nice to hear from you. Is Penny feeling better?" Lacey said.

Cherry Dolan was quick to pick up on the ruse.

"You can't talk right now, is that it?"

"Oh my, yes. Since she's feeling so much better, you'll for sure be joining Steve and me for dinner then? Good. Hurry over. We're still having cocktails."

"I'll get there as fast as I can," Cherry assured her. "Are you in any immediate danger?"

"Not really, at least not for the time being, but I'm anxious to see you both," Lacey replied keeping her voice light and choosing her words carefully.

"I'll bring a backup. I'll hang up now, okay?"

"Terrific, but don't dillydally. We're getting hungry."

She put down the telephone and said with a smile, "Well, Penny and Brett are on their way after all. So let's finish our business before they get here, shall we?"

"You're actually going to give me money?" Steve asked, getting back to the subject that was most important to him.

"A great deal of money, so handle it wisely, because this will be the last," she said, scrapping the idea of an annual allowance. It was safer to lull him into the belief that big money was coming his way. "But you have to agree not to come back when this is gone. In fact, I don't want you coming back here at all. Not ever." She knew she was treading on dangerous ground, but she couldn't help herself. The possibility that he might be the man who had driven the knife into her brother's chest turned the blood in her veins to ice.

"You mean I can't come see my own children?"

"We'll have to see how things go. I don't want to make any other commitments."

"Why? Because of a few telephone calls to a woman who happens to be my legal wife?"

"Do you want the money, Steve?" she asked, making no attempt to mask the threat in her words.

She could tell that he wanted to lash out at her, but for the first time she felt the power that her father must have felt most of his life, the power of money to make even the most intractable people bend to his will. It was a potent weapon, and she felt corrupt using it.

Steve took another long pull at the wineglass, emptying it before he replied, and when he spoke, she knew she had him exactly where she wanted him.

"You drive a hard bargain, Lacey," he said.

"Would you like another bottle of wine?"

"No thanks, I've had enough of that stuff too. Mix me a real drink," he said as he slammed the exquisite Baccarat glass against the brick fireplace and shattered it.

Intimidated by the bleakness of the mood she herself had created, Lacey rang for the butler. She wanted another human being in the room with her.

"I'm not very good at mixing drinks," she apologized. "I never was. Gordon will do it for you."

The butler appeared, and Lacey told him to mix Steve a bourbon and soda.

Steve laughed. "Bourbon? I thought the Gallaghers only stocked the oldest Scotch."

"Whatever you'd like, sir," Gordon said patiently, realizing something was going on.

The doorbell rang.

"Oh," Lacey said, moving toward the door. "That must be Brett and Penny. You make the drink, Gordon. I'll let them in."

"No need, ma'am. Tim's out there. He'll take care of it. He insists that he be allowed to check things out before opening the door."

"Really?" Lacey asked, thankful to be surrounded by so many people. "Well, I'll just go greet them anyway. I'll be right back, Steve."

Trying not to appear too eager, she strode to the entry hall, where she saw Cherry and her partner being allowed to enter.

"Penny, I'm glad to see you," she said loudly, and then lowering her voice to a whisper added, "Follow me upstairs. Hurry!"

The three of them raced up the curved staircase, and when they were all in Lacey's room, she closed and locked the door.

Retrieving the ticket envelope, she handed it to Cherry.

"I came across this by accident. It was hidden in the jewelry case in my mother's room where Steve's been sleeping. Look, he wasn't in Texas the night Scott was killed. He lied."

Cherry studied the ticket carefully for a few minutes, and then she asked, "Can I use your telephone?"

"Of course."

She dialed a number as Lacey and Chuck listened. She identified herself and asked if there was any record of Steve purchasing another Delta ticket on that date. There was none.

She put down the telephone, turned to Lacey, and said, "This might mean nothing, but it's an important lead. We'll check all the flights out of L.A. destined for Texas on that day. You want him out of the house tonight, right?"

Lacey nodded nervously.

"Good. This ticket, which proved that he lied about not being in town, is enough evidence to take him in for questioning. You have any problem with that?"

Lacey shook her head. All of a sudden her knees had turned to jelly.

"Where is he?" Cherry asked. "Tell me. You don't have to be there."

All the strength and the power that Lacey had experienced so recently now slipped from her; she felt like a balloon that was suddenly released, its air whistling away while it whirled dizzily into space and deflated into a limp piece of rubber.

"He's in the library," she heard her choked voice whisper.

"Take it easy now, Ms. Gallagher. Everything's going to be all right," Cherry said, taking note of the terror in Lacey's eyes. If she'd had any doubt about her innocence, it was dispelled in that moment.

"But what about Sasha? He couldn't have killed her. He was sleeping in the same room with JJ that night," she whispered weakly.

"Are you sure he didn't sneak out?" Chuck asked.

"It's possible, but where would he have gotten a car in the middle of the night?" Lacey replied.

"Let's take one thing at a time. Do you have someone to be with you tonight?" Cherry asked.

"Security guards, the servants . . ."

"Call a friend. It's going to be a long night, and you'll need someone with you," Cherry advised. "I'll telephone you in the morning."

The two detectives went out the door and down the steps, but Lacey could not bring herself to stay in her bedroom. She followed them to the library, lagging a few steps behind. She saw them go in and stopped short of the door.

Then the two detectives appeared again.

"There's no one here!" Cherry exclaimed. "Where else would he be?"

Gordon made his appearance and said, "If you're looking for Mr. Haines, I'm afraid he's gone."

"Gone?" Lacey asked startled. "Where?"

"I don't know, ma'am. He started to follow you out into the hallway, and when he saw Ms. Dolan coming through the door, he backed into the library. He asked me which car was out of the garage, and I told him that I believed the Ferrari was still in the driveway. He went out through the French doors there, through the garden."

"Did he say where he was going?" Chuck asked.

"No, ma'am, although I did inquire as to what he wanted me to tell Ms. Lacey. I'd rather not repeat what he said."

"What did he say, Gordon?" Lacey asked, her heart pounding against her chest wall.

"He said"—Gordon cleared his throat—"he said for you to fuck off, ma'am. I'm afraid that's it exactly."

The two detectives were already on their way out to the car.

"Gordon, I'll need the license number, but there aren't that many red Ferraris around so it should be a snap to find him. We'll round him up in no time at all." Cherry smiled encouragingly at Lacey. "Now don't worry about anything. You and the kids stay locked up tight in the house. I'll have a car put outside to—"

"Oh my God! The children aren't here! They're staying at Mary's house. I sent a security guard with them, but they know nothing about . . ."

"Get them on the telephone right now, and give me the address," Cherry ordered. "I'll send a car over there to pick them up. How far away are they?"

"A mile and a half, just a few minutes. Oh God help me, he knows where they are!" Lacey screamed as she dashed for the telephone and dialed the number with trembling hands.

The line was busy. Lacey looked helplessly at the detective.

Cherry took the telephone out of her grasp and dialed the operator.

"Operator? This is Detective Dolan of the L.A. county sheriff's office. This is an emergency. I want you to break into a call." She turned to Lacey and asked, "What's the number?"

Lacey recited it and Cherry repeated it to the operator. The seconds passed like hours as they waited, and then Mary's voice was on the line. Cherry handed the telephone to Lacey.

"Lacey, I'm so glad you called. When JJ took off with Steve he hadn't finished his homework, and I . . ."

53

Although the detectives advised her to, Lacey would not stay at home. Salvador drove her to Mary's house, where Chuck was already questioning everybody. When Lacey arrived, Cherry assured her that the police in the entire Los Angeles and Orange counties had been alerted and were on the watch for the Ferrari. Lacey was not satisfied. She was the only one who knew how cagey and manipulative Steve could be, and she was afraid that he was now extremely desperate.

"Why did JJ go with him?" Lacey asked Mary.

"He told JJ that you brought home a lot of work to do, and he felt like bowling a few frames. He asked Erin to go too, but she refused," Mary replied, feeling guilty for having allowed JJ to leave.

Erin, who was alarmed by the concern in her mother's manner, spoke up. "I told Dad JJ had to study for a test, and he promised to bring him home in an hour, but you know JJ. Anything to get out of studying. What's the problem, Mom? Why are the police looking for Dad?"

With fear rising in her throat and threatening to cut off her air, Lacey nevertheless managed to speak calmly.

"They want to ask him some questions. I'm sure everything's going to be fine when they get back. Now don't worry, honey."

"Did your dad appear to be acting normally?" Cherry asked.

Erin thought for a minute. "He seemed in an awful hurry, and he got angry with me for refusing to go with him."

"Tell us his exact words, sweetheart," Lacey said, trying to keep her terror from showing.

"He said I was too much like you, Mom. I told him I was glad."

"And then they left?" Cherry asked.

Mary spoke up. "Steve asked if he could borrow my car. He said the Ferrari had only enough gas to get him back home, and he didn't want to keep JJ out too long. I gave him the keys, and he put the Ferrari in the garage to keep the dew off it, he said."

"Damn!" Chuck exploded. "Quick, give me a description and license number. We've got everybody on the alert for a red Ferrari."

Mary was so upset that she couldn't remember her license number completely, only that it started with a 2NEN and the registration was in the car, which was a 1988 Plymouth station wagon. She hurried to her desk and searched through her papers to find the car insurance policy. It took her a very long five minutes before she finally was able to furnish the complete number.

Cherry was on top of her every second, and Lacey's heart raced with anxiety. What could Steve possibly be up to? What did he hope to gain by taking his own son hostage? Surely he wouldn't hurt him!

When Chuck finished getting all the proper information transmitted to the dispatching office, he returned to find the women huddled together on the couch.

"Now, where do you think he might have taken your son? Think carefully. We need to move fast before he can get too far away," he asked.

Lacey tried to think, but she didn't have the faintest idea where Steve might be headed.

"I don't know, I don't know. We haven't got any other residential property in Southern California. And he owns nothing but the ranch in Texas. God, I can't imagine where . . ."

"I'll alert the airlines with flights headed for Texas," Cherry said, with the telephone in her hand.

"He's still got my credit card. I've got the number at home."

Confused, Erin asked, "What's going on, Mom? Why is everybody so upset about Dad taking JJ?"

Lacey looked at her almost-grown-up daughter, and it broke her heart to tell her the truth. Chuck, however, did not bother to mince words.

"It's difficult for your mother to tell you, Erin, but your father is now a suspect in the murder of your uncle. We think he might have taken JJ hostage to protect himself."

As Lacey gathered her daughter in her arms to cushion the shock, Erin exclaimed, "Dad wouldn't do that! He wouldn't, would he, Mom?"

When there were no comforting words of reassurance from her mother, Erin was even more distressed.

"Mom! It can't be true. JJ's not in any danger, is he?"

From the other side of the room, Cherry observed the two women closely. Lacey's reactions were giving her important information about her feelings about her ex-husband. Steve Haines must have given his wife reason to be so swift to suspect him.

Holding her daughter tightly, Lacey returned to the business at hand. "Texas is a good possibility. It's his territory, and it might be harder to find him if he manages to get that far away."

"Give me all the addresses and telephone numbers of people he might contact down there. I'll alert the police in that area," Cherry declared.

"Lacey, I think you ought to go home and keep a telephone line open. I'll bet Steve's going to call you and try to make a deal," Mary said.

The detectives looked at her, surprised at her insight and good sense.

"You're absolutely right," Cherry snapped. "You son is valuable for bartering. Let's go."

"Mary, I want you to come with us," Lacey insisted, and the detectives concurred.

"I think it's a good idea. I'll have a detail keep a watch on the house. Let's go." Cherry's voice was authoritative enough to get all three women on the move.

On the way back to the Gallagher estate, Cherry insisted that Lacey ride with her and her partner so they could talk, and Mary and Erin rode with Salvador.

In the backseat of the police car, Lacey asked, "Why was he so quick to run?"

"Running away and taking your son with him was your husband's first major blunder," Chuck, who was driving, observed.

"Ex-husband," Lacey corrected and then added, "no, it was his second really, or his third. He shouldn't have indulged himself in telephone calls to his wife that my son overheard. And he certainly should have destroyed that return airline ticket. God, why would he leave something so incriminating lying around?"

"He didn't have much cash, did he?" Cherry asked.

"He didn't need any while he was living at the house."

"He probably viewed that ticket as an escape valve. He could always use it to get away if he suspected anyone was on to him. If something happened to you, who would become the children's guardian?" Cherry asked.

"Why Steve, of course. Although Tom Brennan would control their money." As she spoke, Lacey's hand fluttered to her throat, and then she whispered, "Dear God!"

"What's wrong?" Cherry asked.

"I just had a ghastly thought. If Steve killed Scott, he probably did it so I would be the one who was blamed. Until yesterday, when he talked to Tom Brennan, he was under the impression that if he ever became the children's guardian he'd also control their money."

"He talked to Brennan about that yesterday?" Chuck asked.

"I believe so."

"We're jumping to a lot of conclusions here," Cherry warned. "Tell me about your marriage."

Lacey looked out into the darkness of the night, and the memories she had tried so hard to suppress filtered through to her consciousness, and as they did, the fear that she felt for her son's safety expanded and threatened to suffocate her. She couldn't speak.

Cherry glanced back at Lacey and saw that the question had seriously unnerved her.

"I really don't mean to pry," she insisted, "but the more we know about the kind of man we're dealing with, the better chance we have of apprehending him."

Lacey could not find the words to express the feelings that were painfully reasserting themselves.

"He's a good person . . . most of the time. He's amusing and enthusiastic, but he doesn't, he doesn't know the children very well, I'm afraid."

"Why not?" Cherry asked, pressing her.

"When I left Texas, they never went back for a visit."

"Didn't he demand visitation privileges?"

"Oh, of course, but he had to visit the children here. That was part of the agreement."

"Courts don't usually deny unsupervised visits with a parent unless there's good cause. Why weren't they allowed to visit their father?" Cherry was absolutely sure that Lacey was holding back on something important.

"My father paid Steve off not to contest the custody arrangements," Lacey admitted. "I asked him to."

"He relinquished access to his children for money?" Cherry asked. She and Chuck looked at each other. Lacey's son was at greater risk than they had presumed.

Lacey nodded. "Steve will do almost anything for money—including marrying me."

"He told you that?" Cherry asked.

Lacey nodded again. "I was a total failure as a wife to him. My father refused to give us any more money to support the ranch. Much as she hated to do it, my mother agreed. Both of my parents wanted me to come home."

"But they didn't want you to bring Steve?" Cherry asked.

"No. They suspected that I was miserable, and they were trying to force me to assert myself and leave him."

"You didn't love him?"

Tears were now falling freely down Lacey's cheeks, and she shook her head.

"I was madly in love with him when we first got married. But all that changed."

"You didn't get along?" Cherry prodded.

Lacey wiped her eyes. "Not really. You see there's something you ought to know about children who grow up in rich families. We're not very emotionally secure. It's so hard to believe that we're loved for ourselves that we eagerly embrace anyone who manages to convince us their feelings are real."

"And Steve convinced you?"

"For a while," Lacey replied, and then in muffled tones added, "but we weren't compatible."

The car was now pulling into the driveway of the Gallagher mansion, and Gordon was waiting to open the doors.

Cherry had one more question before they got out of the car. Lacey was being fairly candid, and she needed an answer.

"Did he abuse you?"

"Not like you think. He never actually hit me—it wasn't like that . . . ," she began, but the car door was opened and their conversation was over.

In the Darkness of the Night

Lying on her stomach with her face buried in the pillow and her arms and legs outstretched and tightly tied, she tried not to think about what was happening to her, but the pain was impossible to ignore. Many times she had tried to participate in his violent sex games, but she could never find any of the joys of passion when pain, her pain, was the focus of the experience, and she found it degrading to be forced to do something against her will.

Then, when she felt she could bear it no more, it was over, and his passion was spent. After a few seconds of recovery, he moved off her and released her arms and legs. He turned over and cuddled her in his arms.

"I'm sorry," he whispered, kissing her tear-stained eyelids. "I wish you could learn to let yourself go and enjoy it with me. Would you like me to stroke you now?"

She pulled herself away from him and swung her feet over the side of the bed.

"No, thanks. I'm not in the mood anymore. I'm going to take a shower."

Lacey padded on bare feet into the bathroom, rubbing the life back into her hands. She snapped on the light and looked at herself in the mirror. She could tell from the deepness of the red marks on her breasts and her wrists and ankles that there would be bruises. Thank God this didn't happen every time.

54

Miss Lacey!" Gordon cried as Lacey got out of Cherry's car. "Billy called from the *Santa Maria*. Mr. Steve's been there!"

"Where's the boat now?" Cherry asked.

"It's docked at berth three, a few yards from the marine bureau's office. Let's go," Lacey replied, jumping back into the detective's car. Chuck placed a red light on the roof, put the car into gear, and they were off. While he drove, Cherry radioed headquarters, directing them to send officers in the vicinity of the boat as quickly as possible.

When she had finished, Cherry asked Lacey if she had any idea why Steve had chosen to go to the yacht.

Quickly buckling her seat belt, Lacey replied, "Maybe he had some mistaken notion he could persuade Billy to take them somewhere, but Billy would never take the boat out unless he got permission beforehand from me directly. He's a good skipper, and he never makes rash moves."

Chuck drove fast. Although Lacey was silent, Cherry asked questions. "Had Tom Brennan been involved in any other shady dealings before this casino thing?"

Lacey shook her head and said nothing. She was too worried about her son to think of anything else.

"The reason I asked," Cherry persisted, "is that the SEC had several complaints about it from investors who'd lost money. All of which were withdrawn shortly before your father's death."

"Tom was expecting a huge windfall when that fake will was probated and the company was sold," Lacey remarked, but it was obvious she had little interest in the conversation.

"The SEC estimated the investors lost close to eleven million. That's a lot of money."

"Where did it all go?" Chuck asked.

"Good question," Cherry replied, and they rode in silence the rest of the way.

Traffic was heavy in the marina, and it seemed to Lacey that it took them an inordinately long time to get where they were going, so anxious was she about her child's safety.

A black and white was already at the dock when they arrived, and two officers were talking to the dazed skipper, who was lying on the forward deck, his head bleeding.

Lacey bounded up the gangway. "Where are they, Billy?" she almost screamed.

"I don't know," he replied. "He and your son came to the gangway and rang. I opened the gate and let them aboard. Mr. Steve said they were only here for a short visit. They went aft and were looking at the Zodiac, so I went back to the galley to fix myself some supper. Then somebody sneaked up behind me and smashed me in the head. When I came to, I called your home and spoke to Gordon."

"The paramedics are on the way," a policeman stated.

"Are they still here?" Lacey asked, rushing toward the ladder to go below to search for her son.

Billy lifted his head and called to her. "Miss Lacey! They're not aboard! They've already searched the boat, and the Zodiac's gone!" He pointed aft where the inflatable dinghy had been tied.

"Good grief, he's gone out in the fog. He's lost his mind! We've got to call the coast guard and the harbor patrol immediately. He can't have gotten very far," Lacey decided. "Billy, was the gas tank filled?"

"I always keep the gas tank on the Zodiac filled, ma'am, for safety's sake."

"What's the range?" Cherry asked.

"Ten miles—give or take a mile or two," Lacey replied, and Billy nodded in agreement.

"I'm going up on the bridge and notify the coast guard immediately. Then I'm taking out the *Lady Maude* to look for them. Billy, where's the rest of the crew?" Lacey asked.

"Per's gone back to Norway for a couple of weeks, and Buck and Earl won't be back from that race in Hawaii until next Thursday. Sorry, ma'am, but I didn't think you'd be needing the boat . . . " Billy began to apologize, but Lacey brushed it off.

"Don't worry about it. You take it easy. I can manage," Lacey called back to him as she led the way to the bridge.

"What's the *Lady Maude?*" Cherry asked.

"Our ski boat. It's fast and has twice the range of the Zodiac. We store it in a slip on the other side of this finger of land. Sometimes we tow it to Catalina."

"Isn't a Zodiac one of those little rubber boats?" Cherry wondered. "Why would he take that instead of a ski boat?"

"We've only had the *Lady Maude* for about three years. I suspect he didn't know about it, and JJ must realize he's a hostage or he would have mentioned it to him."

After notifying the coast guard, it took Lacey less than ten minutes to take the cover off the ski boat and get it started. Chuck was involved in organizing the search and so only Cherry joined her.

"You know how to handle this thing okay?" Cherry asked doubtfully.

"Of course. I notified the coast guard to watch the channel to make sure Steve didn't try to take the Zodiac beyond the breakwater, so we'll concentrate on the marina. There are a thousand places he could sneak into and hide."

"Visibility is really bad out here tonight."

"I've seen fog a lot thicker. We'd better watch out for other boats making their way back into the marina, especially bigger ones that might run right over us without noticing," Lacey remarked. "When I tell you to, get one of those spotlights and turn it on."

"Does your husband know anything about boats?"

"Ex-husband. He learned a lot while we were married and living in this area. He loves to sail and scuba dive. He often said that the only thing he missed when he went back to Texas was the *Santa Maria*."

As they passed the rows of boats anchored in the marina, Cherry asked, "Do you really think he might be hiding around here someplace?"

"Maybe, but he might also try to get out of the area as fast as he can. Ten miles can take him a way down the coastline, and you can dock a Zodiac almost anywhere."

"He could have gone a lot farther in a car," Cherry observed.

"But he knows the police are looking for the car. It's pretty easy to slip away in the fog when you're on the water."

They searched for more than an hour, but they saw no trace of the Zodiac. They encountered the harbor patrol, but they too were having no luck. Lacey was frantic with worry. Steve and JJ and the Zodiac seemed to have vanished into the ocean mist.

Finally, Cherry made a decision. "I think we should go back to the *Santa Maria*. Your husband might be trying to contact us there. It's almost certain he's going to want to make a deal with you. The kid's only valuable to him if he can trade him for money."

Lacey hated to give up the search, but she bowed to Cherry's reasoning.

Much to their surprise, when they arrived at the slip, Pete Cunningham was on the dock talking to Chuck Bascombe. Pete directed Lacey to throw him a line, and he tied the boat and helped them off.

"Pete!" Lacey exclaimed, "what're you doing here?"

"It's on the news already. As soon as I heard it, I called your house and was told you were down here. I came to see if I could be of any help."

"The news . . . ?" Lacey asked, bewildered.

Chuck interrupted their conversation. "Thank God, you came back. Your husband called the boat fifteen minutes ago. He said he'd call back in half an hour."

Without another word, Lacey rushed aboard the *Santa Maria*, followed by the two detectives and Pete.

Someone had prepared a large pot of hot coffee, and cups were passed around. Lacey's hands trembled as she took hers, and it was apparent to everyone in the room that she was not only chilled, she was terrified. Pete moved close and placed a comforting arm around her shoulders.

"It's going to be okay. Your husband won't hurt his own son," he said.

Lacey welcomed the warmth of his touch and his sympathy, but she was not reassured.

"You don't know Steve. He can be very cruel," she said, and having uttered the words, she felt a cold sense of betrayal. For years her silent response to the true feelings she had about Steve had fostered the illusion that Steve really was a nice guy and her parents had broken up a good marriage. It was simpler to blame them for the breakup than to concede, even to herself, that Steve often frightened her with an appetite for violence that manifested itself in his sexuality. She shivered as the suppressed memories took shape in her mind.

All eyes were rivetted on Lacey as she grappled with her internal demons, and there were questions hanging unasked in every corner of the cabin.

Cherry was the first to venture a word of inquiry. "From your experience then, you actually believe your husband is capable of violence. Is that true?"

Lacey looked up into the eyes surrounding her, and she knew that the secrets she thought safely buried had to be revealed. She felt again the humiliation and degradation that Steve had so often visited upon her when she was a young woman. She had endured, but could she bear the revelation that she had been submissive to his abuse?

She looked uncertainly to Cherry, then to Chuck, and she saw that they would settle for nothing less than the truth. Looking up into Pete's eyes, she found encouragement.

"We need to know the truth. Did he ever actually abuse you?" Cherry asked.

Lacey, the strong woman, the daughter of a powerful man, lowered her eyes and nodded. "I didn't know that's what it was at the time. I only knew that he made me feel like a failure as a wife," she said, and the words were uttered so softly that only Pete and Cherry heard them. Pete drew her closer, trying to infuse strength from his body into hers.

"Did he ever hurt your children?"

"Not really. Whenever he tried to spank them, I intervened. He said it was for their own good, but I didn't believe that. My parents never once in all my life hit me."

"This isn't helping find her son," Pete said, realizing how difficult it was for Lacey to talk about such things.

"No, but it's giving us a better idea of the kind of man we're hunting," Chuck stated. "Lacey, do you believe it's possible that Steve Haines might have killed your brother?"

"I didn't before, but now, I don't know what to believe, especially with him taking JJ like that. Oh God, I actually welcomed his presence in my house. I let him stay there and sleep in the same room with JJ to protect him!" If her voice hadn't been so low it would have been a wail.

"We have ten minutes," Chuck said, galvanized into action once more. "Is there an extension on this line?"

Lacey nodded. "In the main cabin below."

"Good, I've already notified them to put a tracer on the line. Cherry, instruct her," he ordered. "I'm going below so I can listen to the conversation. Pick up on the second ring, understand?"

"Right," Cherry agreed. "Now, Lacey, when the call comes in you have only one mission. Keep him on the line as long as you possibly can, understand?"

Lacey nodded, and Cherry continued. "Do whatever you can to keep him talking. Be friendly, be agreeable, don't in any way threaten him. Make him believe you'll do absolutely anything to settle the situation amicably."

"I understand. Do you have any suggestions?"

"It always helps to pretend you've got a poor connection. Whenever he says something, ask him to repeat it. Talk low so he'll have to strain to hear you. That way he's less likely to become suspicious. Can you do it?"

"Of course I can. I'll do anything to get JJ back safely," Lacey responded, stepping out of Pete's embrace and moving toward the telephone to prepare herself.

"Have a few sips of coffee. Think about what you're going to say," Pete suggested.

Lacey did as he said, and after a single swallow, she set the cup down. "What should I ask him?"

"Ask him to bring JJ back to you, and tell him you'll help him anyway you can," Cherry instructed her. "Don't worry about being nervous. He expects that. Make him believe you'll do anything he wants. Let him think he's in control of the situation. I'll be with Chuck listening on the extension." With a reassuring pat on the shoulder, Cherry went below. Pete sat down across from Lacey and smiled.

"You're going to pull this off, Lacey. Everything's going to be okay."

The ring of the phone came like a bolt of lightening. With a sharp, jerky movement, Lacey grabbed at the instrument, then waited for the second ring before she picked it up. She said hello in a voice that was barely above a whisper.

"Lacey? Is that you? Where were you?"

"Steve? Steve? Are you there? I can barely hear you," she answered, keeping her mouth at a distance from the telephone and continuing to speak low.

"I said where were you," Steve repeated. He raised his voice and made an effort to speak clearly.

"I was out in the *Lady* . . . in our ski boat looking for you. Where did you go?"

"I'm going to pass on that one, Lacey. Now listen up because I'm going to tell you this only once."

"Steve, can you talk a little louder? You seem to be fading away," Lacey replied, and her heart beat faster. It was a good technique, but she was afraid it might backfire and he'd hang up.

"Bullshit!" he snapped, very loud, and then he continued. "You're not going to see JJ until tomorrow afternoon, so forget about searching for us. We're in a spot where no one will ever find us. Now I want you to go to the bank in the morning, get two million in cash, go home, and wait for my call." Without another word, he hung up.

Stunned, Lacey was still holding the telephone in her hands when Cherry and Chuck raced up to talk to her.

"Did you have time to trace it?" Pete asked.

"I don't think so," Cherry replied. "Lacey, you ought to go home. We'll stay on this all night, but I think it's fairly obvious that he's not out on the water anymore. Do as he says. I'll be at the house early in the morning. Can you arrange to have the money there?"

Lacey nodded.

"Good. Look, I want to catch the guy, but it's more important even to me that we get your son home safely, understand? Will you trust me?" Cherry asked.

Lacey looked at Cherry and wondered if she could trust even her.

"Come on, I'll drive you home," Pete said.

55

As soon as Lacey arrived home, Erin rushed into her mother's arms.

"Oh, Mom! Thank God, you're back. Is there any news of Dad and JJ?"

Lacey held her precious daughter tightly to her and answered, "I talked to your father. He only wants money."

"Are you sure?" Mary asked suspiciously.

"That's what he said. He told me to get two million dollars in cash and have it ready for him first thing in the morning."

"Can you do that?" Erin asked as her exhausted mother sank to the couch.

"Of course. I'll call Joe at home tonight and ask him to have it delivered. Money is not the problem."

"Dad would never hurt JJ, would he, Mom?" Erin asked, and for the first time since the nightmare had begun, Lacey lied to reassure her daughter and to mask her own anxieties.

"Of course not, honey. I think that the easiest thing to do is give him the money and let him go."

"The police are still looking for them, aren't they?" Erin asked. "Mom, you don't really believe Dad killed Uncle Scott, do you?"

Gordon appeared at the library door. "Miss Lacey. The detectives are here, and Mrs. Marchbanks is on the telephone and wants to speak with you."

"Please have them come in, Gordon, and tell Penny I'll call her back when I get a chance."

Lacey turned to Mary who had joined them. "Mary, why don't you and Erin sleep in the same room tonight? I don't want her to be alone, and I have no idea when if ever I'll be getting to bed. Is that all right with you, Erin?"

"If Mary doesn't mind. We can sleep in my room. It's got twin beds."

Mary smiled and put her arm around Erin and led her toward the door. "Okay, but you'll have to lend me a nightgown."

When Mary and Erin had gone upstairs, Lacey invited Chuck and Cherry into the living room and asked Gordon to fix coffee. Then she said, "Now, before we get started on any plans to capture my husband, I want one thing made very clear. I intend to give him the money and whatever else he wants, and I want no interference from you until I have my son back safely. After that, I don't care what you do."

"You have our promise on that. I assume you can get the money?" Cherry asked.

"I was about to call a good friend of mine. He's the chairman of the board of First Consolidated Bank, and I have no doubt that he can have the cash delivered here in the morning."

"I suggest that you get it here early. Would you like to make the call now?" Chuck asked.

Lacey nodded, went to the telephone, and within a few minutes everything was settled. She put Chuck on the line, and he arranged to have an expert at the bank early in the morning to mark the bills and transport them to the house.

"We're having a tap and a tracer put on the telephone lines here. I hope you have no objection to that?" Chuck asked.

Lacey agreed that was a good move.

"Now, we need to know a little more about your relationship with your ex-husband. Did it ever occur to you before tonight that he might have been the one who killed your brother?"

"Absolutely not! If I had ever thought for one single moment that he might have been the one who killed Scott, I would have told you." She took a deep breath and continued, her voice rising with fury, "And I would never, ever have permitted him to stay in my own house if I had suspected anything, anything at all!"

Chuck looked thoughtful. "I'm curious, Ms. Gallagher. Did you consider any other explanation for the unused ticket other than that he had committed the crime?"

Lacey looked directly into his eyes as she spoke. "No, I didn't."

"Why not?" he asked.

"It struck me like a thunderbolt when I realized that he hadn't gone back to Texas as he said he had."

"Why would he kill your brother?" Cherry asked, and her tone was much more gentle than her partner's.

"Under the terms of the will he got nothing unless I agreed to marry him again, and he knew that I never would."

"Why?" Chuck asked.

Lacey bit her lips and then said, "That's a more personal question than you realize, Mr. Bascombe. When I left my husband, I escaped from a marriage that had turned me into a victim."

"Could you explain that?" Chuck asked, pushing her to tell more.

Lacey hesitated. She hated baring her soul to these strangers who acted as if they had a right to know her deepest secrets. But maybe, under the circumstances, they did. She chose her words carefully.

"Steve is two people. He's an amusing, bright, ambitious person. People like him—especially if they don't know him too well. But he has a dark side to his personality. He has this terrible need to control everyone around him, and when things don't go well, he can be very punishing. He blamed me because my father refused to give him what he wanted."

"What was that?" Chuck asked.

"He wanted position and power at Gallagher's Best. My father stuck him in the sales department. It didn't work. Steve was too arrogant ever to concede that the customer is always right. He and my dad were on a collision course from the moment they met, and I found my parents' opposition to him humiliating and demeaning."

"Why was that?" Cherry asked gently.

"They acted as if I had nothing to offer a big, handsome man like Steve except my money. Maybe if they hadn't opposed him so severely, I might not have felt that I had to assert myself and marry him."

"You mentioned the word *punishing*. Was it just mental or did he hurt you physically?" Cherry asked.

Lacey's lips tightened. She didn't want to pursue this element of the conversation any further, and there was a heavy silence in the room.

"I know this is difficult for you to talk about, but it might help us to know, and it might help you to tell us," Cherry said, encouragingly.

"He'd hurt me," Lacey began at last, and the words did not come easily. "He'd always shield the violence under the guise of sex and lovemaking, but the pain was quite real."

"Did you ever complain about it?" Cherry asked gently.

"Resistance encouraged him. He'd get meaner."

"Was he like that before your marriage?"

Lacey gave a short laugh of derision. "Steve was too smart to tip his hand prematurely. He treated me like a royal princess during our brief and intense courtship."

"Why did you stay with him?" Chuck asked.

"I hated to admit that my parents had been right. Anyway, I got pregnant shortly after the wedding, and things were tolerable while I was living in my father's house. By the time Steve realized he would never get anywhere at Gallagher's Best, we had two children."

"And you went to Texas, where things didn't get any better?" Cherry asked.

"God no. I was happy to go to Texas because I wanted my husband to succeed on his own. Steve, however, had the mistaken idea that if he took me and the children away from my parents, they'd give him whatever he wanted to get us back. He underestimated my mother and father. They were both very tough people. I was welcome to come home, but not with him. Once I found the courage to leave, I knew I would never go back."

"If you'd been convicted of murder, Steve got control of the kids but not the money, right?" Chuck asked, and Lacey nodded.

"We talked about it this afternoon. He was furious when he found out Tom Brennan would control their inheritance. He didn't understand all the implications of the divorce agreement."

Lacey paused before continuing. "There's something else you should know. Steve was completely frustrated when that fake will was read, because it stated he'd get ten million dollars to marry me."

"Why would that frustrate him?"

"He wasn't free. He already had a wife in Texas."

"Is there any possibility that he might have left the house the night of your sister-in-law's death?" Cherry asked.

Lacey thought for a moment and then shook her head.

"Why not?"

"There's a motion detector in the hallway, which was turned on. There was no way he could disarm the security system without walking through the beam."

A significant look passed between the detectives, and Lacey picked up on it. "What's going on?" she asked.

"Nothing really, it's just that we've been considering the notion that there might be two murderers."

"You weren't sleeping in your usual rooms. How would Steve know which one your brother was in?" Chuck asked.

"He was here for a visit five months ago."

"So it would have been possible for him to pretend to leave and then hide himself somewhere on the grounds until everyone was asleep. Did he have a key?" Cherry asked.

"Our butler has a key rack in the pantry. There are duplicate keys to everything there, all neatly hung and labeled. It's always been like that, even when Steve lived here."

"Then he could have gone through the kitchen," Cherry theorized, "picked up whatever keys he needed to get back in, and then found himself a comfortable place to wait until everyone was asleep."

Lacey remembered something she had forgotten entirely. "Yes, and he could have sneaked into my room to get the letter opener sometime during the hours when Scott and I were in the library drinking wine and talking. I noticed my bedroom door was closed when I returned, and I distinctly remembered leaving it open."

"If he'd been here recently, then he also knew about what time Scott's wife went for her morning jog," Cherry reasoned.

Lacey nodded. "Steve's an early riser. He probably saw her."

"Did he come often?" Chuck asked.

"About every eight or nine months, and never for more than two or three days. I paid for the plane tickets and made the reservations. It was a long-enough visit."

"You still have your security guards?"

"Yes, I do."

"Good. We'll post a car outside, and we'll be back by eight in the morning. We'll find out what he wants and take it from there. I know you're not going to get much sleep, but try to rest. Tomorrow will be a tough day," Cherry advised.

Gordon saw them to the door, and Lacey made her way upstairs to say good night to Erin and Mary. Her heart ached when she thought about JJ. Where was he and what was he thinking?

56

As weary as she was, Lacey knew that sleep would be impossible for her until she had her son safely back home, so she was happy to be reminded by a note on her bedside table to return Penny's call. Her friend answered on the first ring.

Penny was eager to hear everything, and Lacey briefly sketched in the events of the evening, without mentioning her conversation with the detectives concerning her personal relationship with Steve. Painful as it was, it had given her no sense of relief or catharsis. She merely felt humiliated.

After she had hung up the telephone, she stripped off her clothes and got into the shower to wash off the salt from the sea as well as the perspiration of fear. She pulled a fresh silk nightgown from the dresser drawer and then put it back. With her son out there somewhere, she wanted to be ready to move at a moment's notice, and so she stepped into clean underwear and then pulled on a sweat suit. She could lie down in it and be comfortable and still be ready to respond to any kind of emergency.

She brushed out her hair and then stretched out on the bed to watch the late news on television. Her heart raced when she listened to the newscaster describe the futile search for her son and his father's demand for ransom. God, did the police have to tell the media every damned detail?

She snapped off the TV and closed her eyes. She would try to nap if she could. Detective Dolan had certainly been right when she warned her there was a difficult time ahead. God, would this terror ever end? She wanted her son back safe and sound, and she closed her eyes and said a little prayer. Dear God, don't let him be afraid, and please don't let him suffer for the sins of his parents.

It was a long night. Several times she found herself nodding off only to be jerked awake by the reality of the situation. At dawn, she greeted the sunlight on the horizon with the cheering notion that perhaps the new day would bring with it the safe return of JJ.

Late in the morning, Cherry and Chuck arrived with the money, which had been delivered to them by Lacey's friendly banker. Gordon served lunch, and although everyone pretended to eat, most of the food went back to the kitchen.

Sensitive to the delicacy of the situation, Mary devoted her attention to keeping Erin diverted. The two of them went out to the kennels to play with the new litter of puppies whelped the week before by Snubby, the schnauzer. When they wearied of that, Mary suggested they take a swim, and after they had showered, she insisted on giving the younger woman a new hairdo. The minutes ticked by like hours. Each time the telephone rang, everyone leapt to attention, hearts pounding with expectancy, but the call they awaited did not come.

Periodically, Chuck and Cherry would check with headquarters to see if anything new had happened, but the answer was always negative. There was no sign of the Zodiac or Steve or JJ.

By midnight, after much consultation with their superiors, Chuck and Cherry decided to leave.

"Lacey, I guess we're going to have to pack it in for today. I don't think we're going to hear from him," Cherry said. "And I think you ought to try to get some rest. This thing might go on for days. Apparently he's fairly secure about the place where he's hiding, because it looks like he's in no hurry."

"Dear God, don't tell me that! I'm not sure I can endure another day of waiting," Lacey exclaimed. "Right now I feel like I'm going to explode."

"I have a feeling that's exactly what this man wants you to do. He's being unpredictable. That makes our job harder and it serves his ends," Chuck observed.

"You need sleep. Have you got any sedatives?" Cherry asked.

"I have some pills that were prescribed for my father."

"Take one, by all means. The house is safe. We're leaving a car at the gate and two officers patroling the grounds, in addition to Tim Coffey's men. We're going to have to wait this man out. You've got the money, and you can rest assured eventually he's going to contact you to get it," Chuck concluded.

Lacey finally agreed to try to rest, and after the detectives had gone, she tiptoed into Erin's room. Her daughter was asleep, but Mary rose from her pillow and whispered, "She's fine, Lacey. Don't worry; I'm not much of a sleeper, and I'll watch over her closely. Go to bed now."

Lacey went back to her room, got the sleeping pills from her medicine chest and started to take one, but as she was about to put it on her tongue, she changed her mind. No, if she really needed to sleep, nature would do it for her. She merely sipped some cold water and climbed into bed.

After a while, the weariness that made her bones ache subsided somewhat, and lassitude crept slowly through her body. She didn't want to give in to it, but she was both mentally and physically exhausted. Clothed in a fresh running suit and with the light shining brightly in her face, Lacey's eyes closed and she surrendered to sleep and to troubled dreams.

She was on the sea again, not in a boat but floating on top of the water. She could not move her arms or her legs but she did not sink into the icy waves. She floated immobile and surrounded by the clammy darkness. Somewhere in the distance she heard a voice calling to her. Sometimes it sounded like JJ's voice, at other times it was her brother's. She tried to call back to them, to reassure them that everything would be all right, but try as she might, she couldn't utter a sound because there seemed to be a heavy weight pressing on her voice box. She struggled to release herself, but the pressure grew more intense, and suddenly, she came to full wakefulness. Her eyes sprang open, but she could not see!

Confused about where she was, she blinked rapidly, and then she remembered with a start that when she had gone to sleep, the light on her bedside table had been shining brightly in her face. Who had turned it off? Groping for the switch, she accidentally hit the glass of ice water she always kept on her night table. With a noisy clatter, it bounced off the table and splashed water everywhere.

"Damn!" she exclaimed as she pulled her wet hand back to dry it on the sheet. She reached for the light switch again, turned it, and nothing happened. The bulb must have blown out, she reasoned, as she peered through the darkness to see if she could read the time on her digital clock radio. Strangely, she could see nothing. By this time she was sitting on the edge of the bed. Fumbling with her feet, she tried to locate her slippers, but she encountered only cold water and ice cubes on the rug.

Furious with herself for being so clumsy, she swore and pulled open the drawer on the night table. She was almost certain there was a flashlight there. She rummaged about and found nothing but a small package of tissues and a tube of hand cream. Frustrated, she fell back on the pillow once more. Where was she going to go anyway? The security guards or one of the servants would undoubtedly deal with the electricity and get it turned on again soon. She closed her eyes and lay still.

Then she heard a sound. Had her door opened?

"Who is it?" she called, but only stillness answered her.

She called again, and this time her voice carried a more commanding tone, "Who's there?"

Moving slowly so as not to make any noise, she sat up again. She was not alone. Someone had entered her room. She could feel the presence, and the silence was hostile. She tried to ease herself off the bed. If she was going to be attacked by an unseen hand as her brother had been, she was not going to lie there and wait for it. Whoever was in the room with her was as handicapped by the inky darkness as she was, and although each movement set up a rustle of the sheets, she kept going. Soon she was off the bed and on her feet. Which way to go? The bathroom? She could lock herself in there and telephone . . . no! She couldn't save herself and risk making her daughter and Mary a target. But they were together in the other wing, and she was here alone.

The door! She would move as fast as she could and get out of the room. There was no point in staying here. She'd run down the stairs and start screaming as soon as she was free. She'd alert everyone in the house.

Dragging her feet across the carpeting so as not to risk slipping on the ice or the water, she traversed the room. She did not hesitate or pause to listen, but she wondered if the person nearby could hear the sound of her heart thudding in her chest.

Her hand touched the knob. The door was still closed. Her mind must be playing tricks on her and she must have imagined that she heard it open, she thought with relief. There was no one here. She was about to turn back and return to bed when she heard a sound that could not be mistaken. Someone was very close to her. She could hear breathing. Panicked, she groped for the knob once more. This time she tried to turn it and yank the door open, but nothing happened. The door was locked! She fumbled for the key, but it was gone.

Then she felt a hand take a firm grip at the back of her neck, and another hand quickly covered her mouth and her nose and pressed so hard that she could not breathe.

"Don't make a sound. If you do anything, anything at all to cause a stir, you will never see JJ alive again, understand?" It was Steve's voice whispering into her ear.

Terrified, she nodded, but she clawed at his hand to pull it away so she could breathe.

"I've got your son in a spot where he'll die if I don't get back there in time to save him—do you understand that? And so help me God, I will let him die if you cross me."

His voice was low, the words were harsh and desperate, and she had no doubt that they were spoken in truth.

She nodded again, and although his hand came away from her mouth, he kept his tight hold on her neck.

"I took the handgun off the boat, so be careful what you do."

"Where's JJ?" Lacey whispered.

"You and I are going to go get him, but you've got to cooperate, understand? If anything happens to me, I'll kill you first, and nobody will ever be able to find JJ in time to save him."

"How did you get into the house?"

"I asked questions." She could detect a note of pride in his answer. "The security people were more than happy to point out ways the system can be circumvented. It was easy."

"But the guards?"

"The night guys play gin rummy when they aren't on rounds."

A beam of light shined into Lacey's face as Steve snapped on a flashlight. The light startled her and hurt her eyes. She winced.

"You look sick without makeup, you know that?" he commented. "But you're dressed, that's good."

"Help me find some shoes. I can't go anyplace in my bare feet." Something told Lacey to talk to Steve and make him feel comfortable. She had no choice but to cooperate with him anyway, at least until JJ was safe again.

He swept the light around the room and focused it on the pair of sneakers she always kept at bedside in case of a nightime earthquake. "There, those'll do. Put 'em on. We've got to get out of here. One of the guys just now passed through the hallway. That'll give us about ten minutes before the next one comes through."

"How do you know they'll be on schedule with the electricity off?"

"I wasn't stupid enough to turn off all the circuits and alert everybody in the house. I only turned off the one this room is on. I'm not dumb, even if you and your father thought so."

"We never thought you were dumb, Steve. On the contrary," Lacey replied as she knelt to tie the laces on her shoes.

Steve turned the light off. "We gotta let our eyes get accustomed to the dark again before we start out."

"Where are we going?" she asked. She was calm now, reassured that she had her fears under control. She had a job to do, and it was obvious that she would have to do it alone.

"We're going out the back door. I left it open. Then, well, you'll see. But first we're going to get the money. Where is it?"

"It's locked up, in the big safe in Dad's study."

"Let's get it. Come on." He grasped her arm, put the key in the lock, and turned it. In silence, they moved out into the hallway and crept down the staircase. Because she knew that Steve did not make idle threats, she intended to cooperate with him fully.

Without making a sound, they made their way to the study, and within a few short minutes, she had opened the large safe and extracted the suitcase filled with money. They moved swiftly on.

The door near the pantry was open as Steve said it would be. He paused at the security panel, punched several buttons, and then pulled Lacey out of the house and closed the door.

"There. Now when those jerks check the security system, which they do about twice a night, they'll see that everything's in perfect order."

"Now where?" she asked.

"We have to walk, but not down the road. Stay on the lawn," he said, steering her toward the grass.

"Why?"

"Because they've stretched wires across the pavement to warn when a car passes over it."

"I didn't know that."

"They did a lot of junk to run up your bill," he said with a derisive snort.

"You didn't learn everything by asking questions, did you?" she asked. She had to keep the conversation going.

"Thanks to you and your stingy father I had to work in Austin three days a week installing security systems to put food on the table," he said, pulling her arm and making her walk faster.

"But I've sent you money on several occasions since the divorce, Steve. I signed the checks myself."

"Those checks didn't even cover the mortgage and the taxes. What was I supposed to eat?"

She tried to remain calm, but she couldn't help thinking that without her help he would have lost the land a long time ago. He had never been the least bit grateful, and it irked her. She wanted to shout at him that she hadn't been forced to help him; she had done it because she didn't want her children's father to be impoverished, but this was no time to have another argument about money. They were approaching the gate. Would he remember that the slightest sound would turn on the lights and the TV camera? Should she tell him? She slowed her pace, thinking.

Steve jerked her arm to hurry her along, and it was almost too late.

They were already in the sensitive zone and approaching the iron gates, which were closed and locked.

"We've got to be really quiet now," he whispered. "We're going to climb over the gates. You first."

She looked up at the eight-foot-high iron gates with the spearpoint tops and shook her head.

"I'll never make it."

"You damned well better," he threatened and gave her a shove. "There are laser beams on top the walls. You haven't got any choice."

Lacey was an athletic woman. In her youth she had been a formidable tennis player and golfer, and she was still a strong swimmer, but the prospect of pulling herself up and over a gate that was two and a half feet taller than she was intimidating.

"I can't do it," she whispered.

"Think of your kid, and you'll make it," Steve replied, grabbing her arm and pushing her upward.

Lacey moved to the side where it wasn't quite so high and began her climb, reaching upward with her hands, and trying to get a grip on the vertical iron spokes. At first she made little headway but then she took Steve's advice and thought about JJ and with a mother's burst of effort she grabbed the top crossbar. With painful effort, she pulled herself up and got one knee on the railing. If she slipped or fell now, she would for sure be impaled on one of the spearheads. She moved with extreme caution. The muscles in her arms quivered with exertion, but she managed to get herself over. She wanted to let go and fall to the ground, but she was afraid she would make too much noise and trigger the lights, so hand over hand, she made her way down the other side.

When her feet hit the ground at last, Steve tossed the valise over, and then she watched him effortlessly pull himself up and over. She was reminded again how much she was overmatched in raw strength. If she was going to triumph and save her son, she would have to use her wits to do it.

As soon as his feet touched the ground, Steve grabbed her arm again and pulled her down the dark road.

"I've got a car about a hundred yards down the way," he said, no longer speaking in a whisper.

She ran with him, her mind filled with questions. The first one popped out of her mouth when she saw the car, a gray Mercedes.

"Where did you get this car?"

"It was parked in the lot at gangway twenty-five. Whoever owns it is probably at sea and won't report it missing until he gets back."

"You didn't have a key?"

"I hotwired it. Get in."

"But didn't it have an alarm or something?" she asked, doing as she was told.

"It's an old car. They're easier." As he spoke, he did something with wires under the steering wheel, and the car started.

"Where are we going?"

"To the *Santa Maria*. You and JJ and I are going on a little trip."

"But you've got the money, what do you want with us?"

"I want the golden eggs and the goose who lays them," he answered with a grin.

"What are you talking about?"

"Once we get down to Mexico, you'll have all the money I'll ever need sent down there. Nobody's going to do a thing about it, because I'll keep JJ under my wing for protection."

His words brought a sickening feeling into her stomach, and for one ugly moment Lacey thought she was going to throw up. She shut her eyes tightly and held her breath until the feeling went away. Oh God, she thought, he intended to keep her son.

They had turned onto the Pacific Coast Highway and were headed to Long Beach before Lacey found words to speak.

"Are you telling me that you plan to keep JJ?"

"You should have never taken my son away from me in the first place. We'll have a great time sailing the seven seas on that beautiful boat of your father's. It was the only thing I ever enjoyed about our marriage."

Lacey ignored the slighting remark. It wasn't the worst thing he'd ever said to her.

"Why did you run away last night when the detectives arrived at the house?"

"I knew you had something up your sleeve, because you were pretending someone else was at the door. When I saw it was the police arriving, I knew you had found the plane ticket. You're such a bitch, Lacey. Any other kind of a wife would have asked me for an explanation first." His voice had an edge honed on hatred.

"Then you did kill Scott?"

"What does it matter? Everybody thinks I did."

"You did kill him, and you wanted me to be blamed. Isn't that right?"

"It was such a sweet deal, I couldn't pass it up. Too bad I neglected to find out that I could never have control of the money. All the responsibility of raising the brats and none of the cash. Live and learn."

Lacey wanted to fling herself at him and drive the car off the road, but she dared not indulge her hatred. She had to save her son.

"Are we going to get JJ?" she asked.

"Yeah. We'll pick him up at the *Santa Maria*."

Steve glanced across and saw the relieved expression on her face, and he laughed out loud.

"Don't look so damned complacent, Lacey. I didn't leave him *on* the *Santa Maria*. He's under it!"

A gasp of fear escaped from her lips. For one horrifying moment she believed that her son was dead and that Steve had been lying to her to keep her in line.

"What do you mean?" she almost screamed, and she was about to leap on Steve, grab the steering wheel, and kill both of them.

"Relax, he's locked to the dock, about eight feet down. I put a pair of scuba tanks on him—he's got at least fifteen more minutes of air." He looked at her and smiled a mirthless smile. "You see, I didn't lie to you. If I'd been caught, he'd be dead."

Her words were as sharp as razor blades as she said between clenched teeth, "Drive faster!"

57

L acey was out of the car and on her way toward the gangway of the berth where the *Santa Maria* was docked. The padlock was still on the gate.

"How did you get on the boat?" she said, whirling around to face Steve.

"Calm yourself. You're getting too excited. We crawled down the rocks and then climbed up on the dock. Everything was left unlocked except the gate, which was lucky for me. What happened to Billy? That little tap I gave him on the head spook him?"

"He's in the hospital with a fractured skull, thanks to your little tap," Lacey said as she gingerly made her way down the rocks. Within seconds she negotiated the precarious descent and then climbed up onto the dock. Although she tore her sweat suit and skinned her knee, she was unaware of it. Running as fast as her legs could move, she sprinted onto the deck and within seconds she had disappeared down the ladder. Steve tried to catch up.

"Where the hell do you think you're going?" he shouted at her fast-disappearing figure.

"To save my son!" she screamed, not slowing her pace.

He caught up with her in the equipment room, where she was frantically rummaging through the diving gear. She finally found a pair of fins; then she found a mask and a tank. With shaking hands she was trying to attach a mouthpiece and regulator when Steve snatched them away from her.

"What the hell do you think you're doing?" he demanded.

"Give me the key to the lock! I'm going down to get JJ now. The diving equipment we keep here is old. Billy only uses it to clean the bottom of the boat. JJ might be in trouble!"

"Relax! I'll be more than happy to let you go down and free him, but you'll go without a tank. I'm not taking any chances on the two of you swimming away under the water."

He put his hand in his pocket and took out the small key, which he handed to her. "You'll need a light," he said, reaching into the cabinet and pulling out a small underwater flashlight.

Without a word, Lacey grabbed it, adjusted the mask on her face, slipped out of her sneakers, and headed topside. When she reached the deck, with Steve close behind, she asked as she pulled on her fins, "Where did you leave him?"

"Aft. Turn on the light. You'll see the bubbles."

Lacey did so, but after a few minutes of scanning the dark water and seeing no sign of life, she began to panic. Suppose she was too late? Suppose one of the tanks had been faulty? Suppose JJ had panicked?

"Point exactly where he is!" she screamed, and her voice registered the terrible tension she was feeling.

"Right there!"

Lacey peered at the water over the spot he indicated, and seeing the bubbles at last, she tucked the small key in the left side of her mouth, back between her teeth and her cheek where it would be safe. She didn't want to take a chance on dropping it. Then she took a deep breath and jumped in. The water was dark and murky, but the flashlight was helpful. On her first breath, she dove about eight feet down, and located JJ right away. He saw the light moving toward him and he reached out to his savior. She gave his hand a quick squeeze of reassurance and pulled him under the dock where Steve could not see what they were doing. She then plucked the key from her cheek, and with some difficulty inserted it into the padlock holding the chain that was wrapped tightly around JJ's wrist. When he was free and ready to surface, Lacey held him back so she could check the pressure gauge with the flashlight. Satisfied that he had enough air to escape from the area, she indicated to him that he should give her a breath of air. Taking the regulator from his mouth, he handed it to her. When she was finished, she gave it back, turned off the flashlight, and pulled him close enough so that her fingers could touch his face. Quickly she traced the letters SOS on his cheek and stuffed the unlit flashlight in his hand. Then she skillfully stripped the fins off her own feet and pressed them into his hands. He nodded his head vigorously so she would know that he understood, and without wasting another moment, he pulled the fins on his feet and took off, being careful not to breathe until he was away from the dock so that the direction of his bubbles could not be traced.

Lacey stayed down as long as she could and then with her chest almost bursting, she swam upward. She surfaced, gulped for air and yelled at Steve as a diversionary tactic.

"Quick, hand me another flashlight! That one went dead, and I can't see a damn thing down there!"

She splashed about gasping for air, and if he was suspicious, he did not show it. After all, he had not lived with her for many years and had no idea how skilled a skin diver she had become. He did as she asked, and she went down again. She stayed as long as she possibly could, moving around with the light so that it would seem that she was searching. She had to stall and give her son enough time to escape before Steve got suspicious. She surfaced, breathed again, and went under once more before Steve could ask her any questions.

When she emerged this time, she took the offensive and screamed hysterically at Steve, "Get your ass down here and help me find him!"

"What are you talking about?" he asked, momentarily confused.

"You lied to me, you son of a bitch! He's not here! I've looked everywhere and I can't find him."

Steve finally began to get suspicious. "Get out of the water!" he commanded.

"No! I'm not getting out until I bring JJ with me. Now where the hell is he?"

"Get out of the water, I told you. Now do it!" She could see that he was now holding a gun in his hand.

She was tempted to dive under the water and swim away, but her concern for JJ's safety was so great that she could not save herself without first doing everything she could to give him the time he needed to get away.

"Steve, stop being such a bastard! Come on down here and show me exactly where he is or at least give me a tank and regulator so I can do a better job of searching," she replied in a tone of voice that was more pleading than demanding. "Hurry!"

Her less-strident approach mollified him somewhat, but he was still suspicious.

"He's there, I tell you. Count the third piling from the tie. That's exactly where I put him."

"I'm pretty sure I checked that entire area, but it's dark, and I might have missed him. The batteries are almost gone on this thing, and I need something brighter. I'll try again, but I wish you'd come help me."

Steve tossed her another flashlight, then she gulped a great breath of air, switched on the light again, and pulled herself down once more, staying submerged as long as her breath held out. She surfaced again.

"He's not there!" she sputtered, gasping for air.

"Get out of the water. We're taking the *Santa Maria* and getting the hell out of here!"

"I'm not leaving here without my son!"

"You bitch! You released him and sent him for help, didn't you?"

"Go to hell!" she yelled, took another deep breath and dove below the surface again. The water was cold and she could feel her body getting numb. The game was played out. She had stretched it as far as it would go. She began to swim.

The next time she surfaced for air, she was on the water side of the boat docked at berth two. Along with her heart, her mind was racing. She had to get far away as fast as she could. She hoped she had done the right thing in sending JJ for help.

She dove again and began to swim harder.

For her next breath, she surfaced at berth one, where she had a good view of the *Santa Maria*. With horror she saw Steve preparing to jump into the water completely rigged in scuba gear, tank, and fins. Good God, he was coming after her! She had to get out of the water as fast as she could without making any kind of disturbance. Without a tank or fins, she was at a dreadful disadvantage.

Trying to quell her terror, she forced herself to relax and look around. A light in the distance reminded her that the marine bureau was no more than a hundred yards away. She was sure that a radio operator was on duty there at all times. She decided to stay on the surface of the water because without fins she could swim faster that way. It was a gamble, but she had to take it. Afraid to swim freestyle because her flutter kick would churn up the water too much and give away her whereabouts, she opted for the quieter breast stroke and frog kick. It wasn't fast, but it would be safer in the long run. A strong swimmer, she was now motivated by fear, and her long, lean body glided swiftly through the water.

She concentrated on breathing regularly and tried to focus her mind on her stroke, but she couldn't help wondering what vicious measures Steve would take to secure money and his freedom if he ever caught up with her. He had already committed murder and put his own son's life in serious jeopardy. What would he do to her if he caught her now? She must not think about it.

Pull, kick, breathe, pull, kick, breathe. Each time her head lifted above the water she saw that she was drawing closer to her destination. Another fifty yards and she would be at the harbor master's dock. She began looking for it, but it was a dark night and she could see nothing. If memory served her right, there was a ladder on the dock that she could use to get herself out of the water, and then she could run the rest of the way. Her overused muscles were beginning to cramp, first in her feet and then in the calves of her legs, but she continued to force them to move.

So focused was she that she failed to notice a light below the surface of the water that was fast closing on her, and as she touched the bow of the *Sea Queen,* a large vessel tied up at the dock, a hand reached out and grasped her ankle.

She tried to shake it off, but the grip was too strong and too tight. She pulled her knees to her chest and with a fierce shove, she tried to push him away, but she couldn't do it. He was pulling her under, taking her down where she could not breathe anymore, perhaps never again. She was too terrified to realize that without her alive, he would be nothing but a fugitive from the law, and she tried to fight him. She squirmed and writhed in the water until she was in a position to grasp his mask. With one ferocious tug, she pulled it off his face. Forced to let her go momentarily while he retrieved and replaced it, she was able to surface and get a breath of air.

Certain that she was fighting for her life, she knew it was futile to try to escape, so she maneuvered herself behind him. Without fins it was difficult for her to move as fast as he could, but she clutched at the valve on his tank. With one quick twist, she shut off his supply of air. He turned around to grab at her, and as quickly as he did so, she groped around his waist, located the weight belt, and with one fast maneuver, she released it. The lead weights sank like a stone. Lacey surfaced fast, gulped air quickly, and then dove down as deep as she could go. Steve was wearing a buoyant foam rubber wet suit, and without the weight belt, it was impossible for him to follow her down.

Knowing that she had bought herself a little time, she moved away from him, swimming rapidly. She did not come up for air again until she had reached the stern of the *Sea Queen.* Fumbling in the darkness, she located a ladder and had her foot on the first rung when a hand shot out of the water and grabbed her once more, this time with such ferocity that she was yanked off the ladder and back down into the water.

Determined to die fighting, Lacey once again got a grip on Steve's face mask, but this time her maneuver didn't work. Raising his heavy flashlight, he crashed it into her skull, and she sank instantly into unconsciousness.

When Lacey next opened her eyes, she found herself lying on the bunk in the forward cabin of the *Santa Maria* with her hands and feet bound. By the sound of the engines and the motion of the boat, she knew they were under way. Where in God's name were they going?

She felt a huge and painful lump on her forehead, and she shivered. Her clothes were still wet. Painfully, she tried to reach down to the foot of the bunk to pull a blanket over herself. She was exhausted, weary, and dizzy. She closed her eyes. Her child had gotten away safely. That was all that was important to her. Whatever happened would happen. It was out of her hands now.

58

JJ escaped as Lacey had wanted him to do. He stayed under the water until he had crossed the channel. He surfaced, pulled himself onto the dock at the Alamitos Bay Yacht Club, stripped off his diving gear, and on legs quivering with fear and cold, he propelled himself to the large building, but it was locked up and dark. He looked around and saw a light in one of the houses on the other side of the yacht club's marina. He ran up to the house and rang the bell. Then without waiting for anyone to answer, he began pounding on the door and shouting, "Please, somebody help me! Please, somebody answer."

After a few minutes of silence, an elderly man peered out the window.

"What the hell . . . ," he began, and then he saw the wet and shivering young boy. He opened the window and asked, "Good God, what are you doing out this late on a chilly night without any clothes on?"

"Please, sir, would you call the police for me?"

At first, the man was tempted to slam the window shut, thinking it was a trick, but the sound of the boy's voice, and the vision of his vulnerable young body made him think otherwise.

"You want me to call the police?" the man asked.

"Yessir, I'd sure appreciate it if you'd just call 9-1-1. Please, please, sir, my mom's in terrible danger. My dad chained me to a piling under the water, and left me there. She set me free and now he's got her on our boat. She sent me to get help."

The story was too fantastic not to be true. "Okay, I'll do it. But you wait out there."

"Thanks, sir, and will you tell the police my name?"

"What is it?"

"John Joseph Gallagher."

The man disappeared and five minutes later he opened the door and invited JJ inside to get warm.

"Come on in, boy. The police are on their way. Here wrap yourself in this windbreaker."

JJ gratefully took the jacket and pulled it on his icy body.

"So you're Jack Gallagher's grandson. Whattya know about that. Your family's sure had a lot of trouble since he died."

268

A squad car was there within five minutes. In the relative warmth of the police car, JJ told them the whole story, and the word was relayed to the harbor patrol and the coast guard.

"I think he's got my mom. She probably didn't try to get away so I'd have a chance to escape." For JJ, the terror was still very real. His once beloved and admired father had turned into a monster, and at this moment in time, JJ believed him capable of hideous things. After all, hadn't he left his only son chained under the sea for more than an hour? It had been an hour JJ would often relive in his thoughts and his dreams for the rest of his life.

"Where's your mother's boat located?" the officer asked.

JJ told them, and the car took off and headed there, but when they arrived, the *Santa Maria* was gone.

"That's her! There, heading out past the jetty!" JJ shouted.

"Don't worry, son. The coast guard will pick her up. Your mom's going to be fine. Come on, now. We'll take you home."

Erin and Mary greeted JJ with cries of relief and tears. It was the first time he could ever remember his sister taking him in her arms and holding him close.

"Oh God, JJ, are you all right?" Erin asked, and there were tears in her eyes.

JJ nodded, and suddenly he began to cry too. He put his head on his sister's shoulder and sobbed in relief, in weariness, and in agonizing despair.

Mary wanted to step in and whisk JJ up to a hot shower—his lips and fingernails were quite blue with cold—but she sensed that this moment of bonding between brother and sister was important. They were, after all, faced with the frightening prospect of having to grow up without a parent.

After a few minutes, however, she suggested that JJ needed to be warmed up and dressed properly, and JJ went up the stairs, promising to return soon and tell them everything.

"I'll get some hot cocoa," Erin said.

In ten minutes, JJ was back downstairs, dressed in warm-ups and wool socks.

"Detective Dolan will be here any minute. She was the one who called and told us about you. We didn't even know your mom had left the house," Mary told him.

"I know. Dad . . . " He said the word, but seemed to choke on it. As far as he was concerned, he no longer had a real father. "He sneaked up behind Billy and hit him on the head really hard."

"What happened then?" Erin asked.

"He took the gun, and then we tried to make a run for it in the Zodiac out past the jetty, but there were harbor patrol boats everywhere. We retreated to gangway thirty-three, which was deserted. Dad sank the Zodiac there, and we walked to the shopping center at Marina Pacifica and went to the movies."

"You went to the movies?!" Erin exclaimed.

"Didn't you have any idea what your father was up to?" Mary asked.

"He told me Mom was threatening to take me'n Erin away from him for good."

"And you believed him, JJ?" Erin asked.

JJ lowered his head. "I didn't know what to think."

"Then what happened?" Mary asked.

"We stayed for two movies. We sneaked from one theater to another and ate two tubs of popcorn and drank three Cokes. It was kinda fun actually."

"And then after the theater closed?" Erin prompted.

"We walked all the way back to the *Santa Maria*. Every time a car passed on the road, we hid. We got to the gangway, the gate was locked, so we climbed down the rocks and then up on the dock. Dad sent me aboard first to see if anybody was there, but it was deserted. What happened to Billy?"

"He's in the hospital with a fractured skull."

"No kidding? It kinda scared me when I saw Dad hit him, but he said he'd be okay in a few minutes."

"Then what did you do?"

"Dad kept me locked up in the engine room for the rest of the night and all day yesterday. Every now and then he'd bring me something to eat and let me go to the head. He didn't let me out until late tonight when he made me put on the scuba gear. I didn't want to, but he told me I had to even though my wet suit was at home and Billy's was too big for me."

JJ took a deep, shuddering breath and continued. "I almost freaked out when he chained me down in the water. He shined the flashlight on his watch and showed me he'd be back in one hour. I had two tanks of air, which I knew was plenty, but I was freezing and awful scared."

Mary noticed the haunted ring of fear around JJ's eyes, and she wondered if it would be there permanently.

Their conversation was interrupted by the arrival of Chuck and Cherry, and JJ repeated his story for them.

"We think your mom's aboard. If she is, we're gonna get her back safe and sound. You can count on that. Now, did your dad say anything, anything at all about what his plans were?" Chuck asked.

JJ shook his head silently.

"JJ, think hard. When you and your father were walking to the shopping center and then back to the dock where the *Santa Maria* was tied, what did you talk about?" Cherry asked.

"Mostly we talked about traveling."

"Traveling?" Cherry asked.

"Yeah, on the *Santa Maria*. He said how swell it would be if we could just live aboard the boat and never stay two nights in the same place. But it was just talk. Erin and I've got to go to school."

A concerned glance shot between the detectives, and they went on with their questioning but elicited no further information of any importance. After a few minutes, they suggested that perhaps JJ should get some sleep.

59

A hand was roughly shaking her shoulder, and an irritated voice called her name.

"Lacey, for God's sake, open your eyes! I've got to talk to you now!"

Lacey opened her eyes and tried to focus them in the bright light of the flashlight shining in her face, but she had difficulty aligning the two faces hovering over her into one image.

"Steve?" she asked, and the voice that came from her lips sounded as if it were coming from far, far away. She must have either passed out again or fallen asleep. She wondered how long she had been lying there.

"Lacey, get with it!" he said with impatience. "I can only stay here a moment. The auto pilot isn't working, and I've got to get back to the wheel. I've got the boat going as slow as it can go, but we'll be on the rocks if I don't get back up there immediately. Look, I'm going to untie you, and I want you to come up to the bridge as fast as you can, understand? I threw the main switch because there's so much damned new electronic equipment that I couldn't figure out how to shut down the running lights. We've got to travel dark until we're clear of the channel."

In an instant, both her mind and her eyes began working.

"You shut down the main switch! The one in the engine room?"

"Of course," he replied. "I thought I saw a harbor patrol boat approaching, and I panicked. Now, I need you to get the hell down there and turn it back on, but not until you've first shut off all the running lights. Do you know how to do it?" The anxiety in his voice was palpable.

"Who in God's name cast off for you?" she asked, bewildered.

"I cut the lines! Now can you do it?"

Lacey's mind was racing. The *Santa Maria* had always been manned by a capable crew of at least five men, and the thought of trying to operate her, even under power, with only the two of them was daunting, to say the least. Lacey tried to remember where the electrical panel was, but she wasn't exactly sure. It had been years since she had actually done anything on the *Santa Maria* except enjoy the ride, but she didn't intend to tell Steve that until he'd set her free.

"Of course I can," she assured him, "but I'll need that flashlight.

Hurry, you've got to get back to the wheel as fast as you can. The channel is narrow, and we'll be on the rocks before you know it. Untie my hands, and I'll release my own feet." She hoped she'd conveyed a powerful sense of urgency.

"How long will it take you?" he asked as he moved away.

"God, I don't know. I'll do it as fast as I can, but it's suicide to travel without lights at night."

"I've got her on the right heading, and it's a helluva lot safer for me to travel dark than risk being located by the patrol or the coast guard. Now move your ass, and get the electricity going again, and don't try anything funny, or I'll come after you, and this time you'll get more than a crack on the head," he warned her.

"I've got to have that flashlight, or I'll never find my way around the panel."

He tossed the flashlight on the bed and disappeared. As soon as he had gone, Lacey hurriedly undid the knot around her ankles, her mind flying as fast as her fingers. When she was free at last, she got to her feet, moving too fast, and the cabin walls seemed to be reeling. That blow on her head had probably given her a concussion. She steadied herself by clutching the table until she was more or less stabilized. She knew that she had a rare opportunity to scuttle her ex-husband's plans if she could manage to think smart and move fast enough.

When she was ready to leave the cabin, she grasped the flashlight in her hand and proceeded cautiously. There had to be something she could do to stop Steve. She was encouraged by the news that the harbor patrol was apparently on the lookout for them, because that meant JJ had made it back safely. They were fast approaching the open sea, however, and on a night as foggy as this, Steve might get lucky and get away. It was a big ocean, and with filled tanks, the *Santa Maria* had a range of more than 2,500 miles, but under sail, they could go much farther. Unfortunately, two years before his fatal illness, her father had retrofitted the sails with new electronics that enabled him to operate the boat with a smaller crew. But even with all that new equipment, it would be damned near impossible for the two of them, unskilled as they were, to sail her successfully.

Nevertheless, she had a precious opportunity to scuttle Steve's getaway, if she could manage to do it without unduly risking her own life. She had no doubt that Steve would get extremely nasty and violent if he caught her trying to cross him.

She made her way down the gangway and into the engine room, and as soon as she was through the door, she swept the beam of the flashlight around, trying to get some inspiration. She spotted the main electrical panel, opened it, and then closed it again. No way was she going to restore the electrical power so he could engage the automatic pilot and come looking for her before she figured out some way to abort his getaway plans. A small window of opportunity had opened for her, and she was damned well going to find a way to crawl through it.

The moving beam of light suddenly illuminated the switch for the fuel pump, and she had the divine inspiration she so desperately sought. "Thank you, God," she muttered as she moved toward it to turn it off. After four or five minutes, the diesels would shut down, and it would be almost impossible for Steve to get them going again. Diesel engines could go on just about forever as long as they had fuel, but once shut down, they were hell to get started again.

Four or five minutes. What would she do with them? She'd go over the side, that's what she'd do, and then she'd swim back to safety! The dark and the fog would be her allies in escaping. Of course, it was also possible that she'd get lost and drown, but even that was better than staying here with the monster who had been willing to sacrifice his own son's life for money.

For an instant, she considered going back to the equipment room and getting herself a wet suit and fins, but she realized she didn't have the time. She must not waste a second of the precious few minutes lead time that she had. Besides, if the electricity didn't go on soon, Steve might leave the wheel again and come looking for her. Without hesitating another second, she turned off the fuel pump, and still clutching the flashlight, she hurriedly climbed up to the main deck, crept to the starboard side, and silently crawled over the rail. She stuffed the flashlight tightly into the waistband of her still damp pants, and without allowing herself a moment of second thoughts, she took a deep breath and jumped as far away from the boat as possible so as to avoid the propellers as the *Santa Maria* swept past her. She was tossed about when she was hit by the prop wash, but she swam hard to get herself clear.

As soon as she was sure that the sailboat was well past her, she treaded water and tried to get her bearings. By her own reckoning they had not gotten too far beyond the breakwater. She could see a brightness on the horizon that she was fairly certain was the skyline of the city of Long Beach. She had no choice but to pray she was right and head in that direction and hope she'd soon hit the breakwater. If she was wrong and was swimming out to sea, then she didn't have much hope. Without hesitating, she flattened her body out in the water and began to swim. She had no time to waste. The water was cold, and in this fog she could easily be run down by a boat or even an oceangoing vessel on its way into the harbor. Then there were the ever-present leopard sharks and jellyfish. God, the thought was terrifying, but not quite as terrifying as allowing herself to fall into Steve's control again.

Trying not to think about how cold and tired she was, she began to swim, moderately slow at first so that her muscles would warm up gradually and not cramp in the icy water.

Lacey soon found herself grooved into a steady stroke. She began to play mindgames with herself so she would not obsess about being cold and in danger. She imagined herself back in the deliciously warm eighty-six-degree water of her own pool, swimming lap after lap, exercising and relaxing her body. Even as a little girl, swimming had been her sport of choice, and she'd always had excellent endurance. She usually managed to outlast any of the boys when she swam laps with them. She had once even flirted with the idea of becoming a channel swimmer, and she had actually trained for a while with Greta Andersen, but Greta made her work out in the ocean, and she hated cold water. Now here she was, swimming for her life in water that felt like the Arctic. Too bad the ocean in Southern California was almost as cold in March as it was in December.

She had been gliding smoothly for almost half an hour, stopping only occasionally to make sure she was headed for the lights, when she suddenly felt a change in the water. It became more turbulent, and for a moment she became rigid with fear. Was it possible that her nightmare was coming true and she was being run down by one of those vast ships? Getting too close to one would be the death of her and she would be sucked under and pulled down. Her heart pounded, and then the most welcome sound she had ever heard came floating over the water. It was the bark of a sea lion! She must be getting close to the breakwater.

She knew she had to exercise caution from here on. Thank God the sea was calm or she'd be slammed right into the strand of hard, unforgiving rocks. She switched to a breast stroke so she could see where she was going. Her hand touched something warm and furry, and she heard a low-pitched grunt. She drew back immediately, realizing she must have encountered one of the numerous sea lions that populated the breakwater. As she attempted to alter her course, she felt a swell push her right into the rocks. She reached out, got a fingerhold, and held on. Pulling as hard as her tired and frozen arms could, she managed to drag her weary body up on the rocks, skinning her shins and knees on the barnacles. As the cold air hit her wet skin, she began to shiver uncontrollably, but she had no time to rest. She reached into her waistband, pulled out the waterproof flashlight, and turned it on so she could see where she was stepping. She had no shoes on, and the breakwater was always littered with dangerous debris, including fish hooks that had washed up on it. Gingerly, she began to make her way in the direction of the colored lights on the big oil island now visible in the distance. When she was in a direct line to it, she would dive back into the water and swim the half mile or so to reach it. Surely there would be a night crew working there.

She was moving along slowly, watching every step she took, and the going was very rough. She didn't want to slip and fall, and she certainly didn't want to step on one of the animals or get a fish hook snagged in her foot. She had gone no more than a few yards when she heard the motor of a boat that seemed to be bearing down on her from the ocean side. She was seized by confusion born of the paranoia of the pursued. Suppose it was Steve in the other dinghy, chasing her? Or what if he had lowered one of the jet skis after the engines stopped and had come looking for her? What should she do? Should she use the flashlight to signal whatever was out there, or should she lay low and stick to her original plan?

Frightened, she turned off the flashlight and crouched low on the rocks. She peered nervously into the fog and tried to see what kind of boat was headed her way. Finally she saw a point of light in the distance that grew bigger and bigger as it approached, and the prow of a boat hove into view. It was too big to be a dinghy. It was either a private vessel heading back into port or more likely in this soupy fog it was a harbor patrol boat or the coast guard.

"Dear God, please let them see me!" she prayed aloud as she pressed the button on the flashlight. Its beam shot out into the foggy air, and she began waving it over her head vigorously as she screamed as loud as she could for help.

Fortunately, the man at the wheel of the harbor patrol boat was watching closely so he would not miss the entrance to the breakwater and wind up on the rocks, and he saw the dancing light. He slowed the boat and switched on his bright spotlight, aiming it in the direction of the moving beam, and he saw the woman dancing about on the rocks.

"Jim!" he called to his partner. "You're never gonna believe this . . . "

60

T he telephone rang at four in the morning, and Erin snatched it up.

"Hello," she said, her eyes connecting with Mary's. Even JJ, who had fallen asleep on the sofa with his head in his sister's lap, came to instant wakefulness. Penny and Brett Marchbanks and Pete Cunningham, who had all gathered at the Gallagher residence to watch and wait through the night, also came to alert.

Erin listened for a moment, and then with relief they all heard her say, "Mom, are you all right?"

Everybody started to talk, but she waved them into silence as she heard her mother say, "I'm freezing, but I'm fine. How's JJ?"

"He's safe and sound, right here on the couch beside me. He's anxious to talk to you. I'm going to put you on the speakerphone so everyone can hear. Where are you?"

"Thank God. I was so worried about him. Honey, I just this minute arrived at the marine bureau. I jumped off the *Santa Maria* and swam to the breakwater. A boat that was patroling the entrance picked me up and brought me here. The police need to ask me some questions and then I'll be home."

"What about Dad?" JJ asked.

"I have no idea where he is at the moment. I turned off the main fuel pump before jumping overboard, so the boat can't go far. The coast guard is on their way to pick him up."

"Mom, we'll come get you," Erin said, and both JJ and Mary eagerly nodded their heads, but Lacey would not permit it.

"No, absolutely not. I want you to stay right where you are. The police will bring me home. They've also dispatched a car to the house to watch over you. I won't have a moment's peace until I know for certain that your father has been apprehended."

The family's elation at the safe return of Lacey was dampened by the reminder that Steve Haines was still on the loose.

"Don't worry about us, Mom. Penny and Brett are here with us and so is Mr. Cunningham, but if it'll make you feel any better, I'll call the security men, okay?" Erin promised her mother.

"You do that. And stay in the same room with them until I get there. Your father slipped past them and through that expensive security system to abduct me. I don't want to frighten you, but I do want you to be careful, understand?"

"I understand. Hurry home. We need you."

His mother's words sent a chill of fear through JJ. He alone understood the depths of his own father's wickedness, and he began to shake. Erin noticed his distress, and she went to him and took him into her arms. If he could have exorcised his fears with crying, he would have done so, but he was too much in shock for simple tears.

Within moments the three security men arrived in the library, eyes wide, hands on their shoulder weapons.

"Is everything okay in here?" the one named Arnold asked.

"We're fine," Erin assured them, and she repeated the phrase when Gordon came rushing into the room, with shirt unbuttoned and shoes untied.

She went on to explain her mother's instructions. She then dispatched Gordon to the kitchen to brew coffee and tea, and when the hot beverages arrived with muffins and cookies, they each took a cup and settled down to wait for Lacey to come home.

61

Lacey had finished her second cup of hot, black coffee when Cherry Dolan and Chuck Bascombe arrived at the marine bureau. She related the story of her abduction and escape, and they listened without interruption. She explained that she had no choice but to go with Steve because he had placed her son in peril, and the only thing important to her was saving JJ's life.

When she finished, Cherry said, "I think you should know that the coast guard has boarded the *Santa Maria* and although they've searched it thoroughly, they have not as yet encountered your husband."

"Steve's a strong swimmer, but I'm certain he left the boat in either the dinghy or on one of the jet skis."

"How do you know that?" Chuck asked.

"Because anybody would drown if they tried to swim with a valise holding two million dollars in cash," Lacey replied.

"Tell me where the money was. I'll radio them to look for it to make sure."

"I have no idea. From the moment I learned that he'd chained my son underwater, I never gave the money a second's consideration. I'm sorry, but I have to go home now." Lacey got to her feet. "With Steve Haines roaming free, I have to be with my family. God knows what other nasty scheme he might be hatching in that diseased mind of his."

"But surely he won't come after you now that he's got all that cash," Chuck protested. "Anybody with any intelligence would concentrate on getting away with the loot."

Lacey shook her head. "You don't understand, Detective Bascombe, you don't understand at all. Now please take me home, or must I call a taxi?"

"Now calm down, Mrs. Haines . . . "

"Please don't call me that."

"Sorry, uh, Ms. Gallagher," Chuck replied. He had never seen her angry before, and he was somewhat taken aback by the fury in her eyes.

"To lay it all out for you, Detective Bascombe," Lacey said, "so you'll comprehend what kind of person we're dealing with here, let me explain to you that my ex-husband considers two million dollars peanuts. Peanuts!'' Her words were spoken so sharply they sounded like glass breaking.

"Ever since the day Steve first set eyes on me, he's had one goal in mind," she continued. "It took me years to figure it out. I was such a foolish, vulnerable wimp, and I believed he loved me. But it was never me that he wanted. It was everything else. He wants it all, understand? Nothing less will satisfy him. He wants the money, he wants the power, he wants control. He killed my brother to get it. He damned near killed my son, and he would gladly kill me if it would advance his cause. He wants everything that my family has or is. He wants, in fact, to be Jack Gallagher. Now, can we go?"

Both Chuck and Cherry were astonished by the fierceness of her words. Lacey Gallagher, the soft-spoken woman with whom they had dealt earlier, had metamorphosed into a tiger. She swept out of the room and past the personnel in the outer office, wet hair pasted to her head, her lips still slightly blue, deep circles under her eyes, and her body wrapped in a brown blanket. This was a woman who'd had the courage to save her son's life and the strength to save her own.

Cherry hurried to open the back door of their car, and Lacey seated herself in the back, but she had one more statement to make when the detectives were also settled in.

"I think you should both know that I am not pleased with the way you've handled this investigation. Why didn't you check on my husband's story that he had gone back to Texas?"

There was a short pause, and then Cherry, who was sitting in the right front seat, turned around to face the indignant Lacey.

"I don't have a good answer for that. You told me that he'd gone back to Texas and returned when he found out about your brother's death, and I believed it. I should have checked, but he didn't seem to be anything but a bystander. It was a mistake, and I'm sorry."

Chuck had something to say too. "We were both at fault. But Ms. Gallagher, I also think you should know that if Cherry hadn't believed everything else you told us, I'd have arrested you the first day and started building a case against you. Everything pointed to your guilt, but Cherry relied on her instincts, and it turned out she was right."

"What about Sasha? Who killed her?" Lacey asked.

"We suspect it was Tom Brennan. She must have told him about her plan to provide you with an alibi, and he decided to stop her. Unfortunately, we haven't yet been able to prove he was with her the night she was killed, and his black Mercedes has been conveniently stolen."

"Is there any connection between him and Steve?" Lacey asked.

"We're not sure. There was a telephone call placed to Brennan the morning of your brother's murder. We're pretty certain Sasha made it," Cherry replied.

"Why do you think it was her?"

"Because of the bottle of pills we found in her medicine cabinet. We think maybe she dosed your brother with the barbiturate before going out on her run. We suspect Scott told her about turning over his legacy to you, and she panicked. She put him to sleep so she'd have time to contact the mastermind behind the scheme and find out how to handle it."

"That makes sense. Do you think maybe Steve killed Scott and screwed up their plans?"

"We think he was trying to do it so you'd be blamed, which suited Brennan fine. It was the next best thing to having Scott inherit the company."

"That's why Tom was already there when the police arrived. I thought perhaps Gordon had called him."

"We thought it was strange that you already had an attorney there, and so we questioned everyone in the house," Chuck stated. "No one admitted to telephoning Brennan. If you recall, we also asked you, and when you said no, I thought you were lying, which convinced me even more of your guilt. Nobody else had a reason to need him there, you see."

"You think Tom killed Sasha?" Lacey asked.

"The conveniently stolen black car makes it likely he was the one. He didn't want her to get you off the hook for your brother's murder. Brennan had a lot to gain by your being convicted," Chuck explained.

"Can you prove he was the killer?"

"It's going to be tough," Cherry admitted. "We think that after sending her over the cliff, he drove to the airport, parked the car, maybe left the keys and the ticket in it. Then he went to a pay phone, called someone in the business, and gave them the location. He got on the next flight to D.C. An hour or two later, the car was picked up and poof, disappeared."

"If we get lucky, we'll find a witness at some hotel or restaurant who saw Tom and Sasha together that night. If they weren't in a public place, we'll be out of luck," Chuck declared.

"You know, Sasha rarely took pills or medications of any kind. In fact, she made a big deal about eating natural foods and treating her body like a temple, but one night, during Dad's illness, she offered me some sleeping pills. I refused and expressed my surprise at her having them, but she said she'd been having trouble with insomnia and Tom had given them to her."

"Were you aware at the time that your brother had developed a relationship with Tom?" Cherry asked.

"No, and I meant to ask him about it, but I forgot."

"What kind of pills did she offer you?" Cherry asked.

"I have no idea."

The car approached the gates to the Gallagher estate, and the police in the squad car standing guard waved them through, but only after checking all the occupants.

As they drove up into the driveway, Erin and JJ and Mary, followed by Gordon, the Marchbanks, Pete Cunningham, and two security guards, rushed out the door to greet them. Lacey got out of the car and was enveloped by her children. There were hugs and kisses and tears in abundance. With an arm around each child, Lacey walked up the three steps to the doorway. The detectives watched her progress. At the door, however, she hesitated, released her hold on her children, and walked back down to where Cherry and Chuck were standing.

"I think you should know," she said, "that Tom's wife has at various times in her life taken barbiturates. My father told me about it."

"Where does she get the stuff? Does he give it to her?" Chuck asked.

"Reluctantly, but she has insomnia and gets desperate and threatens to kill herself."

"Any idea where he gets it?"

"His brother-in-law owns a chain of pharmacies in Orange County."

"What's his name?" Cherry asked.

"My father may have mentioned it at some time or other, but I really don't remember. I'd tell you if I knew. Good night. Thanks for the ride."

Lacey returned to her family and close friends and went inside the house.

62

A t Mary's insistence, the Gallagher's family doctor was called to check Lacey out. Dr. Preston arrived promptly, and after examining her, he advised her to be quiet for a few days, not because of the swim but because of the blow to her head, which had knocked her unconscious. Although he detected no evidence of concussion, he insisted that she be taken to the hospital later that day for a brain scan to check for any lesions. He cleaned up the numerous cuts on her hands, legs, and the soles of her feet, and told her to rest. When he finished, he complimented her on her stamina and suggested a warm bath to relax her tired muscles.

"Make sure somebody's in the room with you so you don't fall asleep in the tub and drown," he remarked with a wink as he left.

Erin came into Lacey's room as soon as the doctor had gone.

"Where did JJ go?" Lacey asked anxiously.

"He's in his bed asleep. After he heard your story, he sort of went limp with exhaustion. Penny's sitting there watching him, and Mary's out in the hall. That nice Mr. Cunningham stayed until he was sure you were okay and then he left," Erin informed her. "He told me you two went to school together. How come you never mentioned him before?"

"It's a long story, sweetheart. Remind me to tell you sometime." Lacey studied her daughter's pretty face and wondered at how adult she had grown during the last few trying days. She reached up and stroked Erin's soft cheek. The older she grew the more she looked like her grandmother, and Lacey's heart ached that Maude could not have seen her grow up.

Then Erin threw herself into her mother's arms and said, "Oh God, Mom, I thought I would never see you again!" They held each other tightly, weeping for all the sadness, all the betrayal, all the violence, and all the fear they had as a family suffered.

When at last they had spent their tears, they looked at each other and smiled.

"We survived, Mom," Erin said.

"Yes, we did, darling, and we're going to continue to survive. Now, the doctor told me to take a warm bath. Will you stay with me so I don't fall asleep?"

"I'll turn on the water," Erin said, moving toward the bathroom.

Three hours later, Lacey was in bed still trying to fall asleep. Exhausted as she was by her ordeal, she could not forget that Steve was still alive and out there somewhere planning to do more evil. How could she ever send the children off to school, knowing that he might try once more to abduct one of them? Would she ever know a moment's peace again?

When her anxieties began to get the better of her, Lacey got out of bed, pulled a pair of wool socks on her cold feet, and then donned a heavy cashmere robe to cover her still chilled bones. It was almost nine in the morning, and she felt restless. She needed to talk to somebody. She'd had enough solitude for a while.

The house was quiet. She said good morning to the security guard sitting outside JJ's room.

"Is Mrs. Marchbanks still in there with my son?" she asked softly.

"Yes, ma'am, I checked five minutes ago. She's sitting in the rocker reading. Arnold's posted outside your daughter's room. Both she and your friend Mary are sleeping there. Everything's under control, ma'am. You really ought to try to get some sleep."

Lacey smiled ruefully. "I thought everything was under control last night, but it wasn't was it?"

"Nothing's perfect, Ms. Gallagher, but we changed all the security codes first thing this morning. That was our big mistake, not changing them immediately after we found out about him."

"I hope you're right, but I'm not sure I'll ever feel secure in my own home again."

"They're going to catch him. Don't worry about that."

Lacey sighed and headed for the staircase. "I hope you're right."

For more than an hour, she sat in the morning room at the small table in the bay window that faced east. She sipped a glass of freshly squeezed orange juice as she basked in the warmth of the early sun's rays filtering through lace curtains. She appeared calm and relaxed, but inside she was in a turmoil of anxiety. So much was unresolved in her life. Her brother's killer, the man she was responsible for bringing into the sanctity of her family home, was still out there, threatening her and her children. Tom Brennan, her father's most trusted friend, had betrayed him, perhaps even to the extent of murder. Could anyone, anywhere, at any time be completely trusted? She was no longer sure.

Above all, however, she worried about Steve and where he was hiding. She tried to put herself in his position. Where would he go? What would be his next move?

She discounted the idea that he would return to Texas. The poor woman who had been unfortunate enough to marry him would probably never see or hear from him again. Perhaps she should call her and tell her the truth so she could get on with her life. Not one to procrastinate, Lacey reached over to the small credenza behind her and pulled a telephone onto the table. She tried to remember the ranch's number, but it was one of those things she had successfully erased from her memory. She called information and within a few minutes, she was talking to her successor.

"Hello, is this Steve Haines's wife?" she asked, although she recognized the voice she had overheard a few days before.

The woman said she was and asked, "Who is this?"

"Lacey, Steve's first wife."

There was a shocked silence on the other end, but Lacey did not dare hesitate and risk the woman's hanging up on her.

"I called you because something has happened here, and I wanted you to know what was going on."

"Is Steve all right?" the woman asked, sounding anxious.

"Well, no, not exactly. What I mean is, well, right now Steve is a fugitive from the law. It seems that he was the man who killed my brother—"

"You're lying!"

Lacey was not surprised by the response, but she was determined to convince her of the truth.

"I understand your not believing me, but hear me out, please, I beg you. Steve kidnapped my son and I paid him two million dollars to get him back. A lot of terribly nasty things have happened, but I wanted you to know that he has the money, and so far he's managed to elude the police."

"You gave him two million dollars—is that all?"

Lacey was startled by the woman's reaction. "All? My dear woman, that's a great deal of money!"

"Not to you, it isn't. Steve told me you were worth billions now that your father was dead, and that you promised him seventeen million."

"I am not worth billions, I can tell you that, and why in the world would I give my ex-husband that much money even if I were?"

"To get him to agree to give up legal custody of the children. He said it was worth that much to you."

"What in God's name are you talking about? The court awarded me sole custody of the children at the time of the divorce! Steve's visitation rights are entirely at my discretion."

"I don't believe you. Steve said he was granted custody because you'd been screwing around with other men. He said he only let the kids live with you because you could give them more than he could. Private schools and all."

Dear Lord, Lacey wondered, why are big lies so easy to purvey and the truth such a hard sell?

"He lied to you, Mrs. Haines, it's that simple. I never screwed around. Never. Not even since my divorce. I've always had legal custody of the children, and that's a matter of record. Now, listen to what I have to tell you. It's a truth that will set you free of a dangerous man . . . "

Lacey went on to describe the previous night's events exactly as they happened, and to her credit, the woman heard her out. When she finished, Lacey asked, "You have children too, don't you, Mrs. Haines?"

"Yes," the woman replied, and by the tone of her voice Lacey could tell that she was completely unnerved. "I have two little boys, four and six years old."

"If I were you, I would pack up immediately and leave the ranch. Go somewhere he can never find you and get yourself a divorce."

Lacey's suggestion was greeted by silence.

"Believe me, Mrs. Haines. This is one mother talking to another," she urged, using as much persuasion as she could muster. "Steve is a ruthless man and very, very dangerous. He was not a good father to his own children. Think how cruel he might be to yours."

"He called me," the woman said.

Lacey was instantly on the alert. "He called you? When?"

"Last night, uh, I mean early this morning. About four o'clock."

Lacey was now certain that the woman accepted everything she had told her, and she was relieved.

"What did he say?"

"He told me you had given him some money, but you didn't want anybody to know about it. He made a reservation for us to fly to San Francisco. He said he'd meet us at the airport there. He said we'd take the kids to Hawaii for a vacation."

"Mrs. Haines, you're not going to take that flight, are you?"

"I don't think so—not now."

"Look, if you'll talk to the police and give them all the information you have, I promise that you and the boys will be taken care of, understand?"

"I don't want your charity," she declared, but Lacey was not offended.

"It's not charity. You've done me the greatest of favors. And when this is all over, I intend to repay you for it. Now, please stand by the telephone. A detective by the name of Cherry Dolan will be calling you shortly. And thank you so much. I can never repay you enough for telling me the truth."

Lacey put in a call to Cherry, and while she waited for her to call back, she ruminated on the basic stupidity of the man who frightened her so. How could he have been so smugly certain that his wife would not betray him?

Cherry returned the call within ten minutes, and when she heard Lacey's story, she said, "We'll be at the airport when that plane arrives in San Francisco. Give me her telephone number and we'll get on it as fast as we can."

When Lacey picked up her glass to finish her juice, it tasted sweeter than ever. She got to her feet and stretched her arms and her legs and realized that she felt much better. She no longer had to worry about Steve lurking outside waiting to snatch her children. The fool was on his way to San Francisco!

Lacey felt exhilarated and tired and relieved all at the same time. Now she could go to bed and get some sleep.

63

L acey looked at her watch and saw that it was almost two-thirty. Time for Chuck Bascombe to be arriving at the airport in San Francisco. She had checked with the airline and learned that the flight from Austin on which Steve had booked his wife and her children would be arriving five minutes late. To make sure that Steve wouldn't get suspicious, a policewoman had been sent on the flight from Texas using Betty Lou Haines's ticket. The San Francisco police were prepared to arrest him if he showed up to meet the plane. In a few hours it would be all over.

Lacey got up from the desk in the library. She'd tried to talk on the telephone with some of the people in her company, but her mind kept wandering and she lost track of the points they were making. Marge had faxed her some papers to read, but the words on the page had no meaning for her. She hadn't been able to concentrate on anything, and she had an uneasy feeling that for her, life would never be completely normal again. She wasn't even sure if she knew what normal was anymore.

She walked into the foyer and climbed the staircase to check on the whereabouts of her children for the fifteenth time that day. Every minute either of them was out of her sight she was uneasy and probably would be for a long time to come. She wasn't sure she'd be able to relax even when Steve was in jail. If they put him to death in the gas chamber, she expected that he'd still be with them, hovering over their memories, haunting their dreams.

How she hated him for what he had done to JJ and Erin! For the rest of their lives they would have to live with the reality of their father's evil. He was a murderer, a cold-blooded killer. If that wasn't bad enough, they'd also have to go through the ordeal of a trial in which they'd all have to testify and be subjected to attacks from his defense attorneys. It would be a media circus. The newspapers and the television would rake over every little detail of their lives and have a field day doing it, because their name was a famous one and they were rich and therefore fair game. Some wretched writer would probably see best-sellerdom on the horizon and write a book delving into all the little secrets of the

Gallagher family, and God knows who would turn out to be the villain of the piece.

What a titillating story it would be, going back all the way to her father's bastard son who conspired to deprive his half-sister of her rightful inheritance and got murdered for his sin. It would probably even wind up on TV.

She peeked into Erin's room and saw that Mary was still there with her. A flood of gratitude warmed Lacey's cold heart. There was, after all, some good in the world, and it didn't spring from money or power or possessions, but from friends, dear, close, caring friends.

"Hi, ladies. How's everything going?" Lacey asked.

"Hi, Mom. Mary and I are planning the baby's nursery. She's going to do murals on the walls, and I'll help her paint them."

"That sounds like fun. What about your homework?"

"All done. Mary and I took turns reading aloud the assigned chapter in American history. I answered all the questions, and I think they're right. She checked over my algebra problems, and we did some sketches for the nursery mural, which I'm going to use as my project for art class. Mom, are you okay? You looked rested at breakfast, but you're starting to droop again. Maybe you ought to take a nap."

Lacey smiled. "Thanks, honey, but I have enough trouble sleeping at night. Mary, are you sure we're not keeping you from your work?"

"Nothing's more important than my family, Lacey. And you're the only one I have."

"Some family."

"Erin and I have been talking it over, and I've decided to take you up on your offer to live here with you until after the baby's born. The baby's health and welfare is more important now than my own desire for independence. I'd have so much help and support here that it would be foolish for me not to be with you. Do you still want me?"

"Mary, if it were up to me, I'd keep you here forever," Lacey replied, tears rising in her eyes. "Right now, I need you a lot more than you need me. Does Penny know?"

Mary laughed. "Of course. You know how uppity she gets if she doesn't know everything first."

"Is she still here?"

"I believe she and JJ are playing tennis. At least they were an hour ago," Mary said.

"Maybe I'll take a walk out there and see how they're doing. I feel like some fresh air anyway."

Mary frowned. "Didn't the doctor tell you to stay off those torn-up feet of yours?"

"It's not very far and I want to get out of the house for a few minutes. What do you say we all meet in the library for tea at about four-thirty?"

"That's the time the plane is scheduled to land in San Francisco, isn't it?" Erin asked, and both Mary and Lacey nodded grimly.

"Is Detective Bascombe going to call us and let us know what happened?" Erin asked.

"Cherry Dolan said she would. She flew up there this morning, and Chuck is joining her about now. They'll take custody after the arrest and bring him back to Los Angeles. I talked to Chuck before his plane left, and it's all arranged." Lacey hesitated, and then continued. "I figured we'd all be watching the clock and waiting for the telephone to ring, so we might as well be together."

"Okay," Erin replied, turning back to her sketchpad. "But no champagne, Mom. It's not exactly a celebration."

Erin's words sent a stab of pain through her mother's heart. Poor child, Lacey thought. It's going to be so difficult for her to come to terms with the fact that her father is a criminal.

"Nothing but tea, darling. And a whole lot of sympathy for everyone involved in this mess," Lacey remarked as she left the room.

Lacey walked down to the tennis court, which was now empty, and her heart turned over. Stop this! she admonished herself. You can't keep your children under your thumb every minute of every hour of every day, as much as you want to. JJ and Penny have to be somewhere on the grounds.

Walking faster than was comfortable for her sore feet, she made a quick circle of the estate. With each place that she investigated and found deserted, she felt her panic growing. Where had they gone?

At the cottage, she encountered Tim Coffee, who was making rounds.

"Tim!" she called, "Have you seen Mrs. Marchbanks and my son?"

"They were on the tennis court ten minutes ago, Ms. Gallagher. Having a pretty rough game, as I saw it. I would guess you'd find them in the showers. That Mrs. Marchbanks is some player. Man, has she got a serve."

"Thanks, Tim. Is everything okay?"

"Sure is. I've put two extra men on until we're sure Mr. Haines is in custody, and they've got two black and whites patroling outside the estate. They've even put a K-9 patrol walking the perimeter. I got one of Haines's shoes so the dogs would know what smell to look for."

"Thanks, Tim. I appreciate everything that's being done."

"I can't tell you how sorry I am security got breached like it did last night. Mr. Haines really outfoxed us."

"Don't worry about it, Tim. Everything worked out for the best. God knows what would have happened to JJ if you'd caught Steve trying to get into the house. I must go now. I'll let you know as soon as I hear anything."

Lacey hurried back into the house. Gordon was heading toward the library with a silver tray of cookies and pastries.

"Gordon," she asked anxiously. "Have Penny and my son returned from playing tennis?"

"I'm not sure, ma'am. I've been in the pantry for the past half hour or so."

As she pounded up the stairs, the pain in her feet reminded her once more of her ordeal the night before.

Without bothering to knock, she burst into JJ's room, and a wave of relief spread over her as she saw her son, sweaty and damp, stretched out across the clean blue sheets on his bed.

"Hi, Mom. Everything okay?" he asked, sitting up.

"Sorry I forgot to knock, but I've been a little distracted today. Where's Penny?"

"She left a couple minutes ago. She was headed down to the library to look for you. As soon as I get my wind back, I've gotta take a shower. Boy, she killed me playing tennis."

"She's tough. You'll have to work harder if you want to beat her. Now, wash up and get dressed. Everybody's going to be in the library at four-thirty."

"Why?" JJ asked, his voice and demeanor unusually sullen.

"Well, it's not going to be a celebration of your father's being appre-hended, JJ, if that's what you're worried about. I figured it might be less traumatic if we were all together when we got the news."

"Okay, I'll be there."

Lacey paused in the hallway to recover her composure. She glanced down at her feet and noticed that a large red stain had appeared above the rubber sole on her white sneaker. She must have broken open one of the cuts in her mad search for her son.

As she gingerly tiptoed back to her room to change her shoes and socks and rebandage her foot, she wondered if she was going to become a neurotic, overly protective mother in the days ahead.

Everyone was in the library well before the appointed time. Although Mary and Penny made a big production out of exclaiming over the goodies on the tea tray, JJ and Erin wanted nothing more than a Coke. They sat off to themselves in the alcove by the big leaded glass window, and as far as anyone could tell, they did not say a word to each other. It made Lacey and her friends ache with compassion for the difficult position the children were in.

Lacey had a cup of tea, but her throat was too constricted with expectancy to swallow anything more. Inadvertently, her eyes kept straying to the telephone, waiting for it to ring. The wait turned out be a long one. It was almost five-forty-five when the call finally came. Lacey did not want to leap for the telephone, and so she waited for Gordon to answer it.

"Miss Lacey," he announced. "Detective Dolan is calling from San Francisco."

Lacey grabbed the telephone. "Yes, Cherry," she answered in a voice strangled with anticipation.

"Bad news, I'm afraid," Cherry said.

"You didn't catch him!?" Lacey exclaimed.

"He never showed. We're certain of that now."

"What in God's name do you mean *now?*"

"We found out that sometime during the night, Betty Lou Haines and her children disappeared. We have no idea where she went. We think this San Francisco thing was nothing more than a decoy move."

"But the police in Texas were supposed to be keeping her under surveillance."

"They had one squad car with two officers sitting out in front of the ranch house watching for any lights or movement in the house. They said it was dark and quiet all night. Apparently Mrs. Haines and her children sneaked through the back door and walked across the field to the highway where they must have been picked up. That's the only explanation they can come up with."

"You want my version?" Lacey asked.

"Shoot."

"Steve called Betty Lou and told her he was being framed. He promised to send her money if she'd throw us a bad lead and give him a little breathing space. That's why she took off in the night."

"Well, you know him better than we do. Nevertheless, we ought to find her. I'll tell the Texas authorities to check and see if she hired a car."

"Where do we go from here?"

"Sit tight and be cautious. Let us know immediately if he makes any overtures to you at all."

"That's what we're doing."

"I have another piece of news for you."

"It better be good for a change," Lacey said with a sigh.

"Afraid not. Jean Atwill made bail."

"What? They released her?" Lacey sputtered. "How could they do that? And why, for God's sake?"

"I don't know. Chuck told me five minutes ago. I'll look into it as soon as I get back to L.A."

"Thanks for nothing, Cherry."

Lacey put down the telephone and hesitated before turning around to tell her family and friends the distressing news. She was beginning to wonder if the police would ever apprehend Steve, and she was extremely worried about the emotional price the Gallagher family might have to pay before the job got done.

And then there was the matter of Jean Atwill.

64

T rue to her word, Cherry called Lacey early the next morning with the news that Tom Brennan had used his political influence and gotten a late-afternoon bail hearing the day before for Jean Atwill.

"How did he manage that?"

"Nobody around here seems to know. It just happened. Anyway, he apparently had two independent psychiatrists examine her, and they both found her fit for release."

"But she's crazy, you know that!"

"Not according to the psychiatrists. They both said she was aware that you were no longer under suspicion of Scott's murder. I heard she appeared lucid and expressed contrition for her attempt on your life."

"So the judge set bail and Tom posted it for her," Lacey concluded. "Son of a bitch!"

"He posted fifty thousand."

"Good grief, why, why did he do it?"

"Well, it certainly wasn't for her benefit, that's for sure. The D.A.'s office informed me that it'll weaken her insanity defense."

"Now what'll I do?" Lacey asked.

"The same as always. Stay home. Be cautious. This siege won't last forever."

"The hell you say," Lacey snapped and put down the telephone. She was edgier than ever.

Lacey gave the news to everyone in the household and warned them to be on the alert. Later that morning, frustrated and desperate to take some kind of action, she telephoned Tom.

"What can I do for you, Lacey?"

"What the devil are you doing representing Jean Atwill? Have you no shame at all?"

"Hey, you've got the woman all wrong. Jean's better now. She had a few bad days there, but I'm convinced she's back to her old self again. I'm only doing what your father would have wanted me to do. After all, the old broad's all alone in the world. She hasn't got any family or friends. Jack wouldn't have wanted her to rot in jail; you know that as well as I do."

"She tried to kill me, Tom, have you forgotten? If my father was still alive, she'd be lucky to see the light of day again!" Lacey took a deep breath and asked, "Where is she now?"

"At her condo in Long Beach. Mamie offered to let her stay here with us, but she insisted on going home. We're going over there to take her out to dinner tonight."

"You bastard! You're not going to get away with this!" Lacey's anger and exasperation were at the point of explosion.

"You've got a lot of nerve talking to me like that, young lady! Just what the hell do you think I'm trying to get away with?"

"You're going to try to get her to recant her story about the changed will, aren't you? That's the only reason you're making nice with her. Well, you're wasting your time. I'll hire private detectives to put a trail on both of you, understand? Every move, every conversation either of you has with anyone will be tracked and recorded. And when I nail you, I'll turn everything over to the authorities. Keep looking over your shoulder from now on, Tom Brennan. I'll be closing in on you!"

Lacey slammed down the telephone and realized that her blood pressure was probably off the charts. She tried to calm herself down.

She paced through the house, but she couldn't get her anger under control. Damn it all. Tom had started the whole mess. He was the one who had faked the will in the first place, and it was that damned phony will that got Scott killed. Then as soon as Sasha revealed she was providing her with an alibi, he did away with her, because he wanted control of the Gallagher fortune. How could her father not have seen what an evil person his trusted friend really was?

Mary found Lacey walking up and down the solarium, talking to herself.

"What's going on?"

Lacey unloaded all the morning's frustrations on her, and Mary listened without comment until she was finished.

"Doesn't Gallagher's Best use other law firms besides Tom's?" Mary asked.

"Sure, but all of them are referrals from him. Most specialize in various fields."

"Then it's time you got somebody who concentrates on estate law and changed everything. Oust Tom as a trustee of the estate. Under the circumstances, I'll bet you could get rid of him once and for all."

Lacey looked at her friend and grinned. "Why didn't I think of that?"

"Because you've been locked into doing everything the way your Dad did. But it's your company now. And your life."

"You're right. Under the circumstances, it's probably also what Dad would do."

"Another thing I wanted to discuss with you. I think I should call Jean. If she's really calmed down and as reasonable and lucid as Tom says she is, I want to talk to her."

"Why get yourself involved in this mess?"

"I know it sounds weird, but I can't ignore the fact that she *is* the grandmother of my child. Finding out that a part of her son is still alive might turn her whole life around."

"You're going to tell her about the baby? What made you change your mind?"

"I realized you were right. Everybody, even Jean Atwill, needs something to live for."

Lacey put her arms around Mary and hugged her as she wondered what had happened to her own charitable impulses.

For the rest of the morning and most of the afternoon, Mary tried calling Jean at her home, but no one answered. She finally decided to give up for the day and take a nap. She went to her room to lie down.

Every time Mary dialed the number and no one answered, Lacey became a little more nervous. The memory of Jean's face as she pointed the gun at her became more vivid with each ring. Was Jean already stalking her, preparing to launch another attack? Was it possible that Tom Brennan had given the woman a weapon and sent her out to try again? How tidy and fortuitous it would be for him if Jean succeeded on the second attempt.

Twice during the afternoon, Lacey checked her security guards and warned them to be on the alert. No matter how humanitarian Mary's motivation was, Lacey felt like a woman under siege, now more than ever. When the telephone rang at four-thirty, she leapt from her chair to answer it. It was Cherry Dolan.

"Any word on Steve?" Lacey asked.

"Only that your suspicions were right on target. We located Betty Lou Haines. She flew to Charleston, where her family lives. I talked to her on the telephone, and you were correct about the San Francisco bit being nothing but a ruse. He promised her money to mislead us. I told her not to hold her breath."

"So he's still out there someplace?"

"Yeah, but don't worry; we'll find him eventually."

"He's not my only concern. We've been trying to call Jean Atwill all afternoon, but she's not at home. Have you any idea where she might be?"

"Funny you should ask. That was my next bit of news. You don't have to worry about her anymore."

"She's back in jail?"

"No. The doorman at her condo got uneasy when she didn't answer his calls all morning. Finally late this afternoon he convinced the building manager to check on her. They found her dead in her bed. Looks like sleeping pills, but we won't know for sure until the toxicology report."

"Oh, how awful! I'm so sorry," Lacey said.

"You are? I thought you'd be relieved. I still can't believe they released her."

"Obviously they made a mistake. Thanks for calling. Keep me posted."

When the call ended, Lacey walked slowly up the stairs to tell Mary the grisly news that Tom Brennan had succeeded. And another person was dead.

65

For two weeks, nothing was heard of Steve Haines. The atmosphere in the Gallagher household had grown increasingly tense. Lacey had once more gathered her children into her own bedroom to sleep, and although Mary remained in the house, Penny went home. When nothing happened, even the police began to feel that Steve had made a successful escape with the money. The marked bills had turned up nowhere. Even the newspaper reporters had ceased to come around the house. The story had grown cold.

Only Lacey was still caught up in the drama. As time passed, she became more convinced that Steve was playing a waiting game. Sooner or later, they would relax their vigilance and go about leading their lives, and then he would strike. Each day she became more and more certain that he intended to kidnap one of her children, and her fear and her vigilance were all-encompassing.

She refused to allow her children to return to school or leave the house. JJ could not go to the swimming pool or the tennis court without one of the security guards accompanying him. When either of the children complained, she simply advised them to get used to it. After all, even the president of the United States didn't have the freedom to move about without security men surrounding him.

Lacey wanted to go to the office, but she felt it would be unfair for her to move out into the world when her children were prisoners at home, and so she had her work brought to her. Marge made at least two trips a day with papers for her to sign, and the scheduled meeting of the board of directors of Gallagher's Best was held in Lacey's library. Brett Marchbanks came frequently to keep her briefed, and although the operation of the company went smoothly, everyone was worried about Lacey's emotional health.

Pete Cunningham worried about her too, and he never missed his evening visit. He usually arrived in time for dinner, and Erin and JJ welcomed his presence because their mother seemed happier when he was there.

Although she talked to Cherry Dolan several times, there had been little to report until the detective came to see her on the Monday of the third week of Lacey's self-imposed incarceration.

Cherry was startled at how drawn and tired Lacey looked. There were deep circles under her eyes, and she appeared to be exhausted.

"Are you all right, Lacey?" she asked.

"How can one be all right and terrified at the same time?"

"He's winning, Lacey. He's destroying you on a daily basis."

"You think I don't know that?" Lacey responded, irritated by the detective's comment.

"Well, I have some good news for a change. Some of the marked bills have been located. He's spent some of the money."

"Where? Where did you find it?"

"In San Diego, close to the Mexican border. He bought a car there, and we think he may have left the country."

Lacey's heart began to pound with excitement. "That's the best news short of his being captured that you could have given me. That means he's not here!"

"Well, it's an indication anyway. I think you should continue to exercise caution, but we're convinced he took the money and ran. Chances are he's trying to put as much distance between him and us as he can manage. He's got the money to buy a forged passport."

"Do you think it would be all right if I let the children go back to school?"

"This case might drag on for years," Cherry commented.

"Anything new on the situation with Tom Brennan?"

"You had to bring that up, didn't you? Well, on the night Sasha was killed he said he had dinner alone at the Hyatt Regency in Long Beach. He paid by credit card so that checks out, but nobody remembers seeing him there. It's possible he might have given the card to somebody else to use, because the signature's not decipherable."

"Dad always said Tom should have been a doctor, his handwriting was so illegible. Was there a tip on the check?"

"Twenty percent, I think."

"Tom never tips more than ten percent. He's really stingy. What about the car?"

"No luck there either. Mercedes parts are easy to sell, so it was probably completely dismantled and peddled piecemeal outside the state. And we questioned his brother-in-law, the pharmacist you told us about. He admitted giving Tom barbiturates for Mamie. He said that he too was afraid she'd kill herself. Our agents went over all his records, and everything else checks out. Other than that one infraction, he appears to be a straight businessman with an excellent reputation."

"What about Jean Atwill? Did she use the same drug to kill herself?"

"No. The toxicology report came back yesterday. She was full of triazolam."

"What's that?"

"According to the report, it's a benzodiazepine hypnotic agent, usually prescribed for insomnia. Halcion is the trade name. She took a massive dose, and it caused cardiopulmonary collapse. They also found alcohol in her body, and that enhanced the effect of the drug. She knew what she was doing, and it's our conclusion that she intended to die."

"Wasn't her condo searched after she tried to kill me?"

"Sure, but we didn't find any of that drug at the time."

"Then Tom must have given it to her."

"He says he didn't. We went back to his brother-in-law, and he swore that he'd never given any Halcion to either Tom and Mamie. It's a controlled substance, but it's easy to get because a lot of doctors prescribe it for their patients. We can't prove he ever had it or that he gave it to Jean."

"You still think Tom's guilty of Sasha's death?" Lacey asked.

"I do, just as you know he tampered with the will even though we have no way of proving which one is valid, since the signatures on both check out."

"I've begun action to have him removed as a trustee," Lacey said quietly. "I've hired another law firm, but he knows nothing about it yet. When the time comes, I'll be the one to tell him."

Cherry got up to go. "We haven't given up on either of these men, Lacey. One of these days, they'll make a mistake, and we'll nail them."

"Do you have a lot of unsolved cases?" Lacey asked.

"I wish I could say no, but I'd be lying."

"But these men are both cold-blooded murderers!"

"I know that, Lacey. I know."

Lacey shook her head and sighed. "Thanks for coming, and thanks for the good news about the marked money. Let me know if anything else turns up."

After Cherry left, Lacey looked at her watch and saw it was almost noon. If she moved fast she could get things organized so Erin and JJ could return to school the next day, and she could go back to the office.

As she hurried up the stairs to tell them the good news, she felt giddy with the prospect of freedom at last.

66

B efore JJ and Erin were allowed to return to classes, Lacey made sure that the faculty and staff at the private school were formally briefed on the danger Steve represented, a precaution not really necessary since everyone had been following the Gallagher drama in the pages of the newspapers and magazines. The fact that no one close to the family would grant an interview made the subject even more titillating to those who knew them.

Following a scenario worked out with the private security company and coordinated with the police, JJ and Erin were taken to school and escorted into the building by two security guards who then patroled the grounds until it was time to bring them home. Lacey, who was not as worried about herself as she was the children, was driven to work by Salvador. Since there was already a security staff at the company, they eschewed any additional measures there.

At first Lacey was nervous and worried, but the second day was a little better, and she began to relax enough to enjoy her work again. Business was good, although the acquisition discussions with Kettlecup were moving slowly. Otherwise, she was confident that the team running the company was as efficient as it could be, and morale was high. Whenever she started to feel good about her life, however, Steve's existence squirmed into her thoughts, like a worm wriggling from the core of a half-eaten and delicious apple, and she became depressed and distracted.

When she returned from lunch, Marge told her that Pete had called. She called him back right away.

"How's it going?" he asked.

"Okay. I'm happy to be back at work, I guess."

"What do you mean by that?"

"Oh, you know. Everything's so, I don't know, unfinished. It's horrible to think I'm going to have to spend the rest of my life looking over my shoulder."

"You need some cheering up. Why don't we go somewhere fun for dinner tonight?"

"I'm not ready to leave the house yet in the evening, Pete. Why don't you come have dinner with us? I'll open a bottle of Petrus."

"Hey, I may be a marvelous and swell person, but I don't think I can live up to Petrus."

"Don't underestimate yourself, Mr. Cunningham. Be there at seven."

Lacey telephoned Gordon and told him to have the cook prepare something special for dinner, and then she went back to work feeling much better.

The rest of the afternoon was a productive one, primarily because the problem of Steve receded to the back of her mind, and she was in the car and on her way home well before five. Upon her arrival, she talked to the children about their day and then slipped into a tank suit and went down to the pool to swim laps while Mary sat at the side and watched her.

Afterward, while she was in the whirlpool relaxing, she told Mary about Pete.

"Why don't you have dinner alone with him tonight for a change? The kids and I can eat early."

"Absolutely not. I want him to get to know my family better."

Mary shook her head. "Most women try to land the guy before they trot out the dependents."

"Mary, Pete's an old friend."

"Correction, old boyfriend. There's a difference."

"There's nothing between us but memories. I'm not looking to sleep with him," she protested, getting out of the whirlpool and wrapping herself in a thick terrycloth robe.

"What are you, a nun or something?"

"I'm not ready for romance. It's caused me too damned much trouble. Besides, I find sex vastly oversold."

As they walked back to the house, Mary asked, "I get the feeling that you and Steve didn't have much fun in bed. Want to talk about it?"

"It's a distasteful subject for me. The only people I ever talked to about my relations with Steve were—are you ready for this—that inquisitive duo, Chuck and Cherry. Can you believe that?"

"Why them?"

"They asked, and in a vulnerable moment I told them that frequently sex with my ex-husband was like assault with a deadly weapon."

"My God, Lacey, did he hurt you?"

"Not all the time. Maybe it would have been better if he had been more consistent, because then I'd have left him a lot sooner than I did."

"Sex for a woman isn't always great, Lacey. Sometimes it's just there, sometimes it's better, sometimes it's wonderful. Listen to me talk. I sound like the voice of experience. I've only been with one man in my life."

Lacey put her arm around her friend. "It's so personal, isn't it? Well, sex with Steve was all heat and no warmth. Understand?"

"I hear that every man's different."

Lacey made no comment, and they walked back to the house in silence. Although Lacey was tempted to tell her that Steve had raped her only hours before he ran, she could not bring herself to say the words.

67

P ete Cunningham always managed to charm everyone in Lacey's household, including the servants. Erin was intrigued by him, and both Mary and Lacey were amused at how flirtatious she became when he was around. JJ never noticed, because he was always too interested in his own conversations with their guest. JJ had started a collection of baseball cards, and he loved talking to Pete about the famous old stars because Pete knew a lot about baseball history.

Throughout dinner Lacey found herself virtually shut out of the discussion as JJ and Erin vied for Pete's attention, but she was pleased that the children were responding to him so well. After dessert, however, Mary took the initiative and got to her feet.

"Come on," she said, putting her hands on JJ's and Erin's shoulders. "You two have a lot of studying to catch up on, and I need to get back to work too. I hope you won't mind if we excuse ourselves. It was nice seeing you again, Pete. Good night, now. Come back soon."

Lacey started to lead her guest to the warmth and coziness of the library, but the remembrance of her evening there with Steve was still too vivid. She decided to continue the conversation where the vibrations were more friendly.

"Would you like to see my mother's greenhouse? Or have you any interest in orchids?"

"Sure, I always enjoy smelling the flowers."

"How about a glass of cognac to carry with you?" she asked.

"Thanks, but no thanks. I have to drive home. The Petrus, as you well know, was spectacular, but I'm not sure if it was the vintage, or the bottle, or the person I shared it with that made it so special."

"It's fun to open an important wine with someone who really appreciates it. I feel at ease drinking Dad's wine with you," she said as she led the way through the hall.

"Why? Are you usually uncomfortable?"

"I shared a couple of bottles with my brother the night he was killed, but I was angry with my father and felt spiteful drinking it. Then I drank some with my ex-husband, and I didn't enjoy that much either, because my father did not suffer him gladly. But Dad always liked you, Pete."

"Probably because he didn't intimidate me. My dad was such a gentle, easygoing guy that I assumed all fathers were the same," he replied as they walked along the garden path.

"Your dad died less than six months after your mother, didn't he?" Lacey asked.

"They were such a close and happy pair. My brother and I knew he wouldn't make it without her."

"I thought I came from a happily married couple, but I was wrong. Isn't it amazing that I didn't pick up on any of the signs of discontent?"

"I don't think you ought to dwell on that stuff too much, Lacey. Your mother and father loved you."

They had arrived at the greenhouse door, and Pete opened it for her. As she brushed past him, he took her arm and turned her to face him.

"You owe me a dance, Lacey." The scent of flowers combined with the heavy moisture in the air to encompass the couple in an exotic embrace. Lacey took a deep breath and looked up into his eyes. She knew if she didn't move he would kiss her, and it wouldn't be a friendly peck. It would be a real kiss. She turned her head away.

"What's wrong?" he asked.

"I'm afraid, Pete."

"Of what?"

"You. All my memories of you are tinged with a pink and purple glow. I've turned you into some kind of a perfect Prince Charming, and I know such a person doesn't exist in real life."

Pete took her in his arms and held her close. He kissed the top of her head.

"I've never been Prince Charming, Lacey, but I do exist. You're going to have to deal with my feelings for you sooner or later because this time I'm not going away. I care about you. I know you've been hurt and you're disillusioned, but I'm nothing like Steve."

With a gentle touch he lifted her chin and kissed her. It was a warm and soft kiss with no passionate demands, and Lacey relaxed in his arms. It had been a long time since she had experienced such genuine and caring masculine affection.

"I've got a long way to go, Pete. Someday I'll be able to tell you what my life with Steve was like."

"I'm in no hurry, Lacey. Let's talk about the night of November sixteenth. Do you remember?"

Lacey smiled. "The night of the hayride."

"It was the greatest night of my whole life," he whispered and held her closer. "Do you remember?"

She looked up into Pete's eyes. "How could I ever forget?"

He kissed her again. This time the affection was still there but so was the passion, and she wasn't afraid of it. She kissed him back.

When he finally released her, she tucked her head under his chin and said, "I've never regretted it for a single moment, Pete. I'm glad you were the first."

"So am I." He kissed her again.

"It's time to go now, not that I want to," Pete whispered.

"We didn't even have a chance to talk about Kettlecup."

"Good. You'll have to keep wining and dining me then."

"Tomorrow night? Same time?"

"I'll be here. And one night, when you feel comfortable leaving, there's a great little restaurant in Santa Monica, right on the beach. The chef's a friend of mine, and he'll treat us well. We'll have the night all to ourselves. Will you go with me?"

"Soon, Pete. Soon." She was astonished at how breathless and young her voice sounded.

"Come on, I'll walk you back to the house."

She didn't want him to leave, but she had to let him go. She looked at him with an invitation for another kiss, and this time it was as passionate and demanding as it had been when they were young. Reluctantly, she pulled away at last.

"Perhaps it's better if we don't go back through the house," she whispered. "We can cut across the lawn to your car."

"No, the grass is damp, and you'll get your shoes all wet. I'll go by myself. I need a little night walk to cool myself down. Go on back to the house. I'll see you tomorrow." He ran his fingertips across her cheek in a gentle caress.

Lacey watched him go, and when he was out of sight, she went back into the greenhouse. She'd noticed a beautiful stalk of cymbidium blooms and decided to cut them for her room to remind her of the wonder of Pete's embrace. She felt very romantic.

Lacey located a sharp pair of pruning shears on the work table and picked them up. If she remembered correctly, the plant she was looking for was near the back wall. She walked down the row admiring the blossoms but thinking about Pete. He had become an important part of her life again, and she felt happier than she had in many years.

She found the plant she was looking for and counted the blooms on the stem. There were fourteen, each one perfect. She was concentrating on making a clean, slanted cut when she heard the door open.

"Pete? Is that you?" she called. The shelves were too tall and she didn't have a direct line of sight to the entrance. There was no response.

"Who's there?" she asked, pausing and moving to a spot where she could see the door. It was closed and there was no one there. Beginning to feel apprehensive and vulnerable, Lacey decided to forget the cymbidium and get back into the house. She had taken no more than two steps, however, when a figure clothed in black appeared from behind a row of plants and blocked her way.

"Steve!" she exclaimed, her heart racing.

"Surprise! Was that the new prince consort? Is he any good in bed?"

"How did you get in here?"

"I've been on the grounds since three this afternoon. I hid in the dry cleaner's delivery truck. It was easy. Then I waited in the old stables. Hope I don't smell too bad."

"You better get out of here. The guards make regular rounds and they're armed."

"Not tonight they won't. They're in no condition to do anything. I sneaked into the room where they play cards and left a box of home-baked cookies for them. They probably won't wake up until morning."

"What do you want?" Lacey's heart was racing and she was afraid.

"I want my son. He's worth lots of money to you, isn't he?"

"You'd have to kill me before I'd let you take JJ!" she declared. The pruning shears were still in her hand, but she kept them hidden behind her skirt.

"Whatever it takes, Lacey. Whatever it takes."

They were glaring at each other when the door to the greenhouse opened again, and Tom Brennan walked in. He was carrying a gun equipped with a silencer.

"Thank God, you're here, Tom. This madman thinks he's going to take my son!" Lacey exclaimed.

Steve turned around and snapped, "What the hell are you doing? You were supposed to wait outside the gate in the car!"

Tom smiled. "I changed my mind."

He approached, and the two men stared at each other. Steve's hand snaked behind his back and he whipped out a gun, also equipped with a silencer. To Lacey's astonishment, Tom's only reaction was a smile.

"Tsk, tsk, now why did you do that, Steve? You're not going to shoot me. We're buddies, remember? I'm the one who's been hiding you all this time. I even came up with this plan to get your kid for you. Now put the gun down."

"What are you up to now, Brennan? We had a deal. You stay out in the car, while I get JJ."

"I couldn't risk it, my friend. She outwitted you before; she'd probably do it again. You're an asshole, Steve, just as Jack always said you were. Only an asshole would have come to me for help. Your stupidity's going to be the death of you." Tom's tone of voice indicated that he was not talking about the nebulous future.

"I don't need you. What's one more murder on my record," Steve retorted as he pointed the gun directly at Tom's body and fired. Tom didn't move. Startled, Steve took a step forward and fired again, but Tom merely stepped back.

Lacey watched the encounter in horror.

"Stay away from me, Steve. I don't want to get powder burns from the blanks you're firing," Tom warned, his lip curling in disdain.

As Steve looked down at the useless gun in his hand, Tom charged. In one swift stride, the older man approached his victim and fired one shot directly into Steve's right temple. With an astonished expression on his face, Steve sank to the floor and died.

"My God, you've killed him!" Lacey gasped.

"I certainly hope so. Now it's your turn." He pointed the gun at her, but she retreated. She couldn't go far, however, because she found herself trapped against a concrete wall that was no higher than her shoulder. With her hands behind her she fumbled for a light switch, and she barely heard herself babbling, "You're not going to get away with this, you know. The night shift of guards will be coming on duty any minute now, and when they find everybody asleep, they'll be all over this place."

"We have an hour before the new shift is due. Nobody's coming to your rescue, Lacey. Certainly not the guards. Mamie baked the cookies, and they were loaded. I doubt if those guys will be awake for breakfast. By the time the police get to this greenhouse, there'll be nothing but dead bodies here. I'll exchange guns with Steve, and it'll look like a desperate and vindictive murder-suicide. It happens all the time when an ex-husband sees his wife frolicking with a new lover."

"You're crazy!"

"Not crazy, just clever. When that fool came to me for help, I thought why not use the son of a bitch to my own advantage. He gave me the gun he took off the *Santa Maria,* and I got a silencer for it. I gave him that movie prop he was using so ineffectively. Then I planted some of his ill-gotten gains in San Diego so you'd relax your vigilance. Pretty tricky, eh?"

He moved closer as he continued boasting.

"Steve's been accommodating too. If he hadn't fired that prop gun, I'd have had to use his finger to pull the trigger, but now he's already got plenty of powder marks on his hand. I think of everything, you see."

"You haven't thought of the possibility that I might resist, have you? Do you think for one minute I'll die without doing something to stop you?"

Her fingertips located nothing but cement wall. Her peripheral vision, however, picked up an electrical cord only inches away from her hand. It was connected to one of the heaters. If she moved quickly enough, she could cut it and break the circuit. Under the newly improved security system, any circuit break in the house would set off the alarm.

"I don't need your cooperation, my dear woman. But don't blame me for this mess. It was that bastard on the floor there who caused all the problems by killing your brother."

"What would you have done if I hadn't come out here to the greenhouse tonight?" she asked, stalling for time.

"My original intent was to kill you in your sleep and then drop lover-boy here dramatically across your body. You're no use to me alive, Lacey. You never were."

"Have you forgotten that my children sleep in the same room with me?" Lacey cried.

"Not really. You've mentioned on several occasions what sound sleepers they were. But it didn't matter if they awakened. It suits my purposes even better if it turned out that their crazy father killed them too. There's a lot of precedence for that kind of family massacre."

"Why did you kill Sasha?" Lacey asked, hoping to keep him talking while she positioned the pruning shears exactly right in her hand.

"The bitch turned on me. If she'd held the line, you'd have gone to jail. But she wanted money, which I didn't have, and she was greedy and impatient."

"You gave Jean the pills to kill herself too, didn't you?"

"She was the only one alive who could prove that I changed the will. My reputation would have been destroyed, and I could have been removed as trustee of your estate."

Lacey was fingering the handle on the shears. They were covered in a substance that felt like rubber. But what difference did it make if she got electrocuted? Better to die fighting.

He was moving closer to her now, and they were staring into each other's eyes. Lacey did not flinch or look away.

"My father trusted you, Tom. He wanted you to help me and look out for me. He was your friend."

"There's no such thing as friendship in this world. Only different degrees of power. And power comes from money."

The blades were ready to cut the cord, and Lacey inched closer to it.

"Stand still! I want to do this with one shot so it doesn't hurt you. That's the least I can do to repay all of your father's kindnesses."

Pressing the handles of the shears together, she reached out in a flash, clamped down hard, and severed the electrical cord. An explosion of sparks was followed by instantaneous darkness. Lacey was knocked to the ground as the lights and air-conditioning shut down. The wail of the burglar alarm splintered the night air.

A shot was fired, but Lacey was flat on the cement floor and the bullet sailed over her and shattered one of the panes of the glass wall. She presumed Tom had a flashlight and would find her if she tried to run. She scrambled to her feet and pitched her body toward him with as much force as she could muster. The two tumbled to the ground.

"Damn you, bitch!" he yelled and pulled the trigger again, but that shot went wild too. She saw the flare from the gun, and with the sharp pruning shears still in her hand, she stabbed toward it as hard as she could. The blades sank deep into Tom's wrist, severing an artery. He screamed and the gun clattered to the floor. She stabbed again, this time higher. She hit him in the shoulder.

She was on top of him wildly stabbing at his face and his body when the lights of Pete's car illuminated the greenhouse and he rushed inside. He had heard the sound of the alarm as he was backing his car out of the circle, and thinking Lacey might be in trouble, he had driven across the lawn.

"Lacey!" he yelled and grabbed her arm.

"Get the gun, Pete! It's on the floor!"

Tom was no longer struggling with her but was using his arms to shield his face and head from her lethal blows.

Pete dropped to his knees and began searching.

"I've got it!" he exclaimed, and Lacey stopped her attack.

By this time the squad car assigned to their district was racing up the hill, sirens blaring.

"Go show them where we are!" Pete shouted. "I'll stay here and watch him."

On shaking legs and covered in Tom's blood, Lacey ran out of the greenhouse and back across the lawn to get the police. It was all over. The nightmare had ended at last.